Movers and Shakers

ELLE RIVERS

Character Design by Allie McGilberry

Cover Design by Elle Rivers

Edited by Kasey Kubica

Proofread by Amanda Oraha

For those who chose to be alone for so long you never got noticed.

Go choose your new family. They're waiting.

A Note from Elle

This work contains themes that some might find upsetting. In this novel, parental abuse and abandonment are present, and some may find that the character's thoughts in this novel equate to emotional cheating. There is *no* physical cheating between the main characters, but one person gets cheated on by their partner multiple times. Anxiety and other mental health issues are present in this novel.

It is also incredibly important to note that Lila Wilde is *not* based on any real-life musician. I have the utmost respect for people who do this as a career, and I would never twist one's life into a romance novel of my own creation. While some may draw similarities to Lila and some stars, this is entirely coincidental.

As always, if I have missed a warning, please email me at elle@ellerivers.com, and I will rectify the situation.

PROLOGUE

Lila

When making a fake identity, I didn't realize how hard it would be to remember my own damn name.

I'm not Rose. I'm Lila. Lila Wilde.

The reminder bounced around my head, but I had a feeling I would struggle to remember what name I answered to.

My eyes searched the crowd for the man I was there for—Rick Thorne, the agent who could change my life. When Dad told me he would be here, I knew this could have been the moment that made my music career take off.

Most people wouldn't have bought a custom-made wig before coming to an open mic event at an LA café, but Mom's wide-eyed, nervous expression followed me around from the moment I told her.

"What if everyone knows your name? Don't you see how stars are treated? You'd have no privacy. I'd have no privacy." Mom's voice had shaken when Dad gave us the news, and for a while, I thought about forgoing my dream of singing.

But then I had a harebrained, wild idea.

Mom couldn't handle people knowing *Rose's* name. But what about a different one?

What about Lila Wilde?

I took a shaky breath. This plan would work. *It had to.* I wanted my music to have a home, but I also wanted Mom to have peace. If I became Lila, everyone would be happy; that was all I wanted.

Slow, quiet applause brought me out of my thoughts as the performer before me exited the stage. I hadn't listened too closely, but I had caught him struggling to manage both playing his guitar and singing.

The poor guy wasn't made for multitasking.

I watched his twisted frown as he breezed past me. Despite his sullen mood, my eyes drifted to his toned jawline and dark hair.

He was cute.

I wondered if he liked what he saw when I was Lila. Gone was my red hair, covered by a black wig. This wasn't my best look, but my skin tone looked decent enough once I paired it with darker lashes and red lips. After I did my makeup like Mom and I had discussed, I barely recognized myself, which must have meant my disguise was good.

I looked at Dad, who gave me a thumbs-up. This was the first time I'd seen him in a while. A few years ago, he left to travel after Mom and his divorce was final. Mom told me he was never the kind of man to stay in one place very long and that I should make peace with the fact that he'd been gone.

When he'd called me and told me about this opportunity, I'd been shocked. I'd mentioned my writing and singing the few times we talked on the phone, but I didn't know he'd remembered.

His planning all of this for me meant more than I could say.

Of course, here, he wasn't *Dad*. He was just a guy who came to see the show. Lila Wilde didn't have any connections to the people who birthed me. On the off chance I did get famous, people would try to find everything they could, or at least that's what Mom was worried about.

I grabbed my guitar and darted up there, wishing she had joined. Most of my songs had been sung to her first, even if she wasn't all that into music. Luckily,

Dad offered to record my performance, which meant she got to be safe and comfortable back in Canada.

And if she was happy, I was happy.

"Hi," I said to the crowd, cursing the shakiness in my voice. "I'm Lila. Lila Wilde." The name sounded odd on my lips. "I wrote this myself. I hope you like it."

I strummed the first chord, pretending I was at home rather than in front of people. It was the only way I could ignore my nerves. All of my fears fell away as I sang. I'd practiced for this. I knew every note to hit, every move to make, and how to get the crowd to melt in my hands. I didn't focus on them, though. I focused on the words I'd written alone in my room.

When it was over, I was surprised by the loud applause. My eyes slid to the agent, whose lips formed a smile.

I stepped off the stage with shaky hands, taking in all the applause. Rick walked up to me the moment I did.

"You wrote that yourself?" he asked.

"I did," I replied. "Was it good?"

"More than good." He handed me a business card. "You know, you remind me of my daughter. She's your age and has the same drive you do. Maybe you could be friends."

I had no idea if I wanted a friend or not, but I did know that I needed to make this guy happy if I was going to hear my songs on the radio.

"That sounds fun," I replied. Rick's smile told me I'd said the right thing.

"I'll be in touch."

He'd be in touch? Yes!

"O-okay. Thank you!"

He smiled at me one last time and then turned. The guy who'd gone on before me was behind him.

"Blaze," Rick said. "You did your best."

But nothing else.

I winced and watched the boy's face fall.

But he didn't stay down for long. His brown eyes moved to me and his smile returned. "You were fantastic." His voice was smooth. He held out a hand. "Blaze Matthews."

"Ro—I mean, Lila. Lila Wilde."

"Was that written about your boyfriend?" he asked.

"No. I don't have one of those."

It was actually written about a day out with Mom, but I'd never admit that. I didn't want to sound naive.

"Are you busy tomorrow?"

Tomorrow, I was supposed to go back home in the middle of nowhere and tell Mom how it had gone. But this was an opportunity. Rick would probably call and I knew it would be best to hang around. I glanced over at Dad, hoping he would be okay with staying one more day.

"I don't think so," I said. "Why?"

"Because I think we could make a good team. I also know Rick pretty well, considering I'm friends with his daughter."

If I knew one thing, it was that I needed to make connections in LA. I nodded, taking all of him in as if I could read his mind from one look.

I could be what he wanted. I could be what *Rick* wanted as well. And if it meant putting away Rose and being Lila, then I could do that too.

This dream of mine was the one selfish thing I was allowing myself, yet knowing I needed to make Rick and Blaze happy was comforting. I did my best work when it was for others and this had the potential to be *everything*.

Barry

"Barry!" Ruth snapped, throwing a pillow. "Get out of my room! I'm trying to study!"

"For what?" I asked. "Another test? Who cares?"

I knew the answer. *She* cared. Tom did too.

And because Dad cared.

I never saw why. If we were going to college, would the admissions office care about *one* test? Wasn't it the cumulative effort? Why did every single detail have to be perfect?

I'd tried to tell Ruth that, but she studied like her life depended on it. She was determined to be better than Tom, who was already top of his class.

"You need to catch up to him," Mom had told her. *"Be better than he is."*

She'd tried that on me, and it had gone in one ear and out the other.

"Just because you don't care about what Mom and Dad think doesn't mean I don't. Go away!"

"Can't we hang out or something? I'm *bored*."

"No!" She threw another pillow.

I rolled my eyes, but they caught on a CD she had in her room. I grabbed it, wondering if theft would distract her from her studies.

"I'm taking this," I singsonged.

"I don't care."

"I really am."

"Just go!"

I slowly walked out of the room, CD in hand. It didn't do anything to curb the disappointment. Sometimes, I could get Ruth to hang out—something I loved since Mom and Dad didn't let us have friends over because we needed to focus on our studies.

This was obviously not one of those days.

When I got to my room, Mom called out that I needed to be working on homework. I ignored her and slammed the door, alone once again.

But at least in the confines of my bedroom, no one was telling me what to do.

I looked at the CD, seeing a girl with black hair and hazel eyes staring back at me.

She's pretty, I thought. I wondered what her music would sound like.

I grabbed my CD player and put it in, knowing I had nothing better to do.

Words filtered over me. It was an upbeat party song with a killer baseline, and the girl singing had a bright voice, in tune at every note, even when she belted.

We didn't listen to music in the Murray household. Tom had tried to once, but then he stopped out of nowhere. Ruth probably listened to this while doing her homework.

The second song came on as I was mulling over the fact that my brother and sister were at our parents' beck and call.

But then the lyrics hit me. They were about the moments of silence when alone, when no one's expectations awaited you.

And they hit *hard*.

I sat up and grabbed the lyric book, flipping to the second song. As I read along, I saw myself in the words and felt connected to this pop star in a way I never had with anyone else.

Suddenly, being alone didn't seem so bad if I got to listen to her sing.

I knew without a shadow of a doubt that I'd use my meager allowance to buy more of her stuff. And Ruth wasn't getting her CD back. I doubted she would care all that much anyway.

No one ever really cared in the first place.

CHAPTER ONE

Lila

Has Lila Wilde Fallen Off?

By Perez Adder

After her last album's release, critics and fans are wondering what happened to the woman we once loved. In the last few years, her music has become increasingly shallow. Of course, her fans are unlikely to care as her music still charts with every release.

But for the rest of us not in her cult, we wonder if she's lost her writing talent entirely. When will we hear her more profound songs again? Is she doomed to be a basic pop-song factory forever?

Fans are awaiting her next album, which is expected to be as shallow as this one. I'll have more news as it develops.

4,658 comments

Babytali: Leave her alone. Her music is so catchy!

A Twisted Theory: No, this article has a point. She's all dance moves and pop now. She used to release stuff talking about fear of fame, feeling alone, and being left behind. Where are those songs?

Bambi: Not everyone wants to be fucking sad all the time . . .

IsaIsa: All of this arguing is missing one thing. Does SHE look happy with her music? I mean, she does all the interviews and stuff, but when was the last time she actually looked proud of what she was singing? Even in concerts, her eyes look dead.

Babytali: You don't know her so stfu

I finished the final song to the sounds of thunderous applause. It was eleven at night and I was on my second encore. I should have stopped, but the cheering fans kept begging for more and I'd always had one extra song for them.

Blaze was in the crowd and people's phones went from me to him, filming his overzealous reactions to my ending.

"Please give it up for my wonderful band," I called into the microphone, "who's played amazingly for you all night. And for my backup dancers too!"

This would be where I would give a shout-out to Blaze in the audience. It had been a tradition since my first concert when I'd been so overwhelmed with nerves that he had to be in the front row, cheering me on.

I could feel the crowd waiting for me to mention him, as if they were collectively holding their breaths.

But I couldn't. The image of his lips on another woman's a few weeks before flashed in my mind. When it happened, we'd been on a break from shows, though I'd still been practicing with my team. This was the first time we were back, and I was expected to perform as usual.

"Thank you all!" I said instead. "Have a great night!"

I exited the stage without another look at him.

My scalp was itchy from wearing the wig for so long. I was ready to get out of this bright minidress. I wanted my fake eyelashes off, but I couldn't do that until I was completely alone.

I took an unsteady breath. I could still hear the audience cheering. The band played the closing notes as the door to my dressing room opened.

"Are you kidding me?" a voice asked. "Way to add fuel to the fire, Lila."

Blaze had come after me.

I'd barely talked to him since I found out. We both knew the final shows of the tour would be hard now that I'd seen him with someone else. So far, none of the fans were aware that anything was wrong, but I expected speculation after this.

"Post the photos of us from spring, then," I said. "It'll distract from the rumors."

"We can't break up," he replied. "You know that you have to get over this, right? There are engagement rumors that we *have* to fulfill. The fans expect it."

I knew. I knew better than anyone else, but I had nothing else to say to him.

"The silent treatment? Really? You better have this together when we go to the next show tomorrow night."

I still didn't answer.

"You're always so immature. I need to find Mia. She'll talk some sense into you."

When he finally walked away, I could breathe again. I needed him to stay gone so I could figure out what the hell I wanted to do.

But Mia was coming and she'd reiterate everything Blaze had just unnecessarily reminded me of.

The fans would be disappointed. He would be disappointed. *Rick* would be disappointed if he were alive. And considering Mia was his daughter, she knew what he'd feel.

It was all too much. My throat was closing up and my chest ached. After shows, I was always a little jumpy, but the reminder that I was about to get lectured made it all worse.

I didn't do this. I didn't disappoint people.

But I couldn't *thank* him when his betrayal was so fresh.

Mia walked into the dressing room, hand on her hip, blue eyes narrowed in my direction. She'd always looked sharp, especially with her severe dark brown bob—even when I'd originally met her at sixteen. But now, her pointy edges *hurt*. "Really?"

"I couldn't."

"You have to. You said yourself that you didn't want rumors."

I pressed my lips together.

"Just get in the car. We're leaving."

"Shouldn't we meet with fans?"

"I canceled that. The last thing we need is for you to make this worse. Come on."

I followed her to the armored car, feeling like a petulant child. Not meeting the fans was the harshest punishment she could dole out. The people who supported me were my everything.

Still, I couldn't wait to get back to my hotel for the night where I could be blissfully alone. Only then could I get out of my Lila costume and be myself for a bit.

The Nashville lights hurt my eyes, and I counted the seconds until we got to the airport.

I'd only been here on tour and I didn't know where I was, but the buildings grew taller, the roads more congested. This didn't match the way we'd come in.

"Why are we going downtown?"

"Have you ever heard of exposure therapy?"

I frowned, but then I saw what she was talking about: Blaze, surrounded by cameras.

"No," I protested.

"Yes. You're going to go on a romantic walk with him down Broadway. Now."

"I can't."

"We all make sacrifices for this. You're the couple. Now, go and be a couple."

She pushed me out of the car and I had a moment before the cameras knew I was there. I was still in my tour outfit, and after singing for hours, I hadn't had any water.

Mia was probably right. I needed to do this. I needed to get over this thing with Blaze. People wanted us together. Our love songs were what sold albums.

But my feet didn't want to walk toward him. I didn't want to do a pap walk. I wanted to be alone and to get out of this damn wig.

So, instead of doing my job, I ran.

I ducked into an alley, hand going to my hairline. It was glued on, as always, before the show. Ripping it off would hurt, but I could get it off and leave it somewhere. Usually, I'd never take this kind of risk, but desperate times called for desperate measures.

Then I heard something in the dark of the alley. I yelped, turning around with my hands raised in some version of self-defense.

But I dropped them when I saw the man before me.

Long, dark blond hair piled on his head in a bun that put any of mine to shame. His brows were darker than his hair and matched the short, well-trimmed beard framing the lower half of his face. He was kept, yet un-kempt. He screamed mess but in an organized way.

And his eyes were widened in my direction. "You're—"

"Please don't say my name," I said breathlessly. "There are reporters just around the block."

"I'm well aware."

I opened my mouth, but I could hear the cameras coming. In the back-ground, I heard Mia calling my name. She was *angry,* and it made me want to hide even more.

"Can I come in?" I asked.

"Do you even know where you are?"

"N-no, but I'd rather be inside and away from *that*." I pointed in the direction of the commotion. This man could have been a serial killer for all I knew, but in that moment, it was better than being seen with Blaze.

He stared at me like I was a fool, and to be fair, I was. But he pressed his palm on the door behind him and opened it wide.

I didn't waste any time darting inside. Once the door was closed, I realized I was alone in a dark room with a stranger.

I should have been afraid, but I wasn't.

The lights flipped on, and I took in my new surroundings. I saw an old tile floor and stainless-steel appliances.

"I hope you don't make a habit of asking men you don't know if you can come into random buildings," my savior said.

"I don't. You must be the exception."

His eyes met mine, and I could have sworn he was seeing through my soul.

"Make sure I'm the only one."

"Why?"

"Because I know I'd never do a thing to hurt you," his voice was low. "I can't say the same for others."

My heart kicked into gear, but for an entirely different reason.

My eyes trailed over his features once more. He was the kind of man who I could write songs about.

A man who's indescribable, yet I wanted to try.

The lyric popped into my head, which had been abnormally silent for the last few weeks, except for the angry, hurt words pouring out of me. This was the longest I'd gone without writing anything *good*.

"I can't thank you enough," I said, voice wavering. "I could, um, pay you for your time?"

"I don't care about money."

"You have to want something." People always did, and I always found a way to give it to them.

"I want to know why you were panicking in an alleyway and running from a slew of paparazzi."

Ah. Well, that was a bit more complicated.

"Would you believe me if I said I was just tired?"

"Probably, since you just had a concert, but you usually do fan meetings."

Just how much did he know about me? He didn't look like my typical sort of fan.

"Those were canceled for . . ." I looked outside, thinking of the chaos Mia had called to photograph Blaze and me in the street. "Don't worry about it. It's really not that interesting of a story."

The corner of his lip quirked up. "Try me."

It had been a while since someone cared about *me*. My career was about others. At first, it was pleasing the fans by revealing the depths of my soul. But then Mia had taken over Rick's place and she'd told me they didn't want to hear me whine about my life. They wanted dance hits.

In my midnight social media doomscrolling, I saw some weren't happy. They missed my old stuff.

But then Mia showed me the records I was breaking, which shut me up.

However, the doubt always continued. No matter what I did, someone was always disappointed in me.

The man standing before me was different than the company I'd kept over the last few years. He'd turned down the money and asked *me* a question. This was a clean slate, someone I didn't know yet, and it was exciting.

That must have been why I answered.

"I was supposed to be seen with Blaze and I couldn't do it."

"Blaze, huh? What did he do to you this time?"

"How do you know he did anything to me before?"

"You try to be subtle in your dissatisfaction with him, but it's a little like a sledgehammer to those who listen enough."

"So you've heard my songs?" I asked, heart skipping a beat again.

"Every word." His voice was soft. "So, tell me, what did he do?"

"He lost focus," I said, eyes closing as I remembered that waitress. "I don't know if I can talk about it."

Not without a nondisclosure agreement at least, and I didn't know how to bring that up to a man I didn't know. Usually, Mia handled that.

Through the door, I heard people searching for me, calling my name. Blaze had joined in, his voice the loudest. They must have been in the alley.

I closed my eyes. I could see the pictures of him valiantly searching for me. It was as vivid as his lips on another woman's.

"You're safe here. They don't know where you are."

The words soothed me more than I could let on. "S-so, where am I? What's this safe place called?"

"A bar. It's called Movers and Shakers."

"One of those legendary country bars I hear Nashville has?"

He chuckled. "Not exactly."

"What else is there here?"

"Nashville's a city of music. All kinds of music. I showcase it all. Plus the occasional dance night."

"You dance?"

"Not really," he said.

I could picture him twirling a woman around a dance floor—one who'd managed to snag his attention.

"What about with the right person?"

"Are you offering?" he asked slowly.

"Oh, no. I'm exhausted from my show. I mean someone who's not . . . me."

"Maybe."

"Then I hope you meet her soon."

His eyes were on mine, and I could have sworn he saw right through me, down to the person I hid. "Anything is possible."

Stormy eyes that matched my soul.

Shit. I would have a whole song before the night was over.

The sounds of the reporters faded. I could have snuck out after they were gone, but I didn't want to.

"What does the front of this place look like?"

"Do you want to see it?"

"Yes."

"And you have time?"

"Why are you worried about my schedule?"

"You're one of the biggest musicians in the world. I assume you're busy."

Musicians. Not just a pop star.

God, I missed that distinction.

"Not really," I admitted. "But I'll steal it."

Robbing myself for borrowed moments with you.

I'd need to get to my notebook the moment I left.

"You don't have to be polite, you know. I'd happily let you go if you have somewhere to be."

Show me more.

I shook my head. "No need to let me go. I want to see the front of the bar."

"Follow me, then."

He walked me into another room. One with vaulted ceilings and a stage. "I bet this place is pretty cool when it's lit up."

Then the lights turned on and I saw pink and teal neon everywhere.

"You get the full service," he said. "Even if we're closed for the night. And don't worry. All the windows are blacked out."

As lights danced above me, my mind memorized everything because I knew I'd return to it in my dreams.

"I didn't know Nashville had a place like this."

"There are interesting things everywhere if you look hard enough."

"That's my problem," I said. "Touring doesn't allow for much tourism."

"I imagine not." He walked behind the bar, grabbing a glass. "What are you having?"

"Soda water and cranberry juice."

"Not a drinker?"

"I'd reveal too much," I said, shaking my head.

"The last thing we'd want is for you to do that." Maybe I'd been imagining it, but it sounded like me revealing too much was *exactly* what he wanted me to do.

And if things were different, I would be happy to tell him everything.

It was a terrifying thought.

Barry

I'd been relieved when we decided to close the bar early tonight. Finally, after a long day of work, no one was around and I could finally think straight.

That was when I saw Lila Wilde in my alleyway.

For a second, I thought I'd been dreaming. What were the odds that the woman I spent most of my lonely hours with was in the alleyway of *my* bar? But then I saw her face full of fear, and I knew that even in my dreams, I never wanted to see that again.

That annoying little voice in my head, one I usually tried to ignore, had whispered, *Save her.*

And I listened.

Now I was staring at the woman whose words I'd listened to a hundred times, borderline flirting with her.

Keep it cool, Barry. Don't fucking blow this.

I'd bought every album since I found her. Whenever I was in a bad mood, I listened to her words to remind me of something better. I'd taught myself the guitar strings instead of doing my homework.

In the strangest way, I felt like I knew her. Or at least, she knew me. Her voice, even when not singing, was the only one I'd allowed in over these years.

And now she was *here*, and I had no idea how to exist with her in my orbit. It was temporary, I knew that. But I could only hope I made it good enough for her to remember me.

"I wish I could be here when it's open," Lila said.

"Can't you?"

She shook her head. "The minute people find out I'm here, you'll be swarmed."

"I could handle it."

She gave me a wistful smile as if she knew I definitely could not. "That might be harder than you think."

"I'm always up for a challenge."

Anything challenging would be worth having her next to me longer.

"It's okay. I'm not going to subject you to it." She took another sip. "So, what do you do for fun, mystery man?"

"My name is Barry."

"Barry? Is that short for anything?"

"Nope. My parents named me after some suit-and-tie businessman."

"I can't see you in a suit and tie."

"I happen to agree."

I didn't usually tell people about my family. My employees didn't even know about the people who raised me, but Lila broke through my walls without even trying. And I couldn't bring myself to regret it.

She didn't know who I was, yet I knew every word she'd sung and put out in the world. I knew her life and I wanted her to know about mine.

It would push her away. No one wanted to hear my sob story, but with the way she was talking, this was my only chance with her.

I wouldn't waste it.

"And what about fun?" she asked. "You never answered that."

"I tend to the bar. I make sure everyone's happy. And . . . I play guitar."

Her eyes widened. "Really?"

"I do. Sometimes I take the stage if an artist cancels."

"Wow," she said. "I bet everyone loves that."

They did, but not because of me. I sang *her* songs and no one could deny her talent. Especially when I sang the ones no one knew. "Not as much as they love you, I'm sure. You'll be releasing a new album soon, right? You do it every few years."

Her eyes fell to her drink. "I should be. We have another tour set up, but I might not meet my deadlines. I haven't written anything my agent's liked in ages."

"I have a hard time believing that."

"Everyone wants love songs from me, but I don't have any left. All I have are *not* what fans would like."

"Can you show me?"

My heart pounded in my chest. I hadn't been able to attend her concerts in the years since I opened the bar.

"I don't have a whole song written." Her eyes lifted to mine. "But I do have some ideas. If you wouldn't mind sharing your guitar, I can show you those."

My heart raced as I nodded. I had one in the back that I'd played tonight.

Once she had it in her hands, she walked on the stage, sitting on the one stool I'd left. The lights seemed to dim despite me not touching them, focusing only on her.

"This is what I have."

She played a chord, which was lower than most of her songs.

And she let out lyrics I'd *never* heard from her before. They were angry and spiteful.

And it could only be about one man.

The song stopped abruptly, her face twisting in frustration. "That's all there is. I didn't finish it because my agent didn't like it."

"Your agent is an idiot," I said, and she slowly lifted her head.

"You liked it?"

"I did."

"But I don't think my fans would. They want love songs. And I'm . . . not in love. So they're hard to write."

I sucked in a surprised breath. She wasn't in love with Blaze? She caught my slip and her hazel eyes trained on me. I carefully placed my calm exterior back on my face. "They would get used to it."

"Then you haven't seen all the fan edits." She handed me the guitar. "He cheated on me, you know. That's when I wrote that."

I jerked back. He cheated on *her*? How did a man have someone like Lila fucking Wilde and then blow it by cheating? And how did she not murder him when she found out?

I'd do it for her if she asked, and the conviction I felt was almost terrifying.

Lila let out a long sigh, looking at her feet. "I'm *so* angry, Barry."

"You should be."

"But I still have a job to do. So, we're pretending everything is fine."

"Nothing is fine. He cheated on you and you're allowed to be angry about it. You're a human, Lila."

She looked out the blackened windows, where people searched for her. "I don't think I'm supposed to be."

"You're always supposed to be human. That's the best part about any of us. That's what's good about your music."

Her eyes met mine again, one corner of her mouth lifting. "My old music, you mean."

"Your new stuff isn't all that bad. You still write it."

"And apparently, it breaks records and puts me in the number one spot."

"No. Don't worry about that kind of stuff. It gets you nowhere."

She blinked at the harsh tone that escaped me. I regretted letting it slip, but the talk about breaking records reminded me a little too much of my parents.

And they'd always be a sore spot for me.

"You sound like you speak from experience."

"A little. My parents are the kind of people who only care about accomplishments. I got out of there quickly."

Her eyes trailed around the bar. "You're doing well for yourself."

Please. Tell me that again.

I'd mastered never needing anyone to compliment me.

Except for her.

"I think I am too. Who needs parental approval when you've built a successful business out of nothing? Besides, I've always given them a hard time."

"How so?"

"My dad wanted me to work at his company. In some suit and tie. It was never for me. But they both never hesitate to let me know that I'm messing things up."

"But *look* at this place."

"They don't see it that way. But I showed them. If you go look out there"—I pointed to the front window—"you'll see a tall building with the name Murray and Sons on it. I put up my sign right in sight of his office so every time he works late, he can see exactly how much I am nothing like him."

"His logo looks . . ."

"Like a dick? Yeah, there's a whole Reddit account dedicated to it. I may or may not have started it."

She laughed. "That's a level of petty I aspire to be." Her eyes went distant for a moment. Then she turned to me. "Do you have a pen and a napkin?"

I nodded and brought them to her. She scribbled down something, dark hair obscuring her face.

"What do you think of this?"

A man designed to live in his father's shadow, all he had were expectations.

So he built a castle in the dark corners, erasing all that preparation.

"Is that . . . about me?"

"Yeah." A small smile crossed her face. "You're inspiring."

"It's . . ." *Amazing. Cherished. Something to literally pass out over.* "Brilliant."

"Really? I could write more."

"Like what?"

"I don't know. Something about your hair or your eyes."

"My hair and eyes are usually a point of contention."

"Why?"

"I don't look like my dad. And to a self-serving narcissist like him, he took it as an insult."

"You look exactly how you should," she said, her eyes trailing over my features.

Having my idol look at me like that turned my insides to mush. I'd met many women, yet none of them had ever made me feel like this.

Her phone beeped and her eyes moved from mine. She frowned as she read the screen.

"Please tell me it's not your boyfriend."

"No, my security guard. She's here to get me."

"How did she know where you were?"

"She has my location in case I ever get lost."

"Do you have to go?"

"Yes. I should probably stop hiding." She handed me my guitar. "Sorry I couldn't stay longer."

"I'm glad I had you even for a few moments."

"I still feel like I owe you something for hiding me."

"There is one thing."

An eyebrow raised.

"Don't forget me, even when you meet more interesting people."

Her lips turned upward. "I can promise you that I won't."

Chapter Two

My red hair fell in waves past my shoulders. I didn't have a speck of makeup on, and my light eyebrows and eyelashes differentiated me from the woman I normally played. In the busy streets of Nashville, no one recognized me.

I was no longer Lila Wilde. I was Rose Hill, the nobody from nowhere.

My tour was over. I'd been given a long break that I wanted to use to catch up with Dad. I was supposed to be writing, but other than songs obviously about the man I met in Movers and Shakers, I couldn't muster anything.

Blaze wasn't happy.

Mia wasn't happy.

And eventually, my fans wouldn't be happy.

I was trying to play cool about it, but anxiety pressed into every inch of my body.

And that led me back to Nashville, to where the man who'd saved me lived.

"Isn't this a great town, Rosie?" Dad asked, smiling over at me. "Listen to all the music playing!"

The last time I was here on Broadway was when I was running from Blaze and paparazzi. That night had been cemented in everyone's memory as the night I was almost kidnapped. Blaze had made a massive story of it, saying how worried he'd been about me and my whereabouts. The official press release said I'd just gone to my hotel early.

And considering I didn't even plan to have a hotel in Nashville, the lie felt wrong.

But now I was back in Nashville as *me*. I hadn't been Rose in . . . forever.

No one was looking for Lila Wilde here. As far as they knew, I was in LA, either spending my time with Blaze or writing my next album.

I nodded along, eyes looking for the bar I'd waited weeks to get us into. Movers and Shakers was incredibly busy, and they limited who could enter to keep the experience exclusive for all customers. I'd joined the waiting list when I found out Dad wanted to visit Nashville and catch up with me.

We didn't talk daily. And despite knowing he wasn't the kind of man who would fix all my problems, I still needed him around.

Mom was the responsible one. Dad was . . . well, *Dad*.

And her always being there for me was the reason why I was so determined to fix *her* problems.

"I hope you're ready for something other than country," I told him as we walked. "Where we're going is different." I had to yell to be sure he heard me. My hand was tight on his wrist and I was worried we'd get separated in the sea of people.

But I also enjoyed it. I couldn't be in crowds like this as Lila.

"I love all types of music equally," Dad said.

And it was true. He was a decently famous songwriter, which was where I got my talent from. When I was a kid, he moved from rental to rental, always chasing his muse. The flavor of the week was Nashville.

After helping me get discovered, he offered more advice about the semi-famous life in the beginning. He'd helped cultivate some of my early songs when we talked on the phone and it helped me grow as an artist. And then he'd leave and do whatever.

I hadn't told him about my writer's block yet. He'd probably tell me to travel.

Dad wouldn't understand the reasons why I couldn't. I had to sneak out of LA to even be here. I doubted he wanted to know my problems anyway.

We walked up to the line for entry and I showed my ID to a very serious-looking bouncer who nodded and let us both in.

It was somehow more magical with people in it. Pop music played on the speakers and people danced without a care. The pink and teal neon lights were otherworldly, lining the tall wooden beams on the ceiling, illuminating everyone in a different kind of light.

"Wow," Dad said. "This is something."

"I'm so glad I finally got in," I replied. "It's why we had to go tonight."

"I'm always free for my favorite daughter. Especially when you're not touring."

"It's nice." I pushed back the doubts in my mind. *Was* he really free? Not usually.

"Do you know what's *really* nice? This music! Come on, Rosie. Let's dance!"

Dad shook his hips like he wasn't a man nearly in his sixties. Instead of following him to the dance floor, my eyes searched the bar for the man I was desperate to see again.

I hadn't ever finished that song. I wasn't able to once he wasn't in front of me, but I'd at least kept his promise to remember him. He just wouldn't know who I was.

Dad was busy enjoying himself, so much so that I doubted he would notice if I wandered off. And I didn't want anyone to see just how hard I was looking for Barry.

Lila might have been with Blaze, but I held to that even as Rose. Though tabloids wouldn't see this, I would, so if I did talk to Barry, it would only be as a friend. If Dad saw me, however, he would have questions.

Despite my not-so-single status, I felt a little freer coming to see Barry like this. I could talk to him as *me*.

Not the pop star.

But all I could see was a bartender with seriously incredible dance moves. As cool as it was, it wasn't what I came here for.

I tried to stop myself from frowning. Where was he?

"Sorry to slow things down," I heard over the speaker. My heart skipped a beat as I turned toward the stage. I found Barry, but he looked different today. His hair was down, falling over one of his shoulders. There was volume to his hair, something I could never manage with mine considering it was constantly shoved under a wig.

He leaned against a stool, eyes on his guitar. His movements were fluid. Barry looked relaxed as if all of the attention on him didn't bother him. *How?* The first time I was on a massive stage, I nearly passed out.

"I had a band coming to play tonight, but the singer lost her voice. They were going to do a pop mix for you all, but I'm afraid you're stuck with me and my guitar."

"Go Barry!" the dancing bartender called.

"Now, this is a song you'll know," he said, "but I wanted to put a new spin on it. A friend of mine gave me this idea. I haven't spoken to her in a while, but I hope somehow she hears this."

He smiled as if he were remembering someone he was very fond of. Whoever she was—she was lucky.

But then Barry played a chord. I recognized it as one of my own.

No. He can't be.

He got close to the mic, singing one of my biggest hits, but slower and in that lower register I'd played for him when I'd been here.

My knees went weak. He played the song like he'd done it a million times over. His voice, low and rough, said my lyrics with ease. It rocked me to my core.

He said he'd listened to *every word* of music. Now, I believed him.

As it came to an end, the crowd cheered for him, and I wondered how the hell he'd been here and not on massive stages in front of thousands of people.

"Oh, what's that look on your face?" Dad asked.

I jumped. "Don't sneak up on me!"

"Sorry. I walked up while the performance was on. You didn't come and dance, so I wanted to check on you, and here you are, staring at the lumberjack onstage."

"Do you think he looks like a lumberjack?" I asked, eyes still on Barry.

"I think you were looking at him like you used to look at *someone* else."

"I'm . . . He's just cute."

"I'd say he's hot. For your age group, of course."

"I can't say that. I'm not single."

"I know, but I haven't seen you look at him the way you just looked at that man on the stage in a long time. Want to tell me why?"

I didn't know why he cared. He didn't have to.

Thankfully, before I could answer, the music started again, drowning out any possible words. Barry got off the stage and was instantly pulled into conversation by one of the women who'd been fanning herself during the performance. I don't know why my chest sank. I wasn't single anyway.

Dad was still looking at me expectantly, so I gestured for him to follow me and led him to the lobby.

"Things with the boyfriend and I aren't great," I said.

"And?"

"And I . . . I don't know. People want me with him. You know how it is."

"I don't tend to look, but I know how much you care. What did Blaze do?"

My throat felt dry. I hadn't told anyone anything yet, and no matter how much I wanted to trust Dad, the words wouldn't come out. "We've just been together awhile. Both of us are struggling to feel the spark."

"Are you sure that's it?"

"Yep."

Dad looked back in the direction of the stage. "Maybe you need a break, then. A break to follow where your eyes lead. If they tell you to go for someone else, there might be a reason."

This wasn't surprising advice. He was the one who went to whatever city he wanted to. He'd followed his heart his entire life. And that included leaving Mom shortly after they had me.

My eyes went in the direction of the main area. My heart was with my fans. They'd changed my life, made it so Mom could quit working and Dad could travel without a care in the world, more so now that I gave him the same stipend as Mom. The fans had made it so Blaze didn't have to worry about money a day in his life.

I couldn't let them down.

So I would stay with Blaze.

"I'm okay," I said. "Want to finish out the night?"

"Is that what *you* want?"

"Yeah, I haven't gotten to dance very much."

"Sounds good, Rosie. I wouldn't mind dancing more."

We walked back in and I took a deep breath. I pointedly didn't look for Barry. Seeing him hadn't filled me with peace at all. It had given me a buzz, and the feeling wanted me to find him and make him mine.

I walked through the crowd, the music taking me over. The DJ was playing some incredible songs and they knew exactly how to play to the people.

I danced, avoiding any routines that would make me look like Lila. It took me a moment to warm up, but eventually, the music invaded my mind, pushing out all thoughts of Barry.

I lost myself, dancing for me and only me, which I hadn't done in a very long time.

My worries were gone for a few blissful seconds, but then a man got a little too close. I stepped away, trying to give him the hint that I wasn't interested.

He only followed.

Okay, it was time to use words.

"Um, no, thank you."

He didn't move, his eyes dark.

My skin prickled as I tried to get away from him. I looked for Dad but couldn't find him. Would I seriously have to punch out a guy in the middle of this bar?

An arm came between us. "All right, buddy. If her pulling away *and* saying no wasn't enough for you, then I'll be clear. She's not interested." *I knew that voice.* It was the same one on the stage just a moment ago.

Barry.

"But—"

"I *will* make you leave." Barry's voice left no room for argument. My eyes trailed over him, catching on his long hair. Now that it was in front of me, I wondered what it would be like to run my hands through it.

"Try me," the guy challenged, puffing up his chest.

Barry moved away from me and grabbed him by the arm. "Gladly."

My jaw went slack as I witnessed them disappear, my skin sizzling with a ridiculous heat just from witnessing Barry's muscles working to remove the man from my space.

He was back within five minutes.

"Sorry about him. Can I get you a drink? On the house."

"You don't have to give me a free drink," I said, shaking my head. My hands buzzed with nervous energy and I twirled my hair through my fingers. His eyes caught on my movements and I stilled immediately.

Some saw it as flirting. I did it all the time. It was the one thing I allowed to be the same between Lila and Rose.

"I pride myself on not letting tools like that mess with people. When they do, the people who get messed with get a free drink."

His eyes were on me and my heart was in my throat. "They do?"

"Yes. Everyone deserves to have a good time," he said, his lips turning upward. Good *God*. His smile had to be illegal. "Now, about that drink?"

His focus on me never wavered. My heart lurched. I watched him closely, looking for any sign that he knew who I was.

But he was as reserved as ever.

"Sparkling water."

He nodded and walked behind the bar. I regretted my drink choice as soon as I said it.

"Can I also get cranberry juice in it?" I asked. He paused, and I wondered if he would remember that cranberry juice and soda water were Lila's drink of choice. He finally nodded. I chewed on my lip as I watched him.

How could I have been so *stupid*? Anyone knowing who I was would ruin everything.

"So, who do I thank for this drink?" I asked when he returned. I obviously knew his name, but I desperately needed to cover for myself.

"Barry."

"Thank you, Barry. For the drink and for telling off that guy."

"It was nothing. I don't like it when people don't respect a no."

"Me either," I said. "I'm just here to dance. And see you perform, apparently. You're incredible."

"I can hold a tune. I was only a stand-in for the night."

"The crowd loved you." The words came out flirtier than I meant them to. I needed to divert before I accidentally gave him the wrong idea. "So . . . will your boss be mad that you gave away a free drink?"

"Considering I own the place, no."

It wasn't a surprise since I already knew, and yet it still sounded like such a feat for him to have built this bar. "What are you, like, twenty-five? Is that even possible?"

"Twenty-six."

"Only four years younger than me," I said.

He smiled, but his eyes shot back to the bar. I knew he was about to leave. My heart sank. He hadn't been like this with Lila at all.

"Enjoy your night."

His reservation made me desperate.

"I'm Rose, by the way."

He turned and I held out a hand.

"Nice to meet you, Rose." We shook and I wondered if he felt the same electricity that I did.

"I liked your song," I blurted. "Lila Wilde, huh?"

Oh, God. Why would I bring up my alter ego?

"Yeah. She's an interesting artist."

"She's popular, that's for sure."

"I'm guessing you're not a fan."

"Why do you say that?"

"You have that look on your face that many people get when they don't like her."

"I wouldn't say I don't like her. But I'm not her *biggest* fan. Her newest songs are . . . repetitive."

It hurt to say, but it was true for many of my longer-term fans. I couldn't seem to make everyone happy.

Barry had hinted he had been a fan for a while and I knew he had to be in that boat. I wasn't a fan of hurting my own feelings, but I had to know his honest thoughts when he wasn't faced with the pop star herself.

He would be nice to Lila—everyone was to her face. But the real opinions were online or when I wasn't around. It was the only way to get the real feedback.

"I guess you could say that. But even the repetitive ones, I like figuring out their meaning. She puts something into each one. You have to listen very hard to find them."

The lyrics he referred to were usually background vocals or some hidden line I snuck into the song that got past Mia's eyes. He had to have listened a lot even to catch that.

"What would you do if you met her?" I asked. I was playing with fire here, but I couldn't stop.

"I'd treat her like anyone else, which is the best I can."

"And what would you *say*?"

"I'd say hello like a normal person."

"But what if this was your *one* chance to say whatever you wanted to her?"

"Why do you want to know?"

"I like to think about the what-ifs." I shrugged, wondering if he was going to answer at all.

"Fine, then. If you really want to know, I'd say that she'd be the one person who gets me, even if she has no idea who I am."

My heart pounded. There was no way I should see this man again—not as Lila. But those words had me rearranging my schedule in my head, wondering when I could come back.

Barry

"That is . . . a very romantic thing to say," Rose replied. Her cheeks were red, and I wondered if it was because of the heat in the building. She was almost as tall as me, but she hunched in a way that made her seem shorter.

"Well, when dealing with Lila Wilde, you have to go all out."

"I think you're right."

I didn't know why her smile was so wide while I talked about another woman, but it was captivating. The woman before me was beautiful with subtle freckles and full lips. If I hadn't just spilled my guts to her about Lila, I'd be considering having an entirely different kind of night with her.

"You should go back to dancing," I said. "You were having fun."

"Oh, yeah. I should probably get back to it." She turned away but then paused.

"What?"

She turned back to me. "I hope you get to meet her one day."

Again, I added to myself.

"Thank you. That's very nice of you to say."

She returned to the dance floor, resuming the smooth movements that had caught my attention earlier. She was beautiful when she danced, reminding me of a certain woman who refused to leave my mind.

I tore away my eyes. I never wanted to be the kind of man who compared women, and I certainly wouldn't pursue anything with Rose because she reminded me of Lila. In fact, I wouldn't pursue anything at all with either of them. I had a bar to run; I didn't have time.

When the bar closed at four, my mind was mostly cleared.

"What a night," Liam said, brushing away his blond hair from his forehead. "Did you like my shout-out?"

"Thanks," I said. "And nice moves. How much did you make in tips?"

"Enough to pay my bills for a month. I love this town."

Everyone wanted to see the dancing bartender, and I didn't blame them. Liam was a local legend; people rewarded his moves with huge tips. He was also one of the fastest bartenders I'd ever met. When I interviewed him two years ago, he was the only person who'd almost outpaced me.

"People are *still* lined up outside," my other employee, Audrey, announced. Liam's eyes lingered on her as she walked in. "The sign says we close at four."

"I can chase them away," I said.

"I've got security on it," she replied. "If you go out there, you might get accosted by a bachelorette party."

"Wouldn't be the first time." Liam snickered.

"You guys are good to go home. I'll clean up shop," I offered.

"Nope," Liam said. "You did it alone twice last week. Let us help."

When I'd hired my employees, I never expected them to offer as much as they did. Movers and Shakers was my venture and I was used to doing most of the work alone. I didn't know how to stop feeling guilty when they stepped in to take over the responsibilities. They didn't have to do extra for me.

"You guys can go," I reiterated. "You did great today and I don't want to overwork you. Maybe you can still have a social life."

With each other, if I had a choice.

It was no secret that Liam had a crush on Audrey, and if I was right, she reciprocated it. I'd been hoping one of them would make a move for a year.

"Seriously," Audrey said. "We can—"

"Enjoy your night," I interrupted. "I can do this alone."

"Fine," Liam grumbled. "But we do it tomorrow. No takebacks."

"I can agree to that. I have my family dinner anyway. Will you two be okay staying—"

"Yes," both Audrey and Liam said. He glanced at her, a blush darkening his cheeks. They were so obvious it wasn't even funny.

"We can take care of the bar," Audrey continued, "even if your dinner goes over."

"You deserve time with your family."

I pressed my lips together. They didn't know I was looking for a way *out* of being with my family. I hated going to see my parents every week, hearing the same lecture over and over again. But Tom and Ruth wanted me to go, and even though I hated every second of it, they were the two people I somehow still didn't want to let down.

They'll come around, that nagging voice in the back of my head said. *Keep waiting.*

I hated that I listened every single damn time.

Tom, my older brother, was there first. But as usual, he was talking about Murray and Sons with Dad.

Out of all of us, Tom was the only one who'd been what our father wanted. He was his right-hand man and the sole one out of the three of us who worked in that glass tower that was the family business. When I first opened the bar, I wondered what Tom would think of it.

And he never said a word.

But I didn't expect him to. When he wasn't working, he was drinking—up until my sister and I told him he had an addiction. After that, we all hadn't talked at all, other than these family dinners.

Some days, I didn't know why I was here. I didn't have to see any of them, but whenever I thought about storming out for the final time, I would remember the last night we felt like real siblings. There had been a tornado and Tom protected us. I didn't remember much of it, but I recalled him hugging us close, being there in ways Mom and Dad weren't.

I wondered where that boy had gone.

Walking into the kitchen, I readied myself for the lecture I'd get from Mom about my lack of a college education. Sometimes, I'd wait for Ruth to get here so she could take over and hear about how much Mom wanted her promoted.

Sometimes, Mom even compared the two of us, pitting us against each other to get us to do what they wanted.

But that trick hadn't worked in years. At least not on me.

"I don't know why you're wasting your life in a *bar* of all things rather than owning up to your maximum potential," Mom said.

Damn it. Where was Ruth?

"Because I don't want to work all hours of the day to be *your* idea of my maximum potential. I want to be happy."

"Don't you want a better life for yourself?" She shook her head. "Stability? Regular paychecks? Insurance?"

"I have all those things."

"From a *bar*," she insisted. "Don't you want something more than that?"

"I'm happy where I'm at," I said. "I always will be."

"You sound so much like—" She stopped, closing her eyes.

"So much like who?"

Her lips pressed together, and for once, I eagerly awaited her answer. But then Ruth walked in and the conversation shifted to her. The exchange stuck in my mind. Just who did I remind her of?

"I know I'm coming up on twelve months," Ruth said, sighing. "I know I need to get promoted."

And she would try. Ruth worked her ass off, probably more than Tom. She worked at some banking company that I didn't care to know the name of, in a high-level position, making either close to or more than six figures with her salary. She'd done it all without her family name carrying her, something that Tom couldn't claim. Out of all of us, she was the most impressive and hardest working.

I would never get why they didn't see that.

Mom didn't let up, even as both of us got tired.

It didn't get better at the dinner table, either. Dad joined in on the questions, and even though Tom made a half-assed effort to try to take the heat off us, nothing would work.

I left dinner annoyed and having not said anything to Ruth or Tom without our parents present. I knew my life wasn't conventional, but I was happy. I got to sing on my stage and manage one of the best bars in Nashville. I always said I wouldn't come back when I was alone in my car.

Stay. For them.

I always told that voice to fuck off. I'd wasted my youth fighting for my siblings. I'd lost my chance to pursue music instead of the bar because I was still hanging around, hoping they'd do something other than what was expected.

And here we were, never changing.

I didn't even know if Ruth had friends or if Tom would stay sober. My siblings had never been to the bar since I opened it. They'd never heard me play guitar. Sometimes, I wondered if they even cared. Maybe they were destined to turn out like Dad.

Once, a long time ago, I finally put down my foot and didn't come to the family dinners. They were desperate for me to return, and I did. For some fucking reason, I did.

I *wanted* them to know something about me. I hoped they would aspire to be more than Dad's little minions, and then they'd see they could have more. That little shred of hope inched closer to death each week.

And yet, I still came back.

Chapter Three

"**Y**ou've got to solve this problem." Blaze threw another piece of popcorn in his mouth. "I can't keep our fans' interest up forever."

We sat in our shared house in LA. Technically, it was only mine, but Blaze had moved in the second I bought it, saying rent in this city was way too high and we needed to move in together anyway since we were a couple. I'd been all for it back then, but ever since the end of my tour, I'd wanted more space from him. All I could muster was telling him to move into the guest room, something he endlessly complained about.

If it wasn't about the water pressure in the en suite bathroom, it was that sunlight didn't hit the windows correctly.

"I'm doing the best I can," I said slowly, trying not to snap.

"You're thinking too hard about the wrong thing. That waitress was nothing to me, and it's been forever since it happened."

I gritted my teeth. I stared at the empty page in my notebook. It *had* been a long time. Months of no progress on either of our ends. Blaze was the perfect man in front of cameras, always trying to hold my hand, always talking up this next album. In private, he was always saying I wasn't doing enough. I needed to write more about him, do more interviews, and be seen more.

Other pages in my notebook were filled with songs, some angry, un-releasable rock songs, but most longed for a man across the country.

Just write something about Blaze. Anything.

All I could feel was anger.

"I can't."

"It was just a little messing around that got out of hand. It wasn't a huge deal."

If I had to hear about this little affair one more fucking time . . . I'd heard everything about it, how they talked about how much he missed me, how the kiss was a slip of his judgment, and how she'd been around when I wasn't.

But I hadn't heard that it would never happen again or that he was sorry.

"Obviously it's a big deal if I can't write songs now."

"Push past it, Lila. Come on."

I twirled my fake hair, feeling the thicker strands run through my fingers. I didn't even want to be Lila right now. Being back in LA grated on my nerves. Everyone—whether it be paparazzi on the street, my fans, or my own team—was begging for more news on the in-progress album, especially since we couldn't stop the rumors of trouble in paradise.

"How about you fucking apologize," I snapped back.

He rolled his eyes. "Don't be dramatic about it. But if you must hear the words: *I'm sorry.*" They were said mockingly. "I couldn't help that you were busy and on tour."

"I was on break and you were traveling *with* me!"

"But you were *always practicing.*"

"Yes, to be sure I could actually do the show."

He scrubbed his hand over his face. "You always have an excuse. I remember when I could simply look at you and you'd want me. My balls are going to shrivel up and fall off at this rate."

"Then you shouldn't have kissed the waitress."

"It's just one hurdle, Lila. We can figure this out once you get over this and get back to writing. I'm your *muse*, remember? You should always be able to write things about me."

"You're not my muse."

"Oh? Then is it someone else?"

My mind flashed to Barry. *Shit.* I didn't need to be thinking of him right now. "N-no."

"Is that *guilt* I hear?"

"No. You're not hearing anything."

"Then let me see the other pages of your notebook."

I instinctively went to grab it to protect it, but he ripped it out of my hands. "Blaze!"

"Chill, Lila. You're so dramatic." It felt like my soul was being examined as he flipped through the pages. "Huh. Looks like I was right. These aren't about me."

Shit. I was in trouble.

"Give it back."

His dark brows rose as he surveyed the lyrics about a man with hulking arms and long hair. "Have *you* been cheating, little Miss Perfect?"

"Absolutely not," I said. "You've just been a little less interesting to me since *you* cheated."

"Of course. You always have to take the moral high ground."

"Don't you care that I'm not attracted to you?"

"Oh, honey, you *have* to be attracted to me. It's what the fans want." And he wasn't wrong. People loved that I'd only written about him since I was discovered. They all said it was amazing how I never lost him as I got caught up in the glitz and glamour of music. "We'll just change the lyrics a bit," Blaze added. "This can work."

"I'm not changing the lyrics," I said. "Or making a song out of it."

"This has the bones of a good song. If it were about me, Mia would love it." He threw my notebook down on the table. "Write more like this."

"Wh-what?"

"Write. More." He said it like I was a clueless child. "Wherever you found this guy, go back. Make an album, and then we'll make it about me. I can work on growing my hair out to match your lyrics." He ran his hands through his hair. "I'm already blond."

There was a huge difference between his platinum bottle color and what I assumed was Barry's darker, natural shade.

"You want me to write an album about another man?" I asked. "Why would I—"

"Because it's what the fans want. They want an album and we can make it about me like you always do. Besides, you're in your head about me kissing that girl, and this is your way of getting revenge. So have it, and then come back to me like the good girl you are."

My stomach lurched. I hated every second of this. "I won't do it. I'm not going back to Nashville or to Movers and Shakers to write anything."

Blaze laughed and pulled out his phone. Was he *texting* someone? "Now you are. I'm having Mia get you a hotel in Nashville."

"*What?*" I nearly yelled. "I can't just *go* to Nashville."

"Take your bodyguard. You'll be fine."

I groaned. As much as I liked Juno, having her there meant I'd never be able to step foot out of the hotel as Rose. She was a hulking mountain of a woman that would catch me instantly.

"I *can't*—"

"You can for your career," he said, turning toward the door. "This is what you signed up for—and I'm not losing all of this because of your *morals*."

He waltzed out, leaving me to my fate.

It looked like I was going to Nashville.

Barry

The last thing I expected was to run into a woman in front of my office door. She stood as tall as me and wore the most serious expression I'd ever seen. She was a huge figure who had even me wondering if I could get her out of the bar if she were causing problems.

But it was the end of the night and no one should have been here.

The bar had no guests in it and I'd told Liam and Audrey to head home as I cleaned up.

I'd never been a paranoid person, but I didn't like the idea of a stranger being close to where I kept my cash. My fists balled and she caught my reaction.

"Relax, I'm not here to rob you."

"Then why are you standing in the back room of my bar?" I asked suspiciously. "No customers are allowed here, so I'd suggest you get out."

"You're fierce, huh? I like it. Makes me feel better about bringing her here."

"Who?"

She gestured into my office and I poked my head in.

I never thought I'd see Lila again. But there she was, sitting at my desk, twirling her hair between her fingers.

My throat closed.

Her black hair was straight today and her dark lashes were stark against her hazel eyes. She looked up and her gaze landed on me immediately.

"Barry," she said. Her voice sounded exactly like it had in that alley where she'd been running.

"What happened?" I asked.

She took a shaky breath and then looked at the woman guarding the door. "Juno, can you give us some space?"

That must have not been a sentence she was used to hearing. "You know I'm not supposed to—"

Lila's face fell. "Just shut the door, at least."

"Okay." I walked into the room, feeling odd that a woman I didn't know was shutting my office door behind me.

"I . . . I don't even know how to explain why I'm here. But long story short, I need to write an album."

I took in her frown. "Why do you look upset about it?"

"Blaze saw that I'd written snippets about you."

"Oh. Was he angry?"

He should have been, but I wouldn't feel guilty. This was what he deserved.

Lila's lips pressed into a thin line. "No. He wasn't. He sent me here to use you to write the album and said we'd change the lyrics later."

"What? Is that . . . what you want to do?"

"No. Not at all."

"Then don't."

She let out a long breath, eyes falling to the floor. "I have to. I *need* an album. We have a tour booked and ready to go. Everyone is waiting for *me* to write something so we can get started."

"Why don't you write one about what an asshole he is?"

"That's even worse. Fans want us together."

"What do *you* want?"

"I want my fans happy." She said it like it was obvious.

"Why?"

"It doesn't matter. Blaze thinks you can help me and I . . . I agree. The only song close to being finished is about you."

"About *me*?" That sent a jolt straight to my heart.

"I can show you if you want." She pulled out a notebook and opened it to a page filled with scribbled words.

I took it with shaky hands, reading it slowly. It was a love song, or so I hoped. If it wasn't, it was the most charged friendship track I'd ever heard. As I made it through the lyrics, my eyes caught on one line.

"'A man with a voice better than mine'—that line. What does it mean?"

"Oh, um, it's about when you sing onstage."

"You saw me sing onstage?"

Her eyes widened for a moment as I scanned through the last times I'd performed, trying to remember when she could have been here. "I heard you did. From a friend of mine."

I tried to hide my disappointment. I wish she'd seen it herself.

"So you'll make this about Blaze? As far as I know, he can't sing."

"I don't know how . . . For now, I need *something*."

"Did he come with you?"

And can I kick his ass?

"No, he has a modeling gig in LA."

"He sent you here alone, then?"

"He said I could get my revenge for the waitress." Her shoulders fell and she looked defeated.

"He's an ass."

"Maybe. But he's *my* ass."

My fists tightened and my teeth ground together. I shouldn't have been jealous of Blaze Matthews, of all people, yet here I was, wishing I was the one who was hers.

After years, I thought I would be good at being alone. I thought I would never feel jealous because I never got close enough to people to have feelings for them.

Lila was the exception.

To everything, it seemed. I should have said no and went back to my life of being alone. It was what I was good at, after all. But when Lila Wilde asked to spend time with me, I knew turning her down wasn't an option. She'd been with me through everything.

"Let's write more."

She looked at me, eyebrows raised. I didn't blame her for her confusion.

What kind of self-respecting man would let someone write songs about him and then use them for someone else?

Me.

Because I knew I wouldn't sleep at night if I turned her away now.

There was a stupid, almost useless hope that if I showed her what a real man could be, she might leave Blaze.

"Are you sure?"

"I am."

"Even if nothing between *us* can happen? I'm not like Blaze—I won't cheat on him, no matter how gorgeous you are."

She looked at the ground and I had the distinct feeling that she was *not* supposed to say that.

I hoped she'd say *more* like that.

"I understand. I do have one condition, though."

"And what's that?"

"I want you to write one song that tells *exactly* how you feel about Blaze. You don't ever have to release it, but write one. And then I want to see it."

"I can make that work," she said. "We could get started now if you wanted to. I have a lot of scattered lyrics about him."

"Yeah, let's start there."

She smiled but then paused.

"Would you kill me if I asked you to sign an NDA?"

"Not at all. I hear they're standard."

"They just feel weird to ask about, but I need to cover myself so . . . What's your email?"

She looked sheepish, but this was the least of my worries. I wouldn't tell anyone, just like I never told anyone anything.

Once I signed the digital copy, I turned and took the extra seat shoved into the corner of my office. I sat across from her, looking at what she had.

And we got to work.

CHAPTER FOUR

It was nearly six a.m. and I was dozing off. We'd been at it for hours. All-nighters were easier when I was younger, but now, I was dragging, even though I still had all of my inspiration.

"Lila?" Barry asked. "Are you okay?"

"How do you have any energy? We wrote lyrics for"—I counted the pages in front of us—"four songs. In *one* night."

I didn't know if all of them would be usable. The song about Blaze definitely wasn't, but it was a start, which I hadn't managed alone.

"It's interesting," he said. "But you need rest."

He also owned a bar and probably did this all the time. I was perpetually exhausted from all of my years of touring. I cursed the energy that others my age seemed to have.

"I know." I rubbed my hand over my face, hoping it would miraculously wake me. My hand, adorned with mascara, reminded me of exactly who I was. "I should go shower."

And be Rose for a bit.

"I think your bodyguard is asleep on a chair out there."

At the mention of Juno, I shot up. "Shit. I owe her a bonus for staying this late." And for the fact that I was about to sneak out around her. I *needed* a break.

"I'll remind you next time."

Next time. I was going to see him again. "I'm sorry I'm asking you to do this."

"Don't be. I get time with Lila Wilde. Not many can say that."

I smiled. "Thank you. You'll definitely get songwriting credit. Hell, maybe this could be your part-time job. I bet many other up-and-coming artists would love to work with you. You'd make a lot of money—"

"I don't need money." He shook his head. "This is enough."

My body heated.

"I should give you my number so we can meet up more. We'll have to work around the bar's schedule."

"Yes, of course," I said. "I'll gladly take your number."

My mind went to *other* places where I could use his number, but I shook off those thoughts immediately.

Once I had it, I gave him a wave and headed for the door.

"Can I see you tomorrow?" he asked.

"Sure. When are you free?"

"Before the bar opens. I'll be at my apartment."

"And where is your apartment?"

"Upstairs."

My eyes trailed to the ceiling. I wondered what else was up there. Didn't most bars in Nashville have a rooftop? Maybe he used it just for himself.

God, I couldn't wait to see his home. "Convenient." I tried to play it cool, but my smile spilled into my words. "I'll see you after eight hours of sleep."

I only got six. I woke myself up, eager to take a break from Lila. I'd peeled off the wig in the comfort of my room the second I got back.

Juno was asleep in her adjoined one and I'd told her I would be getting a full eight. I double-checked outside, ensuring no paparazzi had found me, and left the room.

My heart pounded. If Juno caught me, I'd be dead. And while I trusted her, I also hadn't told *anyone* who I was.

They didn't need to know. Mom had always told me *never* to let anyone know my secret. If one person knew, then more would, and that slippery slope could lead to *everyone* knowing that I led a double life.

It hadn't been hard at first. When I'd met Blaze, he only liked Lila. Mia too. Eventually, Lila was all I was to people. Anytime I called Mom, she asked me if I'd let it slip, and so far, I could tell her my secret was safe and sound. She still looked at me gratefully when I mentioned being Lila instead of Rose.

She couldn't have handled this.

I couldn't, either.

Rose Hill walked the streets of Nashville, feeling free. No one knew who I was and they didn't need to. I found a small coffee shop within walking distance of my hotel and felt good about myself as I walked in.

It was busy with people lined up back to the door. I couldn't see the menu yet, so I distracted myself with people-watching, which Lila only did when hunting for paparazzi.

I saw a couple having a heated discussion in front of me, a tired dad with a group of kids eating cinnamon rolls, and a person outside with a camera.

Wait. *What?*

I turned so fast it almost sprained my neck. They were in all black—classic for paparazzi. Their camera was pointed into the coffee shop, taking pictures in my general direction.

What was someone doing here taking pictures? Had I been sloppy with my switch-up?

My heart pounded. I needed to get out of here before anything else went wrong. It didn't matter if I was Rose. Maybe someone picked up on the hotel I left out of, maybe they followed me.

Maybe I was about to blow my cover.

I rushed back to the hotel, red hair flowing behind me.

I realized how stupid I'd been. I should have kept Rose a secret the whole time. I should have accepted that I was Lila forever and not risked it.

Mom was going to *kill* me.

I darted through the hotel's back door, using my room key to get in. I gasped for breath, but I knew I wasn't safe until I got to my room. Running up the stairs, I threw the key against the door, begging it to open.

The red light blinked at me and the door stayed locked.

"Shit." I tried again.

Still nothing.

"You might want to step away from that door if you know what's good for you."

I froze as I heard Juno's voice.

I'd been caught.

Maybe for the *second* time.

I slowly turned, cheeks aflame. Juno stood at her full height, eyes narrowed on me in full bodyguard mode.

Perhaps futilely, I wondered if I could get out of this. "Wrong room?"

But Juno looked me in the eye, brow raised.

"Then what room is yours?"

"Uh, that one?"

Her eyes narrowed. "Why do you sound like . . ." She trailed off.

"I just have one of those voices."

"Fine, maybe you do. I hate being rude, but if this isn't your room, you need to move on. My job is to be sure the woman in *that* room is not disturbed."

Had I done it? Had I convinced her?

"O-of course. Sorry."

Juno still looked pensive as I backed away. I went down the hall, wondering if I should get a room as Rose, but then my phone rang.

Needing a distraction as I turned from her, I pulled it out only to gasp when I saw *Juno's* name on my screen.

Lila's phone screen.

Because in my rush, I didn't leave her phone at the hotel.

Fuck. I really had been sloppy.

"Huh," Juno said slowly. "Either you've stolen someone else's phone or you happen to be the very woman I'm supposed to be watching."

I slowly turned back to her.

"I can explain," I said.

"Yeah." She crossed her arms. "I think you definitely *can* explain."

"You snuck out in a *wig*?" Juno's voice was ice. "No wonder I saw your phone out of the hotel. I thought it had to be a fluke and you wouldn't sneak out, but obviously, I was wrong."

"I should have left Lila's phone here," I muttered. I'd been in such a rush I hadn't even thought about it.

My secret stayed intact because I never snuck out. Rose and Lila were separate, and I was just reminded how bad I was at lying.

"So, you have a second one for . . . this version of you?"

"Yes," I admitted quietly.

Juno rubbed her face. "Take off the red wig, Lila. It's not going to work for much longer."

"I'm not in a wig right now," I said. "*Lila* wears the wig."

Juno froze and turned to me. "How have you been an international pop star for many years and no one has caught on to that?"

"The bangs," I said. "And I have very nice wigs."

"So, the makeup . . ."

"Another way to throw people off my trail."

"Oh my God. Why wouldn't Mia mention this?"

"Because she doesn't know."

"Wha—what about Blaze?"

"Nope."

"How have you told no one?"

"My parents know."

"So you have two whole lives. Why?"

"For sanity?" I didn't want to mention Mom to Juno at all. My bodyguard was thorough and she didn't leave stones unturned. And if she ever found Mom, I'd be in trouble.

"Why don't I believe you?"

"The point is, I keep it a secret from *everyone*. Listen, I'm sorry I snuck out, but the plan was *not* to get caught."

"It didn't exactly go to plan, did it?"

"In more ways than one," I said softly. "I saw cameras at this coffee shop I went to. I ran the minute I saw them."

"Cameras? Did they follow you?"

"No. No one did. I'm hoping they were on some other celebrity and they didn't recognize me. How many celebrities can Nashville have?"

"You know you're at the country capital of the world, right?"

"So, then a lot? Maybe no one saw me?"

"*No,*" she said firmly. "You're not going to think that you got out of this unscathed. You can't go around by yourself, Lila."

"I'm not Lila!" I snapped. "I'm Rose right now. No one knows who she is and I plan to keep it that way."

"My job is to protect you," she said. "Which I'm already spread thin doing because it's only me protecting a person worth more than my entire life."

"I'm not worth more than you, and one person is enough. No one knows I'm here, and if there's *one* person, then it's easier to be Rose."

Her glare told me I'd said the wrong thing.

"I'm safe, okay? And if I'm not, I wouldn't blame you. I just . . . I can't be Lila all the time. I can't live my life with eyes following me everywhere. It's too much."

"But—"

"Juno, put yourself in my shoes. You know that whenever I leave the house, I have to have you or some other security around because people either want to photograph me or kidnap me for ransom. This way, I can be a person without anyone knowing."

"But what if they did?"

"The only way they could would be if you told them. My parents have kept this secret for years."

"I'm certainly not telling."

"Then we're good."

"What if someone recognizes you?"

"Then I say we have the same face, but I find that as long as I don't draw attention to myself, no one knows. I don't have any unique features and I've doctored enough makeup-less photos that no one would believe it's me."

"You've thought this through."

"Yes. I have. This isn't just something I've done for fun. I *need* to keep my lives separate."

Juno's shoulders fell. She must have heard the desperation in my voice. "I guess I . . . I guess I can see how it would be. Even I've wondered how you manage it. Now I know."

"Please don't tell anyone."

"I won't. You can trust me."

"I hope I can. I don't exactly have a choice anymore."

"I've kept secrets for you too, just like that guy you're so obviously attracted to."

"I'm with Blaze."

"And he sent you here," she reminded, one corner of her mouth quirking upward. "I won't argue with you about Blaze, but I *will* argue about your safety. Do we have a deal?"

"We do."

"So you need to let me go with you when you're like this."

"Wait, no." I shook my head. "People know you're my security guard. There are memes about you."

A shadow crossed over her face. "Trust me, I know. 'Mountain of a woman' isn't really a compliment."

"I think it's less of an insult and more like they want you to step on them."

Juno turned red and looked away. "O-okay, so maybe I *am* well-known. But at least let me know where you are so I can be near."

"I can do that," I said.

"That is, *if* you weren't caught today."

My shoulders sank. I'd managed to forget my mistake for a few minutes. "Fuck. I hope not."

"Let's lay low. Stay in this hotel room until we know whether or not your cover is gone. Just for a few days."

I let out a long sigh but nodded. "Okay, fair enough."

"I'll keep an eye on the news, but we'll both be in hot water if this gets out. You know Mia is ruthless, right?"

"Yeah . . . Sorry."

"Why do I have a feeling you're about to make me go gray, Wilde?"

"It's Hill when I'm like this. And I have no idea. I'm *very* well-behaved."

She didn't look like she believed me.

Barry

Lila: One attachment.

Lila: Stuck in my hotel room and can't hang out, but I have this. Thoughts?

"Who are you texting?"

I nearly dropped my phone. Liam leaned against the bar next to me. I had been preparing to open the secondary serving area since tonight was another full night. "Jesus fuck, Liam. Warn a guy."

"Sorry, I can't help that you were staring at your phone like it had all the secrets of the universe on it," he said. "Is it a *woman*?"

"I can't tell you."

"Come on. I just want to know if you have a lovely lady in your life."

"Like what you have with Audrey?"

His cheeks reddened. "You know what I call that? Deflection."

"*You're* deflecting."

"Maybe, but I'll readily admit I have a crush on Audrey, even if I'll never ask her out because she's scary. You'll admit nothing." As he spoke, I pressed my lips together. He wasn't going to let up. "Is it that woman you rescued a few weeks ago?"

"The woman I rescued?" Then, the memory came back to me. Red hair. Freckles. A man far too close.

"Audrey said you put someone on the no-enter list for her." He raised an eyebrow. "And that you talked to her after."

He did this with every woman I talked to as if he were hoping I'd wake up one day and suddenly have a girlfriend.

"Someone was bugging her and she was very grateful." *But she's not the one.*

"And you got her number?"

"I . . . It doesn't matter, okay?"

Liam hummed, but I knew he didn't believe I was telling the truth. I could have denied it further, but it was easier letting him think it was a woman I'd never see again rather than what was really going on.

"What are we talking about?" Audrey asked, walking into the room.

"Barry has a girlfriend."

"I do not!"

"Ah, perfect. You're fighting like kids." But a smile crossed her face and she looked at me. "Who is she?"

"Guys—"

"The woman you thought," Liam said, slinging an arm around my shoulders.

"You two are the worst," I grumbled. "I need to go approve the guest list for next week."

"Already done," Audrey said, crossing her arms. "*And* Liam finished the schedule for the bouncers for the next few days."

"That's right," he added. "We took care of it all, so now you have no excuse to get away."

My heart skipped a beat. I'd had employees before, but never like these two. They never shied away from helping and jumped at the chance to do the menial things I never wanted to do.

This is what a family business should have looked like. Not that Dad ever would have known that.

"Thank you, guys, for the extra help." I wasn't sure what to say, so I held up my phone. "So, I guess neither of you would be mad if I went to talk to who texted me."

"Come on. So, not the woman you rescued?"

"I seriously can't say."

"And no hints?"

"It's confidential," I said. "But I'm helping a friend with a music thing."

Liam gasped and jumped. Audrey's jaw dropped.

"A music thing?" Liam asked. "Yes!"

"We always knew you had a knack for it," Audrey said. "Even if you only listen to pop."

"It's not a huge deal. I'm just helping."

"Just helping? Barry, you're incredible onstage," Liam said. "You should have been a rock star."

"I'm a bar owner, and I'm happy. This is just something I'm doing *once*."

"Sure, boss." Audrey let her arms drop to her sides. "You'll do it just once."

"I will," I said firmly. "Now, am I good to go?"

"You better tell me what album it is so I can buy it!" Liam exclaimed.

I shook my head and went up to my apartment, but my mind hung on Liam's words.

You should have been a rock star.

I would have loved that—if only things had turned out differently.

CHAPTER FIVE

"**Y**ou got lucky," Juno said. She handed me her phone. "The cameras were there for some guy named Knox Price. Not you."

I looked at the article. "That was the couple in front of me." I let out a breath of air. "Thank God."

"Your disguise is good. Your hair's in the photo's background, but you're so hunched over that I couldn't even tell who you were."

"I've been doing this for years," I said. "It's like second nature."

"Good. But we still need to be careful."

"I know, but I *needed* to leave this hotel room. It's so stifling being Lila."

"And it doesn't help that someone is following you everywhere."

"Yeah. Not that I don't like you, it's just nice to be alone sometimes."

"I'm not a complete stick-in-the-mud. I know how hard this life is for anyone, especially someone as kindhearted as you. Every day, I wonder how you weren't eaten alive by the music industry. You're so *nice*."

She wasn't wrong. Being nice was the one thing I was good at, though sometimes, it felt like the one thing that caused the most pain.

"I try."

"Your manager, however, is very much the opposite."

"Mia?"

"Yeah. She called me today to check in."

"She called *you*?"

"She wants answers from everywhere. I've gotten used to it, but she's the most intense woman I've ever met."

"It's mainly because I'm behind schedule. That reminds me, I should go to the studio and record now that we know my secret isn't blown out of the water. I have some new lyrics."

"You could relax for a bit," she suggested.

"Now, what would Mia say about that?" I shook my head. "It's fine. I know what I'm here for."

I walked to the bathroom and put on my full Lila getup. Even with my years of practice, it was a long process. I had to prep my skin for makeup, put on lashes and a wig cap, and layer the wig over everything else.

"You know," Juno started, "I've heard some of the stuff you're working on. It's got to be about Blaze, right?"

"Yep."

"Blaze would look terrible with long hair."

I smiled. "With how fried it is, I doubt he could even get it long."

"Only certain people can pull it off."

"Barry can," I said.

"Yeah. He's not my type, but he *is* a fine specimen. What do you think he benches?"

"I have no idea," I said. "Why? Do you think you can out-bench him?"

"I'd like to try."

Days later, I was still writing. Everything was inspiring, whether it was something beautiful for a love song or another thing I hated about Blaze.

He'd done an interview, talking me up as he usually did. But something about how he described it made me feel like he was subtly complimenting *himself*.

When I heard it, I immediately had the perfect melody for this anti-Blaze song, and I needed to get to a guitar to play it.

Technically, I had a guitar here, but what I really wanted was to play it on Barry's.

Lila: Are you awake?

Barry: Yes.

Lila: Can I come over?

Barry: Any time. We can meet at my apartment.

I told Juno to drop me off and stay on call. She agreed and said she would wait outside and stay very close.

Barry met me by the door leading up to his place. His apartment was smaller, with a love seat and a few books stacked on the side tables. His guitar sat next to one of them, in perfect placement for him to reach out to start playing while relaxing on the furniture.

Everything here was ideal for a single person. There was only one stool at the overhanging bar, one chair at a small dining room table, and one set of keys on the hook by the door.

"Lila," he said. "Welcome."

Barry wasn't wearing a flannel this time and my eyes trailed to his arms. Them being on full display made my stomach do a flip. When was the last time I'd ever felt this way over a man?

"Thanks for letting me come over. I love your place."

"It isn't much," he said with a shrug.

"Does it have a rooftop area too? Most of the places here seem to have something."

"I keep that for personal use. I'd show you, but I have a feeling it wouldn't be safe for you to go up there."

"You're right about that." I couldn't imagine what would happen if I got caught. "So, all of this is for you? You have good taste." I eyed the artwork with music notes and the LED lights behind a record player. "What records do you have?"

"Mostly yours," he said. "Plus some Fleetwood Mac and Taylor Swift."

I looked at his collection, and true to his word, many of my albums were there. My cheeks burned at how much of a fan he truly seemed to be.

"So," I said, determined not to overthink this, "I have some ideas for my anti-Blaze song. Can I borrow your guitar?"

"She's all yours." He handed it to me.

I played a melody that was lower than I'd usually go. "I was thinking about this, but with a harsher electric guitar."

He paused to consider it. "Not bad. It's very different from your usual sound."

"This is what I resonate with right now. I almost wish I could release it."

"Maybe one day."

I wished I could say yes, but I busied myself by writing down a few more notes. When I looked up, Barry was watching me.

"What?"

"It's nice to see you in your element."

"Scribbling words in an old notebook? Is that a compliment or an insult?"

"A compliment. I wouldn't dare insult you."

"Thanks," I said. "But I must say, this isn't me at my best."

"I like it anyway."

My cheeks heated again and I found my focus pulled from songwriting to him. "How did you find my music anyway?"

"My sister liked you."

"You have a sister?"

"Yes. And a brother."

"What are they like?"

"They're completely different. My brother is a high-up businessman and my sister is working her way up the ladder in the banking world."

"Your dad works in the big building, right?"

"He does. I'm surprised you remembered."

"It's a good revenge story."

"Not as good as this song you're writing."

I doubted it. My life had grown boring once everyone knew everything about it—at least Lila's side of it anyway. But Barry's life, a man who came from a harsh family and made something all on his own, sounded much more like a story I wanted to tell.

He didn't seem interested in opening up about that side of him, though. And I didn't have extra time to push him in the ways I wanted to. I needed to get this album done.

Desperately.

"You know, I've been writing other things. Softer things, I mean. Want to hear something else?"

He smiled. "I'd love nothing more."

Barry

Never in my life did I ever imagine I would be hearing Lila Wilde sing a new song for me and me alone. This had to be a dream, one I would wake up from and wish was real.

The words were soft and melodic. But I could hear how she would speed it up and make it another hit. I could see her twirling around the stage, singing it to . . . anyone but Blaze.

Maybe me.

At least in my dreams.

One day, it was going to be changed. All mentions of me would be scrubbed and I would be replaced by the man she stood beside.

She stopped strumming and her hazel eyes looked up at me. She didn't look like a pop star when she did. With her hunched shoulders and shaky smile, she looked scared.

"It's amazing," I told her.

"Really? You're not just saying that because you think you have to?"

"I truly think it is. I really liked the line where you ask me not to break your heart."

"Well, I had to have something about Blaze in there."

I laughed, but the reminder of him made me ask for one thing. "Can you record the original version and send it to me?"

She smiled. "I can make that happen."

Her phone rang and I saw the name *Mia* on the screen.

"You need to go, don't you?"

"Yes. My agent is calling. I should probably be at the studio too. I have a few ideas I could record. And this song, of course."

She handed me the guitar and walked toward the door. My heart lurched, and I knew she couldn't leave without me saying one other thing.

"Lila," I started, and she paused.

"Yes?"

"I know you're with Blaze. And I will always respect that. But if you're ever not with him and want anything different, I'll be waiting."

Her breath caught in her throat. "I don't know if I could ever leave—at least not until my fame dies down."

"I'd wait that long."

"Really?"

"If you're on the end of it? Then every single day would be worth it."

Her eyes grew misty and she slowly nodded. I hoped she would stay. If she did, I'd do the impossible and stay away from work, but her smile fell and she walked out the door.

CHAPTER SIX

Lila

"**Y**ou've been busy," my producer, Sasha, said over our video call.

And I had been. Over the last two weeks, I'd written many songs. The lyrics weren't changed yet, but it was easier to get the song on paper to record rather than force myself to change it. I could rerecord singular lines to be better.

Or at least that was what I was telling myself.

"What do you think of what I've given you?"

"These are good. It reminds me of the stuff you used to write when we first met."

"They do?"

"Yeah. And Mia approved all of these?"

"Not . . . exactly. She's more worried about me making progress than the content of the songs."

"So that's why they're good."

I didn't know why, but I felt the need to defend both myself and Mia. "What I was writing before wasn't *bad* . . ."

"It just wasn't you. For one, you sound like you're actually in love here."

"Um, yeah. Rekindling a flame and all."

"Rekindling? More like finding a new one. There's no way these songs are about Blaze."

Sasha had always been perceptive. She was the first to tell me some of my fans might not like my dance-pop hits. She'd been right, but Mia had vetoed her. And then I'd broken records.

"Nothing is going on. He told me to get inspiration from other places."

"He *told* you?" Her dark eyebrows were near her hairline. "I thought he wanted to be your only inspiration."

"He usually does, but these are different circumstances."

Sasha hummed and looked back at the screen, which presumably had the songs I'd sent her. "Do you want me to work on these as is?"

"Yes," I said. "We can change them later."

"If we do . . ." It was almost muttered.

"We have to. You know how the fans are and—"

"Okay, okay," Sasha said, holding up her hands. "We'll see how it goes. But I like this. I like your sound here. Except for this one."

"Which one?"

"It's titled 'the revenge track.'"

My eyes widened. Did I forget to take that out? "I wasn't supposed to send that."

"I'm going to call this a happy accident," Sasha said.

"Happy accident? You said you liked all of them but this one."

"Because I *love* this one."

"Oh."

"And by the way? Fuck Blaze."

"I . . . It was supposed to be for me only."

"Why?"

"It's not a huge deal."

"Is it not? Because from the sound of this, he cheated on you."

"He did."

"And you're still with him?"

"I have to be," I said. "My fame is *rooted* in my love for him."

"Or it's your talent. You didn't get to where you are just because of your relationship."

"Sasha, it's the music business. People have to have something to root for. That's what Rick and Mia believed, and unfortunately, I can't deny it's worked."

"Are *you* happy with how it's worked?"

I opened my mouth to say I was, but the words wouldn't come out. "Others are," I managed to say. "That's what matters."

Her eyes narrowed, and it felt like she was seeing right through me.

"So we don't release this track," she said after a moment. "But can I at least add some stuff to it? Only for your ears, of course."

That was a bad idea, but I could admit that hearing my revenge song as an *actual* song would feel good. "Fine. If you want to."

"It would be my pleasure."

Barry

Monday night rolled around, but things had been off in my family.

Ruth had been going through it, and it all started when her former rival returned to town.

Knox Price was a genius inventor who graduated with her at our old high school. He was the smartest kid in class, and Ruth always tried to knock him out of his number-one spot. She'd hated him because she never could manage to beat him consistently.

Mom and Dad quickly figured out that comparing Ruth to him was far more effective than comparing Ruth to Tom, who was in college. They mentioned him at every turn while she was in high school, shoving his success in her face to give her a reason to push herself impossibly harder.

And it continued into adulthood. Knox was now a billionaire and the head of some company he'd started. Whenever his name was anywhere in the news, Mom brought it up to Ruth.

It felt like Mom loved Knox more than her own daughter. Even I saw it.

So when Ruth was in the news with Knox last week, I knew she would face many questions. And she had from the very second she'd walked in the door.

And in a twist of events, Ruth said no. She didn't tell them *anything*.

Our parents were mad—furious, even. But she'd managed to escape relatively unscathed since she'd left early. Now, it was a week later, and our parents had seven days to think of ways to break her.

I dreaded it.

Though I was prouder of Ruth than I ever had been, I didn't expect her rebellious streak to last long.

When I saw her at dinner, on time as always, I readied myself to be disappointed again.

But then she leaned over to me and cracked a *joke*, of all things, which I couldn't help but return, and I wondered if I'd gotten my sister wrong.

Mom and Dad questioned her as expected, but she held to what she said last week. She *wasn't* talking about Knox. Instead, she was brave enough to try to talk business with Tom and Dad.

But he wasn't having any of it, especially not when she managed to call him out on being money-hungry.

"And *that* is why you're unmarried," he said, shaking his head. "That attitude of yours."

For a second, I wasn't sure that I heard him right. Why was he bringing up marriage? He didn't care about our social lives, only our professional ones.

"Unmarried?" she replied. "Since when do you care about my marital status?"

"Since you crossed over twenty-eight with no prospects in sight."

"Todd," Mom hissed. "We agreed not to talk about this."

"She's almost thirty!"

"What are you saying?" I asked him. I had an idea, but surely our parents wouldn't be *this* cruel.

I should have known not to underestimate them.

"I'm saying that your sister is nearly too old to have kids. She should be worried about that."

"I have more to worry about than children, Dad," Ruth cut in.

He scoffed. "Not in my books."

"Todd," Mom pleaded, "we agreed to let her try to have a career."

"And what has she made of herself? She's refusing to talk about the one man who can make her into something, and she's a menial director of a shitty banking company."

Ruth argued back, but I was too busy trying to deal with the fact that Dad was also a sexist piece of shit as well as a god-awful father.

Well, he did always want to exceed expectations.

When I finally tuned back in, Dad was confirming that he thought Ruth was only meant to be a housewife, that Mom had pushed for her to be treated equally to us, and that she was some evil, man-hating feminist.

Ruth hated many men, but mainly the ones who talked to her exactly like Dad did.

Even though I knew she was angry, I wouldn't have blamed Ruth if she backed down. After all, she'd just found out that all she'd worked for was for nothing.

But then again, this was Ruth Murray.

Dad ordered Mom to sit and be quiet. Then he tried to turn the same energy to Ruth. But she only glared at him and said, "Fuck you."

"You will do as I say!" Dad snapped in an ear-splitting yell, one designed to strike fear into anyone it was directed at.

I became numb to it long ago, but I wasn't sure when Ruth did the same.

Her jaw only tightened. "Why should I? You're more of a failure than I am. I believe you were a director at thirty, Dad. You didn't become a CEO until Grandpa died and handed you the company. You didn't do shit to get where you are. Everything was handed to you."

That was an absolutely badass line and I almost wanted to clap for her because she was *exactly* right.

"I will not tolerate this from you!"

Impossibly, his anger was escalating and now his fists were clenched. These weren't good signs.

"What are you going to do?" Ruth asked. "You gonna scream? Slam things around? I'm not scared of you."

"And if you touch her," I added, "you'll have me to answer to."

Dad wasn't a dumb man. He knew he couldn't go against us both. So, he tried to hurt us in different ways.

"You two are the biggest disappointments in this family."

It wasn't news, so it rolled off my back like water.

"Fuck this," she snapped. "I'm leaving."

"Excuse me?" he bellowed. "Ruth Murray, you do not get to leave—"

"I don't know if you know this"—she spun around to look at him again—"but I'm a grown-ass woman. I don't listen to people like you."

I only had a second to feel proud of my sister *finally* throwing her snark at our parents before she ran out the door. I saw her face drop as she did and I knew her bravery was waning.

I turned my glare at Dad. Ruth had given her all to make him proud. She'd studied. She'd worked her ass off. She was better than anything he could be.

And none of it mattered to him.

I couldn't even feel joy that Ruth had finally seen Dad for what he was. All I could feel was rage.

"You're an asshole," I said.

"I speak the truth."

"That Ruth isn't good enough because she's a girl? She's better than all of us." I looked to Tom, hopeful for backup, but his lips were pursed.

I don't know why I even had hope for him.

Maybe Ruth was the only one who would see this fucked-up family for what it was. I should cut my losses and be grateful that she even realized what was wrong.

See? that voice said. *She was always going to see it.*

"No, she isn't." Dad's voice pulled me back into the present moment. "She needs to learn her place." He went for the door.

"Dad, don't—" Tom began, but I stood in his way.

"You leave her out of it," I said. "She's had enough of you."

"I'm her father."

"I wish you weren't."

"Move," he demanded, eyes narrowing at me. "Or I will move you."

"Try it."

The moment his hand landed firmly on my shoulder, I punched him in the face.

Chaos ensued, and I decided to take one from Ruth's book and run out the door. It was a cowardly move, but it was the only thing that kept me from laughing at Dad's flabbergasted face.

I wasted no time getting into my car and pulling out onto the road.

But then I heard a truck rumbling behind me. In my rearview mirror, I saw it was Tom.

I pulled over onto the shoulder, unwilling to let my asshole brother follow me all the way home. I got out of the car to face him. "I don't regret it, and you won't make me."

Tom got out too. "Are you going to check on Ruth?"

The thought hadn't occurred to me. All I wanted to do was go home and pretend I didn't even have a family.

And find a lawyer.

"Do we need to? Ruth isn't the kind of person to have her mental breakdowns in front of her brothers."

"She was just told that everything she worked for was for nothing. Why wouldn't we at least be sure she's okay?"

"It's *Ruth*."

"Barry," Tom snapped. "She's our sister."

"Oh, and you care so much? You didn't even stand up for her."

"I have reasons I didn't."

"Like what?"

"Come with me to check on Ruth and I'll tell you."

I narrowed my eyes, wondering why Tom, of all people, was here instead of back at the house stroking Dad's ego. I should have told him no so I could return to the safety of my bar and be alone.

But, damn it, I was *curious*, of all things.

"Fine," I groaned. "We'll go check on her. But you better have a good fucking explanation for staying silent. And for suddenly changing your tune the second you were out of Dad's sight."

Ruth wasn't at her downtown apartment. Tom let us in with a key that she had apparently given him some time ago. I'd never been inside it, but it reminded me of our parents' house. Cold, undecorated, and boring as hell. When we saw the place empty, Tom texted. She didn't answer until he threatened to hunt her down and she finally said she was fine.

I knew for a fact she was lying.

Eventually, she agreed to a sibling meeting. When the front door to her apartment finally opened, I expected to see the same woman who had stormed out of dinner.

Instead, I saw one with red-rimmed eyes and a sad expression. Her hair was down, making her look younger.

And Knox Price was in tow.

I had a million questions, but we didn't get long to talk about this significant change in Ruth's life because Tom steered us right to the topic at hand.

"We need to talk about what happened with Dad." Tom glanced over at me and I knew he was probably mad about me throwing that punch.

"I'm not apologizing for what I did." And I wouldn't.

"What did he do?" Ruth asked. She didn't look like herself. She didn't look like my fearless sister anymore. She was *just Ruth*. I could tell she had been crying, and with the way she'd come in with *Knox,* of all people, I figured he'd been there for her.

Which was what she had needed.

"He punched Dad in the face when he tried to follow you."

"What?"

"Nice," Knox remarked. I smiled at him.

"No, no," Ruth snapped. "Not nice. Why?"

"He said he wanted to knock some sense into you," I replied. "So, I decided to do it to him first."

Knox reacted in the way I would have: pure anger. I didn't know when he'd gotten so close to Ruth, but I was happy for her. She hadn't been alone through this. While it would have been *my* preferred way to deal with my family drama, I didn't think it suited her.

"It's what he deserved," I muttered.

"He could press charges," Ruth said.

Tom shook his head. "He won't. He's going to be tied up with something else very soon."

"I don't think there is enough revenue in the world to make Dad not go after Barry," she replied.

She was right. I was about to be in big trouble and no one was out there to save me.

Still, I didn't regret it.

"It's not revenue," Tom replied. "It's a lawsuit making him take a leave of absence as CEO. I left the papers HR drafted on his desk tonight."

"You *what*?" Ruth and I asked at the same time.

Tom left it on his desk? Tom, the perfect child?

Knox said something, but I drowned it out as I processed what I'd just heard.

There was no way this was happening. I didn't think Tom would ever do anything out of line. He was the favorite, so why would he?

"What did he do to get put on leave?" I asked.

"He sexually harassed multiple women. I found the emails when digging in our archive system."

Jesus. I had always had low opinions of Dad, but this was low, even for him.

"*You* found this?" I asked. "You went looking for it?"

"I did. Ever since I stopped drinking and doing whatever he says, I've seen him do very illegal things. This is why I wanted us to wait a week. I needed to get everything together."

"Oh my God. You played a double agent." Ruth's voice was quiet.

This couldn't be real. I'd gotten him all wrong. I thought the boy who'd protected us from that storm was gone. That he only did the bare minimum out of duty.

But *he* would be the one to take Dad down.

"He's not going to take this lying down," Tom said. "He has access to the greatest lawyers. I have a feeling he will find a way around it."

Knox chimed in, saying he had a few lawyers that might help. I didn't listen. I was too busy coming to terms with what Tom had done. The world was tilting and everything I knew was wrong.

See? You're glad you came, aren't you?

And somehow, I really was.

CHAPTER SEVEN

Lila

*L*ila: You free tonight?

   Barry: I am, but it's been a long day. I don't know if I can help you with music tonight.

   Lila: What happened?

   Barry: Long story.

   Lila: I could bring tea.

   Barry: I don't want to bore you with my family drama.

   Lila: Please? I want to be sure you're okay. We don't even have to talk about it, but I don't want you to be alone.

   Barry: Fine. I'm at my apartment.

"How long am I staying for?" Juno asked.

   "No idea."

"If it's an all-nighter again, please just text. And give Barry my number. I want him to have it in case either of you need backup."

"I will," I said. "Thank you, Juno."

I grabbed the box of tea she had purchased for me and walked to the door of Movers and Shakers. When I knocked, he opened immediately.

But this was not the man I knew. A shadow had fallen over his face, making him seem darker. I'd only seen Barry angry when he talked about his family.

What had they done to him?

"Are you okay?"

"Tonight isn't a good night."

"You said as much. Do you wanna talk about it?"

"Not really."

"Okay, then tea it is."

I brushed past him and went up to his apartment. I was in helping mode and I didn't want him to be alone with whatever had happened. "Sorry, not sorry, but I'm going through your cabinets to find mugs. I hope you don't have a dildo collection hidden here."

"Why would I put that in my kitchen cabinets?"

"I don't know. Maybe you sanitize them in the dishwasher."

A tiny, almost imperceptible smile crossed his face, and I took that as a win.

I busied myself with warming up some water. When I brought it to him, he looked at me like it was the kindest gesture he'd ever experienced. "Thank you."

I sat on the couch next to him. "Do you want to talk about it now?"

Barry let out a long sigh. "There isn't much to say. Other than the fact that my dad is a sexist asshole, and I hit him for it."

"You . . . oh." My pulse thrummed. I usually didn't care for violence. But Barry? Maybe I wouldn't mind seeing that, especially if the person being hit was a sexist asshole.

"It's a lot," he muttered. "It's always been a lot. But I think we're finally done with him."

"That's a good thing, right?"

"It is."

"How are your sister and brother doing?"

He let out a low groan, dragging his fingers over his face. "They're fine. Probably. It really was a long night and I don't know how much more I can think about this before I lose it. And you and I only have so much time together . . . I can't let them take up that time too."

"I don't mind," I insisted.

"No, I just can't. I want to help you write, not sit here wasting time talking about shitty people doing shitty things."

I paused. Should I continue pushing him? Would it even help if I did?

"Okay," I said. "We don't even have to work. We can just sit here."

"I think I want to hear your voice. Whatever you've got."

I hadn't planned to sing, but if it would help him, I could do anything. "Then I'll play you a song."

He leaned back, his shoulders sinking in relief. "That is *exactly* what I need."

Barry

When Lila performed, I forgot everything.

She played a slower version of one of her hits, the very first song that made me feel seen by her. She couldn't have known how much this track meant to me, yet it felt like this lucky guess was balm for my soul.

I didn't know how I'd ever go back to vinyl after seeing her sing live.

I thought tonight was going to be a wash. The plan was to put on my favorite Lila record and be alone, just like every time my family had hurt me.

But now I had her, and terrifyingly, I didn't know if being alone was enough. She finished the song with a nervous look in my direction.

"Did that help?"

"Yeah," I said. "It did."

"Anything for my biggest fan." She gave me a teasing smile that I was *almost* ready to return. "Oh, I almost forgot, Juno wants you to have her number."

"Why?"

"Because I spend so much time with you. She says you might need backup."

I couldn't imagine when I would ever need that because Lila couldn't be seen with me, but I also knew that anything could happen. "Okay, I'll put it in my phone."

As I did, I scrolled past Dad's number, and all of the night came rushing back.

"Is what happened still bothering you?" she asked.

"A little."

"Do you want to write something?"

"I don't think I have the focus."

"It always helps me." She paused as if in thought. "It doesn't even have to be about your family. It can be about anything."

"What if it's about you?"

Her cheeks turned a beautiful shade of pink. "I mean, we *can*."

"I know this won't ever be anything," I said slowly. "But just for a moment, I'd like to pretend it could."

"So, a love song?"

"One love song."

She bit her lip and I was certain she'd say no. I wouldn't blame her if she did.

"Okay," she agreed. "One song. But if it's about us, I might have a hard time changing it."

"Then don't."

"It might not make it on the album, then."

"It doesn't have to. For once, we can write without reason."

A slow smile spread on her face. "I haven't done that in years."

"How about we start now?"

She slowly nodded and took a notebook out of her bag. "Do you want to do the honors?"

I gingerly took it from her, hands shaking. I wrote down a few thoughts and passed it back to her. "Is it any good?"

"It's great," she replied. "This could really be the beginning of a good song. Here, let's try this."

We passed the notebook back and forth, adding to it line by line.

"What kind of chords do you want this to have?" she asked once we had about half of a working song. "Maybe a . . ." She played a slow and smooth progression.

It was perfect.

We lost the night together. We worked on the song. Lila started it out and I had a heavy hand in the second verse. By the time we were done, she was rubbing at her face again.

"I should go, but this was good. Now to do the other million things on my list."

"Are you behind?"

"A little." She shrugged. "But I'll be okay."

Guilt settled over me. I'd taken her from her songwriting, which was far more significant than just me.

"I want to help with the rest of it. Tomorrow? We can work as long as we want to."

"I think I'd like that. Maybe we could even give it a name. I like this theme of everything being for this one night."

"We could use that. Something like 'On This Night.'"

Her eyes lit up. "That's perfect."

Chapter Eight

Lila

Two months later, I was still in Nashville. We'd traded out the hotel for an Airbnb in Juno's name, which gave me a little more breathing room. Juno proved to be incredible with wigs, helping me put one on every time I went out as Lila. I gave her a raise during the first month she was here.

The album was coming along slowly, but I still hadn't changed the lyrics. At first, Mia was angry, but Blaze had offered to change his looks to match what was in my album, which curbed my agent's rage. I'd seen paparazzi photos of his new muscular build.

Unfortunately, those pictures did nothing for me.

I hadn't gone back to LA once, yet no one had gotten wind of me being in Nashville either. Blaze talked like I was with him every second of the day. I knew I should have felt bad for sticking in Nashville so long, but instead, I felt like I could breathe here. I didn't realize how much Mia and Blaze stressed me out. Talking with them on the phone was far easier than being in person.

Still, I wasn't blind to the fact that Juno was stuck with me. She didn't talk about her personal life much, but being away from her home for this long had to be weighing down on her.

"If you need to go home and see some family," I told her one morning over breakfast, "I won't stop you."

"I'm only going back to LA if you're returning."

"I can just hang out here as Rose."

"And miss time with Barry where you're working on the album? No thanks. And besides, my family isn't the biggest fan of me." She looked at her coffee cup like it had offended her.

"Oh, I'm sorry."

"Don't be. I know I'm not supposed to make anything about me when I'm guarding you—"

"Who said that?"

"Mia."

I sighed. Mia had a habit of talking to anyone who worked for me before I did. "It's fine. I don't mind if you tell me things. We're spending all of this time together anyway."

"I work for you."

"So? I'm a chill boss. Except when I sneak out as my other identity."

"I'm still mad about that," she said, leveling me with a sharp stare. "But thanks. I don't have much to report since I don't talk to my family, but it's nice to know I don't have to be a wall of protection at all times."

"Or a stick-in-the-mud."

She laughed. "You know, when I took this job, Mia made it sound like you were the most selfish person on the planet. It's *so* not true."

"She made me seem selfish?"

"She's done it with everyone. It's like she has a vendetta against you."

I frowned. Had I done something to her without realizing it?

"Or maybe she's just like that." Juno shrugged. "She never seems content with anything."

"That's true," I said. "Even when I break records, she asks when I'm going to break the next one."

She rolled her eyes. "I know she's your agent or manager or whatever—"

"She's kind of all of them."

"But she could stand to be nicer."

I nodded. "It's nice being here where she can only call me. It's probably why I've been working so much."

"Speaking of working so much, would it be rude of me to say your voice is sounding a little rougher than usual?"

"No." I rubbed my throat. "It happens when I sing too much."

"Do you need more tea?"

"Yeah, but I want to go get it. I need to not be Lila for a bit."

"I'll go with you."

"I can—"

"I need some milk anyway, but I'll keep my distance. I know the rules."

"Still, I want to talk to you at least. Maybe we can while we're driving there?"

"I can work with that." She smiled before I walked to my bedroom to throw on clothes.

Juno told me bits and pieces about her family as we drove. I would have listened longer, but she paused when we pulled into the store parking lot, telling me to go in first and she'd follow.

She stayed an aisle away while I went to find the tea. In the unfamiliar surroundings, it took me a second to find my favorite brand. I normally had it delivered to my LA house, but here, searching for it in person was taking longer than I'd have liked to admit.

I was about to grab the box when I felt someone walk up next to me. Out of habit, I looked to make sure it wasn't someone with a camera.

But then I did a double take because I knew the man who was only a few feet away.

I'd seen Barry only a few days ago when he helped me write yet another song that could easily be a hit. I knew the crease between his eyebrows, the way one laugh line was deeper than the other, and the way his eyes squinted when he smiled.

Well, *Lila* knew those things.

But I wasn't her right now. I was Rose, who he had only met once.

My eyes moved over to where I knew Juno was and I found her looking at us like someone would look at a train crash.

But then she ducked into another aisle and I imagined it was because she knew if Barry saw her with me, there would be questions.

I turned to him, heart in my throat. "Fancy seeing you here."

He looked over at me, a slight smile on his face. It was the exact opposite of how he usually looked at Lila.

"Sorry," I said, laughing awkwardly. "You might not remember me. I was at your bar and you—"

"I remember you." His voice was low. "But I don't make a habit of bothering someone at the grocery store."

My face flamed. "I didn't mean to bother you. It's so rare to see someone you know out in public."

"You're not bothering *me*. I just know how some women might feel about a stranger talking to them."

"Good thing you're not a stranger," I said. But then I cursed myself. The best thing to do would be to let this go and not talk to Barry as Rose.

I was bad at doing what was best for me. Something about him made me want more.

He changed the subject with a fond smile on his face. "That's a good brand of tea. A close friend of mine really likes it."

There was no doubt in my mind he was talking about Lila. My heart flipped at his gentle tone.

I fanned my on-fire cheeks. "Is it hot in here?"

"It's pretty chilly for October. Usually, the heat hangs around, but we're having a false fall."

"I'm from Canada, so this is summer weather for me."

"What are you doing in Nashville then?"

"Work, but the city is charming me."

"You'd be surprised at how many people love it here. My sister's boyfriend just moved here permanently."

He was talking to me about his sister? Besides the few tidbits I'd gotten from him as Lila, Barry usually avoided the topic.

"Maybe I'll join them." And I truly wanted to, especially if Barry would talk to me more about his personal life.

I wanted to keep the conversation going, but his phone rang.

"Speak of the devil," he said, a faint smile on his face. "I should take this. I'm trying a new thing where I answer my sister's calls."

"I won't keep you then." I gave him an awkward wave. With a smile, he walked away, the same tea that I came for in his hand.

"That was close," Juno said, coming to my side. "If you're going to talk to him as two different people, you'll have to work on your poker face. You looked at him the same way Lila did. And you stopped shrugging your shoulders as much."

I knew she was right. It seemed I wasn't the best at pretending to be two people where he was concerned.

"I'll work on it."

"You're used to being Lila around him. But Rose is a very different person."

In more ways than one.

It was like he was embarrassed about his family when it came to Lila. Like he didn't want me to see him at his lowest.

And I got it. If I was meeting my favorite pop star, I'd be the same way.

But I wondered if we could have been more if Rose had met him first.

As I listened to Ruth's fifth run-on sentence in the call, I stopped her.

I was walking back to my apartment. She called often these days, but she was never *this* scatterbrained.

"Is everything okay?" I asked. "I know we're supposed to talk about life, but you seem . . . off."

"Yeah, of course I'm okay!" Her voice was high. "There's no major news or anything."

I narrowed my eyes. "Then why mention major news?"

She groaned. "I would tell you, but I don't think I *can*. It doesn't affect you, though."

"Then we don't need to talk about it."

"But it is about our brother."

I paused in my walk. What could be going on with Tom? He and I hadn't talked since I found out he had outed Dad. But why would we? Tom and I never had a close relationship; he wasn't like Ruth. He didn't seem to *want* to be. The man was allergic to connection.

"I'm sure everything is fine."

"That is definitely *not* the case," she said. "Our family is fucked."

"You can say that again."

"Our family is *fucked*."

A shocked laugh startled out of me. We hadn't been doing this for very long, but Ruth called me crying when worried about Tom. I'd been so shocked that I agreed to reconnect.

That little voice had won out once again.

I couldn't bring myself to regret it. Ruth was hilarious when she tried to be, and now that she was focused on living and not just working herself to death, I enjoyed it.

But I knew that I would never have this with Tom. He'd always been the kind of man to do his own thing.

Then again, so was I.

I didn't like seeing the similarities. Being like him went against everything I'd set out to do. Moments like this were why I didn't look too closely at him.

"He'll figure it out," I reassured. "I wouldn't worry about it too much."

"But he was the one around Dad the most. That did damage."

"Poor him, being around Dad."

"Yes, *poor him*. Imagine always being around those lectures. It's awful."

"Are you helping him, then?"

"Only because I forced my way in. You could do the same."

"Not my style."

"Come on, Barry. What if he needs us?"

"How about this, *if* he asks for help, I will help." It was more than I would usually offer, but this was *Ruth*, and she seemed to genuinely care. "But I'm not the kind of person to do more, and besides, I doubt he'd want me to."

"I guess I can agree to that," Ruth said.

"Now, can we take a break from talking about Tom? I can only do so much family talk."

"And yet you're on the phone with your sister. *Fine*. What's new in your life, Barry? Have Liam and Audrey gotten together yet?"

"No, but they've been around each other more since..." I trailed off. "Since I've been busy."

"Busy with what?"

Lila Wilde.

"Nothing too important," I said. "Don't worry about it."

"You know I will."

"It isn't a big deal. But I can't talk about it. An NDA is in effect."

"Oh, okay," she said. "I fucking hate NDAs, but I can admit they're useful. Will you tell me when it's over?"

Lila's NDA was very long-term. "Eventually."

"I guess I'll have to guess until then. You coming to the family dinner?"

It wasn't with *our* family but with people Ruth met and liked. My skin still itched at the idea of another family dinner, regardless of who they were. I didn't doubt that Ruth cared about these people, but now that I was free, I wasn't interested in returning. "Not this time. Maybe soon."

"I'll hold you to that. I promise it'll be fun."

I wanted to believe her, but the idea of a family was ruined for me a long time ago.

Chapter Nine

The album was *so* close. I'd called Barry to the studio after becoming Lila again, but we were both tired after working for many hours together.

I needed another song. I'd already recorded the ones that we enjoyed, the ones we could easily change. I'd invited Barry to the studio a few times because his input was more helpful than he knew, but this time, both of us were stumped.

We were trying to make a song work that wasn't all there. Even I could admit that this one wasn't as good compared to some of the other songs we'd written.

"I wish we had another like *our* song."

"We *could* just use that one."

I twirled my hair between my fingers. The song was perfect as is, and changing it would gut me.

But it would *fit*.

"Are you sure? I mean, it's *ours*. And this album is about . . ." I trailed off, unable to say it.

"Yes, but this song is incredible. And I'll know that you'll think of me whenever you sing it."

He was exactly right. I would always think of him first.

"It's just . . . it's *ours*."

"And it always will be. I'll know it."

I bit my lip. I had refused to think of this song as ever being released, but now that he was giving me permission, I knew it would fit perfectly. "Okay, we can add it."

"Just let me hear it first. Those are my only terms."

"How about you get to hear me record it?"

"That's even better."

I pulled out my notebook and flipped to the page. I'd doodled on it, adding rough sketches of hearts as I went through the lyrics in my head.

"You've come back to it, huh?"

My cheeks burned. "Shut up."

He laughed but said nothing else. Little did he know, just the sound of that chuckle sent my heart into overdrive.

God, I wanted this.

I wanted *him*.

Only him.

I wouldn't do it, though. Even if Blaze had cheated, I refused to stoop to his level.

Barry exited the recording booth, as per usual for when I was about to sing. I took a measured breath and put my notebook on the stand.

I knew I loved it the second I started recording.

Up until the second verse.

"It doesn't sound right," I muttered, pulling off my headphones.

I was tempted to slump over, but Juno had given me a long lecture about not letting Rose slip in, so I clenched my teeth and looked at my feet.

"Try it in a different key," Barry urged through the mic, his low voice patient.

I did, but my tone sounded wrong. I tried to lower the notes to match, but I couldn't quite get there.

"While that would work," I said slowly, "I need a lower voice."

"Hm," he said, and it hit me that *his* voice was perfect for this.

"Barry, can you sing this part?"

"I don't think I should—"

"It would get the song down. You'd sound good."

"How do you know?"

"I've heard many people say you're good at singing, and I trust them."

His mouth twisted and I waited for his answer with bated breath.

"Fine," he said. "I'll record it."

He stepped into the studio and I knew I should have left him to it, but I couldn't bear to walk out.

"Is this how duets usually go?" he asked.

"N-not really, but do you mind if I—"

"I never mind if you stay," he said lowly. "But you'll have to tell me if I sound terrible."

I nodded, eyes on him as he began singing. His low, rough voice was far better up close and my skin erupted in gooseflesh. How was this man not famous? How was he not onstage every single night on tour like I'd been?

"How did that sound?" he asked as he finished.

It took me a second to answer him. "Great. You're . . . incredible in person."

"I'm not trained or anything, so I'm sure—"

"That's exactly what I like," I said. He opened his mouth to argue, but I wouldn't hear it. "In fact, I like it so much that we should sing the chorus together."

"Are you sure?"

"Very."

We started again, and this time, I joined in.

Our voices meshed perfectly.

I'd never sung with anyone. When I had features on albums, I would have them record their studio separately and maybe meet up with them to work on the ending sound.

But *this* was different.

It felt more intimate than sex ever could. It felt like knowing someone so close.

"It's perfect," I said when we were done. "It's exactly what we need for the album's last song. I don't know if Mia will like that I brought someone in, but . . ."

"It's fine," he said. "You do whatever you need to with it."

"She'll have to deal. It's a great song and a perfect closer."

"What's going to happen now that the whole album is done? Are you going back to LA?"

I wanted to say no. I wanted to stay here and record more with him.

But it was already going to be a fight to even *keep* this song. Mia would want someone else to feature.

"I'm sorry." It was as close to an answer as I could give.

"No, don't be. This was always the deal, right?"

"Yes."

"Then go back. Just remember your promise. Don't forget me."

I didn't know it would be so hard to get ready to say goodbye, but my throat was thick with emotion. I'd felt at peace here in a way I hadn't in a very long time.

Before I could overthink it, I hugged him tightly, pressing my face into his firm chest. "I could never. You know that, right?"

His arms wound around me, pulling me in impossibly closer. "I think I'm starting to."

I was already in a bad mood when Tom texted.

Saying goodbye to Lila weighed heavier than I could have imagined. I foolishly thought I could change her mind about leaving.

And I didn't.

She was going to go back, make those songs about Blaze, and people would admire how he inspired her *once again*.

And damn, did it make me angry.

Tom's text wasn't much. But it was the final straw to my shitty day.

Tom: Can you tell me about Lila Wilde?

He knew. He had to.

And if he knew, others would too.

Lila had been very firm about this being a secret, and if I'd fucked it up and my brother somehow found out, then her memory of me wouldn't be good.

Barry: Exactly what do you want to know about her?

Tom didn't answer and I wondered if this was some shitty manipulation tactic made by Dad to get me to talk. I was sure I'd heard of something like this before.

I knew where he lived, and while I told myself I would never go over, this was a conversation to be had in person. If he was going to betray me, he could at least look me in the eye and do it.

I pounded on his door. He opened it, and when I caught sight of my perfect older brother, a mirror image of Dad, my rage boiled over.

"Why did you ask about Lila Wilde, of all people?" I snapped. "What do you know?"

He dared to blink in shock. "What? I don't know anything except that she was in your bar."

I didn't believe him. "Then why would you be asking about her? You don't even listen to music."

"I'm getting into it."

"That isn't like you." And I wasn't going to fall for his little charade. "Why?"

"For reasons."

"Really?" He had to have broken his sobriety. As much as I wanted to believe he had stopped drinking, I didn't. I leaned in, using my nose to try and detect any of his favorite habit.

"Are you smelling me?"

"I'm making sure you're not drunk."

"I quit."

Okay, maybe I was wrong.

"You could have broken," I said, "but I forgot how stubborn you and Ruth can be." My anger was fading at his sheer confusion and now I doubted he knew a damn thing. "Just forget I was here."

His hand clamped on my shoulder. "Why would you come visit me because I asked about Lila Wilde? Was it just to see if I was drunk?"

Why was he touching me? Why was he even being *nice*? Weren't we supposed to hate each other? I shrugged it off and he pulled away. "It's nothing."

"It?"

I turned to him. "Since when is what I do of any interest to you? Aren't you too busy running the family business?"

"It's not that hard to run it."

"Dad made it seem that way."

"I'm not Dad."

I appraised him. "Head of the company? Telling me running it isn't hard? Could have fooled me."

I expected him to snap back. I certainly would have if I were in his shoes.

But he didn't.

"Fair enough," he replied. "You don't have to tell me anything. I'm sorry I bothered you."

I didn't expect to see his eyes on the ground. He looked smaller, like he was filled with *regret*.

And he'd never looked less like Dad to me.

"Really?"

"Yes. I already asked Ruth about her and she told me to come to you, but I should have known you wouldn't want to be bothered. I'm sorry. For both bothering you and for pushing you to talk about your life."

You accused him and he's *apologizing?* that little voice said. *Come on, Barry.*

"No." It hurt to admit I was in the wrong, but it was the right thing to do. "I'm the one who should be sorry. I came over here in the wrong headspace."

"Because I asked about Lila Wilde?"

"Yes. You asking—you even just texting me—came out of nowhere. I thought that if you were drunk, you might be using the fact that she's been in the bar to get something from me." And she'd just left, souring my mood even further. Clarity felt like a bucket of cold water. "But that's a Dad move. Not you."

"Why would anyone care if she's been in a bar?"

For such an intelligent man, I didn't get how he wouldn't see it.

"A major pop star? In a small bar in Nashville? It's not like her. Her fans would pick it apart and they'd find me. Do you know what would happen if Lila was connected to anyone other than that boyfriend of hers?"

"I don't."

"It would be like what happened with Ruth, but twenty times worse."

"Okay, I can see why that would be a problem. But I'm not going to tell anyone. Your life is your life."

"I agree, but I remember a time when everyone told me what I *should* be. Including you."

I didn't want it to affect me. I thought it wouldn't once I wrote off Mom and Dad. Yet I was so angry.

"I won't do that again," he said. "I was genuinely curious."

"Why? You're busier than ever now that you run the company."

His lips pressed together. "I work all day and come home to a quiet apartment. I just thought . . . music would fill the void."

"That doesn't sound like you." I took in his newly tense shoulders. "Are you trying to hide something from me?"

Was it what Ruth knew?

"Someone I care about likes her," he said slowly.

"Like a girlfriend? I didn't think you did commitment."

"It's not a girlfriend . . . It's complicated."

"Does it have anything to do with why Ruth's been acting weird?"

"How do you know Ruth is acting weird?"

"We talk. Sometimes." I pretended to be nonchalant about it with a shrug.

"Really?"

"I'm trying, okay? So whatever this is . . . just tell me. You give a little, I'll give a little. About Lila, I mean."

"I seriously doubt that," he muttered, looking away again. "In fact, you'll probably find it funny for two seconds and then hate me."

"The only thing I'd find funny is if you were wearing heels to be taller than me."

"I—why would I do that?"

"Ruth does. *Dad* does."

"He what?"

"I snuck into his closet one day and found them. All of his boots have heels so he's as tall as Mom." It was one of the few good memories I had of home. I knew Dad was insecure about his height and I wanted something to knock him down a peg.

"How did I never know this?"

"You and Ruth zoned out when I got yelled at for hinting I knew about them. It was worth it, though."

"Huh. That must be why he never took them off at home."

"We got off topic again." I shook my head. "I believe you were about to give me information?"

He looked pained. "I need to know for a . . . child."

"A child?"

"*My* . . . child."

I froze. Tom had a *child*? A real, living, breathing *child*?

And he never said anything?

"You have a kid?"

"Yes."

"How old?"

"Eleven. Almost twelve."

"Fuck. Almost twelve? You managed to keep that a secret for this long?"

"I didn't know about him."

"What do you mean you didn't *know*?" I was realizing just how much worse this was.

"I mean, I was told. But I turned her away, I guess."

"There isn't any guessing here, Tom." I'd thought lowly of my brother, but I always hoped that he wouldn't do this.

There was no way he would *leave* a child out there. Dad was a piece of shit, but even he didn't *leave* us, even if it would have been better if he had.

"She told me through an email that I don't remember," he explained. "I've tried to, but I don't. I don't remember most of college."

"I wonder why." I rolled my eyes. "Alcohol is a dangerous thing. A little is fine, but you were getting smashed every night for years. That does lasting damage."

"I know. And I've stopped."

"Yeah. Good for you. Except it's twelve years too late. Knowing about Lila Wilde, even if this kid is her biggest fan, isn't going to fix this, you know."

At least he had the decency to look like he felt bad about it.

My conscious was wrong about Tom. I shouldn't have stuck around for him. Only Ruth was worth it. I needed to get out of here and never talk to him again.

"I know." His voice was hard. "There is no apology, no gift, *nothing*, that can make up for it. All I can hope for is to know him for the time that his mother is tolerating me. I can't make up for what I've done, what I've missed, but I can't sit here knowing about him now and leave him."

"Then how could you have done it all those years ago?"

"I don't know!" He snapped, his voice loud like Dad's but shaking in a way I'd never heard before. "I don't *fucking* know. She was . . . I remember her. I remember the one day we had like it was yesterday but *nothing* else. I wish I had done something different. If I could go back in time and shake some sense into younger me, then I would. But all I know is at that time, Dad was on my ass about being the only Murray he deemed worthy, and I probably hid it so I wouldn't disappoint him, or worse, get smacked around by him. It's not an excuse, but I just want to *try* to be a good person this time. And I don't know if I can."

You're still not wrong about him, the voice said. *He regrets it.*

Son of a *bitch.* Just when I thought I knew him, he surprised me again. My family was good at that, apparently.

"That's the most words I've ever heard you say."

"What? Aren't you supposed to yell at me some more?"

"I could, but you seem to know how bad you fucked up." And then I did the math in my head. "And that was around the time that I started acting out so . . . maybe that was why Dad was harder on you. So, I'm sorry for that."

I'd always annoyed our parents, but it really ramped up in ninth grade when Dad downplayed yet another one of my passing grades in favor of Tom's and Ruth's perfect performances. That was when he figured out that I would never be like him and I realized I was fucking done.

"It's not your fault. It's Dad's, and it's mine. I own up to it."

"You're being more mature than most." I gave a small sigh as my feet pushed me forward and I took off my jacket. "Which is why I'll tell you more about Lila, even the things most people don't know."

"I appreciate it," I said. "But they have to be kid appropriate."

"Duh." What kind of a person did he think I was? "I mean the things real fans know."

"How about which album to start with? I'm wanting to listen to her, and to music in general. It's just overwhelming."

"Why?"

"You don't remember when Dad laid into me at dinner when he thought me listening to music caused me to get a B on a final?"

"I dimly remember it. All of Dad's yelling blends together."

"It ruined music for me. And now I don't even know where to start."

"Maybe start with her softer stuff. It's not as popular, but her deep cuts are what are really interesting. She has this way of subtly hinting at something going wrong in life. If you were to like anything, it would be that."

"What songs?"

"I'll make you a list," I said. "I think it's cool that you're trying to get into your kid's interests."

"He's worth it."

And I hoped he was being genuine because if he were, then he was already steps ahead of Dad.

Chapter Ten

Lila

Mom: *Oh my. That dress seems so uncomfortable for a night being surrounded by people. I hope you have fun!*

I sighed as I saw Mom's text. *I hope you have fun* meant she probably didn't want to hear more about my wild night. She'd grown increasingly distant from this part of my life ever since I moved to LA. Whenever Lila was involved, she stayed out of it.

All I wanted was to talk to someone about my night. My dress, while beautiful with its bright colors, was itchy and heavy, and there were sequins everywhere.

And now I dreaded going to a movie premiere I should have been excited about. Months ago, I recorded a song for a movie a friend directed. While it wasn't my best, I was excited to see the scene that it was featured in.

I'd hidden in my room after squeezing inside to get one photo of myself to show her what I was up to, but I should have known her response wouldn't have been helpful.

I'd been told I needed something eye-catching since Blaze and I were supposed to be seen together at this premiere for the first time in the nearly three months I was in Nashville.

The problem with eye-catching in LA was that *everyone* went for it. And then everything was all too much. We were still in the car, but I could see the glam from our spot at the curb.

I'd stick out more if I were wearing leggings and a T-shirt at this event, but Mia would never let me leave the house like that.

I said yes to getting dolled up for this because Mia told me Blaze's interviews hadn't fully calmed fans. They were dying to know if everything was okay. I'd checked social media myself the second I was back in LA, and she was right. They wanted to see us together.

In Nashville, I hadn't focused on social media nearly as much. But here, I was reminded every day of everything I needed to be in order to keep people happy.

There were more paparazzi than guests at this premiere and everyone was waiting to see me walk down the red carpet.

I didn't know how I was supposed to pretend to be in love with Blaze when my mind was with Barry back in Nashville, but everyone was done with my delays. Especially Mia.

"No more of this mood you've been in," she had said as I got dressed. "You had your break and now we're back in business."

"Right."

"Stand close to him," Mia instructed. "Cover your left hand. We want to spark some engagement rumors."

I promised myself I wouldn't mess this up.

I tried to push back the feeling of disgust that I felt when I saw Blaze waiting in the limo. He wore a designer suit with a multicolored tie that matched my dress. Once upon a time, I would have loved that we were in similar colors. Now, I wanted to change my outfit and sink into being Rose.

My fists tightened. I didn't usually have this hard of a time making people happy. The fans were going to love seeing us together.

But I knew I didn't want to. This feeling of defiance was new to me.

If Barry were here, he'd tell me to do whatever I wanted. He'd tell me to change, to say fuck Blaze, and follow my heart, which was in Nashville.

I imagined it for one second: the feeling of leaving and finding something better. But after that second, I pushed it away and walked to the car where Blaze was. As I got in, his eyes were on his phone.

"Look," he said. "Our fans are waiting."

Our. Because Lila was nothing without her muse.

He had a live stream on his phone, showing everyone waiting to see what we wore. On the outside, we looked like a cohesive couple.

But I didn't know if I could even call him my boyfriend. I hadn't touched him since I caught him with someone else, and I didn't know if I ever could again.

This didn't feel like a real relationship. What sort of partnership could we have when I didn't even want to be near him?

Do it for the fans. They want this.

"This dress is so tight," I said, trying to make conversation as we headed for the venue.

He didn't even look up. "You probably didn't work out enough in Nashville and now you're paying the price."

"I think this is just how the dress is designed," I muttered.

The cameras saw us as we pulled up. Flashes blinded me through the tint as everyone yelled our names.

Blaze grabbed my hand and hauled me out of the limo. I had to remind myself not to pull away. We slowly walked the red carpet, people desperately trying to get our attention.

"Doesn't she look *great*?" Blaze asked, laughing. "My girl knows how to dress up."

My stomach twisted. He didn't even say that in private.

He didn't even *look* at me.

For the man who'd complained about me not spending enough time with him, he sure didn't seem to care now. I wondered if he'd found someone else to spend his nights with, to cure his "blue balls," as he called it.

I wondered if people could see how uncomfortable I was growing. I wondered if they would pick up on how much I didn't want to be next to him.

And though I shouldn't, I hoped that they did.

"Lila!" a voice called, and I turned to see Sasha waving at me. I smiled at her. I wanted to go say hello, especially since she'd helped me with the song that was in the movie.

Blaze's grip tightened on my hip as if he were trapping me.

"Come here, girl!" Sasha said. "I want some photos with you."

The cameras turned, ready for me to move. It was a smart move because now I *had* to go.

"Coming!" I replied.

"Lila," Blaze snapped.

"She's my producer," I hissed before walking away.

If the cameras had caught that, there would be a field day about it. I could only hope they'd been distracted.

"How are you?" she asked. "You're glowing!"

"It's the dress," I said. "And I'm okay. Happy to see this movie's premiere."

"And happy to be back in LA?"

My face fell.

Her eyes left me and went to Blaze, who was gladly continuing to pose in front of the cameras. "Why don't we walk in together?"

"I don't know if that's a good idea."

"We made the song," she said. "We can do what we want."

She put her arm around me and led me to the doors. My smile felt brighter. A few reporters interviewed us, and it was far easier to talk about my work when I didn't have Blaze in my ear telling me all the things *he'd* done to support me.

I liked it when things were less about Blaze and more about my work.

"I can't wait to finish this album with you." Sasha winked before she went to her seat. "Especially the lyrics. Oh, and by the way, there's a cheater incoming." The words were muttered as she went to her seat. I only had a second to process them before Blaze was on me.

"Really?" he snapped. "Do you know how stupid you made me look?"

"I just walked in with my producer."

"After I gave you months with a man who isn't me, I thought you'd be more grateful."

"Keep your voice down!" I hissed. "Who knows if any of the reporters are here? And I didn't do anything with him. I'm not you."

"Hold on to your moral righteousness if you need to. Both you and I know that everyone wants *us* together. Not some fucking nobody in Nashville."

He walked ahead of me, going to our assigned seats, and I glanced at the door, so tempted to leave. But the director of this film, a woman I called a friend, wanted me to see it.

And I always did what people wanted—including staying with a man I was starting to hate.

Barry

The bar had barely opened, but people were filtering in. I had my phone in my pocket and it burned a hole through my leg.

I wanted to check on Lila.

She was walking the red carpet tonight at a movie premiere that included a song she wrote.

And I was desperate to see her.

In the near week since her departure, I missed her. I found myself seeing life as she did, as a lyric waiting to be written. I wanted to make more, but I wondered if I would ever be able to find connections who would take a chance on me.

Besides, I had the bar, which should have felt like home.

"Hey, Barry, can we—" Audrey paused when she saw me. "Ooh, never mind."

"What?"

"It's nothing. You look like you're thinking about something pretty hard over there."

"I'm not," I lied. "What's up?"

She turned to me, lips pursed. "It's a work question. A kind of big one, so if you're not in the mental space to handle that, then it can wait."

"I'm fine. Go ahead and ask." My fingers drummed a beat on the table in front of me. I needed to know or else I'd spiral. If she were quitting, I'd be fucked.

"I think we need to up the dance nights."

"Oh." At least it wasn't *bad* news. "Why?"

"Check the sign-up sheet," she said. "We have a wait list triple that of the other ones. People *love* the dance nights."

"But we'd have to cut the singer-songwriter performances."

"Not really," she said. "Some of the singers *want* to do a dance night. They'd jump at the chance to do pop covers and medleys. Hell, even some K-pop groups want in when they're in the US. We can keep the idea of this being an artist-first space and do more business. Scoot over." She nearly pushed me out of the way and opened Excel. "I know you don't care about revenue all that much, but I made a graph of the potential increase here. It's worth looking at."

The jump was enough that it would even interest Dad.

I shook off the thought about him the second I had it. *Why* did I still think about him?

"You looked into all of this?" I asked slowly.

"I had help." Her cheeks darkened. "Liam's the one who talked to the artists. I just made the graph."

I could have made a joke about her and Liam working together on this, but another question was on my mind. "Why?"

"Why not?"

"You just work here. You don't *have* to do all of this."

"Because I care, and I manage the guest list, so I see these things. There may not be much in it for me, but I know you want the bar to do well, and I want to see you succeed so . . ." She shrugged. "I just thought I'd help."

I stared at her. I should have known she'd jump at the opportunity to do this. She and Liam always did it for other things, but this was above her level.

"You're right," I said. "We should implement these things. And *you* should be a manager."

"Wh-what?"

"Do you think I'd let you do all of this with nothing in it for you?"

"You know I didn't do all of this expecting a reward, right?"

"I do know. That's why I'm giving you one."

"Thank you, boss. I accept."

"And I'm doubling your pay."

Her eyes widened. "Double? But you already pay so much!"

"And you get a bonus if this change pays off."

"But—"

"Question me and I'll do more."

She sighed but didn't look annoyed at all. "Fine. I *guess* I'll deal."

"Thank you, Audrey."

She left, and I was in a distinctly better mood. I'd almost forgotten what I had been mulling over before.

Then I remembered.

Lila.

I took out my phone and opened the browser, searching for her name. She was plastered everywhere in a shiny, beautiful dress.

But my eyes were caught on her face and how miserable it looked. I should have let her be, but I couldn't help but text her, wondering if she'd even remember to reply.

CHAPTER ELEVEN

Lila

Barry: You deserve someone who can make you smile a real smile.

Lila: Thank you. I'm guessing you saw photos from the premiere.

Barry: Yes. You looked miserable.

Lila: It was. But the fans loved it.

"This line won't work," Mia said, shaking her head. We sat in her office, reviewing the album I'd recorded. I dreaded every second of this meeting and I was right to. Sasha had tagged along for moral backup, but I didn't know how she would fare against the hurricane that was the woman who curated every aspect of my life. "I knew you shouldn't have recorded them without my approval first. Do you know how hard it'll be to change it now?"

Very. But not because nothing else would fit.

The song seemed perfect as is.

All the relaxation I'd felt was gone now that she was in front of me. It was made worse by the fact that Blaze was still at my house and showed no signs of leaving.

"All the love songs are set in *Nashville*," Mia continued after my silence. "You two have never been there, not for any meaningful time. Not only that, but these aren't the pop hits your fans expect."

"They *are* pop hits," Sasha said. "Just not mindless ones."

Mia glared at her and I jumped in.

"We'll figure it out."

"Blaze has been covering for you for *months*. And this is how you repay him?" Mia shook her head and stepped away. "I can't believe you."

"He's the one who sent me to Nashville! And I did what was asked. I made an album."

"An unmarketable one. God, I can't believe you're letting down my dad because of one measly kiss."

I winced. Rick's death a few years ago had taken a toll on her.

And me, if I were being honest.

Things hadn't been the same since Mia stepped into his place.

"I knew you were harsh, Mia." Sasha's voice was cold. "But that was too far."

She only rolled her eyes, completely unfazed. "Whatever. I'm going to go blow off some steam. Take these and make them into a number-one hit. *Now.*"

I slowly nodded, no words coming out of my mouth. She slammed the door behind her, which made me jump.

"She's a piece of work," Sasha remarked.

"Yeah, she is," I muttered. "But her dad gave me my big break."

"And you owe *her* something for that?"

"He taught her everything he knew. And she's been good at what she does. My last two albums—"

"Did well, but were repetitive."

They were, and it hurt seeing some of my fans call it that. It wasn't my best work—even I could admit it—but it was what the majority of everyone seemed to want.

"Lila," Sasha said, walking toward me, "I say this only because I care about you. Nashville was where you were happier. This music is the best you've ever made. And you shouldn't have to change it."

My hands played with my hair. "You're right. And if it were only me I was singing for, then I wouldn't change a thing."

"But it *is* only you."

"Not where the fans are concerned."

"The loud ones, maybe. But plenty would love to hear this."

"So, *what*, I just tell them I fell for someone else? While Blaze was saying all these great things about me?"

"Great things about what *he* did for you."

She wasn't wrong, but disappointing anyone, especially those who had given me all of this, made my throat close.

But then I thought about how I felt at that damn premiere, how miserable I'd been.

"You're conflicted," she said, "and you have a right to be. But the music is *yours*."

And Barry's. What would he do if he were here?

A tiny spark of defiance grew within me.

"I'm . . . I'm not going to change some of them. I'll fight harder for them."

"Yes," Sasha said. "That's the right call. And I'll fight for them too. Whether Mia likes it or not, I know more about music than her."

I grabbed my bag and stood, determination filling me. "I'm going to go home and decide what I'm keeping. I'll face Mia tomorrow."

"Good idea. I'm proud of you."

Anxiety rose in my stomach and I didn't feel proud at all.

Just terrified.

But I knew I was doing the right thing. Worst case, we could say Blaze and I had gone on a vacation in Nashville. But I wouldn't change the heart of it. Even if this wasn't a "number-one hit" according to Mia, this was *my* work.

I said my goodbyes and walked out to the car. When I got in, my shoulders slumped and I felt like Rose Hill, not Lila.

"You okay?" Juno asked.

"I'm fine," I said.

"You don't look fine."

"You were at the studio when I recorded my new album. What did you think?"

"I'm far from a music expert."

"I don't need an expert, just someone who listened to it."

"Please don't take offense to this, but I think you mass-produced hits before you went to Nashville. And sure, it worked, but it wasn't like the stuff you wrote a long time ago when you first started. Your best work is when you're genuine, especially your softer stuff, and lately, you haven't been making that."

"Until I worked with Barry."

"Exactly. I don't mean to make you feel bad about your last albums, but—"

"You didn't. You just made me feel better about what I'm about to do."

When we got home, Juno pulled into the garage. She asked if I wanted dinner, but I was ready to pore over the album and devise the perfect plan to win over Mia. I had loads of ideas, ones to prove to her that this could be *good*.

Blaze's car was here and I hoped he would entertain himself while I worked.

"Do you want me to go in with you in case he gives you a hard time?" Juno asked.

I shouldn't need protection from my boyfriend of all people, but I nodded anyway.

She walked ahead but paused as she got to the door.

"What?" I asked her.

"I think I hear something."

I leaned in, putting my ear on the door. I heard repetitive wet, slapping noises.

"What *is* that?" I asked. "Is he watching porn?"

"This loudly? In your living room?" Juno's voice was tight and I realized just how embarrassing this was.

God, why couldn't he be normal?

"I'll handle this," I muttered, readying myself to enter.

"Wait," she said, and a second voice joined in just as she did.

One that I knew.

"Yes!" Mia's voice said. "Go harder!"

"You know it, baby."

I felt like I could faint.

Blaze's and my sex life had been nonexistent for a while, even before he'd cheated. But after I discovered him with the waitress, he told me he wouldn't do it again. He swore they hadn't even had sex. It was only a kiss.

My horror climbed to impossible heights.

Was *this* the steam she was letting off?

"Lila," Juno said, "maybe we should—"

I threw open the door.

Blaze was buck naked and Mia's pantsuit was strewn around the apartment. Her legs were in the air.

"You're always so tight!" he grunted.

Always.

"Are you *fucking* kidding me?" I yelled.

Blaze turned, covering himself in a useless attempt at modesty. Mia yelped and tried to hide under the nearest blanket.

Which had *our* faces on it. A fan had given it to him years ago.

"Lila!" he said.

"You and *Mia*?"

"It's . . . it's not . . ."

"It's not what?" Mia asked, crossing her arms. Juno came in behind me, the door shutting. "Great. The mountain is here."

"Why are you in Lila's house?" Juno boomed. "Last I checked, neither of you are on the deed."

Mia rolled her eyes before she settled on me. "Aren't you supposed to be working?"

I wanted to scream. Maybe throw up. She was just caught fucking my boyfriend and she was asking why I wasn't *working*?

"Fuck you," I snapped.

"You two need to get out," Juno instructed.

"Lila," Mia said, ignoring Juno, "it's not that huge of a deal."

My eyes widened.

"Mia," Blaze said. "Maybe that's not what we should say."

"Who are you to lecture me on what to say?" Mia snapped. "I let you handle her and she wound up in Nashville with some other guy!"

"How long?" I croaked out.

"Not long," Blaze said.

"Oh my *God*!" Mia snapped. "Lila, it's always been a thing, okay? We've always been together."

"S-since . . ."

"Since the beginning, yes."

"What? But—"

"Your first song about him made you a mainstream pop star and then Dad told me you two were the selling point."

"So, it was all a *scheme*?" I asked.

"I mean, like the sex parts were good," Blaze said.

"And it worked," Mia added. "How do you think I feel seeing you two together all the time?"

"Don't make this sound like a *sacrifice*." I felt like I couldn't breathe. "How dare you?"

"You wanted fame. I made it happen and let you fuck around with my boyfriend."

"He's *my*—" I stopped, realizing how petty I sounded. He was my boyfriend, but I didn't want him to be.

My rage turned into conviction. Sweet, sweet conviction.

Suddenly, telling them I wasn't changing my damn album wasn't enough. I was done with *all* of it.

"You can have him, then," I said. "Juno, get them out."

"Gladly."

"Wait, what?" Blaze asked, sounding panicked.

"You're not coming anywhere near me again."

"We *have* to."

"Fuck you both. Mia, you're fired."

"Excuse me?" she hissed. She dared to look offended. "I have a contract."

"Who cares? I'm done with it."

"And the contract doesn't cover you being in her home when she's not here. Get out or I will drag you out myself." Juno started toward them and Blaze finally got up. He threw on his underwear and a shirt.

"You can't—" Mia began, but Juno grabbed her by the arm, pushing her to the door. "I'm not even dressed!"

"Too bad. Wear your shame like you deserve."

When they were gone, I let out a shaking breath.

"Lila, I—"

I held up my hand. I expected the normal feeling of guilt to settle in, but I was only angry this time. And I would use that anger for as long as I could.

"So, I *am* going to be changing some lyrics," I began slowly, "but not in the way I thought. Can you go to the car and get my notebook?"

"Yes, why?"

"I'm about to work on my revenge song again. It's time to update it. Can you call Sasha for me? I'll need to be at the studio once I finish."

"Of course." She went to grab the notebook but then paused. "Are you okay?"

"Right now, I'm pissed. But everything else will hit me later, I'm sure. And by that time, I'll have a new song and be on my way to Nashville."

"To see Barry?"

"Yeah, it's time to go back to where I'm my happiest."

Barry

I was getting ready to go down to the bar for the night when I heard a loud knock at my door. I checked my watch, wondering if Liam or Audrey had already encountered a problem.

But then I opened the door and my heart skipped a beat when I saw Lila instead. At first, I thought this had to be a dream come true, but then I caught sight of her red-rimmed eyes and how her lips trembled.

"What happened?"

"Can I come in?" Her voice cracked.

"Of course." My eyes slid to Juno.

"I'm going to ensure reporters aren't around so you two can have privacy."

I let Lila into the apartment as Juno descended the steps. That was when she broke down. She sank to the floor, tears escaping her. For a moment, I froze. I was terrible when it came to people crying. The Murrays didn't do well with emotions that didn't drive us to improve. I was reminded of when Ruth cried about how much distance was between us.

But I couldn't just let her sit there.

I knelt to be on her level. "What happened?"

"I walked in on him fucking my manager."

I had to take a second to process her words. "You *what*?"

"They're 'in love' and always have been. I feel like such a fucking fool."

"Why wouldn't he just be with her, then?"

"Because Blaze and I sold music." She let out another sob. "He wasn't the best man, but he told me it was one time. I never thought he would cheat on me for *so* long."

Rage clouded my vision. I never wanted to pummel a man more than I did him.

But I wanted to be there for *her* more.

"He never deserved you," I said slowly.

She nodded and wiped a tear from her cheek. "I rewrote the revenge song."

Now *that* I didn't expect. "You did?"

"And I'm releasing it at midnight. I don't know how I'll hype it up, but I have to do *something*."

"And the album?"

"I'm releasing it as is."

It hit me then that she was a free woman, which changed everything. She'd come back in her darkest moment to be with *me*. There was a chance this could be something more. "I think you're doing the right thing."

"I knew you'd say that," she said with a smile. "It's why I came back."

CHAPTER TWELVE

Lila

Lila Wilde's Agent Was Spotted Leaving Her House in Only a Blanket?

By Perez Adder

The world of Lila Wilde has been awash with drama lately. After looking uncomfortable at her most recent red carpet, people have been wondering if things are all roses with her and Blaze. Though sources have said things are happy, we all know those statements come from her agent, Mia Thorne, the daughter of the agent who discovered Lila.

Mia has done a lot for Lila and she wears many hats in the Wilde world of one the biggest pop stars. Now, we are wondering if this relationship is continuing.

Why would Mia be at Lila's mansion dressed in only a blanket, much less a blanket with Lila's and Blaze's faces on it? Are Mia and Lila having a torrid affair? Or are Mia and Blaze?

5,682 Comments

Highvirtue: I hate gossip rags so much. There is no way this actually happened.

Lauraobviously: there's photos . . .

Highvirtue: Photoshop exists.

Buttlicker6969: these photos are SO hot

*Mmmfantasy: GUYS CHECK LILA'S INSATGRAM! NEW
SONG?*

Ciya: PR as usual . . .

"So, besides nervous, how do you feel?" Barry asked as he handed me tea, the same one Rose had seen him get. I took it from him, trying not to think about my alter ego as Lila's life fell apart.

"Excited. I'm hoping maybe people will like this, but I'm terrified I'll regret releasing it."

"Why would you regret it?"

"Because . . . for once, I'm doing something for me."

"Anyone who would be angry at you for doing something for you isn't worth your time."

I wanted to believe him, but I wasn't sure if I could. My entire life had been making others happy, and this was making no one happy but me.

And Barry.

"Come here," he said, and I leaned into him. His arms came around me, pulling me to him tighter. He smelled like leather and patchouli, almost like home. I'd only hugged him once when I was saying goodbye, yet it had cemented in my mind as one of the most incredible hugs I'd ever received.

"I've got you. I've always got you."

His arms were so comfortable, but then I saw the time. "You need to be at the bar."

"Yes, but—"

"No buts. It's important to you."

He looked pained. "I can stay."

I shook my head. "You don't have to. I should call my parents anyway. They should know."

"Are you trying to get rid of me?"

"Not at all, but you have a life and I don't want to derail it more than I have. If I need you, I'll call you."

"You promise?"

I nodded. "I'm fine. A hug from you can heal almost anything."

"I do need to be sure my team's okay, but I'll be back as soon as the bar closes."

"Okay. I'll be here."

Barry's lips pressed to my forehead before he left the apartment. The feeling of the simple action lingered and I had to take a moment to collect myself before I pulled out my phone.

It was time to call my parents.

While I knew Mom would always be angry with Dad, she was civil, and I needed to let them know what was happening. I didn't do joint calls very often, but I couldn't bear to tell them separately and repeat what happened more than once.

I texted them both and waited for their reply. Mom called and then Dad did. Once they were combined, I let out a sigh of relief. "There. Now we can all talk."

"A joint call with your mom? Is everything okay?"

"Yes, dear," Mom said as she came on the line. "I'm worried about you."

"I don't even know how to start this," I muttered. "But I'm releasing a new song tonight."

"Oh, good!" Dad said. "What's it about?"

"Blaze and I . . ." My breath quivered. "We're over. I dumped him."

"Really?" she asked. "I saw something had happened at your house, but I wasn't sure if it was true."

"What did you see?"

"That your agent was outside of your house in a blanket?"

I cringed. So someone *had* seen that. I bet Perez Adder was all over that, as he was with everything in my life. The comments on that were going to be *wild*.

"Yeah, that's a part of it."

"People are all up in arms about it."

"Blaze was cheating on me with her."

"What?"

"For how long?" Dad asked.

"For many years," I added.

"*Years?*" Dad repeated. "I'm glad you dumped him or else I would do it for you."

"I can't believe he would cheat on *you*," Mom said, but then she sighed. "It's going to be huge news, isn't it?"

And *there* were the words I was thinking. The news would be big and I wondered if Lila would get any privacy. I'd have to stay away from Mom for the entire time. She hated it when my name, even my fake one, was everywhere.

"It'll fade," Dad said. "Don't worry about it, Linda. Now, Rosie, is that why you were upset when I was in Nashville?"

"Kind of. I'd caught him with someone else that time. But this thing with Mia is . . . worse. I left right after."

"I knew I never liked him."

"Really?"

"All he cared about was fame," Dad said. "He only approached you after Rick said you were the best there."

"He didn't—" I began to say, but I stopped myself. Maybe he *had* always cared about the fame. Maybe he realized he couldn't achieve it on his own and focused on me to get a foot in the door. And I'd been too blind to notice.

"But you seemed happy," Mom said. "For a while."

"Where are you now?" Dad asked. "Do you want to come stay with me, Rosie?"

"I'm in . . . Nashville."

"Why are you there? You knew I left for Portland months ago."

"Um," I said, "I came back for Barry."

"Who's Barry?" Mom asked.

"Wait, I know the name," Dad said.

"He was the bar owner. The one I had the eyes for."

"Oh, really?" he asked. "Are you spending more time as Rose, then?"

"N-no. He knows Lila."

"But I thought you liked him as *Rose*?"

"I've met him mostly as Lila. But also as Rose."

The line was silent.

"Is that a good idea?" Mom asked.

"I can't switch now."

"But you talked to him as Rose."

"Yeah, but he *likes* Lila."

"Okay," Mom said slowly. "But what if you get the story mixed up?"

I closed my eyes, knowing that my secret identity kept her sane.

"I'll be sure no one knows. Everything will be okay." I wasn't sure if I was reassuring her or myself.

"Rosie . . ." Dad's voice was soft in a way I hadn't heard before. "You can't be Lila forever."

Couldn't I? I'd been Lila for the last decade and more.

"A secret like this is worth millions," Mom said. "Do you trust him?"

"He hasn't told anyone he's even met me."

"Do you see yourself staying with him?" Dad asked. "I told you to follow your heart."

"I could."

"Is this the life he wants?" Mom asked. "To be tied to fame?"

And my heart crumbled at their questions. Mom wasn't wrong and neither was Dad. Rose was supposed to be the *real* me, but he only knew the fake side.

The one who could ruin is life if people found out about him.

"Linda," Dad started, "let her live her life, especially if she likes this guy."

"I'm trying to be sure I can stay safe, Archie," Mom said. "I can't do this like you and Lila can."

"I'll be safe," I promised. "No one will catch me."

But even I knew I wasn't always being safe. Not by a long shot.

Barry

"Um, Barry?" Audrey's voice shook when she found me working in the back. "We've got a problem."

I blinked. She could figure out almost everything by herself, so if she was coming to me, then it meant something big.

"What is it?"

"You should follow me."

We went to the front door and all of the bouncers were gathered around one person. I took a second look, noticing that some of the security wasn't even my own. Was this some major celebrity trying to get in?

"What's going on here?" I asked.

"Barry Murray." One of the bodyguards moved out of the way and I saw a vaguely familiar woman. She had dark hair, blue eyes, and a sharp bob. "I'm here to get my star back. I believe you know who I am. The name is Mia."

It dawned on me then. Mia was Lila's agent, and judging by the look of this, my secrets were about to get blown out of the water.

"Let's go to my office," I said. "We can talk more there."

Audrey and all of my security staff looked at me incredulously. I knew she wasn't going to take this sitting down. There were going to be *a lot* of questions about what was happening.

But first, I needed to deal with the person who had hurt Lila. That was more important than anything else.

Mia and her entourage followed me to my office. Out of the corner of my eye, I saw Juno peeking around a corner, eyebrow raised. When she saw who was following me, her jaw dropped.

I wouldn't have been surprised if Lila left my apartment within minutes. Juno was very protective and I couldn't blame her.

"I hate to disappoint you," I said as I shut my office door, "but she's not—"

"Can it," Mia stated abruptly. "I am well aware that she was here writing her next album, considering you match the guy in her songs, and her phone was here almost every day. Once she disappeared, I knew she would come running to you. Now, talk some sense into her before she does something incredibly stupid."

"Incredibly stupid? Or do you mean incredibly brave? Because the way I see it, she's entirely justified to do exactly what she plans to do after what she witnessed tonight."

"So, you admit that she's here."

"I admit that I know *exactly* what's going on."

"Oh, do you? Have you ever considered that she could be lying?"

"The only thing I'm considering is publicly kicking you out and making sure you never return. I won't be telling you a damn thing about Lila, much less let you take her back to LA where she's miserable."

"I wouldn't be making threats," she said. "I've been making media statements for her for longer than you've owned this shitty bar and I can twist this into whatever I want."

"And I've been dealing with manipulators like you for just as long. Listen carefully, Mia. I. Don't. Care."

Her eyes widened a fraction and I prepared for her next wave of bullshit. But the door to my office opened.

And Lila barged in.

"You have a lot of fucking nerve coming here." Her voice was like ice.

"You have a lot of nerve firing me," Mia retorted. "But thank you for coming out of hiding. That means I can more easily drag your ass back to a jet." She grabbed Lila's arm tightly. Rage tunneled my vision.

"Don't fucking touch her."

She turned to me, a cruel smile on her face. "Try to stop me."

I was tempted to step in physically, but something in the back of my mind told me Mia was expecting that.

I wasn't sure what to do for a moment, then I remembered what Ruth had done when her boss illegally fired her.

"You're cool with me recording this, right?" I asked as I took out my phone.

Mia froze, and I hit the button to start filming.

"Cool. So, let's continue. You were dragging Lila Wilde out of my office against her will?"

Lila wrenched her arm out of Mia's. "Yes, she was."

"Anything else to say?" I asked Mia.

She slowly turned, glowering at Lila. "You're coming back to LA with me."

"No. Not after what you did. I fired you for your inappropriate behavior. You shouldn't be here."

"You have a contract with me. I'm not fired."

"I can break the contract."

"Oh, you definitely can't. I made that thing ironclad. You're stuck with me."

Lila blinked, mouth open. It was time for me to step in.

"A contract, huh?" I asked. "I think I know a few lawyers who can look at it."

"Huh?" Lila said. "You have a lawyer?"

"Not me, but a celebrity in my family does. He's pretty good, actually. He's going against many powerful people. What's one more?"

"You're bluffing," Mia said.

"Not really. I don't know if you've looked up my family, but you should. My sister's dating one of the smartest people on the planet. Behind her, of course. And my brother's currently dethroning our father of a billion-dollar business through a very public legal process. Usually, I wouldn't throw my family into it like this, but I would for *her*. Walk away. Now."

"This all is out of nowhere. I didn't do anything." Mia's eyes were on the camera as if she were pleading to a jury.

"Here's the truth," I began, "you fucked Blaze Matthews for years behind her back and used your dad's name to become Lila's PR agent, and then did more than you should have to control every aspect of her life. You forced her to produce empty pop albums for years and came here planning to take her *against* her will to a different city. Is that right?"

"It's right from my perspective," Lila said. "I don't want to go with you."

Her face went beet red and her nostrils flared. "You little *bi*—"

"And remember, everything you say is on record."

Her mouth snapped shut.

"I wonder what her fans would say about everything I just accused you of. It certainly would hurt your reputation."

"I underestimated you."

"And it'll be the *last* time you ever do that. Now, get the *fuck* out of my bar."

Chapter Thirteen

My heart was pounding, but not with fear. Watching Barry stand up for me in front of Mia was doing unfair things to my body. He'd used his connection to his family for *me*.

"Thank you," I said. "You didn't have to do that."

"I think I did. She wasn't going to take no for an answer, was she?"

I bit my lip. I'd never seen her like that, but I'd also never pissed her off before. I'd heard from other artists that she would stop at nothing to get what she wanted, but seeing it for myself was entirely different.

"You beat her at her own game. You said that was your sister's move?"

A smile crossed his face. "Yes."

"When did she use that?"

"I think we have bigger problems than my family," he said, shaking his head.

I deflated. I wanted to know more about this man who dominated my mind. He would give a little, but he wasn't entirely opening up to me.

But all in all, he wasn't wrong. I *did* have bigger problems, such as figuring out how to separate myself from Mia as soon as possible.

I let out a long sigh. "I need to contact my lawyer and see if I can get out of this contract."

"Do you need help with it? I wasn't kidding when I said I had connections."

"No, I'll be okay. I have someone I can ask first."

He nodded. "When do you need to leave?"

As much as I wanted to say never, I was worried about how Mia seemed so certain that she couldn't be fired. I'd signed my working contract with her when we were all grieving Rick's death, so maybe I'd overlooked some things.

Mia wouldn't delay anything. She was probably heading to a lawyer right at this very moment.

I didn't have time to waste.

"I should probably go now. God, but I don't want to. How could this get any worse?" My phone buzzed and I saw Juno saying that paparazzi had begun showing up in Nashville looking for Mia's car. "Oh, that's how. The paparazzi found me. I need to go before they find the bar."

"I don't care if people know you're here. Me and my security team—"

"I wouldn't put this on anyone. Thank you for everything you did tonight, Barry. I'll see you once all the buzz dies down."

Barry

The bar closed at its usual time of four a.m., and I foolishly thought I was free from questions when Audrey and Liam seemed more focused on straightening up rather than talking to me.

But the minute the floor was mopped and everything was clean, Audrey found me.

"What was that?" she asked. "Why was Lila Wilde's agent here yelling at you?"

Liam raised his eyebrows. "Was that who it was? I knew it was something big when you went to get Barry."

"Uh, yeah," Audrey said. "She said she wanted her star back. She had to be talking about Lila, right?"

"She works with other artists," I muttered.

"Was it another one, then?"

I didn't know how to answer.

"Is *that* who you're working with?" Audrey asked.

"I can't say."

"That's not a no."

"Guys, I really can't say. I signed an NDA."

Audrey's eyebrows shot up.

"So, we can safely assume that Audrey's right," Liam responded. "But you just can't confirm that."

He was exactly right.

"Holy shit!" Audrey exclaimed. "You're, like, her biggest fan."

"I wouldn't say that."

"You cover her songs all the time. Trust me, it's obvious."

"How did this even happen?" Liam asked, shaking his head. "*The* Lila Wilde was here and we didn't even know?"

I didn't answer, no matter how much I wanted to.

"God, I'm dying to know the details."

"You can't tell anyone. Both of you know that, right?"

"Of course." Liam rolled his eyes. "We kept that one big rock star who did a secret show here on the down-low. We aren't gonna tell a soul."

"But I *am* buying that new album," Audrey said. "I can't believe you worked on it."

"I didn't," I lied.

"Yeah, yeah. NDA and all of that." Audrey waved her hand. "When does it come out?"

"A single was dropped a few hours ago."

"*What?*" Audrey pulled out her phone. "Why is it called 'Goodbye, Good Riddance'?"

"Let me see that," Liam said. "Holy shit, it is."

"Is this about Blaze? Is that why Mia was so mad?"

I shrugged.

"I've got to listen to this." She pushed play on the song I was hoping to listen to in the comfort of my apartment where I could fully get lost in her music.

But the second her song played, I knew I wouldn't stop it.

I was dying to hear what she'd written about him, after all.

Harsh electric guitar was the first thing I heard, then her voice—but this wasn't the commercial sound of in-love Lila Wilde, rather a fast-paced, lyrical middle finger.

What was even more interesting was that she didn't pull *any* punches. She called him out for cheating on her, saying it was in her own home with someone she thought was a friend. It was like it was her mission to make everyone hate Blaze.

And it was going to work.

"Holy shit," Audrey muttered. "Has she ever released anything like this?"

"No," I said. "Never."

"The guitar, that was *you*, wasn't it?" Liam asked.

"How do you know it was me?"

"One, it's a lower pitch, and two, you play like that, even if it's on your acoustic."

"I may have contributed a *little*."

I just didn't know Lila would use it in the end. She never ceased to surprise me.

And I doubted she ever would. I knew I needed to go listen to this a hundred times until I had every note memorized.

This new version of Lila was more addictive than I could ever imagine.

And I could only hope I got to spend more time with her now that the album was done and she was finally free of Blaze.

CHAPTER FOURTEEN

Lila

I didn't get to see what people were saying about the last twenty-four hours of my life because I was too busy trying to get away from Mia to even worry about it.

When I'd signed with her after Rick's death, I'd trusted her not to screw me over and that was my mistake. Her contract was ironclad, just as she had said, giving her more permissions than she deserved. My lawyer blanched when reading it over and then advised me never to sign anything else without consulting with them again.

I had to get Barry's recording of her inappropriate behavior to build a case to break the contract. I'd be able to with a large settlement, which I paid out immediately, but it was so high it made me wince.

All of that to say that I was agentless right when my new song was out. Mia had done most of my outreach as well, and her services carried over far more than most. I hadn't posted about it, but I knew my fans had to be freaking out.

After my meeting, I turned on my phone to a million messages, but most notably, a call from Sasha.

I returned that first.

"Girl," she said instead of a greeting. "People are loving this new single."

"Are they? I've been . . . busy."

"Hopefully preparing for some performances."

"Mostly on breaking my contract with Mia. She handled all of that."

"She was your PR manager *and* publicist?"

"Yeah. Before that, it was Rick."

"That's a lot of control to give one person."

"I know. Trust me, my lawyer had a *lot* to say about it. But it worked for a time. I'll have to figure out a new person for the job soon."

"Well, then. I might have a recommendation for you. My cousin Malia is an agent. She's been wanting to help you for a while."

"When is she free?"

"For Lila Wilde? Any time."

"Then let's set up a meeting."

I refused to go home and see the couch where I'd found Mia and Blaze, but being out and about as Lila Wilde made it very dangerous. Juno was already grumbling as we drove to our next stop. The paparazzi were eager to catch any glimpse of me, and my jet had been tracked back to LA, which meant they knew I was here.

And they'd somehow known I was going to the studio. I noticed a car seemingly following us and assumed it had to be one of them, and judging by the way they jumped out and ran to me, I was right.

There were flashes of cameras and calls of my name. I ducked down and ran inside, knowing I'd stirred the pot by doing this.

Sasha was waiting with another woman next to her. They looked so much alike that it was like they were twins. They had the same dark skin and eyes. The only difference was that Sasha's hair was in a natural afro and the woman beside her had box braids.

"Hi," I said. "Malia, right?"

"Yes. That's me. Nice to meet you, Ms. Wilde."

"Lila, please," I said.

"Okay, Lila," she replied. "How are you?"

"Um, busy. I've been working on a new album, which I'm still figuring out a name for, and my single just dropped—"

"But how are *you*?" she asked. "I know your work. It's incredible, but you've just separated from an agent who was the daughter of the man who discovered you and just broke it off with your long-term boyfriend."

I blinked. Mia never asked about me.

"I've been better. I feel a little lost, actually."

"I'm sorry," Malia said. "Let's see what we can do to help."

She worked for an agency that specialized in all aspects of management. While she would be my main contact, I would also work with other people for different parts of my career. I'd have an entire team rather than one person overseeing everything.

The idea sounded better than anything Mia could have ever offered. As I listened to her explain in detail how she would help me, my stress lifted.

"How's this sounding?" Malia asked.

"More than okay. I'd love to work with you."

"Great! I'll draw up the paperwork. Then we'll talk PR for this most recent news."

I nodded gratefully as she led me to the table.

"And maybe exactly what we'll be putting in the album," Sasha added. She'd let her cousin talk for most of the meeting, but her smile told me she was also excited. "Because I am *ready*."

I signed all of the papers after sending them to my lawyer who gave me a confident thumbs-up, feeling a sense of relief. "Now, I just need to see how the fans are reacting to this."

"And how do you do that?" Malia asked.

"I usually check social media."

"Oh, and do you like that?"

"Sometimes the truth hurts, but it's good to know what the general consensus is."

Malia and Sasha glanced at each other as if passing words between them.

"What?" I asked.

"I have surveys I can send out," Malia explained. "Maybe it would be best to shelve social media while you're finishing this album. After all, you've been through a lot and the last thing you need is to have your creative flow interrupted."

"And you'll let me know if I need to change anything?"

"Of course."

"Okay," I said. "I don't even know if I *can* stay away. I always go back to it when I'm bored."

"Have you considered deleting the apps from your phone?"

"Uh, no. I honestly hadn't even thought of doing it. Thank you for that suggestion, Malia. I think it's a great idea."

Lila: Hey, Barry. My life is a little less of a mess right now. I got a new publicist. The single is doing so well. People love it.

Barry: Glad you're okay.

Lila: You helped me so much with it. I could give you songwriting credit so you'd get paid for it.

Barry: I don't need the money. Helping you with it was more than enough.

Barry: Are you okay? I know you haven't been able to have a moment of peace in LA. I keep seeing paparazzi pictures of you everywhere.

Lila: Ugh. I'm fine. I'm used to it, no matter how much it sucks.

Lila: Also, I have this song we sang together. Want me to add your name to the album?

Barry: I don't need to be named.

Lila: But you wrote the song? Don't you want your glory?

Barry: I don't need glory. I got everything I wanted.

Barry: Will you be coming back to Nashville anytime soon?

Lila: Well, I can't leave my biggest fan hanging. When I finish the album, I'll come and show it to you.

Barry

The last time I'd seen Lila was over two months ago. My life had been busy between running the bar, finally giving in to joining Ruth's newfound family dinners, and watching Tom repair his relationship with his son Max—but Lila was always on my mind.

So when she randomly showed up at my front door, she looked like no time had passed at all; her hair still past her shoulders and her lashes dark, but her smile was like a breath of fresh air after being underwater.

She was wearing a simple T-shirt, jeans, and a hat. I knew people were dying to get a glimpse of her, as they had been ever since the breakup went public, so she had to hide, even when she was in a new city.

I let out a long breath when I saw her.

She'd come back.

For me.

She smiled as she saw me. "Wow, your hair is longer."

"I still let it go even when I get my regular trims," I said, stepping to the side to let her in.

"So, are you ready to hear this album? I have an interesting new featured artist." She winked as she walked inside. But then she saw the changes I'd made to the apartment. "Wait a second. Did you redecorate?"

Her eyes trailed to the table, now with two chairs and a full-sized couch. It hadn't been planned on my part, but when she said she would return to show me the album, I knew my bachelor pad of an apartment needed more room for her.

"In a way."

"There's two of everything."

"Call it wishful thinking, but I hoped I'd have a guest soon."

"Like a night guest?"

I shook my head. "Like a pop star guest."

"You did this for *me*?" Her jaw dropped and her eyes shot back to the newly furnished apartment. "Oh my God. I don't know what to say."

She didn't know what to say? She was a world-renowned songwriter. I didn't think it was possible.

But I was still ridiculously proud of myself. "You don't have to say anything."

"I owe you at least a thank you. Unless it was for a different pop star. Then I might die of embarrassment."

"It's for you. It's always for you."

She turned to me again, eyes wide. "Wow. That's twice now you've left me speechless."

"How are you?" I asked. As much as I would love to keep torturing her, I knew she'd been through a lot in our time apart.

"I'm good. I've been busy dealing with the fallout of everything. But it's fine."

I raised an eyebrow. "Really?"

"It's an adjustment. All of it is. I've deleted all of my social media apps from my phone, which has helped. Malia told me she would let me know if there was anything I needed to see."

"Good. You don't need it anyway."

"And how are you?"

My family was better than ever, for once. Tom was a good dad. Ruth was living her best life. Mom was trying to get me to come out to her new place in the middle of nowhere, but I'd turned her down. While I was fostering a slight connection with my siblings, it was because they were the only ones I'd seen make a decent effort to change.

"Everything is good."

"It is?"

"Yeah, for once."

"That's good!" she said. "I know for a bit there it was tough."

"Ruth and Tom got away from our parents. They seem . . . happy these days."

"Really? God, I want to know *everything*."

"How much time do you have?"

She paused and her face fell. "Not a lot, and the album is long, but—"

"Let's play the album," I said.

"But—"

"My family isn't as interesting as the pop star in my living room who has an album for me. I'd rather listen to that. Maybe we'll have time to talk about Ruth and Tom later."

"Okay," she said softly. "Then let's get this listening party started."

She turned to start the record she'd brought and I felt a jolt of excitement like I always did when she released something new.

But nothing could have prepared me for the first song. It was a completely different point of view from our first meeting. While I had been worried about screwing something up, she sang that she didn't want to leave and she hated the idea of going back to her old life.

As the first song ended, I had to pause to catch my breath. I'd often thought over our first meeting. I told myself it wasn't as important to her as it was to me.

And I'd been wrong.

"Do you like it?" she asked.

"This is the *first* song?"

"It is. I figured I'd tell the story as it happened."

"This is about when we met. I remember some of these lyrics."

"Yeah," she said. "I mean, coming here was the falling domino that started it all, so I owe you a thank you for that. What do you think?"

I didn't know how I was going to listen to the rest of the album when the first song had nearly destroyed me.

"It's good."

"Do you want to keep going?"

"I think I need a moment."

"Why?"

"It's not every day a man's dream woman writes a song mentioning him."

She blinked as if she didn't know exactly who she was to me, but then her lips pressed into a slow smile. "You're hyping me up."

"I'm not. I don't know why you don't see how amazing you are."

"Maybe it's because you haven't seen all of me."

"I'd love to see every part of you, Lila."

She froze but then looked down at her feet, breaking our eye connection.

"Hey," I moved closer to her. "What's wrong?"

"Nothing, this is just . . . It's different now that I'm not with Blaze."

I wouldn't lie and say I hadn't thought about it. We'd agreed not to be anything when she still was attached to him, but now that she wasn't . . .

Anything was possible.

"Besides," she continued, "it's nice that you're also not making this about you."

"Why would I? It's *your* album."

"But you helped, and in the past, when people helped . . . they took a lot of the credit, so much so that it never felt like *I* did it, but this time is different. *You're* different."

"Anyone who makes you feel like you aren't enough isn't good for you."

"And anyone who *didn't* is. Like you are. I was hoping that now that I'm single, and you're here that we could . . ." She trailed off, looking up at me with those shy eyes.

"Are you sure? So soon after Blaze?"

"Fuck it. You're my type anyway."

"And what's your type?"

"Long-haired men. Bar owners. Men who look like Thor."

"You think I look like Thor?"

"Very much so. It's doing something for me."

"Come here." I couldn't hold back any longer. I desperately needed her in my space.

Her blush darkened at my muttered command, but she did so, moving in close. My mind worked in overdrive to take in every detail of having her here. I saw her dark lashes and red lips framed by long black hair.

"If I kiss you, will this red lipstick rub off on me?"

"No, it's very kiss-proof."

"That's a shame," I said, running my finger over her lips. True to her word, it came back clean. "I'd gladly let you leave a mark."

She leaned forward, capturing my lips with hers. She hovered over me and I grabbed her by the hips to fully sit on my lap. I heard her breathing stutter as her hands ran through my hair, nails scraping against the scalp.

All I could do was focus on kissing her and not messing this up for myself. She was a solid weight in my arms, a reminder that this was real. She was really here and she was kissing me, of all people.

Her hand moved up, tangling in my hair. I moved mine to do the same, but she pulled away.

"S-sorry. I don't mean to be a hypocrite, but my hair is . . . delicate."

"What about the rest of you?"

"Do what you want."

I didn't need to be told twice. "Message received."

"I'll leave your hair out of it." She began to move her hand, but I grabbed it.

"No. You can touch whatever the hell you want. No limits."

Her jaw dropped and my mouth returned to hers. She was all I could see, all I *had* seen in ages.

And now I had her right where I wanted her.

I nipped on her bottom lip and she let me in. Our tongues clashed as the kiss turned heated and she tugged on my hair.

"You said I could leave a mark, right?"

"Anywhere you want," I replied, nearly forgetting to breathe as her lips clamped down onto my neck. The sting of pain only made the pleasure better and I could feel myself grow hard. I had no doubts she could feel it too.

Her hand left my hair to cradle my neck, but her fingers slipped under the hem of my shirt and I was struck with the desire to remove every single piece of clothing from my body.

Once her lips finally left my neck, I ripped off my shirt. Her eyes trailed over my chest and she licked her lips.

"You're gorgeous," she mumbled, hand trailing over my chest.

"Not compared to you. Can I take this off?" My fingers grazed over the hem of her shirt.

"Please," she urged. I pulled off her top, revealing her beautiful breasts.

"No bra?"

"Sometimes they're uncomfortable, so it's nice to go without."

"I'm not complaining. It makes things way more fun for me."

She had been out of reach my entire life, and now that I had her in my arms, I had no clue where to start. "You can touch me," she said. "Wherever you want."

I kissed her again. Then I trailed down her jaw and neck with my mouth. I cupped one breast in my hand and latched my mouth onto the other.

I heard her gasp as I did it and her chest arched to give me more. I gave her nipple all of my admiration before I moved to the other one.

"Fuck, Barry." Her voice was low in a way I'd never heard before. Her fingers gripped my neck, keeping me close.

Breaking contact, I lifted her and laid her down on the couch, her dark hair fanning perfect waves around her head. My fingers trailed downward, gripping the waistband of her jeans, pulling them off with one motion.

She was wet and waiting for me. And I wanted to make her feel good in ways she hadn't before.

I could see her breath coming out in short stutters as she waited for whatever I could do next. I wondered if she had some lyric in her head, and suddenly it was my goal to make her forget every word she knew, but in a very different way than I had before.

"I'm going to get on my knees," I said into her ear. "And I'm going to taste you. Is that okay?"

"Yes," she gasped. "Please."

I angled her off the couch, bringing her pussy right in front of me. I put my mouth on her core, tasting her sweet scent and moving my tongue up to circle her clit.

"Oh my God." Her fingers dug into my scalp. I dared to look up at her and she was arched up on the couch as if begging for more. I returned to my work, tasting every flavor of her, giving her the sweetest torture I could muster. "Barry, I . . . God, I . . ."

She wasn't a lyrical genius here. And *I'd* done this to her. I'd made her forget words and be completely lost in pleasure. I couldn't help but smile into her as I continued my relentless assault.

Lila came with a soft moan. The only sign was the way her core tightened as I pushed one finger into her. She jerked around me, gripping my digit like a vise as she orgasmed.

"Was that good for you?" I asked, looking up at her.

"Y-yeah. So good." She was struggling to catch her breath as her eyes closed. "That was incredible. I should return the favor." But a yawn broke away from her.

"You're tired."

"I'm always tired."

"Then rest."

"But—"

"We have time, sunshine. All the time we need. I'll carry you to bed myself."

"I don't think I qualify for the name sunshine when I look like this." She gestured to her dark hair.

"You're the sunshine in *my* life, so I think it works."

Her jaw dropped and she had no other arguments for me. I lifted her, carrying the woman of my dreams to my room, where I wished we could stay forever. I pulled her to me as we lay down, knowing she could be gone by the next day.

CHAPTER FIFTEEN

Barry was gone when I woke up.

Disappointment curled in my chest. When was the last time I'd woken up in someone else's arms? I'd hoped that this would be the first time that someone stayed the entire night.

I slowly got up, checking the windows for any signs that people knew where I was. A truck and a sedan were parked outside, but they didn't look to be camping out waiting for me.

When I opened the door, I could hear voices in the bar. I slowly crept down the stairs.

"Barry, this is life-altering news. We wouldn't be here for something small."

It was a woman's voice and I wondered if it was his sister. I paused, knowing I shouldn't listen but couldn't help it. My desperate curiosity about his family was too much to fight.

"Whatever it is can wait until later, okay? I have something that I need to get back to." Barry's voice was tight.

"Barry," a male voice said.

"No. I'm not having you guys ruin it by bringing more family drama for her to see."

"It's okay," I said before I could stop myself. Everything went silent, but I refused to let him turn away his family for *me*. "Whatever it is sounds important."

"Shit," he muttered under his breath. He turned to where I was half hiding. "Go back to bed. It's nothing."

"It's obviously not nothing," I insisted. "And they know someone is here."

"Wait," the woman said. "I know that voice."

"You might as well come on out," Barry said, his tone flat. "Ruth is going to figure it out any second now."

Ruth's eyes widened. "Wait. Barry, are you sleeping with—"

"Lila Wilde?" I asked, coming fully into view. "Yes. Yes, he is. And now that you two have seen me, you're about to have to sign the most extensive NDA you've ever seen. Sorry about that."

I shouldn't have walked out of there, but I needed to know what was happening. A sibling meeting that I got to take part in? It seemed too good to be true.

At least I'd remembered an NDA. Malia and my lawyer would be happy with me.

To Ruth's and Tom's credits, they handled it well.

Ruth, with her sharp features and dark hair, only covered her mouth. Tom stared, his face nearly as unreadable as Barry's.

"Okay," Ruth eventually said. "Well, this complicates things."

"You weren't supposed to know she was here," Barry muttered. "And you should sign the NDA."

"Is this the same one you told me you're under?" she asked.

"Yes," he said, running a hand over his face. My heart skipped a beat. Maybe I shouldn't have said a thing. It wasn't my place to step in. The last thing I wanted to do was piss him off by getting involved in something I shouldn't.

"Wh-what're your emails?" I asked slowly, trying to focus on one thing at a time.

Once Tom and Ruth had sent it back, Tom looked over at me. "My son is a huge fan."

"Son?" I asked and then gasped as I turned to Barry. "You're an uncle!"

"Yeah, yeah. Things have been wild lately with these two."

"And I'm not helping anything, am I?" I asked.

"It's fine."

"So, how do you two know each other?" Tom asked.

Barry looked at me, eyebrow raised.

"He's helping me with my next album."

"What?" Ruth said. "Wait, *the* album? The one that everyone is dying to have?"

"How do I get myself in these situations?" Tom pinched the bridge of his nose, looking much like Barry had only moments ago. "But that isn't what we're here to talk about. It's something bigger."

"It better not be any more shit about Dad." Barry's voice was harsh. "If you two have forgiven him—"

"We haven't," Ruth interrupted. "And we won't. But we did go see Mom."

Barry sighed. "And let me guess, she's sorry for not standing up sooner even though she was just as bad as Dad was."

"Kind of. We got to see Grandma and Grandad," she added. "But Mom wanted you there."

"I'm not interested."

"And that's fine," Tom said. "We're okay with that. But she told us something that you should know."

His eyes met mine and I could see the invisible question. *Do you want to hear this?*

I stayed rooted to the spot, mesmerized by the inner workings of Barry's family.

"Can you please make this quick?" Barry asked.

"This is *big*."

"Mom cheated on Dad," Tom said bluntly.

"Wow," Barry said. "Good for her."

"Barry, she cheated on Dad twenty-seven years ago."

"Why should I c—" He paused as he put the numbers together. "Wait a second."

"Our dad is not your dad. She just told us."

Barry blinked, not breathing as he took in the news. A long, painful silence stretched out between all of us.

Then he shrugged. "Okay," he said, but his voice was choked. "That's fine."

"But—"

"It's fine," he repeated. "Just another shitty thing Mom did to add to the pile. Whatever. It doesn't matter anyway."

"I think it does," Ruth said.

"No, it doesn't. My conclusion is the same. I'm better off alone."

"You don't want to meet him?" she asked.

"No, I don't. But I guess you want to tell me I should."

Her lips pursed and I wondered if she would.

"What Barry does is up to him," Tom said in a soft voice. "I'm sorry we had to tell you this way, but we will respect whatever you want to do."

"Good. Then I want to be alone."

The words weighed heavy as he turned from everyone, including me.

My throat went dry. I could see why he'd not want me around. I wasn't foolish enough to think some kissing and one orgasm was enough to forge a bond where he'd want me to stay after he found out his father wasn't his actual father.

"Okay," Tom said. "But we're here if you need us."

They shuffled out and I followed. I looked at the ground, and when the daylight hit me, I realized I had left with *no* plan.

"Lila?" Ruth asked. "You followed us?"

"I don't think he wants me around." I shrugged, trying to play it cool even though my heart had sunk into my stomach. "I'm just a one-night stand."

Ruth and Tom looked at each other and I almost hoped they would tell me I was more.

But instead, Ruth asked, "Is it safe for you to be out here?"

"No. Not at all. My hotel is two blocks away."

"I'll drive you there," she offered. "Hopefully, no one will see, but if they do, I guess it wouldn't be the first time."

"You know another celebrity?"

"My boyfriend is Knox Price." She smiled. "We've been the subject of some news. I'm sure you wouldn't know—"

"I remember that story," I said. "You were in a coffee shop."

And Rose was behind you.

"Oh wow. So, you've heard of me in a weird way. What a small world."

"Small indeed," I said. "Thank you. I'll take you up on that."

She showed me to her white Honda. Tom, who had been quiet, gave her a wave. Then his eyes fell on me.

"It was nice meeting you. My kid is going to kill me if he ever knows I met you and didn't tell him, but it was still nice."

He'd looked scary, but he didn't seem so scary now. Barry's family was . . . not what I expected. He hid them from me, but with these two, I didn't see why.

"Sorry you had to see that," Ruth said as I got into her car. "And that Barry kind of kicked you out."

"It's fine." And it was. I'd already blown into his life like a tornado and then inserted myself into a conversation where I didn't belong. "I'm just glad that you handled me being there so well."

"It was a shock, but if anyone was going to do it to us like that, it would be Barry. He's always been different. And I wonder how he'll handle this." There was a small smile on her face, but it fell. "Will you check on him for us?"

"You guys might be better for that."

"I doubt he wants anything to do with us right now. Please?"

I couldn't say no to Ruth's face.

"I'll try my best."

I was dropped off at the hotel and I wondered what I could do for a man who wanted to know my life but obviously didn't want me to know his.

Juno did a double take when I walked in. This time, we had a suite because she wanted to be closer to me with all of the fanfare around 'Goodbye, Good Riddance.'

"What are you doing back? Weren't you supposed to call me?"

"Things got a little wild. Someone else gave me a ride back."

Juno frowned. "That's not the safest idea. I knew I should have stayed."

"It's fine. I don't think anyone saw me, and it wasn't planned. Something big happened for Barry and he wanted to be alone."

"Oh," she said. "Is everything okay?"

"I don't know. I want to go check on him later."

Juno nodded and glanced out the window. She cursed and slammed the blinds shut.

"What?"

"Paps. I don't know if they're here for you, but they're here."

"Damn it," I cursed. "How long do you think they'll hang around?"

"Too long. I'm sorry, but I think your plans are dashed."

"*Mine* might be, but I have another trick up my sleeve."

"*No.*"

"Yes. It's time to be Rose for a little bit."

"We're on borrowed time," she said, shaking her head. "You were supposed to be here just to see him for a day."

"I can't help that something happened. I'll just move some meetings. I can't leave right now."

"And what if he recognizes you?"

"No one has so far and I'll go to the bar tonight. The low lights will help."

She pressed her lips together, still unhappy, but I knew I couldn't leave Nashville yet. Not after what I'd seen.

"Fine, but I'm staying close this time."

"Deal," I said. "Thank you, Juno."

Barry

Lila left.

Because of course she did. No woman of her caliber would want to stick around while I found out my father, the man who tried to ruin my life, wasn't even related to me.

I stared at the space she occupied, wondering if she'd somehow come back.

But as seconds trickled into minutes, I turned away, ready to accept that I would be alone.

It was fine. I liked it that way.

I spent the day looking for something to do. There was a loose plank in the back floor, so I secured it. The menus, though they were rarely used since people normally knew what they wanted, needed cleaning, so I did that too. As the day gave way to the evening, I found myself running out of things to do.

Once upon a time, I would have never been able to stop, especially when the bar first opened, but now that it had been around for years, I was starting to think someone had fixed all of the problems.

"Evening, Barry," Liam greeted as he walked in. "Are you working tonight?"

"Yes," I grunted, looking back at the list of people approved to get in.

He raised an eyebrow. "Is everything okay?"

"Yep."

"It doesn't seem like it is."

"Your station could probably be sanitized. Can you go do that?"

Liam frowned but nodded. I felt bad sending him off, but I didn't want to talk about what had happened today. None of it needed talking about. My family sucked. That was all there was to it. So my dad wasn't my dad. It wasn't a big deal. I'm sure the man who really was wouldn't want anything to do with me anyway. He was living his life, wherever the fuck he was, not giving a shit about me.

But where? Where does he live?

The curiosity shook me to my core.

I didn't need to know, though my heart begged me to.

Come on, it said. *Look into it.*

I refused to call up my siblings to ask more questions, just like I refused to think anything of the man who I didn't know. I didn't need any of this, so why was I focused on it?

I lingered at the front, not having anything of substance to do, trying to distract myself by watching who came through the door.

I heard a woman say to the bouncer, "I've been here before. Is there any way I could get in again?"

My eyes shot to her because her voice sounded so familiar.

Red hair. Freckles. It was the woman who ordered Lila's drink. The one in the store who'd been looking at Lila's tea.

It wasn't fair to compare her to Lila. She was her own person, but the similarities kicked my heart into gear.

"Sorry," the bouncer said. "We're—"

"She can come in," I said. "I know her."

She blinked as if in shock. If I squinted, I could see the woman I desperately wanted.

Don't be an ass, Barry.

Just because the woman of my dreams had walked out today didn't mean I could see her in other ones who walked into my bar.

"Thank you," she said as she sidestepped around the bouncer.

"You're lucky I was here. Usually, we don't let people in on short notice, even if they've been here before."

"I've heard. You don't have to treat me like I'm special, though."

I smirked. "Too late. I already let you in, even though I never usually do that."

Her cheeks heated. "Why me, then?"

My smile fell. Why did I say it was okay? Was it some part of me mourning Lila's leaving and wanting something—*someone*—who reminded me of her to be around?

I couldn't keep a woman around because she reminded me of someone else. That was a shitty move and I refused to be that guy.

I only shrugged. "I keep running into you, I guess. It was the least I could do." It didn't appease the pang of guilt in my chest. "Let me get you your drink. A cranberry juice and soda water?"

"You remembered?"

"I try to. Let me get it for you and then you can enjoy yourself."

And I could get away from this conflicted feeling around her. But could I? Whether with her or not, there wasn't much in my life that I wasn't conflicted by.

The thought sank into my chest. I was a fool to think she wouldn't notice it.

"Are you okay?" she asked loudly. "You seem . . . off."

"How would you know if I'm off?"

"Let's call it intuition. Want to talk?"

Say no. It would be easy to, but she *looked* like a person I could open up to. A feeling overtook me, one I didn't know how to deal with.

"Yes." No one was more surprised than me as I said it and her eyebrows raised as if she didn't expect that answer herself.

"Can we go somewhere quieter?"

"I have just the place."

The rooftop was just for me. It was a place I desperately wanted to take Lila to, but with her fame, I knew she couldn't. I sometimes sat out there when the weather was comfortable and watched everything.

Small fairy lights illuminated the space. Rose looked around with wide eyes. "Wow, this is better than I imagined."

"You imagined it?"

She blankly stared at me, then blinked away the expression. "I mean, most places have something like this . . . I thought maybe it was for VIPs."

"I didn't want to be like the rest."

"That's what you're good at." She gave me a smile, one that could have been flirty.

And if she had dark hair, I'd flirt right back.

I broke eye contact, looking out at the city. Where was Lila? Was she okay?

"Barry?" she asked.

"Sorry," I said. "I have a lot on my mind."

"Tell me, then. I'll listen."

I didn't do this. I didn't let anyone in. I tried not to with Lila since she had so much more going on, but having her near made me *want* to. I was spilling at the seams, and while Rose wasn't the one I desperately wanted, she was here.

Which made me feel even worse.

"It's . . . I . . . I don't even know how to begin."

"Probably at the beginning. Wherever that is."

"That might take a long time."

"I have it."

"Really? Didn't you come here to have fun?"

"Maybe listening *is* fun to me. You were so kind to me last time I was here, so why wouldn't I repay that?"

It was a good reason. I took a shaky breath and said the words that had been bothering me all day. "I just found out that my father isn't who I thought he was."

"Wow," she said, eyebrows raised. "That must have been hard."

"It was. It *is*. But this is in line with what my family does. We hurt each other, but considering I left them long ago, I thought I was free of it. Looks like I never will be."

"Everyone in your family hurts each other?"

Yes should have been my answer, but it was no longer completely true. "My brother and sister are *trying* not to. But my mom and my dad . . . I mean, the guy who raised me. *Fuck*, I don't even know if I should call him my dad anymore."

"What's his name?"

"Todd. Todd Murray."

My eyes went to the building that I'd built this bar in the shadow of. The "and Sons" was no longer lit ever since Tom decided to rebrand. That was no longer Todd Murray's tower, yet I hated it all the same.

Murray. Was that even my last name anymore? I truly didn't belong to that family. I never had.

"What is he like?"

"A *complete asshole*. He ruined my brother and tried to break my sister."

"Then it's a good thing you're not related to him, right?"

"Of course, but my siblings are. And now they're not all that related to me, just when—" I stopped myself. These were words I hadn't even admitted to myself yet, but as they rose in my throat, they got stuck.

Just when I thought we were a family.

"You still are, through your mom."

"But I'm the odd one out. Just like always. And I thought that was what I wanted, but . . . I don't know anymore."

"What do you want?"

Lila. To get to know Max. To see Ruth smile more.

"For everything wrong in my life to right itself." I paused. "You know what's the most fucked up about all of this?"

"What?"

"That I might not be my father's son, but he still sunk his claws into me somehow. I have friends, but I keep them at arm's length."

I looked over at her, wishing to see black hair and red lips.

And then I felt even more like Todd Murray's son.

How did evil do this? How did it invade me when all I wanted to be was free and different?

A warm hand touched my shoulder. "I don't think you're your father's son. If you were, you wouldn't have stepped in to make sure I was okay."

Reality came crashing back in at Rose's reminder. "And my dad certainly wouldn't own a bar. I mean, Todd. God, what do I call him?"

Her hand squeezed. "Anything you want. Asshole works."

A laugh escaped me. "I wish the news didn't even affect me. I thought I wrote off everyone."

"You rightfully wrote off the man who you thought was your father. What about the one that is?"

I blinked. "I-I know nothing about him."

"Do you want to?"

"I fucking do," I muttered.

"Then you have your answer."

I looked back at her. I knew she wasn't Lila, but I had shared things with her as if she were.

And I didn't regret it.

"I thought I would be alone forever."

"Being alone might work for some people, but it also means missing out on some of the best parts of life," she said. "Like people you care about. And sure, maybe you haven't met anyone you *want* to care about yet, but you will. They're out there. Maybe they're even in this bar."

My heart skipped a beat. *Or maybe they were once in this bar.* She was right about most of it, but wrong about one thing.

I'd met someone I cared about *very* much.

But I pushed her away. And while I wanted Lila, she wasn't here. Rose was.

"So, what, I go meet my dad with someone?"

"Yes. Is there anyone you trust?"

Lila. But was it even possible for her to go out into the country to meet my dad? Probably not.

"I don't have many people in that category." Glancing back at Rose, I noticed she was absentmindedly touching her hair, lips pursed.

"I know we've only met a few times," Rose said, "but I would love to be someone you trust. I could go with you."

"You'd do that?"

She shrugged, gazing down. "Yeah. I would. I'd need your number first."

"I think I can make that work."

She pulled out a phone. "Shit," she said and immediately put it away. "Wrong one."

"Wrong phone?"

"I have one for work. I don't let them overlap. Things get complicated when I do. I have another one at my hotel."

"Hotel? You're not from here?"

"I visit. For work and sometimes pleasure. But I'll make time to be here. I kind of like it in this town."

"Oh, that's right. You've told me that before."

She gave me another one of her smiles and my heart skipped a beat. How could I have forgotten when she said she wasn't from here? I still couldn't remember *where* she said she was from. I needed to do better by her and listen when she talked. She had a beautiful voice, after all.

If we stayed here, I might have told her more. I might have gotten lost in her hazel, almost golden eyes and it felt like a betrayal for a woman that wasn't truly mine.

"Can I get you another drink before I get back to work?"

Her glass wasn't even halfway empty. "No, I'm okay, but thank you. I'll let you get back, though."

I led her back to the dance floor, and as I busied myself with things I didn't need to do, I wondered if I would catch her dancing.

But I never did. It was almost like she'd had fun just talking to me.

Chapter Sixteen

"So, how did that go?" Juno asked the second I walked in the door. I nearly jumped out of my skin.

"I told you that you didn't have to wait up for me." I put down my purse.

"One of the most famous women in the world went to a bar with different-colored hair and I'm her bodyguard. Of course I waited up."

"I'm fine," I said. "Really."

"And what happened?"

"He opened up to me way more than he ever did as Lila." I could still feel the way my heart loosened as he did so. Some of those caged thoughts were free and I was able to *finally* help him with them.

"Oh."

"I think he could trust this version of me more."

Juno was silent for a long time. "I'm . . . happy for you, but seeing him as *Rose*? This is risky."

I looked at my hands. She wasn't wrong. It *was* risky and Mom would be so upset if she knew I was blurring the lines like this. But then I thought about that rooftop bar, unseen by Lila's eyes.

"But this feels less complicated when I'm *me*," I said. "All of it does."

"So you plan to have one side of you ghost him?"

"He still has to hear the rest of my album."

"Okay, then ghost him as Rose."

"I *can't*. I've promised to help him meet his dad."

Juno blinked. "You did *what*?"

My cheeks heated. "The point is, I'm entangled."

"That might not be a good thing," she said. "People could get hurt here. Barry could find out and think you're playing him. Or worse, someone sees you going to the same place Lila is and notices that you seem similar."

"It would be easier if he knew. I bet Barry would know a way out of this." I rubbed a hand over my face.

"You're not thinking about telling him, are you?" she asked.

"Maybe that's a good idea."

"No. That's not a good idea."

"Why?"

"Because what if he tells? Your NDA doesn't cover anything as *Rose*."

"He didn't say anything before he signed one."

"Yeah, when he *met* you. Think about how much a secret like this could sell for."

Mom had said something like that once. And the idea of someone selling my secrets haunted me. A simple picture of me with the wig in my hand would earn a lot of money. I didn't think Barry would sell me out, but he would be angry.

And people did say stupid things when they were angry.

Like I had by releasing a song detailing how Blaze had cheated on me.

"Pick a version to be and stay there." Juno's words were firm.

I thought about how it felt to write those songs with Barry, how it felt to sing for him. Then I thought about the rooftop terrace—a new side of him—one where he knew me without all the strings.

"I don't know if I can."

"Think of all the people who could be hurt. *Him* included."

I bit my lip. "I have no clue what to do."

"Lila knows him best."

"But Rose comes without all the issues of fame." I sighed.

"So then be Rose."

I looked out the window, unable to answer. Neither option felt right and I wasn't sure what to do about this stupid situation I'd put myself in.

Barry

Barry: What was this guy's name?

I texted Ruth and Tom and threw my phone on the couch. I paced the floor, wondering if I should tell them not to worry about it. Then grabbed it, hoping they'd responded. When I saw nothing, I tossed it again.

I checked the time. It was early afternoon and I knew neither of them would fuck with me during their work hours.

But then there was a knock on my door.

And they were both on the other side.

"What the fuck?" I muttered. "Don't you two work?"

Ruth rolled her eyes. "Haven't you ever heard of a day off?"

"Have *you*?"

"Yep," she said. "Now, you texted for info?"

"You could have just answered."

"Barry," Tom said softly. "We know you aren't the kind of person to ask something like this without a lot of thought."

I glared. He was right.

"*And* we want to check on you," Ruth said. "That involves seeing you with our own eyes. So, how are you?"

I thought of my conversation with Rose, a session I didn't quite regret, but I didn't know if I had done the right thing. "I'm making it."

"So not good," she said. "Can we come in?"

"How did you get into the bar anyway?"

"You keep a key under your mat," she said. "The same way I do even to this day."

"I tried to tell her it was still breaking and entering." Tom sighed. "But she wanted to check on you."

"And you?"

"I did too. This couldn't have been easy news to hear."

I wasn't sure they even cared. I was their half-brother, which meant they only had to *half* care.

"And we do have information on your actual father," Ruth said, and any thoughts I had disappeared in the weight of that revelation. "His name is Wilfred."

"Where is he?"

"Mom's town in West Tennessee."

"I . . . can't remember where that is." I never thought I would need to. She'd buried that part of herself.

"Lyles," Ruth said. "It's tiny, but she's living next to him."

"Do you know anything else?"

"No, but we can reach out to her and get more information," Ruth offered. "We get it if you don't want to talk to her considering . . . everything."

"It's the last thing I want to do, but yes, thank you."

"Are you okay?" Tom asked. "You can tell us anything."

"I'm giving this one chance," I said. "But if it goes south, then I'll stay exactly where I'm at. I don't *need* anyone."

But even I didn't believe that. And judging by the way Ruth and Tom looked at each other, I didn't think they believed it, either.

"Okay," Ruth said. "Now, get your keys."

"Why?"

"Because we should have a nice family lunch, if you're free."

All I'd been doing was sitting with my thoughts.

"What do you want to have?" I asked.

"There's a brunch spot not too far from here," Tom suggested. "It's pretty good."

I almost didn't know who the fuck these people were.

"Come on," Ruth said. "We won't talk about work."

"And what would we talk about?"

"How I had to put out an oven fire last week, maybe?"

"What?" Both Tom and I said at the same time.

"See? I'm basically a hero."

"I *do* want to hear this story," I said, and I went to grab my keys. "Let's go."

Chapter Seventeen

Lila

Blaze Matthews SHOCKS in New Tell-All about Lila

By Perez Adder

The music world was rocked when Lila Wilde surprise-dropped her newest single, "Goodbye, Good Riddance," about her long-time muse, Blaze Matthews. The lyrics are devastating, accusing him of falling for someone and lying to her for years about it. She accuses him of cheating on her in her own house.

Many eyes have been watching for her rare public appearances, or at the very least, an interview about the shocking song, but she's stayed busy on her new album, which should come out any day now . . .

But today, we finally heard from someone involved. A representative for Blaze reached out to clarify a few things.

"Obviously, this isn't the full story. Blaze was faithful in his dedication to her from day one, but Lila began to grow complacent and found comfort in other places. He supported her when she went to Nashville to work on her new album and even encouraged it. This single is like a betrayal of the worst kind. She's probably there now, focused on her new, shiny muse while Blaze has been trying to get over her."

There you have it. Lila has been in NASHVILLE of all places, the country music capital of the world. Is she about to go country? I don't think it would suit her . . .

3564 Comments

Potstirrer: Not surprised. Women always cheat.

JuliusSneezer: But like . . . did she cheat? God, there's so much drama. This next album is gonna be LIT.

RealLilaFan247: There is no way. Blaze is such a liar!

HairyPoppins: I need new pics of her. Where is she?

I'd figured out that Malia was not the kind of agent to call me. Unlike the barrage that I was used to from Mia, she handled things silently. So when I saw her name flash across Lila's phone, my heart skipped a beat, and rightfully so.

"Lila, are you in Nashville right now?"

"I am," I said. "Why?"

"Blaze's team released a statement and they mentioned where you might be."

My heart stopped. "He didn't."

"He, unfortunately, did. He also mentioned some other things, but that's the only important thing. I wouldn't recommend reading it. You might want to lie low. I've heard that paps are coming out of the woodwork to find you."

"Damn it," I muttered.

"I'm sorry. We'll handle it and make him look like the idiot he is. Tell Juno she can call someone from our bodyguard services if she needs backup."

"Should I come back to LA? I know I have a lot of work to do."

"Right now, you should just disappear for a bit, and that's almost impossible to do here."

"But I have work to be done."

"We can shift it to be virtual. Find a place to relax while I deal with this."

"Do I need to do anything else?"

"No, I've got it. You focus on your work."

I was still adjusting to the way Malia handled things. Mia would have thrown me to the wolves or told me to bask in the attention.

"I will," I said slowly. "Thank you, Malia. Seriously, thank you."

"It's no problem. Get some rest." She said her goodbyes and then hung up.

"I just heard," Juno said, walking into the room. "He's an asshole."

I looked at her and sighed. "Lila needs to disappear. So, I guess this makes my decision for me."

"Do you think so?"

I slowly nodded, ignoring the way every part of my being hated this. "Yes. I should cut off this thing with Barry now."

"Let's invite him over," Juno suggested. "The last thing you need to do is leave and be swarmed. Then we switch to Rose."

"Yeah," I said, though I felt a dread I couldn't place. "Let's get this over with."

I texted Barry and then rushed to get ready. I tried to avoid all my thoughts about this decision. Fifteen minutes after the texts, he arrived just as I was finishing putting on my mascara.

"He told people where you were?" Barry asked the moment Juno opened the door.

"Technically, Mia did." Juno shook her head and gestured to where I was on the couch, biting my lip.

My throat went dry the second I saw him. Juno looked between us, asking a silent question.

"Can you give us some privacy?" I asked.

"Of course. I'll be outside in case anyone shows up."

"Paparazzi are coming, aren't they?" Barry asked.

"Yes, a lot. With the album nearly done and this news, they're dying to get the first photos of me. I can't be seen."

"Or you can tell them to fuck right off like they deserve."

I let out a long sigh. "That doesn't make them stop. They all just want photos. It's easier to give them that and keep walking."

"Okay," he said. "Does Juno need help with that? I could—"

I closed my eyes. Of course he'd want to help. Of course he wouldn't be scared off.

"Barry, you can't."

"Why?"

"Because this life is like a . . ." I remembered the words Mom called it many years ago. "This is like a tornado. It will rip apart every aspect of your life if you're seen with me."

"I don't care."

My heart pounded in my chest. He didn't *care*? When life was like this, it was miserable being Lila. It would have ruined my life if I hadn't done this the way I had. I thought of Mom's panic attacks from when she saw me getting stormed by the media. I thought of everything I'd done to separate Rose from Lila and how it could ruin everything with Barry.

Besides, he said he didn't care *now*, but he would in five months when it never let up.

Yet, I was *so* tempted to say fuck it all and agree with him. It would have been so easy to.

"I can't ask you for that," I said slowly. "I just can't."

"But I can offer it. I'd love to be with you, Lila. As *you*."

The words hurt so much that I looked away. I wanted it too. More than he knew.

But I wasn't *just* Lila, and he could have so much more from me if I were someone else.

"And I can't take you up on that," I said.

"So, what, we stay in the shadows forever?"

"No. *This*, us, can't be anything. I'm . . . this was fun, but with everything, it's too much."

He blinked, but then his lips pressed together. I wouldn't blame him if he yelled at me for cutting him off like I was. I never imagined I would be doing this, but I couldn't risk him, and I couldn't risk Mom.

And he'd still have me. He trusted Rose, after all.

"So, it's over."

"Barry, I'm—"

"Don't apologize. Let's end it like adults."

"O-okay."

"But be honest. Was it me?"

I shook my head. "No. It wasn't."

"My family?"

"*No,*" I insisted. "This just wasn't going to work. I can't ask this of you. Of anyone."

"Fine. I'll respect what you want." He turned away but paused. "But for the record, I would have stood by you through everything, tornado or not."

The words broke my heart. "I don't think you know what you're offering."

"I've seen tornados, Lila, and I've survived them. But at least with this one, there would have been you at the end of it. Like sunshine after a storm."

Barry: I want you both to know I just got dumped by Lila Wilde. Go ahead and fucking laugh.

I had texted Tom and Ruth in a rush of emotion after I left Lila's place. A part of me hoped one of them *would* laugh; that way, we could start a fight, and maybe I'd feel a little better. I didn't know *why* I had texted them in the first place. It might have been the fact that they'd signed an NDA so I could talk about her with them.

It also could have been the conversation we'd had at brunch just hours ago. We'd *laughed*, of all things, talking about anything but work. They'd even been nice when I had to bail early, telling me that they hoped everything went well.

Instead, there was no answer, which was almost worse. I got back to my apartment, feeling my fists clench. Maybe I needed to work out or maybe I needed to throw something. All I knew was that everything fucking *hurt*.

Then, there was a knock at my door.

Shit. I had forgotten that my siblings tended to show up instead of texting back. I thought that maybe if I ignored them, they would go away.

But I also had forgotten that you simply couldn't ignore Ruth Murray.

"Barry!" Ruth's voice was loud. "You're gonna answer and we're gonna talk about this."

I threw open the door. Tom rubbed his forehead, looking sheepish.

"Good. We're coming in." Ruth breezed past me and I turned to glare, but I caught her simple outfit of a casual PATH T-shirt and jeans. Tom had on shorts and a T-shirt.

"Sorry," Tom said. "She does this because she cares."

"You changed clothes?"

"I was out for a run with Max."

"You should spend time with your kid. Not me."

"He gave up within five minutes. And then told me to come. So here we are."

"Oh, great," Ruth said. "You have tea."

"Don't," I hissed. "Lila gave that to me."

"Okay, cranky. You get water. Where the fuck are your cups?"

I desperately wanted to be angry that she was riffling through my cabinets, but I couldn't find it in me.

She gave me a full glass of water and sat on the couch. "What happened?"

"If you feel up to talking about it, that is," Tom added.

I looked in between them, wondering why they seemed to care so much, wondering why they made the drive through traffic in downtown Nashville, *again*, because I'd called. I was the odd man out and they'd always cared more about their own goals.

Until now.

"You can talk to us," Ruth added at my silence, sounding much kinder than she had moments ago. "And we won't laugh."

"And we've signed NDAs about Lila," Tom said. "So you literally *can* talk to us."

"Are you two trying to *logic* me into talking about it?"

"Would it work?"

"Nothing is going to work. I'm *fine*."

"Can you say that without the muscle in your forehead twitching?" Ruth asked.

I glared at her, but it had no heat in it. Because, despite everything, I *did* want to talk to someone.

"Her ex leaked her location," I said. "I offered to help and she said no."

"What kind of help?"

"The kind where I was there. For everything."

"Oh," Ruth said. "Did she say why she said no?"

"She did, but I have a feeling how I acted when I found out about the dad thing contributed. I didn't mean for *her* to leave."

"She wasn't mad," Ruth said. "She did agree to come check on you."

"She did?" I asked. "I never saw her until recently."

"She's got to have a lot going on. Maybe she was waiting for a break to come and see you."

"Or she was truly mad," I said. "I'm not good at emotions around people. It's why I choose to stay alone."

"Emotions are messy," Tom said. "But it's important to have them, or else you'd do what I did for years and drink them away."

My conviction faltered. "I did try to shield her from any other drama after that. Do you think that was the wrong move?"

"If you're offering to be there for everything, then it's a two-way street," Ruth said. "So, kind of."

"Then the damage is done. She said she couldn't be a tornado in my life."

"It would be hard," Ruth said.

"I told her that I've seen tornados before. She'd easily be the best one."

The room fell silent. None of us had talked about the tornado since it happened.

"But they're still scary," Ruth said slowly.

"I wasn't like you two. I was fine."

"You were left to process it alone," Tom reminded. "That wasn't right."

"You both were scared too."

"I mean, it wasn't right of our *parents* to do that."

"Only one of them is related to me." I was unable to look them in the eyes.

"Dad thought you were his and he still sucked as a dad. I know you handled that storm—all of it—better than Ruth and I did. You've always been ahead of us when it comes to things like this. But you've got one thing wrong. You're *not* alone."

My heart pounded at seeing my normally tight-assed brother be so open.

"The kid and sobriety did you good, huh?"

"We've all finally caught up," Ruth said. "And Tom's right. Maybe it didn't work out with Lila, and it sucks that it didn't, but you have us to talk to about it. And you have your bar and your friends. Lean on us."

Any other day and I would have said no. But on *this* day, when my heart had been stomped on, I couldn't hold back anymore.

And so I told them *everything*.

CHAPTER EIGHTEEN

Rose

"This feels so fucking wrong," I said once Barry left.

"You did the right thing," Juno replied. "You don't want to put everything you've worked for in jeopardy."

My hands went to my hairline, yanking off the heavy wig and wig cap, letting my red hair tumble down. The plan was to move to an Airbnb in Rose's name. We'd gone back-and-forth on where I should hide out, but Mom wouldn't want to see me—even as Rose—with all the heat on Lila's name, and I wanted to see Barry again.

It was risky to stay in Nashville, but Lila would disappear for now. We were working on borrowed time as it was, so I packed up even though my heart ached.

Weren't decisions like this supposed to feel *right*?

When we got settled in our new place, Juno was looking at me like I was a grenade with no pin and I grew tired of it.

This decision ate at me, filling me with buzzing energy with no outlet. I needed to leave, to do something close to fixing the mess I'd created.

"I'm going to Movers and Shakers," I announced.

"Is that a good idea?" Her voice wavered, but I knew I would lose it if I stayed.

"I'll be fine. I need to see how badly I've broken Barry's heart. I won't even talk to him."

Probably.

"Rose," Juno called. I only paused as I was halfway out the door.

"What?"

"Be careful," she warned. "This is . . . dangerous."

"Everything will be fine." But I wasn't sure who I was trying to convince.

I walked out of the new place. I was in a completely different part of town, but I'd persuaded Juno to let me buy a car—a sensible Toyota—so I would have some freedom. When Juno didn't follow me, I let out a breath of relief.

The line for Movers and Shakers was long, and as I approached the bouncer, I wondered if Rose would somehow be removed from entry. Lila would have deserved that after what happened today. I knew that Barry didn't know everything was blending together.

"Congrats," the man said. "You're on the permanent entry list."

"How do I get on that?" the woman behind me asked.

"You know the owner," the bouncer replied. "Right?"

I nodded, a blush rising to my cheeks. Rose didn't know the owner all that well, but I must have made some impression on him if he'd gone through the trouble of adding me.

When I entered, I let out a breath of air.

Barry was tending the bar next to the famous dancing bartender. I walked up, getting in line for myself. I didn't even need to talk to him; I could see him and then leave.

As I got to the front, my favorite drink was set down in front of me.

My jaw dropped and when I looked up, Barry was focused on me. His lips pursed and I wondered again if somehow the anger he must have had for Lila carried over to Rose too. But then the dancing guy turned to him and said something in his ear, and he left the bar, coming toward me.

"Hi!" I said loudly.

"Is this going to be a regular thing?" he asked loudly back.

"You added me to the permanent entry list, so I guess so."

"I keep taking up all your time talking about my life. It's the least I can do. What are you here for?"

"I was in town for work. I figured I'd check on you."

He blinked. "You have impeccable timing."

Only because I did this to you.

"Wanna catch up?"

He thought about it for a moment before turning to the other bartender. The man gave him a thumbs-up and Barry gestured to the back.

We climbed the stairs to the rooftop and I couldn't resist the smile that spread onto my face. *This* was where I wanted to be.

"How are you?"

"Not the greatest," he admitted. "But on the bright side, I . . . I think my siblings and I might be getting along for once."

"Really?" Relief hit me. At least he hadn't been alone. "That's good."

"Yeah, and I'll probably go see my dad soon."

"Still want me to join?"

He looked at me, expression unreadable. "I could use the moral support. I'd ask my brother and sister to go, but I imagine it wouldn't be fun with them since they're still related to the asshole that raised us."

We hadn't talked about the real thing, the reason why I'd come here. Maybe I should have left it, but my mouth opened anyway.

"Did anything else happen?"

Barry huffed out a laugh. "Can you read my mind or something?"

Nope. I just know what I did.

I managed a noncommittal shrug, swallowing around the guilt in my throat.

"Have you ever fucked up something that could have been really good?" He asked it slowly and I looked at him, feeling more like Lila as I answered.

"Yes. Very recently, actually. All we can do is move forward and learn from our mistakes."

He looked out at the city skyline and I wondered what he was thinking. My heart picked up speed as I waited. I didn't have the words to describe what it felt like to wait.

Then he turned to me. "You're right, and I shouldn't waste the time you're here by thinking of someone else."

"You know, we only ever have these hard conversations."

"We do, don't we?" He shook his head. "You should go downstairs, then. Have some fun."

"What if you went with me?"

The question hung in the air.

Please say yes. Choose Rose.

He slowly turned. "Why me?"

"I get the vibe that you have this bar and you've never enjoyed it yourself."

"I enjoy it."

"Really? What do you do here, then?"

"I mostly . . . work." He cringed as he said it. "Man, I sound too much like Todd. Maybe I should enjoy it for once."

"Come on." I grabbed his hand. "Let's change that."

We went downstairs where the music was loud and infectious. Bathed in these lights, everything felt different.

"Listen to this music," I said, bobbing my head to the beat. "Doesn't it make you want to dance?"

"You can. I'll watch."

"Where's the fun in that? Isn't the point that we're supposed to do it *together*?"

"I don't dance."

"Can you at least twirl me? No dancing required for that."

Barry paused for a moment and I wondered if he would change his mind, but he held out a hand to me, spinning me around. I couldn't help the giddy giggle that escaped me.

"That was surprisingly coordinated."

"It's fun! Do you want to try?"

"I don't think the guy usually gets twirled."

"Come on," I said, rolling my eyes. "There are no rules."

"Fine. Just once."

I stood on my tiptoes to do the same to him. He spun faster than I did and landed facing me. "See? Fun."

"It was," he said. "And now I see why the dance nights are so popular. I'd never experienced it for myself."

"One twirl isn't enough to experience a dance night." I shook my head. "Let's do the real thing."

I held out a hand, hoping he wouldn't turn me down. And when he didn't, the joy I felt could have lifted me right back onto the rooftop.

We went deeper into the crowd. My feet moved in accord, tapping to the beat I'd danced to onstage, but I let myself mess it up. I let myself dance for fun and not for perfection. I wasn't onstage here. I was simply a woman in a bar.

And I was having *fun*.

I lost time, dancing to a mix of songs, some of which were new to me. As I moved, occasionally Barry would twirl me, making me feel like a princess in a ballroom.

When we finally stopped after nearly an hour, both of our chests were heaving. "You're very good at dancing," he said.

"You too. Incredible, actually."

I wasn't usually this sweaty unless I was at the gym or onstage. It was amazing to let loose and dance for a while as someone who wasn't Lila.

My phone chimed and I saw that Juno was checking on me. "I should get back. But thank you for hanging out with me."

"You're welcome here any time."

The corners of his lips moved upward and I smiled back. It had been worth it, breaking it off as Lila and being Rose instead. My secret was safe and now I had this all over again. I'd done the right thing.

Or at least I hoped I did.

Barry

"Since when do you dance?" Audrey asked after the bar had closed.

"I don't," I said. "That was an exception."

"You were almost as good as me!" Liam exclaimed.

"And you two looked good together. Happy," Audrey added. "But what about *you know who*?"

Even thinking about Lila hurt. "It's over. She broke it off."

"I'm sorry. I know how much you liked her."

"Don't be. I . . . messed it up. I wasn't open with her about the things I should have been."

"So, Rose?" Liam asked. "She's different."

And she was—but only I knew the truth. I was making it work with her because of who she reminded me of. "Yeah."

"And she has *moves*. If I squint, I would say she's as good as a certain pop star you know."

"Guys," I said, sighing. "She's a different person."

Even if I forgot it.

"Fair enough. She definitely doesn't *look* like her, that's for sure. You have a type."

"And what's that?"

"Dancers."

"That was just for fun. Besides, I could have done better."

"Who cares about doing better? It's just fun, like you said."

And that it was. Rose seemed to bring that out of me. She didn't worry about perfection, and after trying to be that for Lila, it was nice to let loose.

"When are you seeing her again?" Liam raised his eyebrows.

"No idea."

"It should be soon. I've never seen you like that."

I didn't want to admit it, but I'd never *felt* like that either.

Ruth: I got Wilfred's number from Mom. Do you want it?

I woke up to the text and groaned. This was the last thing I needed to deal with.

Barry: Did this have to happen the day AFTER my day from hell?

Ruth: Unfortunately, this is how emotional growth happens. All at once. I also asked her weeks ago, and she was nervous about talking to him.

Barry: I wonder why.

Ruth: Hmm, maybe the lying?

Ruth: Anyway, she told him about you. He was as pissed as expected. But he wants to talk to you.

Barry: Talking to fathers who are pissed has not worked out well for us.

Ruth: Fair enough. You don't have to message him.

Barry: But I fucking want to for some reason.

Ruth: Then you have his number. Let Tom and me know if you need us.

The number in her text stared innocently at me and it made my skin crawl. I got up, content to ignore the feeling, but it only grew.

I thought about asking Ruth and Tom what they would say, but I knew they would be at work, and I'd already distracted Ruth enough for the day.

I flipped to a new text chain, finding Rose's name.

Barry: Hey.

Rose: Hey! Fancy another dance night?

Barry: This is more for advice. What do I say to him? My father.

Rose: A simple hi would be good. Maybe say who you are.

Barry: Do you have a good father?

Rose: He's mostly a good guy.

Barry: What's it like?

Rose: We hit a rough patch when he decided he wanted to be on the road again and he left me with my mom. But once we got past it, he's been pretty good. I know I could call and he'd answer.

Her words sounded eerily familiar, like one of Lila's first songs.

Fuck. I did it again, thinking of Lila as I talked to Rose.

Barry: I'll let you know what he says.

Rose: Please do. I'm busy this morning, but I'm always available by texting!

Barry: I might need that.

I flipped to the new number and took a deep breath.

Barry: Hi, Wilfred. It's Barry.

My phone rang. I stared at it, unsure of whether or not I should answer.

Do it, my conscious begged. *Answer.*

"H-hello?"

"Gosh damn it," a deep voice said. "I meant to text back. How do you text? I knew these bloomin' fancy devices weren't for me."

A shocked chuckle escaped me. "Saying 'gosh' before 'damn it' is a new one."

"My mother would come out of the grave if I said the other version. I swear it. One time, I hammered my thumb and let it slip and all my begonias died."

"Wow." It was all I could utter. This was not how I expected this conversation to go.

"We can go back to texting," he said. "Sorry about bothering you. I know a lot of people don't like being on the phone."

I had an out. I could cut this here. But he'd said *sorry*. I'd never heard Todd say that word.

Stay, my conscious begged.

"No, it's fine. Sometimes, we have to jump into things."

A chuckle came through the line. "I see a lot of things that way," he said. "Listen, kid. I'm about twenty-six years too late, but I'd like to get to know you."

"You're not late if you didn't know."

"I consider myself late. But it doesn't matter. What matters is how *you* feel."

"I . . . I think we can try. But I don't know how to do . . . *families*."

"I don't know what it's like to be a dad. So I guess we can try to figure it out together."

"Yeah. Maybe we can."

CHAPTER NINETEEN

The album was finalized and the announcement was ready to go. It was all about new beginnings, but it felt wrong now that Lila was done with Barry. I'd convinced myself that Rose got that new beginning with him, but the feeling of guilt still nipped at my heart.

The only time I was Lila was when I was doing video calls to plan my next few months. Once the heat on my name died down, I would be due back in LA—something I dreaded.

"I don't know how you're doing it," Malia said one day as we were wrapping up another meeting. "There's not been one hint of you."

"I know how to disappear," I said, already itching to be out of the wig. "And I'm good at it."

"No kidding. Keep it up. The mystery is good."

"And people still love the single?"

"It's charting and radios are playing it everywhere. Critics love it."

I took an uneasy breath. "Okay. Good. I was worried people would be heartbroken that Blaze and I split."

"Don't worry about that," she said. "Focus on the music. That's what matters and this is easily one of your best that I've seen."

"I can't thank you enough."

"It's never a problem," Malia said. "I'll let you get back to your break. Stay off social media and enjoy it."

I turned off the camera, head resting against the wooden table I sat at. After a few breaths to collect myself, I slowly pulled off the wig and cap, shaking out my hair.

"You okay?" Juno asked.

"Yeah, I was just talking to Malia about the single. She says it's doing good and that people aren't that torn up about it."

"Oh, good." Juno's voice shook on the last word.

"What?"

"Nothing," she said. "Nothing that matters anyway. You've gotta be tired from all of these meetings. I made you tea."

"Thank you," I replied. "For everything, even when I'm Rose. I never thought I'd tell anyone but my parents, but I'm glad you know."

She smiled and sat next to me. "Want to do something to get your mind off of it?"

"Anything."

"I found a puzzle in one of the closets," she said, pulling it out. "It's kind of nerdy, but it could be fun."

"That sounds so nice. I need to do something other than think about work."

Or my mistakes.

She laid it out on the coffee table in the living room where we worked on it together in the quiet of anonymity, playing the day away.

Lila's phone was in the depths of her purse, untouched, and for once, I didn't feel like I was missing anything. I instead kept Rose's phone, which proved to be fruitful when Barry texted a few hours later.

Barry: Sorry I haven't gotten the chance to reach out in a bit.

Rose: You're busy, I understand.

Barry: I'm going to West Tennessee to meet my dad in person. Want to join?

Rose: I'd love nothing more.

Barry

I picked up Rose in a trendy neighborhood in Nashville. It was one of those older houses that was renovated for an Airbnb. I knew she was only traveling for work, but I was happy to see she was in a safe neighborhood at the very least.

As I pulled to the curb, I thought about walking up and knocking, but the door opened and she came tumbling out of it. I noticed her first, especially the way her red hair shimmered in the sunshine, but then I also saw a prominent figure that gave me pause.

It looked oddly familiar.

"Do you have someone traveling with you?" I asked as she got into the car.

"Oh, yeah. A coworker of mine. She's nice."

"What's her name?"

"Jun—June. Just June."

"Huh," I said. "She reminds me of someone."

My mind went back to Lila and Juno, her bodyguard.

"She doesn't speak English," Rose rushed to say. "This is her first time in America."

"I hope she's enjoying it," I said slowly. "I was going to walk up and grab you. Maybe I could have said hello."

"Oh, she's antisocial. Even the two of us have to communicate through translators. A third person would be so much more work, even if you just say hello. Don't worry about it."

I nodded, trying to ignore the bothersome feeling that I was missing something important. It wasn't like I was upset that Rose had someone staying with her, even if it had been a man. We weren't anything to each other, so she could do what she wanted.

But it still nagged my mind, and I wasn't sure why.

"This is a weird day," I muttered as I pulled away from the curb.

"It's not every day that you meet your real dad. You're allowed to be a little off."

"Thanks for coming, by the way."

"It's so weird seeing you in the day and not in the bar, but I like it. This is our first hang out somewhere else."

"We saw each other in the grocery store."

"Oh! That's right. But this is an *intentional* hang out." Her lips curved into a smile that once again reminded me of Lila's.

"True. To new beginnings, then."

Her smile grew as if I'd said something funny.

"To new beginnings," she replied. "Let's do this."

The drive was easy. As the city gave way to rolling hills and blue skies, I found myself growing nervous about the man I was going to meet.

Wilfred was truly awful at texting. He used a mix of 2000s lingo and was the victim of autocorrect more times than I could count. In a way, it was funny to see a man who wasn't so tied to his pride. And seeing him mess up made going to visit him easier.

"Are you okay?" Rose asked as I grew quiet.

"I am," I replied. "Mostly."

"You're drumming one hell of a song on your steering wheel," she pointed out.

I stilled my fingers. "Sorry. Nervous habit."

"It's fine. Do you want to talk about it?"

"There isn't much to talk about. I'm meeting my real dad for the first time. My mom apparently lives next door and this could go great, or it could go like everything else has in the past with my family."

"We don't know yet," she said. "But what I do know is that I'll support you either way it goes. Hopefully, that counts for something."

"It does, but this could get messy."

"Life is messy."

It was, even when I wanted it to be relaxed and easy. I'd wanted that with Lila, but it didn't seem to come to fruition.

But Rose had seen most of it and she was still here. And as much as she reminded me of Lila, she was still different.

Easier to talk to, somehow.

"I hate for people to see me when dealing with my family. I built a life away from them for a reason."

Out of the corner of my eye, I saw her eyes widen for a moment, but it was gone just as fast as it had arrived. "That sounds lonely."

"I used to think being alone was good," I said. "But now I'm not so sure." I snuck a glance over at her, hoping I wouldn't see the ghost of Lila.

But I still did.

We pulled in moments later. The driveway was gravel and muddy. A small house sat on a hill with plants surrounding it. In the distance, I could only see one other house, which was where Mom and my grandparents were living. I didn't give it a second glance, knowing I didn't need to think too long about the woman who'd caused all this.

This was so different from the hustle and bustle of Nashville. Mom always hated it because it seemed lowly, but in a way, it was also peaceful. While I loved my bar and being in the city, there was a certain charm to this too.

The screen door opened with a loud squeak. A man, tall with broad shoulders in a flannel, walked out. His hair was nearly white, but I could see its tips were blond like mine. He had a long beard, which had grayed as well, and his face was weathered.

But he looked exactly like me.

My heart pounded in my ears and I had no idea what to say.

"Y'all want some salsa?" Wilfred's accent was deep and rough. I'd heard it on the phone, but it was far more pronounced when I was seeing the rest of him for the first time. He fit the image of a country man perfectly, and I could see why Mom didn't want to be around him. Once Todd sunk his claws into her, what he hated was what she hated—including her humble upbringing. "I mean, it's great to see you, Barry. I'm glad you came, but I'd like to skip the awkwardness and bond in my favorite way: food."

"I would love that," I said slowly.

"Who is this?" Wilfred asked, his eyes sliding over to Rose.

"I'm Rose, Barry's moral support for the day."

"It's nice to meet you, Rose. Now y'all come in. I'll pull up an extra seat."

CHAPTER TWENTY

Rose

Wilfred's house felt like an old log cabin. The only light filtered in from the front windows and the dimmer space was small but packed. An old, well-loved couch sat in one corner, a small table in another, and through a small doorway was a kitchen. Next to the table were racks of home canned goods and Wilfred picked up a red jar.

"I made this using tomatoes and jalapeños from my garden. I sometimes sell some at farmers markets, but I always keep a little bit for myself. I made homemade chips as well."

"So, you like cooking?" Barry asked.

"It's one of my favorite pastimes. It's only second to sharing the food." He set down a plate of chips paired with a bowl of salsa.

"Thanks," I said, taking the first one. The chip was crunchy and salty, but the salsa tasted like it had just come out of the garden. "These are great."

"Thank you," he said. "How was the drive?"

"Um, good."

A silence fell over us, broken a moment later by an awkward laugh from Wilfred.

"Shit, kid," he said. "I'm bad at small talk. And polite talk."

"Me too," Barry admitted.

"Got it from me, I guess."

"You know what usually worked for me when I met Barry?" I asked after another silence fell over them.

"Getting hit on by a weirdo?" Barry asked.

"Ask him about his bar," I stage-whispered to Wilfred. I glanced at Barry, and my heart sank when I saw his jaw tic. I knew the bar was not a good subject for his usual family, but was it also banned with Wilfred?

"Right, the bar."

"You know about it?"

"I looked it up, once I figured out how the Google works. It's one of the few bars on the main strip that isn't all country, right?"

"Yeah, that's it. It's called—"

"Movers and Shakers. Cool name. Miriam and Bill have a hard time remembering, but I tried to commit it all to memory."

"Who?" I asked.

"His grandparents," Wilfred said. "I'm good friends with them, even after everything. They keep tabs on that bar. They did on all of you kids. You are one impressive bunch."

"Ruth and Tom are the impressive ones."

"No," I said. "You are too."

"I mean in the *normal* way. Owning a bar isn't really what anyone had in mind for me."

"It's amazing, kid. And from what I can tell, you've hosted some famous people in those four walls. I want to go, but I, uh . . . don't know how the website works."

"You want to go?"

"It sounds like a fun place. I'd like to see what you've been up to. You . . . all of you made names for yourselves. I wish I could say that I had a part in your upbringing. That man . . . *Todd* . . . must have been good for you three."

Barry's lips pressed together and I wondered if I should step in to say that Todd had been the opposite of good. He'd been evil.

"Did I say something wrong?" Wilfred asked.

I wondered if Barry would tell him what Todd had done to them. But his eyes fell to the floor, and when he looked up, all the emotion was gone.

Just like when I'd been Lila.

"No, you didn't. We're still getting the hang of this, that's all."

Wilfred smiled, unaware of how Barry had shoved all of his pain into a box. But I saw it.

And I hated it even more when it wasn't directed at Lila.

Barry

"So, Rose"—Wilfred turned to her as she'd been watching me like a hawk—"how did you and Barry meet?"

Rose's eyes slowly slid from me and I knew she had seen what I'd just done. I didn't know how she caught it, but she always seemed to.

"His bar," she said. "It's a funny story, actually."

"Something to do with being hit on by a weirdo?"

"She was there one night and a guy came on too hard to her. I kicked him out."

"And then I followed him like a lost puppy until he talked to me."

"That isn't how I remember it."

"Maybe my desperation didn't show, but I felt it." She shrugged, a smile on her face.

My heart, even when down, skipped a beat. If it hadn't been for Lila, I might have felt more.

I cleared my throat. "She's been a good friend," I said. "A great part of my support system."

Her grin fell and I wished I could offer her more than friendship, but I knew I wasn't ready, not after Lila.

"We all need that," Wilfred said, oblivious to the meaning that Rose had picked up on. "Now, can I show you my garden? I think you'll like it."

I nodded, letting him lead me outside. The air was warm even this early in spring. He had just started pouring new dirt onto the old, telling us about his plans to get tomatoes, peppers, and other vegetables once the risk of frost was gone. It was nice to see a man doing something he enjoyed.

Peering around the side of the house, I saw a massive pile of split wood and an axe. I may not have known much about country life, but I knew there was no reason to split it when it was warm. A question bubbled up, but I shook it away. I doubted he would want to tell me.

Then Wilfred caught my line of sight.

"So you've seen my pile," he said.

"Is wood splitting a fun pastime?"

"I do it when I'm mad, and after I found out about you . . . Well, I had to process it somehow. And I can still use it in the fall."

I looked back at the pile. I was glad I hadn't told him about Todd. If he'd already been this mad, just how much worse would it have been if he knew how awful it was?

"I felt the same way," I said. "Let's not mull on it."

"Definitely not. The sun is setting and you probably have to go back to the bar."

"I do."

"I won't keep you, then, but I also won't let the two of you leave empty-handed. Come on, I have food for you."

Wilfred sent us both home with salsa and chips. Rose offered to drive back, which allowed me to think.

I wondered what Ruth and Tom were going to say. We'd spent our entire lives in competition with each other and I questioned if they would be secretly jealous, or if they would be, once they knew it had gone well.

I would have been.

"You did good," Rose said as we pulled off the smaller highway and onto the main interstate to Nashville.

"It doesn't feel real."

"To have a nice parent?"

"Yes," he said. "I've never had one before."

"Why didn't you tell him about the man who raised you?"

"I don't think he needed to know. He was already angry."

"You don't have to hide things to protect people, you know."

"It's a habit I'm trying to break." I let out a sigh. "Doing it already messed up something once, but it's hard when I look up to someone. I want to be easygoing."

"Who did you look up to?" she asked slowly.

"It doesn't matter. It didn't work out and now she's across the country."

"Did it really affect you that much?"

I knew I should tell her it didn't, but I also couldn't lie.

"I fear I'll never be able to look at another woman without comparing them to her."

"Oh." Rose's eyes went wide. "It was that serious?"

"I tried to focus on her, but in the end, it only pushed her away. It's why you and I can't have anything more. I'm sorry."

She was silent for a long time, and when I looked over, her lips were pursed. "It's okay."

"You're disappointed."

"Not in you," she said. "Just in some choices that were made."

"By me."

"By the woman who broke your heart," she said. "I feel it like . . . like *I* did it."

"But you didn't. She's a different person."

"Yeah." Her voice was low. "A different person."

Something about her tone set off alarm bells, but I couldn't place *why*.

"I won't make you hear about her if you don't want to. Hell, you don't even have to be friends with me if you don't want to."

"I want to be friends with you. I'll take anything you give me."

"I don't know if I deserve that."

A half smile was on her face. "You do."

"I'm sorry. I feel terrible about . . . us getting closer while I'm not being open to dating."

"You have nothing to apologize for. You really don't. I'm just glad you hang out with me at all. That woman before . . . she was that special?"

"She was, but that doesn't mean I don't like you. If I'd met you first, then things could have been different. This feels natural, but going into something with you when I'm thinking of someone else isn't fair."

She slowly nodded, but she was still thinking about something.

I desperately wanted her to share it so I could say anything to make this better. She'd been kind to me from day one, letting me open up to her and even coming to meet my real dad. She'd done so much.

"Are you okay?"

"I will be," she said. "I just need to think for a bit."

"Okay," I replied. "Take all the time you need."

"Time is something I don't have much of."

We lapsed into a silence, broken only when she pulled up to her house.

"Have a good night, Rose." She gave me one last sad smile before she got out of the car. I watched her until she walked through the front door. Then I sighed and got in the driver's seat.

I didn't pull away immediately, in case regret hit me. If it did, I'd go to the door and take it all back. I'd push past this thing with Lila and start something new with Rose, the woman who *wasn't* the tornado in my life.

The feeling never hit.

As I pulled away from the curb, I was only sure of one thing: I was desperate to hear Lila's voice. I turned on her music, letting it fill the quiet car.

She sounded as she always did, but familiar in a new way. It had to be because of how much time I'd spent with her. She'd infected everything, making me hear her even in Rose.

But that was a ridiculous idea and I didn't know why I kept returning to it.

Because they were *obviously* two separate people.

Right?

CHAPTER TWENTY-ONE

Rose

I slammed the door when I got inside the Airbnb, making Juno jump. My heart was in the depths of hell and I felt like I'd ruined everything.

No, I *knew* I had.

"Is everything okay?"

"He wants Lila," I muttered, falling face-first onto the couch. "He turned me down so nicely because he's too hung up over *her*."

"Oh," she said slowly. "So, you can reach out to him as Lila—"

"No," I said. "No more lies. Going back and forth feels *awful*."

"You're protecting yourself."

"With lies? This is wrong, Juno."

"But there isn't another option."

"Of course there is. I could have *told* him—"

"No," she said. "Do you know how much that would upset people?"

"People? Like who?"

"Your mom, for one."

I opened my mouth to tell her Mom wouldn't know, but then I paused. "How do you know my mom would be upset?"

"I—"

"I haven't told you anything about her."

Juno sighed. "You didn't, but *she* did when she tracked me down."

"How?"

"It started when I went looking—"

"No. I didn't want you to go looking."

"What if you had a husband and kids and they needed protection? I wanted to know the whole story and I found out about a woman named Linda Hill in Canada. She was the reason you've been leading a double life, right? You wanted her to have peace."

"Yes, which is why I didn't tell you."

"I didn't plan to do anything with the information. I only called her to see if she was a real person."

"You called her? She never answers the phone."

"I know. Her voicemail told me all I needed to know."

"What does her voicemail say?"

"I don't know if you want to hear this. Or if I want to call again."

"I do."

Juno pulled out her phone and brought up her contacts.

"You have reached a number that is no longer in service," Mom said in a bad impression of an official phone notice. "The woman here has moved on and *cannot* be found!"

"Oh, boy," I muttered. Her anxieties over my life were obviously getting worse and it seemed splitting myself into two hadn't been enough. But what else could I do? I was trying my best, yet I still messed up somehow.

"Yeah. I was done after that."

"So, how did she find you?"

"She has a private investigator looking into every call she receives and that investigator somehow tracked down both my phone number *and* my social security number, which she recited the second I answered the phone."

"She *what*? How does she have a private investigator?"

"You didn't know? I assumed you pay for it."

"No, I don't pay for it. I give her a decent amount of money to live off of, but that's it."

"And how much is a decent amount of money to you?"

My cheeks heated. I knew I was privileged with more money than I could ever use, so I spoiled my family with it, but I also had no idea how much was too much. "Like twenty thousand?"

"A year?"

"A month."

Juno's eyebrows raised. "Well, we figured out how she can afford the private investigator. And why you pay me so much."

"I'd rather other people be cared for, but I didn't think she'd do *this* with the money."

"Unfortunately, that's not all of it."

"What else could there possibly be?"

"When she called me, she told me to make sure no one else found out about Rose Hill. If they did, she'd tell you to fire me. I thought it would be best if I listened so you didn't get stuck with someone who didn't know your secret."

"So that's why you were against me telling Barry."

"I still am."

"What if Barry doesn't tell?"

"What if he *does*? You're right, this was wrong, and maybe we should have gone back to LA once you broke it off with him, but what's done is done, and if he knows, then he might speak out, especially if he's mad."

"He wouldn't—"

"Have you seen him angry yet? Like truly angry?"

I had, and it was when he'd found out about his father. He'd kicked me out then. But he still didn't tell anyone.

I closed my eyes, feeling the now-familiar wave of guilt. "I don't know what to do."

"Sleep on it," Juno suggested. "And then you'll feel better."

"I don't know if I'll ever feel better," I muttered. "All of this is so wrong."

"It'll work out." Her voice was soft, meant to be comforting. But I didn't think anything would make me feel better.

Not when I'd fucked it all up with the perfect guy.

I went to my room, still feeling uneasy about this whole thing. The correct answer was to tell him, I knew that.

But what if he told everyone?

Maybe you deserve that.

When the thought hit me, I fell on the bed. I *did* deserve it. I deserved every ounce of his anger and I didn't know if my self-preservation was enough justification to keep lying to a man who'd done nothing wrong.

I tried to think of Mom and how she would react. That usually snapped me back into line, but even the fear of that was nothing compared to the guilt I felt. I'd promised her I would never do this, but my guilt was morphing into something else.

Conviction. Painful, righteous conviction.

In my dream, the bar was different. The pink and teal neon lights faded together and I had a drink in my hand, something I'd never done since my first year owning the place. I took a sip, expecting alcohol, but all I got was fizzy tartness and fruit.

Cranberry juice and soda water.

"Don't steal all of it," a lyrical voice said. "It's my favorite."

My eyes snapped up and I saw Lila in front of me. She gave me a heart-stopping smile and grabbed the drink out of my hand. Her hair looked different today—a slightly lighter shade of black.

"Did you dye your hair?" I asked.

"Come on, you'd know I'd never do that. My hair has been the same for over a decade."

And it had. She'd never shown a sign of roots or an outgrown haircut. She'd always been the same. She'd always been *Lila*.

She handed back the drink and the song turned into the one we'd written together. The angsty rock song about Blaze wasn't dancing music, but she laughed as if she had entirely moved on from the pain I'd seen her in. She twirled, and in the shifting light, her hair had red strands.

When she stopped, the red was more prominent, but like this, she didn't look like Lila at all.

I blinked, thinking I must have been losing my mind. When I opened my eyes, Lila would be back.

But then she wasn't.

It was Rose.

Her red hair glistened in the light, just like when she came out of her house to see Wilfred with me. Her lips weren't painted red like Lila's, and it hit me how similar they were to the pop star's.

My eyes went to Lila's, and I realized they *also* had the same shade of hazel.

"Come on, Barry," Rose said, but her voice mixed with Lila's. "Come dance with me."

My legs followed of their own accord and the horror rising in my chest did nothing to stop me. Her hair was red in the pink lights and freckles danced on her skin. In the green, it was darker and she was the pop star I longed for.

But she was somehow both.

"You're the only one I'm like this with," she said, two voices somehow one.

And I couldn't say it back because I was opening up to *two* women.

But now I was dreaming that they were one.

I woke up, breath heaving. It was nearly noon the following day, and I'd never been known to sleep this late—yet I felt the opposite of rested. My dream played in my mind on a loop, one that didn't allow me to think of anything else.

I might finally be losing my mind. Because there was *no* way Rose and Lila could be the same person and my brain had to be playing a cruel trick on me.

Slowly, I got up, trying not to think of my cursed dream. I desperately needed to find something to do, so I worked on social media for the bar, which I usually never touched.

Then I went downstairs to meet Liam, who had come in early for deep cleaning, to ask if he needed help opening his station. When he said no, I went to Audrey, hoping for something to do.

She didn't need me either.

"Your woman is here," Liam called out right after the bar opened.

My eyes found her immediately. Her hair was braided today and my dream flashed behind my eyes.

Same shade of hazel.

Same lip shape.

"Hey," I said, giving her a weak smile.

She chewed on her lip. "We need to talk."

"We do?"

She nodded, one firm bob of her head. "And considering it took me almost a whole day to sneak out to meet you? We only have a few minutes."

I eyed her. She didn't look like herself. Her shoulders were straightened and she stood tall at her full height. I'd always seen Rose with slumped shoulders.

She reminded me of the version of her and Lila I'd seen in my dream.

"Let's go to the rooftop."

"No one can hear anything from there, can they?"

"It's never been a problem before. Are you okay?"

"Not at all, but let's do this anyway." She gestured for me to lead.

I followed and Liam wiggled his eyebrows at me. Everyone expected me to end up with Rose. They hadn't even met her and they liked her.

But I'd told her no.

After my dream, I didn't know if I regretted it. I didn't know anything.

"Oh, God," she said once we were alone on the rooftop. "I don't even know how to begin."

"What's going on? I've never heard you like this."

Rose let out a humorless laugh. "You definitely have."

"No, I don't think that's true."

"It'll all make sense in a few minutes." She let out a quivering breath. "But I guess I should start by saying that I didn't mean for this to happen."

"What?"

"All of this. And once you know, you'll be mad, which I deserve, but . . . before you are, know that I didn't mean to hurt you."

"What, did you contact Todd or something?"

"It's not about your family."

"Then I don't think you can do anything to make me mad."

"I doubt that," she said. "You know, when I was a kid, I dreamed of being a pop star."

I blinked at her change of tone. Her voice now sounded clearer, more lyrical. Like Lila.

"You . . . what?"

"I did."

"You look like a very famous one, so maybe I can see it."

"Lila Wilde, huh?" Her smile was sad.

"I guess you've heard that before?"

"No, but that's by design. No one's supposed to look at me and see Lila Wilde. That was the point of it all. And no one has looked long enough to see her in me for a long time."

My mind spun as my dream popped into my head: red hair fading into black. My heart kicked up in speed as I started to draw one *very* impossible conclusion.

"You're not about to tell me you *are* Lila, are you?"

She looked down and reached into her bag, pulling out a black wig. "Yeah. That's exactly what I'm telling you."

I stared for a second. "This is a joke, right?"

"No. Unfortunately, this is *very* real."

CHAPTER TWENTY-TWO

I watched Barry carefully. He stared at the wig, jaw tight.

I'd been up all night figuring out how to word this. The rehearsed speech was gone the moment I got in front of him.

Seconds stretched out. I wanted to beg him to say something, yet I was terrified of what he was thinking. I deserved whatever he had for me—that much I knew.

"You're the *same* person," he said slowly.

"Yes."

"So, I first met you outside the bar, not when you came in and got hit on."

"Yes."

"And you *dumped* me."

"I . . . as Lila, yes."

"What the *fuck*?"

There it was. The anger I deserved.

"I'm sorry," was all I could say.

"For playing me?"

"I didn't mean to play you. None of it was done with the intention of it going this far."

"So why did you do it at all?"

"Because you seemed to like Rose more."

"How? How did I like you as Rose more?"

"You opened up to me, Barry. You kicked Lila out when you found out about Wilfred and then told *me*. I came in to check on you to see how you were doing, but I never expected you to show me this rooftop and open up. And once you did, I thought Rose would be better."

"I meant for Ruth and Tom to leave. Not you."

I blinked. "But . . ."

"Why would I kick you out?"

"You kept diverting the conversation when it was about your family."

"Because you're *Lila Wilde*. You didn't have time to hear about my melodramatic, broken family. You're a pop star, an international sensation. Why would you care about me?"

"Because you're interesting? Because I care about people in general? You have such a perfect impression of me that it was harder to get you to see I was a normal person. And Lila is just a wig anyway. She's not real."

"So, it's all a lie?"

"The feelings weren't."

"Why didn't you tell me until now?"

"I . . . there're a lot of things that happened and—"

"Just answer this: was it because you didn't trust me?"

"I trusted you."

"Then you should have told me."

I opened my mouth to try and defend myself, but nothing came out. There was no way to justify it.

Besides, the damage was done. Barry looked at me like he hated me, and I couldn't blame him.

"I guess I have my answer," he said. "You didn't actually trust me. Don't worry, though; no one will know. Whatever you think of me, I know the kind of person I am."

I opened my mouth to tell him that it was far more than *trust*. But my phone rang.

And it was Juno.

I cursed. She'd found me. When I was quiet this morning, she had been worried about me, but I told her I wanted alone time.

Not that I was coming here.

"I have to go," I said. I had no idea what she would say if she came up here. She, like Mom, was going to be *pissed* that I did this.

"Then go," he said. "Go live your double life."

"I . . ." But my phone rang again.

"Go," he said. "Go so I can fucking *think* for a minute."

His words hurt, but I knew I had no basis to argue. I stuffed the wig in my bag, slowly nodded, and brushed past him.

And I let him go.

As I descended the stairs, I knew I'd messed this up in a way I'd never be able to fix.

I went through the hordes of people, trying to ignore the stinging in my eyes. I met Juno out on the sidewalk.

"Why are you here?" she asked suspiciously.

"We need to get back to the Airbnb."

"What did you do?"

"I want to go home," I snapped. "Then you can be mad at me there."

Just like everyone else was.

She did what I asked. She waited until we pulled into the driveway before she started. "You told him, didn't you?"

"Yes."

There was a long sigh. "This is bad. Really bad."

"I couldn't do it anymore."

"Well, good for you."

I turned to her. "This was *my* secret, Juno. I can do what I want with it. And don't worry, I won't fire you over calling Mom."

"I do care about *you*, you know. Not just the consequences of what your mom could have done."

"Sure, but maybe I need someone to support my choices, not be one of the millions of people begging me to do what they want."

She was silent for a long time and I readied myself to hear all the reasons why she was right and I wasn't.

I didn't expect her to agree with me.

"Okay, yeah. I should have been better about supporting you, not telling you what to do."

I glanced over at her, eyes wide. "Don't you have more to tell me, though?"

"About what?"

"About how I'm wrong?"

"All of this is a little wrong. It's not a black-and-white situation, especially when so much rides on this. The one thing that is one hundred percent true is that it *is* your secret. Not mine."

I'd said that in anger and I was ready for it to be torn apart. Nothing was ever truly mine.

Until now.

"What did Barry say?"

"He was pissed, as he should be."

"What do you think he's going to do?"

"He said no one would know—that he knew he was trustworthy, even if I didn't."

Juno blew out a breath. "Wow. That's . . . a good response, I guess."

"Why can't I do anything right? No matter what I do, people are upset."

"They always will be. This is life."

"I thought I could be different, that I could make everyone happy."

"Every people pleaser learns they can't, eventually. And I'm sorry I contributed to it. You have a right to do whatever you think is best, Rose. And you can piss people off."

"At least my fans aren't mad. I don't think I could take that."

Juno went silent again and I wondered if she was lost in thought. I wanted to ask if she could show me a few posts of fans being happy, but my phone rang.

It was Malia, which meant something was needed from Lila. I sincerely hoped Blaze hadn't done anything else. That was the last thing I needed.

"Hey," she said. "I hope you're doing well."

"I'm . . . okay. What's up?"

"Your newest single is number two on the charts right now."

"Wow, that's great." I hoped I sounded excited because numbers didn't make me feel anything on this god-awful night.

"If you're up to it, we *need* to monopolize on this. I have an offer for you to perform your new single on daytime TV up in New York City. You could maybe do an acoustic or something. You're incredible when you perform live."

"When is it?"

"Tomorrow. Think you can be there?"

That was so soon. I almost said no, but then I remembered that Barry wouldn't want anything to do with me after this. He'd told me to leave, and maybe I should.

And I was on borrowed time anyway.

Nothing felt right and I wasn't sure it would ever again. I needed to focus on my job. At least the fans would be happy.

"Yes," I said. "I'll be there. Thanks, Malia."

I hung up and looked over to Juno.

"Time to go to New York."

"What, why?"

"To perform. It's time to go back to being Lila."

"But what about Barry?"

"Be honest: would you ever talk to me again if you were in Barry's shoes?"

Juno's stricken face was my answer.

"Exactly. Performing always makes me feel better, and according to Malia, this'll be good for me in the long run. I want to just do one thing that makes someone happy. This is one way I can do that right now."

Barry

I barely slept. I was too busy trying to put the pieces of my sanity back together. But not sleeping didn't help and I was exhausted when I finally woke up out of my mostly restless slumber.

My anger was interrupted by a phone call. It was Tom.

"If you're calling to ask how I am, then the answer is not good."

"I was calling to check in, but I was also calling to see if you wanted to go out. We're getting breakfast. Want to join?"

"You and Max?"

"Yep. Selena's in Atlanta visiting her best friend."

"I . . . I don't know if I'll be any fun."

"Trust me, Max will be enough fun for us both."

Usually, I would stay alone and wallow in this. People didn't get to see me when I was *this* upset.

Seeing the second dining room chair was a reminder of how things had gone so downhill. Max was a cute kid who'd proven to be a bundle of laughter and joy anytime I saw him, so maybe going out with Tom and him would do me some good.

"Okay. Where do you want me to meet you?"

"Have you ever been to Biscuit Love?"

"No, but I know where it is. I'll meet up with you in a few."

I slowly got dressed, putting my hair up into a messy bun. I drove to the restaurant in pure silence, unable to listen to anything. I pulled into a spot, seeing Tom getting out of a *car* of all things.

"Is that a new car?" I asked.

"Yep. The truck, even with airbags, is a safety risk."

"It's nice," I said. "At what point are you getting the minivan?"

The joke felt wrong, considering my shit mood, but it helped.

"On kid three," Tom said with a straight face.

"I want a sister!" Max said.

"Let me and your mom get married first. Then we'll talk."

"Little man knows what he wants," I said, able to crack a small smile. Max was so happy, it was infectious.

"Oh yeah," Max said. "I've been an only child for too long, and honestly"—he lowered his voice—"Mom and Dad need something else to focus on."

"Too strict?" I asked.

"There's just too much love."

"Sickening," I replied, but I smiled at Tom.

The restaurant smelled like biscuits and citrus. It was decorated in pink and white with a touch of dark stained wood—a Nashville classic.

"I want an orange juice," Max said immediately. "They make it fresh here."

"You can't say no to fresh-squeezed," I replied.

We got our meals and found a table; I was happy to be out of the apartment for a bit. Max was content to talk about everything. And it was nice to listen to a kid and not relive Rose's and my doomed conversation over and over again.

"Dad said you were in a bad mood," Max said in between sips of his drink. He looked up at me with innocent eyes. "Wanna talk about it?"

"I don't think that's a good idea."

"Even doing it a little can help. You don't have to tell us the *details*, but we're here for you, Uncle Barry."

I looked at Tom.

"Does he get this open nature from you?"

"I'm pretty sure he gets that from Selena," Tom said. "Not us."

"You're nice too, Dad. You wouldn't *believe* how much he talks about his feelings." Max looked at Tom and then back at me. "And when I was mad at him, us talking really helped."

"You were mad at him?"

"For lying and not telling me who he was for a bit. It sucked."

I blinked. That was almost exactly my situation. "And you got over it?"

"I did. I mean, they should have told me from the start, but they also wanted to protect me." He shrugged. "We all make mistakes when we care about people. It's what we do afterward that makes the difference. You can stay mad or you can see if they won't do it again. And as far as I know"—his eyes slid to Tom—"you haven't done it again, right?"

"I mean, there's some stuff I *can't* tell you." Tom eyed me. "But that's only because I really can't."

"What did you say it was again?"

"Nondisclosure agreements."

"Yeah, that sounds super legal. But you told me that might happen not too long ago. And I get it."

I leaned back in my seat, thinking about Max's words and my situation. He was right, but I wasn't sure I was ready to hear it.

"You're a really smart kid."

He perked up. "Thank you."

"I tell you that all the time," Tom interjected.

"Yeah, but it's cooler hearing it from my *fun* uncle."

"I'm the fun uncle?" I asked. "Do you have another one?"

"Knox, but he's the *smart* one."

"I like being the fun uncle."

"You know what would make you the *super* fun uncle? If we hung out more. That way, Uncle Knox doesn't dethrone you." He raised an eyebrow and he looked so much like a happier, younger version of Tom—I had to laugh.

"You know what? I'll have to take you up on that. Once I figure out what the hell to do with a twelve-year-old."

"I like pretty much anything. I'm an easy kid." He shrugged. "I like Centennial Park, pop music, and roller skating."

"That's a new thing," Tom said. "He's pretty good at it."

"We'll have to figure out something different, though. I want our hangouts to be special."

"That would be *so* cool. As long as you can hold up your promise, though. I'll be waiting."

I let out a huff of a laugh. "Can you believe this?"

"I can. He's a mess." Tom reached out to touch his hair.

"Dad, don't even dare. I will scream and ruin breakfast for everyone if you mess up what I worked on for ten minutes."

Tom's hand stilled. "He's sensitive about that."

"Mom does it all the time! Do you know how much effort it takes to style this?"

Tom shook his head, still smiling. "Fine. I'll be a decent dad and leave you alone. Speaking of dads, did you ever meet up with Wilfred?"

Shit. I hadn't even thought about it. "I . . . did. It went okay."

"What happened?"

A pit of anxiety settled in my stomach as if telling Tom about Wilfred would set us off. "He's nice. I didn't talk to him too long."

"Who is that?" Max asked.

Tom looked at me, a silent question in his gaze.

"He's my dad. My real one, that is."

"You have a different dad?" Max asked. "Congratulations. It must be a relief."

"Kind of," I said. "Family stuff doesn't really bother me."

Max narrowed his eyes and I had a feeling he saw right through the lie.

"We can't go in too hard on Barry. Let him have time to process."

Relief hit me at Tom's words. Sometimes, he was a decent brother.

Or all the time, as of late, it seemed.

"Thanks," I said.

"When you're ready, we'll be there."

"Can I be included too?" Max asked. "I'm invested now."

"It depends on how south this goes."

"You know, working out helps me process," Tom offered. "After breakfast, I was thinking about heading to the gym."

"Ew," Max said. "Please leave me with abuela. I'm still recovering from the run we went on."

"Is she even free?"

"For her favorite grandson? She better be. I'm still teaching her how to play Mario Kart. You two can have all the fun you want to at the gym. I have my own mission."

CHAPTER TWENTY-THREE

Lila

I wrote on the plane ride to New York City. As much as I was tempted to redownload and doomscroll social media in a feeble attempt to make myself feel better, I kept my phone on airplane mode to focus.

Plus, Malia had told me not to and I couldn't take disappointing anyone else.

As we neared the city, I realized performing was going to be next to impossible, considering I'd written most of the song with Barry and it was going to be a constant reminder that he was mad. I was tempted to cancel, but then I'd be sitting in misery, which seemed worse.

I jotted down what I wished I had said to Barry when I was on the bar's rooftop. I poured my heart and soul into it, feeling only a little lighter once it was done.

Immediately, I knew the chords I wanted to use. I knew how the bridge would go. It all snapped into place.

When the plane landed, my heart was in my throat. I knew there were some paparazzi here. There always were whenever Lila's jet landed. I'd had it stocked in another state for a bit but flew in under my other name to switch it up. Because people tracked it, I sometimes used a rental to avoid others knowing where I was.

Malia was waiting for me at the airport and smiled when she saw me.

"You flew out to New York?"

"I wanted to see you perform." She gave me a tight hug. "How was hiding out? Did it help?"

"Kind of."

"I don't mean to push you, but we do have to start talking about touring soon if you want to have it ready in time for the scheduled dates."

"Right, we have lots to do." I knew I couldn't stay in Nashville for long and it seemed my time was finally up. "But first this performance . . ." Dread filled me at the idea.

"Not excited?" she asked.

"I . . . I'm not in the right headspace. I don't think I'm angry. I'm sad. I even wrote this." I showed her my notebook, and her eyebrows raised.

"This is good. Sasha would love it."

"It's what I'm feeling. I messed up something good in Nashville but had to leave before I could say I'm sorry."

Malia's lips pressed together. "You know, your fans are happiest when you *feel* what you sing. You could perform this."

"It's not even on the album. Plus, you said I should monopolize on 'Goodbye, Good Riddance' being number two."

"But it could be a bonus track—if you go record it right after this. And any performance you do is going to make waves."

"That isn't how I usually do things," I said. "But . . . I'd love to perform it."

"Do you have everything you need to do it?"

"I do," I replied.

"Good. We can have it out in a few days. Let's go get ready."

I nodded, and as she walked off, I thought of Barry. I doubted he would even see this or if he would even care. But it was my apology, and until I knew he was okay with me apologizing in person, this would have to be a good start.

Barry

"Jesus, man," Tom said, lifting the last weight. "You're probably the only one who works out more than me."

I refused to admit it, but my arms were sore too. I just didn't want to feel the mix of all the emotions from the day.

Tom looked across the empty gym. "Want to talk about it?"

"It's a long story."

"Yeah, but I have time. Max said that teaching his grandma to play Mario Kart was a long process."

I sighed. "It's just . . . still hard to open up about things."

"Take all the time you need." Tom started to walk away, but the words spilled out of me before I could stop them.

"I got lied to by Lila. And I'm mad."

He stopped and turned. "What did she lie about?"

"She has a . . . secret that I found out. She said she hid it to protect me, but I didn't need that protection."

Tom's lips twisted. "I get how easy it is to say you're protecting someone when really you're just scared to admit the truth. It's a coward's way out, but I've taken it before. You have the right *not* to forgive her, but know that her life has to be a whirlwind that we can't even imagine. You saw what happened when Ruth was just *seen* with Knox, and he's not even a mainstream celebrity."

I blew out a breath of air. "I know. I get it. And with this secret, it makes it all the more complicated."

"Did she apologize?"

"Yes."

"Did she promise to do better?"

"We . . . we haven't gotten there yet. She had to go because she's . . . you know. *Her.*"

"You probably needed time to cool off, which you're taking."

"Until she goes back to LA and it's over."

"Barry, you didn't see the way she watched you when you found out about Wilfred or the way she promised Ruth to check in on you after you found out. Even if she didn't do it—"

"She did, actually. In her own way."

And I'd opened up to her as Rose.

What was her real life like when it wasn't split in two? What was *she,* the woman behind both Rose and Lila, like? What were the moments in between the two?

And in that moment, I knew I wanted it more than anything else. I still needed time to process, but once I was ready, if she could promise to be honest with me and hold true to that, I would be more than happy to know every part of her.

"Then—" Tom frowned and pulled out his phone. "Hang on, Max is texting." His eyes widened.

"What did he say?"

Tom turned his phone around so I could see.

Max: DAD THIS IS NOT A DRILL

Max: LILA PERFORMED ON GOOD MORNING AMERICA

Max: SHE DID A NEW SONG!!!

"A *new* song?" I asked. "I thought the album was done."

Another text came in and Tom moved his phone so we could both see.

Max: It's like an . . . apology song? It's really sad but I stg if this is her apology to Blaze I will gag.

"Maybe you should look up this performance," Tom encouraged, and I couldn't grab my own phone fast enough.

The video was trending. Lila was performing on a morning show, wearing dark clothes. She only had her guitar, no band. As she sang, the lyrics were powerful. She blamed herself in the song, wishing she'd shown a mystery man every side of herself instead of lying about it. She apologized for his pain and said she wished she could redo it all.

As far as apologies go, it was the best one I'd ever fucking heard.

"I'm going to LA." The announcement blew out of me the very second the video ended.

"Barry, wait—" Tom began.

"I need to talk to her. Don't try to stop me."

"I know better than to do that," he said. "But let's think about this. How do you know she's in LA? She would have performed in New York City."

"Her house is in LA and I know for a fact that she hasn't recorded that song yet. She'd go back to do that."

"Okay, so you *do* know where she might be. Have you been to her house?"

"Well, no."

"Then how do you know where she lives?"

I bit my lip, but then I remembered I had Juno's number. I never thought I would need it, yet here I was. "I might."

"Start there. See if you *can* get there."

I took out my phone and called Juno. She answered on the third ring.

"Barry?"

"Yeah. Can you talk for a second?"

"For a second, maybe. I'm about to board a flight."

"Is Lila there?"

"Yes, but she's finishing up her song right now so she can record it."

"I want to see her," I said. "Where's she going?"

I expected her to say no, or to keep me away from her. I got the vibe that she didn't like me very much.

"LA. She'd want to come and see *you*, but—"

"I'll go to her."

"You'll *what*? Just fly out to LA?"

"After a song like that? Yes. I will."

"And you haven't told anyone?"

"Not a soul," I replied. "And I won't."

Juno was silent for a moment. "Then she was right to trust you." It was admitted quietly. "Okay, I'll give you her address."

"I'll be there as soon as I can." I wanted to get there as fast as possible, but I was due to work tonight and I needed to talk to Liam and Audrey about it. "I'll need to wrap up a few things with the bar, but I'll be there."

"And for what it's worth, I'm sorry."

"For what?"

"For my part in all of this. I was part of the reason she didn't tell you. I told her it was a bad idea because a member of her family threatened my job."

"Oh . . . I didn't know that."

"It's a long story. I'm sure she'll tell you it all when you get here. She'll be happy to see you when she gets back and settled in. See you soon." She hung up.

I looked up at Tom, who had a smile on his face. "Figure it out?"

"Yep, and now I have a lot of things to take care of. Sorry to cut this short, but—"

He held up his hand. "Don't apologize. I'm just happy I could help."

I thanked him, still in a state of disbelief over the man Tom had become, before going to my apartment to shower and wait for Liam and Audrey to come into work.

When six rolled around, I was nervous, thinking of all the things I could do if they said no.

"Hey, boss." Audrey gave me a wave. "Ready for a long night?"

"Actually, I have something to ask you," I said to the two of them. "Can you manage the bar for a few days?"

Liam's jaw dropped. Audrey's eyes widened. "You want us to watch the bar?" she asked. "By ourselves?"

"Yes. But only for a few days. I know it's a lot of responsibility, so I won't ask for more than that."

"When?"

"I have to get a flight and everything, so maybe tomorrow?"

"Yeah, of course we can," she said with a smile. "Where are you going?"

"Across the country to . . . see a friend."

"Rose?"

"Y-yeah. Rose. She's out of town and needs me. If it's too much—"

"No, it's not. We have it all taken care of."

"Are you sure?"

"Very. Now go get ready to get your woman."

Chapter Twenty-Four

Lila

When I finished, I felt the words through my soul. I didn't know if any of it translated, and the audience clapped, but I knew they had to.

I wondered what my fans would say about this. For the first time in weeks, I was hit with the urge to see their reactions to all of this.

I loved singing with emotion. I loved putting my heart out there and processing my life through music. I also loved coming up with surprises. The show's producers had nearly passed out when I told them my plan and they rushed to make sure the hosts knew.

Despite my misery, I was still excited. And that excitement carried over until everyone was clapping and I was exiting stage right.

Malia was waiting for me, applauding as well with a huge smile on her face.

"That was *fantastic*," she said. "Really."

"Do you think everyone will like it?"

"I do," she replied. "But we need to get you to the studio. I called Sasha and she'll meet you there."

I nodded and we left the building. My work would keep me busy, but it was rooted in what had happened with Barry. It was going to drain me and I could only hope that I was going to come out of it feeling better.

On the plane ride back, I fine-tuned the song, making notes on exactly what I wanted it to sound like. Having all of this prepared meant that Sasha and I would have an easier time getting it recorded.

"You've been busy again," Sasha said the second I walked into the studio.

"Yeah."

"I'm guessing you're really feeling this one?"

"I am."

"Come on, then. Let's process it like we did last time. With singing."

I was more than ready to get into the booth, and when I started recording, I felt every word just like I had on that stage. When I'd gotten most of it recorded, Sasha went to work making it sound perfect.

We worked all night, coming up with a stripped-back song to release.

I should have felt relieved, but my mind was swirling with all the unknowns.

I was swarmed when I left the studio, even though it was early in the morning, and I knew I'd be followed around every time. Being back felt like my world was a chaotic storm of dust and debris now that I'd sung that song. They asked if it was about Blaze, just like everything else had been.

I hadn't thought about him for a while.

But *they* sure had.

They wanted to know why I'd broken it off and if we were getting back together. I didn't know how to begin to answer a single one of their yelled questions and I didn't get a second to breathe because they followed me back.

As I pulled up to my house, I knew the wig wasn't coming off for anything. As I took a measured breath to center myself, Juno offered to lock up the garage.

Then I darted in.

I was used to my house being the way I left it. I wasn't a messy person, so when I tripped over a pizza box, red flags raised in my mind.

"Ah, you're back."

Oh, God.

My eyes trailed up. Blaze was in my house, shirtless, with a beer can in hand.

"What the hell are you doing here?"

But it was a stupid question. I knew why.

"I live here."

"When we were *together*. This is *my* house."

"You never said I couldn't stay."

"It was implied!" I turned to call out to Juno, but his hand clamped around my wrist.

"Don't call out to her. Come on. It's just you and me right now."

I could have gagged. "Don't try to come onto me when you *cheated* on me."

"Was it really cheating?"

"Yes!"

"Lila," he groaned. "This has been torture."

I eyed the mess that was my house. "Seems like you had fun to me."

"It would have been better if you were here. I might even be able to deal with your boy toy."

"Don't call him that," I said.

"I'm trying to meet you in the middle here. But I guess you're still hung up on him."

"Just like you're hung up on Mia. Who you could live with. Get out."

"I didn't wanna play this card, but I will. I *could* clap back and tell everyone the truth."

No, he can't mean . . . "What truth?"

"See? I knew you'd be worried. How would everyone feel if they knew you cheated too?"

"I didn't cheat."

"But I can hint that you loved another. And I'll do it in your favorite form. Song."

Technically, this wasn't the end of the world. At least he didn't know who I really was. But it still wasn't *good*.

"I-I don't care. Write what you want."

"But—"

"Juno!" I called. "I need you!"

"Damn it," Blaze muttered.

Juno came up the stairs, eyes searching for the reason I'd called her, and when she saw Blaze, she blinked as if she couldn't believe he was here.

"What the—Blaze? You're not authorized to be in here."

"Ugh. You're so serious for nothing. Both of you are."

"Do I need to throw you out myself?" she asked.

He rolled his eyes. "Fine, but when the fans are even more upset, you'll regret not making it work."

He ambled out the door with no other word and I turned to Juno.

"More upset?" I asked.

"He was probably making stuff up as he always did. Don't worry about it. We have a mess to clean up."

I wanted to worry about it, but she was right. This place was disgusting and I refused to relax with Blaze's litter surrounding me.

Juno and I made it through two trash bags of garbage before my phone rang. I would have ignored it except it was Dad.

I hadn't heard from him in a while and I missed him. I told Juno I needed a break and took the call.

"Hey, Dad. What's up?"

"Hey, kiddo. Both your mom and I are on the line."

"Oh, a joint call? Is everything okay?"

"We're just checking on you."

I let out a breath of relief, glad there wasn't any news that made them call together.

But then I remembered what Mom had done.

I wasn't prepared to talk to her so soon after finding out everything, but knowing she was on the other line opened the door to questions.

And I needed some answers.

"Hey, honey," Mom said, her voice wavering. "How are you? We've seen . . . a lot going on."

"A lot *has* gone on," I said. "Including my bodyguard being threatened."

The line was silent.

But then Dad spoke up first. "By who?"

"Probably some deranged fan," Mom rushed to say.

"No. By you, Mom. You told her you'd get her fired if she didn't keep my secret from Barry."

"*What?*" Dad asked, an edge to his voice I'd never heard before. I'd never heard him get angry. In fact, I didn't even think it was possible.

"Wh—well, can you blame me? You're slipping."

"Linda, you overstepped."

"If she let her bodyguard know, then imagine who else she could tell! When Juno mentioned that man she kept working on the album with—"

"Barry," I said. "His name is Barry."

"I knew she would tell him eventually."

She wasn't *wrong*. I did tell him.

"He's not going to let it slip."

"He knows?" Mom gasped. "No. He can't."

"Why?" Dad asked. "Nothing traces back to you."

"Have you *seen* what people are saying? They're hungry for anything, and he could sell it—"

"He won't sell it," I snapped. "And what are people saying? I've only been told they're saying good things."

"You don't know?" Dad asked. "You usually keep up on that social media stuff."

"Malia banned me from it."

"Oh. That's definitely a good thing."

Or maybe it wasn't. In just one day, *three* people had mentioned my fans. Something was off.

"We need to talk about this random man knowing about Rose's secret identity." And just like that, Mom reminded me of the problem at hand.

"Rosie, did he say he would keep it a secret?"

"Yes."

"Then there's nothing to worry about."

"Yes!" Mom hissed. "There is!"

"It's all worked out. What else could there be?"

"How about how *I* feel about it?"

"I mean this in the nicest way, but you're not the most important person here, Linda."

Silence on the line again. I closed my eyes, knowing where this was leading.

"Guys, don't fight."

But it was too late.

A sob erupted from Mom. "Archie, how could you say something like that?"

"Linda—"

But she hung up.

"I'll call to apologize," Dad said, sighing. "Give me a minute."

They were gone and I felt like the worst person in the world. My phone burned a hole in my pocket. In the silence, I was finally able to remember what Blaze and my parents had said. Biting my lip, I redownloaded a social media app. The curiosity was killing me.

Once I got back into my account, I was able to search my name and see what people were saying.

And my heart stopped at what I saw.

Lila Wilde's Newest Single

By Perez Adder

"Goodbye, Good Riddance" came out with a bang. We've never heard Lila quite like this. She's been a pop phenomenon with a hint of deeper lyrics until even that faded away. Now she is back and better than ever. This new style of pop rock is incredible. I only hope she does more of it. We are eagerly anticipating her newest album, Goodbye, Hello.

Unfortunately, her rabid fans do not agree with me. They do not like that she's dumped Blaze Matthews, nor are they happy she's got a new sound. They're the same as all fans, always wanting the same old, same old.

At least I finally have a Lila song I like.

5189 Comments

BiggestLilaFan: The song is NOT her! There is no way she would do this to Blaze, and there is no way he would hurt her! This is all a PR stunt for this new album. I'm so disappointed in her.

BlazeandLilaforever: How could she do this to us? How could our parents be broken up?

BlazeStan: She's manipulative, I bet. Just like Blaze said. I for one will NOT be listening Goodbye, Hello. *#lilawildesucks*

RealLilaFan247: This is . . . something ig

RealLilaFan247: I TAKE IT BACK I CAN'T STOP LISTEN-ING

Barry

LA was different from Nashville. The warmer weather aside, the traffic alone was enough to give me a headache, but then I saw the houses. Nashville had its nicer neighborhoods, sure, but they were nothing compared to the sprawling mansions that LA boasted, especially as I got closer to Lila's home.

The man who picked me up at the airport was a part of Lila's security team. He seamlessly weaved through traffic as if it were nothing. Meanwhile, I wondered how we didn't get into a wreck. Even in the back neighborhoods, people were not paying attention while driving.

Lila's house was massive. Todd would have choked just at the sheer size of it. I knew I came from money, and I'd left it behind for the bar, but *this* was huge, even for me.

If Mom were here, she'd be telling me to marry this woman immediately. I grabbed my bag, refusing to be intimidated in the face of Lila's well-deserved success, and thanked the driver.

Juno answered the door on the first knock as if she'd been waiting on me.

"Hi, Barry," she said, gloves over her hands.

"Do I even want to know?"

"Blaze," she said.

"Blaze? Here?"

She rolled her eyes. "He's an idiot who doesn't know when he should leave his ex's house. Don't worry, he's gone now."

"Good. I'd hate to add another punch to the face to the reasons my mom is disappointed in me. Where's Lila?"

"In her room. She just took a break. And maybe fell asleep. She's been back there for a while. I think her parents called her and if it was her mom . . ." Juno shook her head.

"What did her mom do? Wait, wasn't she the one who told you not to tell me?"

"That's her. Rose's mom is . . . stressed. More so than I've ever seen in a person."

"So the double life is for her mom?"

"Kind of. I mean she *does* deserve some time to herself as Rose, but I think it started there. And I have a feeling her mom doesn't exactly instill calmness in Lila."

"So the conversation probably didn't go well."

"What do you know about her dad?"

"Not much. I know she has a rocky relationship with him."

Juno raised her eyebrows.

"It was something Rose said."

"Huh. Looks like you weren't the only one who opened up."

"Yeah. Let's just hope we stay that way after this."

"I think you two are good together, even if it took me a minute to see it."

I laughed. "Thanks, Juno. That's nice to hear."

"Just be careful around her mom."

"I'll be fine. I've dealt with *a lot* of family confrontations. This is the one thing I'm an expert at."

CHAPTER TWENTY-FIVE

Lila

Lila: Why didn't you tell me my fans were so upset?

Malia: What did you see?

Lila: The comments. Most of my fans hate what I've done.

I'd never felt like this. While I knew how much my fans thought Blaze and I belonged together, I thought it was fine. I thought they'd accepted it.

Malia had told me everyone was happy and that I'd done well with this album, but *this* told me I'd made a mistake.

They all wanted that apology to be about Blaze. They wanted to see us doing events again because he was the thing that made me my best.

I'd gotten it all wrong.

And now I saw why Blaze thought his threat of an album would be devastating. Judging by many of the comments on my videos, they were waiting for him to speak out in song about what I'd done.

Maybe he was the one who was going to come out on top.

Tears gathered in my eyes. I was frozen, unable to consider what to do to begin making my fans happy again.

Every single thing in my life was wrong. This was why I lived for everyone else; the second I was selfish, people got hurt.

There was a knock at my door. I shut my eyes, knowing it was Juno wondering where I'd gone. She needed help cleaning up Blaze's mess, yet I was stuck here like a fool.

"Juno," I said. "I still need a minute."

"It's not Juno."

When I heard the voice, I thought I had to be dreaming.

Because it sounded like Barry.

But there was *no* way he was here in LA.

However, when the door opened, the man himself peeked inside.

"Well," he said, "I'm glad you're not naked, or else I'd have a lot to apologize for."

"Barry?" I asked. My voice cracked as all of the regrets I felt mixed with pure confusion. The tears threatened to fall; he saw them immediately. When he did, his entire demeanor changed.

"What's wrong?"

I didn't get it. Why did he even care? I'd hurt him. He was *mad* at me. Didn't that mean he was done, that he'd leave and never look back?

"Why are you here?"

"I'm here to talk. You can't just write a song about me and expect me to sit back in Nashville and not come find you."

"You came across the country just to talk to me?"

"Sunshine, I'd do a lot more than that for you. Just say the word."

My jaw dropped. "But—"

"No arguments."

"No, you shouldn't be nice to me. You shouldn't *care* about me. Not after what I did."

"You know I never listen to what people tell me I should do. I do what I want. And I *want* to be here, Lila." His lips twisted. "Rose? What do you want to be called?"

I blinked, still baffled by everything that he was doing. "I . . . I don't know. My mom only calls me Rose because she doesn't really like Lila. My dad lets my name slip *sometimes*, but I'm not around him enough for him to call my name often."

"That's not confusing at all."

"Yeah, sorry. Just call me whatever person I'm playing."

"You're the same person no matter your hair color," he said.

"I'm not supposed to be."

"But you are. I thought I was losing it, but I saw the similarities."

It should have worried me, but the fact that he still saw *me* made me feel better than anything else today. "That's why I don't let people see both sides of me, but you've always been different. God, I'm *so* sorry I didn't tell you. I'm sorry for all of it. Breaking up with you and then reconnecting as Rose and then waiting so long to finally admit it and—"

"Breathe," he instructed. "We can talk about it all. Just do me a favor and don't come up with any other alter egos, okay?"

"I have no more."

"And be honest with me. Even if you're telling me you never want to see me again. I don't need to be protected, okay?"

"Of course," I said. "I don't think I can ever lie again. At least not to you."

"Can I know the story of how all of . . . this happened?"

I nodded, sitting up. My phone was forgotten on the bed.

"I got my songwriting talent from my dad. He's a songwriter. A free spirit too. But those were the two things my mom hated, especially the fame he had. It only got worse when I wanted to be famous too."

"Juno told me a little about her. And it's . . ."

"Yeah, it's bad. She keeps moving farther and farther away from cities to escape the idea of anyone knowing her, and that's even when I'm hiding who I am. If I didn't . . . who knows. Maybe she would have stopped talking to me. Being two people was better for us all. I told no one."

"Blaze didn't know?"

"Nope, and neither does Mia. Juno only found out because I was trying to get into Lila's room as Rose at one point, and even then, when Mom found out, she begged me not to tell anyone else. But I'm not the only one. She told Juno not to let me tell you either. And *threatened her*." I shook my head, trying not to think of the conversation that had just happened.

"You were just on the phone with her, right?"

"Yeah. She's not happy that you know, but it was the right thing to do. It was a mess—everything was. But I know I should have stuck to my guns and told you the minute I knew you wouldn't tell anyone, but I tried to make Mom and Juno happy." I shrugged. "It didn't help."

"You don't need to make others happy. The only one that matters is you." It seemed to work for him. He'd found the balance of being kind to others and living for himself. I just didn't know if that kind of life was even possible for *me*. "I've been thinking about how it went down. I *was* treating you differently because you're Lila Wilde."

"I don't blame you. She's interesting. And has all of this." I gestured to the things around me. "Rose is . . . just Rose. It makes sense that you were beguiled by Lila and not—"

"Remember what I said in the car? I said I liked Rose, but I met Lila first. Now I don't have to worry about it. The *two* women I like are the same one."

I blushed, looking at the ground, but then a thought hit me. "Just so you know, once you're seen with Lila, Rose is off the table."

"Wait, why?"

"Because if you're in Lila's orbit, your privacy is gone. You're seen and then you're followed. And if you're seen with Rose, then you're a cheater, or someone will see who I am and then—"

"They might put it together."

"This, *all of this*, is a mess. Even more so now that I've released these damn songs."

"Wait, what's wrong with the songs? Is that what you were upset about?"

"Have you seen the fan reaction?"

"No. I don't pay attention to that stuff."

"It's bad," I said. "So bad that I feel like I've ruined my career because I'm mad at Blaze."

"Let me see."

I wordlessly handed him my phone. I was still on social media, looking at all of their reactions. As he read them, I waited for understanding to dawn on his face. Instead, his brows furrowed.

"Why are these people worried about *your* relationship status?"

"They're my fans and I've always been with Blaze."

"But it's none of their business. Why do they get any say in your life? They don't know what went on behind closed doors."

"They gave me everything."

"*Everything?*" he asked. "Did you not do any of it yourself?"

"I-I mean, I wrote the songs and danced onstage."

"Don't you hold the record for the longest note held during a dance number? Against Broadway professionals?"

"Yes, but what does that have to do with the fans?"

"You're forgetting that your *talent* got you here. Sure, your fans bought your albums and saw your shows, but you made the thing they love. If you want to do more, then you can write more and do more shows, but only if you want to. But your personal life? That's *yours*. No one else's. And besides—" He looked at my phone again. "Did you not see the ones who love the album?"

He turned my phone to me, displaying a comment saying that they loved the new sound.

"I saw some, but the bad ones outweigh the good."

"Why does the bad outweigh the good?"

"Because they're the ones who I need to get on my side. That's how I got to where I am. I made everyone happy. It's what—" As I started to say it, I stopped. It was what *Mia* and Rick had told me to do.

"Exactly," he said. "You made an album from your heart. *That* is what you owe the fans. Nothing else."

"But Malia didn't even tell me some were upset."

"I can think of a few reasons why she didn't."

"But it was wrong not to tell me."

"Yeah, it was. She did it to protect you, which historically, never works out."

I looked at the ground, knowing *I* had lied to protect someone, whether it be Barry or Mom.

"Come on," he said. "Let's go talk to Malia."

"Talk to her? Why?"

"Because I find getting everything out in the open does *wonders* for making someone feel better."

I let him pull me to the door, wondering if he had all the secrets to the universe. Because having him here made my problems seem solvable.

"Okay, let's try it. But before you do," I rushed to say, "maybe we should hide your hair or something."

"Why?"

"We haven't really decided *who* you'll be with. If you wear a hat and maybe some sunglasses, you'll look like part of my security team. It won't work forever, but it will for a bit."

"I don't mind being seen with you and I don't care what kind of shit people say about me."

"I know, but this is a big decision. My life is a mess and I'm overwhelmed with everything and I'd hate to rush into something that we might regret later on."

"Fine," he said. "But I don't know if a hat will work."

"Oh, I can make it work. I am the *queen* of hiding long hair. And Juno can be getting the car ready while we're working on you."

Malia was able to see me immediately. She guided me to her office and I sat with a nervous tremor shooting through my whole body. While I'd confronted Blaze, I'd been furious. This time, I wasn't in the same headspace, which made this terrifying.

What if she was like Mia? What if she told me off for even feeling the way I did?

"Lila," she said. "It's good to hear from you. Who is this?"

"I'm Barry," he said. "A friend."

After I'd meticulously gotten his hair into his hat, he looked like a different man. His jawline was more pronounced with his hair up and so were his stormy eyes.

"Nice to meet you, Barry." She smiled and then turned to me. "I know we have a lot to talk about."

"Why didn't you tell me about all the controversy from this album?"

"Because Sasha warned me that you were nervous to make it."

She wasn't wrong.

"But I should have known."

"Would it have stopped you from making it?"

"M-maybe, but—"

"None of the buzz is really *that* bad. Some people are upset and some people are calling it a conspiracy, which they always do. They're social media comments."

"But I take them to heart."

"I know you do, and that can be dangerous. I'll admit that I wasn't sure if not telling you was the right call, and I'm sorry I upset you. But you're so talented that I didn't want you to water it down because of people you don't know."

"I could have changed things to make it more palatable."

"Have you ever had an album that everyone liked?" Barry asked.

I looked over at him. "No, but I'm sure it's possible. Other people have done it."

"No one has made everyone happy," Malia said, shaking her head. "It may seem like it, but every artist has someone who hates them vehemently. We don't often notice it because it isn't us."

"Mia said it was possible, though."

"She has a history of not being truthful," Malia reminded. "Though, I know I'm not perfect either. I should have asked more questions about why you were so worried about opinions rather than making the decision. This is a new working relationship and I made a bad call. But this album is great, Lila. It's true to *you*, and you were happy making it. You deserve to release it, no matter what the world might think."

I looked at my hands, knowing she was at least correct about that. I glanced over at Barry who was somehow staying by my side despite my own misguided lie to him. If he could do that for me, then I could try again with Malia.

"I don't want to be lied to again," I said. "I want to know if there's controversy. But not the details. I *was* happier without seeing the comments."

"I will be sure to let you know," she said.

"So then, what is the general consensus? The good and bad? What I saw were people *begging* me to get back together with Blaze."

"There are a lot of younger fans who feel that way. They think this is you straying from your roots, but many feel this is a great new direction for you. What is *your* consensus about the album?"

"I like it," I said, and I glanced over at Barry again. "I got to write it with a good friend."

Malia's eyebrows rose and I wondered if I should have even made the comment in front of her, but she didn't say a word.

"That's good, then. Your opinion is the main one I care about. You deserve to be happy with what you release."

"She's right," Barry added.

I looked between them, feeling more grounded with the two on my side. "Okay, then. I'll try to focus on me more."

"So, Barry," Malia asked. "How long are you staying?"

"Only for a few days. I have a . . . thing at home I have to get back to."

"Well, I'll be the first to say that I'm happy Lila has some good support. She definitely needs that."

I did, and selfishly, I wanted him here for longer. I was sure he was stretching it by being out as long as he was, but it still didn't feel like enough time.

Maybe it never would.

Barry

"Do they ever lay off?" I asked from the limo. I'd been told to go with Juno, before Lila, since she didn't want anyone to pick up on who I was. I'd grumbled about it but listened since she was the one who would be affected if people *did* catch on.

"No," Lila said. "But it's worse than usual right now because of the buzz about the album. They're just trying to get a reaction."

"I don't like that they treat you like a piece of meat."

"To them, I'm just a way to get paid." She shrugged. "I've made my peace with it."

I didn't like seeing her walk with her head down as she avoided their gazes. She stood tall, as she always did when she was Lila, but she nearly ran to the limo.

"So this is how it always is for you?"

"Yes. And if it's too much, I can send a car for you."

"I didn't mean for *me*. I can just see why you guard this secret with your life."

"Yeah." She nodded. "Did I tell you about my first outing in Nashville by myself? I went to this coffee shop and I saw a camera and *panicked*. I thought they had somehow tracked me down. But they were there for Knox Price."

"Knox Price? Like my sister's Knox Price?"

"Is there more than one?" She laughed. "I think it's funny I encountered your sister and her boyfriend before I even knew who they were."

"They weren't dating then. Knox was just annoying her like he always did."

"Are you sure? They *looked* like they were."

"Ruth is stubborn, and he knew that from the day they met."

"How did they meet?"

"They went to high school together, but they were rivals then. Well, Ruth thought he was her rival, but he didn't feel the same way. I don't think he ever did."

"I'd love to meet them both officially someday."

"You can. Maybe come back as Rose."

Her smile grew wider. "Thank you for coming out here."

"It's no problem. It's nice to see a different part of the country. In a different life, maybe I was a guitarist that toured the world or something."

"You'd be incredible at it, but I think you're incredible at most things you put your mind to."

CHAPTER TWENTY-SIX

Lila

Lila's New Bodyguard . . . Would You Bang Him?

By Perez Adder

We all know of Lila Wilde's usual bodyguard, Juno. She's buff, tough, and doesn't let anyone mess with her woman. When our favorite pop star is roaming the streets, Juno is in tow.

But this time, there was a new bodyguard with her.

Now, it's not unusual for Lila to require backup. We've seen other security join Juno in the quest to keep the multiple Grammy winner safe. But this one is HOT.

Can we expect a little bodyguard romance? Do you see him with Juno or Lila?

3856 Comments

Temptaction: Neither. He's MINE

LilaandBlazefan56: Def not Lila. She belongs with Blaze.

Hissgorl: Boo. They're done. He cheated on her.

LilaandBlazefa56: He did NOT! It's all PR to get hype up.

I shut the door, closed every blind I could, and triple-checked that no one was on my street corner. I'd been avoiding taking off the wig for a while, but it was quickly becoming too much.

"Do paparazzi even get past the security here?" Barry asked.

"Yes. And there are drones these days, so that doesn't help."

"Jesus, all for a photo of you?"

"Yep," I muttered. "Okay, I think I'm good."

I took off the wig and cap. I felt free like I could breathe for a second.

"Wow," he replied. "That's wild."

"Wait until I get the makeup off."

"Aren't there photos of you makeup-less?" he asked. "You still didn't look like Rose then."

"It was by design. I used non-lengthening mascara and darkened my lips just slightly."

"Smart."

"Thanks," I replied. "This is always the best and most terrifying part of my day."

I went to the bathroom to remove the rest of my makeup. Once I was done, Barry picked up the remaining litter on the floor.

"So, that song . . ."

"Oh, yeah. It's coming out at midnight. It won't be on the physical record because I got to it so late. What did you think?"

"When did you write it?"

"On the plane. I hated how we left it, but I know you needed time."

"I did, and I saw my family, actually. It was kind of nice."

"What did you do? And don't try to get out of it now. I *want* to hear about your family."

"I wasn't going to try to hide. I've learned my lesson." He leaned against the counter in the kitchen. "I hung out with Tom and Max."

"With Tom? I thought you were closer to Ruth."

"I thought so too," he said. "But he became a different person once he met his son. It was good for him."

"I need to meet him again when everything isn't terrible. I only really got to say a few words."

"A few words used to be all he would say." Barry shrugged. "Things are different now. And I don't think I mind it."

"Good. When we met, you hated your family."

"They grew. Finally. Just like you did by leaving Blaze. Did he really make all of this mess?"

I rolled my eyes. "Yes. I've already changed the locks. It's too bad *Goodbye, Hello* is done or else I'd write another song dissing him over this."

"We never did finish listening to it."

I thought back to the night we'd only gotten through one song. I couldn't bring it in me to regret what we'd done instead.

"We have time now. Do you want to finish it?"

"More than anything."

We continued through the last bits of cleaning and then I made popcorn to snack on while we listened to the album. As we sat on the living room couch, I pulled up the version Malia had sent me, hooked it to my speakers with Bluetooth, and pressed play.

Last time, he'd loved the first song and I could only hope he would also love the rest.

Barry

It felt odd to listen to a Lila Wilde album with a different version of the same woman in the room with me. Usually, I listened to them the moment they came out, alone in my apartment.

But this time, her eyes were trained on me and I wished I could have kept a straight face, but the songs were *so* incredible that I couldn't.

I usually hid this kind of giddiness from people. When I was a kid, it was a nuisance, and when I was an adult, everyone looked up to me as their boss. But I couldn't hide the joy I felt about listening to *Goodbye, Hello* before everyone else, and the fact that some of the songs were about me. I knew what some of them would be, and while I loved hearing parts my own style—I loved hearing what she did on her own more. It was a window into her thoughts, something I'd been curious about since day one.

Lila was very clear about how she felt. She was excited about being away from Blaze and hoped that she could be with someone else who was nothing like the people in her past. One line stuck out, and it hit like a freight train.

I hope that he can see all of me,

The sides that I've hid,

And like it all.

They were the final words of one of the songs and I wondered if she'd put it there on purpose. My eyes went to hers, and I found her still watching me.

"You wanted to tell me, didn't you?"

"I'm not a very good liar. I just thought it would never happen."

"And here we are, listening to you serenade me in your new album. Subtlety isn't your strong suit, is it?"

"I've written about a lot of my life, even if it was in code. Besides, it couldn't get much worse than the fuck you I wrote to Blaze."

"Is that really the only song about him?"

"He didn't deserve any more of my time. He had me convinced that I wasn't a good songwriter unless I was writing about *him*. I decided I was done with that. I decided I would prove him wrong."

"And you did that and more."

"Thank you for coming," she said. "Especially after how we left things. I think I needed you here. You remind me that I don't have to care about what everyone else thinks."

And she was the reminder that I wasn't alone anymore, that I didn't want to be.

Now that I saw the whole picture, I could see how Rose and Lila were melded. She did surface-level things to hide who she was, like shrugging and making sure her face looked different, but she couldn't hide her sparkling personality—at least not from me.

"So," she started, nervously twirling her hands through her fingers. "Should I get you a hotel room?"

"Doesn't this place have a hundred bedrooms?"

"Five," she said. "And you can stay here, of course. I just don't want you to feel like you *have* to. If you need space, just say the word."

I'd had my entire life to be alone and it wasn't all that interesting anymore. "I'll stay here, but maybe not in whatever wing you put your guests."

"The second floor," she said.

"A whole world away."

"If you wanted to . . ." Her eyes darted down the hallway where the master suite was. "You could just stay in my room."

"I was hoping you'd offer that because that is the exact place I want to be."

"Really?" she asked. "Even after everything?"

"I think writing an apology and singing it on TV was enough."

"It doesn't feel like enough. I could shower you with gifts, but I have a feeling that isn't your cup of tea."

"Not really, no."

"Then what do you want?"

"You. Just you."

Her cheeks turned red and I loved how I could see that when she was Rose.

"Let's go to sleep," I said. "I'll need to head out tomorrow, but I'll be back."

Her face fell at the mention of me going home, and I wished I could stay with her forever, whether it be in the mansion or in my apartment in Nashville.

She led me to her room, a huge space in its own regard with a massive bed. We could have stayed on opposite ends of it as we fell asleep and never touched. But she moved to the middle and I joined her.

"I don't know if I deserve you," she said as the lights went out. Her head was on my shoulder and my arm held her tight to me.

"I do, and I'll do my best to prove it to you."

CHAPTER
TWENTY-SEVEN

Lila

A month later, the album came out with a supernova explosion. I took over people's entire social media accounts as they dissected every part of it.

They wanted to know who the mystery man was who joined me on "On This Night."

They wanted to know who the hopeful new beginning was with.

They wanted it all.

I wanted to disappear and become Rose, but I couldn't leave LA.

Because I was *busy*.

With the tour scheduled and all of the buzz around me, I barely had time to think. We were rushing to get everything together in time to hit the road to bring my new album to life in concert.

Malia had connected me with another person at her talent management, Justice, who had taken over making everything perfect.

The first order of business was to decide on the setlist. I planned to do most of the new album, but I knew "On This Night" wouldn't be the same if I were the only one singing it. After some back-and-forth, it was one of the ones that got cut.

Neither Malia nor Justice had been too happy about it, but I had to do right by the song. It wasn't one I could do alone and it wasn't like Barry would be on the tour with me.

After we finalized the setlist, we focused on the dance moves. Since we had so little time to prepare, I was going to use a lot of the ones I already knew from previous tours, and the new ones would all be very similar. While I was getting into shape and memorizing the choreography, my team focused on getting the tour visuals ready.

Everyone, including me, was working around-the-clock to get this done. And I knew I couldn't let anyone down.

I shouldn't have even had time to miss Barry, but I did. I missed him while I was running on the treadmill, while I was dancing and practicing, and when I finally crawled into bed at night, exhausted. We texted, but it wasn't the same as having him here, especially now that he knew everything.

The closest thing I could do was focus on my team and my band. I knew most of these people from my previous tours and the familiar faces made this more possible. We already had a set rhythm.

Which meant I also knew if someone was off.

Jason was my rhythm guitarist, and I'd worked with him for my entire career. He was in his mid-thirties and was always the light of the tour. He made jokes and cut up with other band members during breaks.

So, when he went two weeks without talking to anyone, I was worried.

I'd asked everyone else about him, but they told me not to give it too much thought. I tried to do what they asked, only for my concern to come back tenfold.

I hated the idea of someone on my team being miserable, especially someone I'd worked with for so long.

Maybe it was my people pleasing rearing up, but when I mentioned it to Barry, he'd told me that he would be worried too. His crew was like a family, so he took care of them.

Eventually, after another day where Jason was quiet, I decided to ask him directly.

"Hey," I said. "How are things?"

"They're good." He made a move to go around me, but I didn't give up so easily.

"You can tell me if it's not, you know. I care about everyone on this team, including you. If something is wrong, even if it's something I did, I want to hear it."

He slowly turned back to me. "It's not you. It's family stuff."

"What's going on?"

"My mom is sick and she lost her job."

"Because she's sick? Is that legal?"

"They blamed her performance, which I *think* is legal, but we don't have the energy or time to fight it. She needs to be focused on getting better, and this tour pays enough for me to pay for her treatment outright."

"But you're not going to be with her."

He shrugged. "We all make trade-offs."

Not like this one, though. I shook my head. "No, you should be with her."

"I can't just stop everything. I can't afford it if I'm not working." He gave me a sad smile that told me he'd thought this through.

"I'll pay for it. All of it."

His eyes widened. "What? You would do that?"

"Absolutely."

"But the tour starts so soon. Will you be able to find someone else in time?"

Justice was going to be mad. Malia too. This would make everything more complicated, but I couldn't let Jason go through with this, not when I could do something for him. He, and all of my band, had given me their time and talent for many years. They all deserved more than a paycheck. I usually gave bonuses and food through the tour, but there was something more I could do for Jason.

I'd deal with people being mad. The right thing was more important.

"Don't worry about it," I said, feigning nonchalance. "I'll figure it out."

I did not, in fact, figure it out. Justice had gone pale when I told her of my decision, but thankfully, she didn't tell me off. Instead, she called Malia, who jumped in to help set up replacement auditions. It was going to be tight with how little time we had. No one was angry with me, which was surprising, but I could tell this might change everything about the tour.

Everything ground to a halt while we looked for someone else. We were able to tell the team they could have some well-deserved time with their families, but we all knew it was because we needed someone new.

And fast.

"So, what do you need me to do to organize auditions?" I asked the day we told everyone they could go home.

"Nothing," Malia said. "We've got it."

"But I did this. I should help fix it."

"Yeah, but you don't have to jump in and fix it," Justice added. "Everyone did need a break and you do too. When was the last day you *didn't* run two miles on a treadmill?"

I couldn't remember. "It's been a while."

"Get some rest," Malia said. "Maybe go see Barry."

My cheeks heated. I didn't expect Malia to remember Barry at all.

"I don't know if he's free—"

"For you? He will be."

"One day, I'm gonna need all the info about this Barry guy," Justice said. "But not today. I have other things to do. You go enjoy some time to yourself, Lila. We'll call you in about two days."

"O-okay," I said, shocked they were willing to let me go at all. I thought I'd be pulling all-nighters to fix this, even if it might kill me to do so.

And yet, once again, my new team surprised me.

The first thing I did when I left Malia's office was call Barry. It was early in the day, which meant he wasn't busy with the bar yet.

"Hello, sunshine," he greeted. "To what do I owe the pleasure of you calling me?"

He always talked to me like I was his whole world. I didn't know if I would ever get used to it.

"For once, it's good news. I have two days off. Mind if I come for a visit?"

"I would love that more than anything. But how do you have two days off?"

I winced and explained what happened with Jason, up to the moment Malia and Justice forced me into a break.

"So you *were* right that something was wrong. I think you did the right thing."

"I know I did, even if it's making a lot of other people's jobs harder. Why can't the right thing just feel *right*?"

"The world would be a different place if the right thing was easy, but it's hard, which makes it more incredible that you did it in the first place."

I rubbed my warm cheeks. "I don't know if I'll survive seeing you in person again if you say things like that."

"Hop on a plane and we can test it."

"Are you even free?"

"I have a family dinner planned, but I can cancel."

"Not with your parents, right?"

"No. Ruth and Tom host something every week. I don't always go, but they tend to beg me if I don't. They'll understand if I tell them something came up."

"No, you should join them."

"I'm not losing any time with you. Why don't you join me? We can enjoy the benefits of you being Rose a bit."

"Are you sure? I don't want to intrude."

"I doubt you will. They all invite different people each time. I swear, finding love made them all so *social*. It's weird."

"I'm sure they're happy."

"They are, and they'd be even happier to see you."

I bit my lip as I thought about it. I needed the distraction. If I thought too hard about the tour, I knew I would feel the weight of everything on me again.

"Let's do it," I said. "I'll hop on a plane right now."

"And I'll be waiting for you."

Barry

I waited in the airport, watching the exit closely. I was sure Rose would be walking out those doors, but I had prepared just in case Lila showed up.

But then I saw a flash of long, red hair and my heart skipped a beat. She looked just like everyone else. When I got out of my car to wave her over, a smile broke across her face. She burst into a run, slamming into me to give a tight hug.

It felt right to have her in my arms and I didn't want to let her go.

"Did you come in on a regular flight?" I asked.

"Still first class, but yes. No one even batted an eye at me. It helps that Lila is supposed to be practicing for her tour and that I let Juno join me."

"Where is she?"

"Flirting with a flight attendant. She knew you were waiting on me, so she let me go. And family dinners aren't her thing. She has free rein to do whatever she wants tonight."

"Can I also have that?"

"You'd do what you want anyway. But if you're talking about free rein with *me*, then yes."

"I'll hold you to that." I checked my watch. "We should go before Ruth starts blowing up my phone."

I opened the car door for her, which made her cheeks darken.

Now, *that* was one of my favorite things to see.

Rose and I were the last to arrive. I could see Tom's newer car parked next to Ruth's and Knox's.

When we walked in, the house smelled warm and inviting and the cool air was a welcome reprieve from the near-summer heat outside.

Ruth was cleaning off the dining room table when we walked in. "Oh, hi, Barry. Welcome in." When she saw Rose, she paused. "I didn't know you were bringing a guest."

"Is that okay?" I asked. "Normally, you say I can bring who I want to."

"Yeah, of course, I just thought it would be . . . never mind."

I opened my mouth to question her, but I was interrupted by Max running into the room.

"Uncle Barry's here!" he yelled. "And he has a friend!"

"Are you making sure they can hear you from space?" I asked, though I was smiling.

"I'm making sure Mom and Dad can. Sometimes they get into their own world and it's just gross." He turned to Rose. "Hi, I'm Max."

"Rose. It's nice to meet you."

"I'm Ruth," my sister greeted. "Sorry, I'm just not used to Barry having friends. It's nice to meet you."

She walked over and held out a hand to Rose, who shook it. I watched, hoping she wouldn't look too closely.

I should have known better.

Ruth had a pretty good poker face, but I saw her eyes linger on Rose's features for half a second too long. Maybe she didn't notice how much Rose looked like Lila, but I doubted it. She was far too observant.

"You know," Ruth started, "you look *so* familiar."

"I just have one of those faces," Rose replied, but her voice wavered.

"You two also like the same coffee shop," I replied. "Maybe you've seen each other there."

"That must be it," Ruth said, looking away. "And props to you for remembering the coffee shop I liked."

"You got caught there with Knox."

"So you *did* see that. Thanks for not mentioning it at the time. That whole situation was a nightmare."

"I bet," Rose replied. "It's nice to actually put faces to names. I've only really met Wilfred."

Ruth's jaw dropped. "She has? When?"

"She went with me to meet him," I explained. "Moral support and all that."

"Yeah, because you're so quick to ask for moral support," Ruth said. "Did you blackmail him to make him trust you? Be honest."

Rose laughed. "No. I just annoyed him into it."

"If only that worked for me, but then again, I've annoyed him in so many other ways that I think I should spare him. How did it go, meeting Wilfred?"

"Um, good," I said. "He was all right."

More than all right, but I didn't want her to know that just yet. Not when we were finally getting along.

"Uncle Barry, I hate to pull you away from your conversation," Max said, "but we have much to discuss."

"About?"

"Our favorite singer."

I paused and could practically feel Rose's eyes shoot to me.

"Oh, yeah."

"*Goodbye, Hello*? The future album of the year? *Amazing.* Easily the best thing she's ever put out. I can't stop listening to it, especially with the mystery man. I *need* to know who it is."

"Mystery man, huh?" Rose asked. I could hear her smile. "I wonder who he could be."

"Hopefully someone who makes her happy," Max said. "Are you a fan too?"

"Sometimes I am."

I nearly rolled my eyes. She knew *exactly* what she was doing.

"Barry!" Knox called as he entered the room. "Welcome in. I'm glad you could come. It feels a little empty since my parents couldn't make it."

"Why couldn't they make it?" I asked.

"They're having a date night."

"I planned it," Ruth added. "They deserve some time to themselves, especially with how hard they work."

"So it's just us nonparents. Except for Selena and Tom, of course."

Tom came into the room and I introduced Rose to him. He didn't have the same reaction Ruth had, thankfully, which meant we would make it through this dinner with her secret intact—as long as Ruth believed my explanation.

I thought she had, but as we sat to eat, I could see her constantly glancing over at Rose.

Max talked about Lila, which meant Rose was too busy tossing teasing looks my way to notice Ruth's attention. Apparently, she found the way I talked about Lila with Max hilarious.

But eventually, as Max talked about how happy Lila sounded, she leaned into my ear.

"Can I do something?" Rose asked.

"What?"

"I was going to offer for Lila to meet him."

"That might not be the best idea."

"He's such a sweet kid, Barry." She nearly pouted, which meant she would get anything she wanted.

"Fine, but I'll offer it," I whispered back, "and say I know Lila from the bar."

"Good idea."

I looked up, only to see Ruth watching us with narrowed eyes.

"Um, Max," I said, clearing my throat. "I do have something kind of cool to share."

"What's that?"

"I might have a . . . distant connection to Lila Wilde."

He choked on his drink. "What?"

"Yeah," Tom said, his eyebrow raised. "What?"

"I met her once through my job. And I . . . might be able to have you meet her sometime."

"You *what*?" Max nearly yelled. "How could you keep this from me?"

"I had to make sure she would be willing to, and I wanted to surprise you."

"Oh my God, yes!"

"You really know her?" Selena asked, her eyes wide.

"I do."

"C-can I meet her too?"

"Of course."

"You're always full of surprises," Ruth said, and I glanced over at her. The smile on her face was more curious than anything else. I knew Lila would have to play this perfectly if she wanted to escape with her secret untouched.

But Rose's smile was so wide that I didn't regret it.

"No one else can know," I said. "But I figure if Tom trusts you, then I can too."

"You're lucky I've learned how to keep secrets," Max said.

"Where did you learn that?" Selena asked. "I didn't teach that to you."

"Yeah, but I see what you do when you're hiding something. Diversion is really easy."

Selena sighed. "Yeah, that was gonna happen eventually."

"How about tomorrow?" I asked.

The house nearly exploded with everyone sharing their plans. Ruth mentioned she would bring Lynn, Knox's mom, and Max and Selena talked about what they would say. I leaned back and glanced at Rose, raising an eyebrow and giving her one more chance to back out.

But she looked just as excited as everyone else.

Chapter Twenty-Eight

Rose

Barry drummed on the steering wheel as we drove back to his place.

"Nervous?" I asked. "Or excited?"

I knew I was. It had been too long since I'd met fans in person. I'd been working so much that I almost forgot what it was like to see them. In the sea of the angry ones online, I was glad to see that some liked the album.

"I think my sister might figure you out."

My mood instantly deflated. "What? Why? *How?*"

"She's smart. Way too smart. And I saw the way she kept looking at you at dinner."

"I mean, people look at me all the time."

"Ruth is not most people. Plus, she saw us whispering before we brought up Lila."

"What are the odds that she'll figure out we're one person, though?"

"I have no idea," he said. "But I know it's risky. You can cancel if you think this is a bad idea."

"And disappoint Max? No way. Do you think the explanation of the coffee shop helped?"

"Maybe."

"I could even mention the day I saw her as Lila to throw her off the trail even more."

"That might work, but be careful. Be fully Lila tomorrow. She may not be watching every second, but she picks up on stuff."

"I'll do my best. I've been doing this for over ten years. I've got this. I'll even have Juno come to tell me if I'm acting too much like Rose."

That seemed to help. His drumming slowed. "I just don't want to ruin this for you. This privacy you have, despite your fame, is . . . incredible."

"Thank you, but I think it'll be okay. Ruth will officially meet Lila Wilde tomorrow, not just running into her at Movers and Shakers. She'll be busy with that."

"You're probably right," he said as we pulled up to the bar.

All thoughts of our plans for the next day dropped when we saw how hectic things were. People were in line, more so than I had ever seen.

"Audrey was right about the dance nights," he said. "They're always this busy now."

"Do you need to go check on things?"

"Yeah, I should. Will you be okay in my apartment?"

"Of course I will, especially since you bought me my own chair and everything."

Barry laughed and pulled me into him, his lips slotting over mine. My heart could have stopped, but he let me go soon after.

"I'll walk you up there," he offered.

I nodded and got out of the car. As he opened the back door, I was already thinking about what to do with my free time, but then two people were in the doorway, as if waiting on us.

The woman had black hair and thick eyeliner. She looked catlike in this light. The guy with blond hair I dimly recognized as the dancing bartender.

"You have some explaining to do," Liam said.

The woman elbowed him hard, eyes on me.

"Liam, Audrey," Barry said slowly. "Do you guys need help with the bar?"

"No, we have employees on everything," Audrey said. "And I guess we can talk about this when you don't have a guest."

"Rose was just going up to my apartment," he said. "So we can talk work."

"It's not work related," Audrey said. "But we *do* have questions."

"I'll just go," I said. "See you upstairs."

I walked off but stopped around the corner, half listening to see if it was bad news.

"When were you going to tell us you *recorded* a song with a certain famous woman?" Audrey asked.

I froze. Technically, this was about a *version* of me. This was the second time Barry was confronted about something with Lila in one night and I owed him a major thank you for all of this.

"Why do you think that's me?" he asked.

"Because we know how you sound when you sing," Liam said. "And we've listened to it a hundred times to make sure. It's you. There's no way it's not."

I heard him curse.

"Barry," Audrey said, "why didn't you put your name on this? It's awesome!"

"I didn't feel the need to."

"But you sound great. You could make more."

"I have a job to do here. I can't juggle both songwriting and this. You both saw how much I wasn't here when I was working on this album."

"And the bar ran smoothly."

"The bar is my responsibility. I refuse to shirk it off, no matter how much I enjoyed it."

"It was only for a few weeks," Audrey said. "We handled it. What if you got another chance like this?"

"I *don't* have another chance like this. Guys, it's fine."

But my mind was spinning. He *could* have another chance. He could step in as my rhythm guitarist while we practiced. He would fit.

Barry didn't want the fame and he wouldn't have to leave full time.

The idea was perfect. I knew Malia and Justice's process of holding auditions and dealing with the legalities of a contract would have us stopped for far too long. There had been talk of having Jason come back for practice, but his mom had taken a turn for the worse, so he couldn't.

I just needed to convince him of my idea, which would be hard, considering how much he loved the bar.

I thought I would have more time to come up with a valid argument, but Barry rounded the corner.

"O-oh," I said, rubbing the back of my neck. "I thought you were working."

"I didn't hear the door up the stairs shut. Did you hear all of that?"

"Sorry. I figured it was about Lila, so it was *kind* of okay."

"It was, but you don't need to worry. They don't know anything."

"I wasn't worried about that. I trust you. It's just . . . you *do* have another chance, you know."

"For songwriting?"

"For . . . something in music. My tour needs a guitarist."

He immediately shook his head. "I can't—"

"Not full time. I know you can't leave things here and I won't ask that of you. But you can help us practice while we look for someone. Maybe only for a few weeks."

He considered it for a long, hopeful moment, but then shook his head again. "I can't leave. I'm sorry, but I can't."

"But your employees just said they can handle the bar. What does it hurt to ask? It's not for forever. I won't pressure you if you truly don't want to do it—"

"I *do* want to do it."

"Then bring it up with them. What's the harm in trusting your team and letting them take care of you for once?"

His lips pressed together and then he let out a long sigh. "I'll ask. I can't promise anything."

"That's enough," I said, smiling. "Thank you, Barry."

"Go upstairs. I'm going to make sure they're really okay."

"I'll talk to Juno about tomorrow."

I called her after Barry shut the door behind him. She answered on the fifth ring, which was late for her.

"Hey, what do you need?"

"I hope I'm not interrupting anything," I began.

"Not at this very second."

"Did it go well with the flight attendant?"

"Very. Now, what's up?"

"I'm going to meet some people in Nashville tomorrow and it might be good to have my bodyguard there."

"Yeah, I'll be free."

"And also, it's Barry's family. And I've met all of them as Rose."

"Wow. Um, is that a good idea?"

"Not really, but Barry's nephew is so sweet and loves Lila. I don't want to let him down, but I need to watch myself closely and be sure Rose doesn't slip tomorrow."

"I can help with that."

"And watch Ruth. She's apparently very smart."

"Watch you and a woman named Ruth. Got it. I'll come and get you tomorrow."

"Thank you. For both doing this and not lecturing me about how this could be a bad idea."

"You'll have Barry with you, so he'll help too. Besides, you deserve to do some things you like. I know that now."

I couldn't help the smile that bloomed on my face as I thanked her once again. I let her get back to her night and I worked on relaxing.

And that turned into songwriting. I was too inspired being in Barry's home in a city of music. I was still thinking of that kiss from earlier, the one that was far too short.

I was jotting a few lyrics in my notebook when Barry walked in the door.

"So they weren't lying," he said, "they don't need me."

"Did you ask them about coming to LA?"

"Not yet. They might have the bar under control, but they were incredibly busy. What are you up to?"

"Writing a song," I admitted.

"Aren't you supposed to be on a break?"

"My inspiration doesn't take those, unfortunately."

"What are you writing?"

"Something I don't think I can ever put in a song. The lyrics are . . . horny."

"They're *what*? Let me see."

I handed over my notebook, cheeks warming.

I didn't write sexy stuff since my fans were younger, and I doubted I would change that. Some people *still* complained that I'd started cursing in my work. This was only for me and I hoped Barry didn't think it was too much.

"You should definitely make a song out of this."

"Really?"

"For one thing, it's great. And for another, I wouldn't mind the world knowing that you feel this way for someone, especially if it's me."

"Of course it's you." I rolled my eyes. "You're the one who gave me that kiss in the car. It was only like a second, but it was enough."

"If you come here, sunshine, I'll finish the job."

And just like that, I was a woman who followed orders. My notebook was forgotten on the counter the second I stepped into his space and pressed my lips against his again.

In seconds, I was desperate to have more of him. His woodsy, warm scent enveloped me, flushing all my senses with his presence.

My hands moved down his broad shoulders, feeling the taut muscles flexing underneath my touch. His mouth opened in a groan. I deepened the kiss, my tongue grazing his, and he pressed into me farther.

My skin was on fire, lit by him and him alone. He moved off of me only to slide his hand to grip my ass, pulling my hips flush with his.

"Is hair still off the table?" he asked. "Or was that just a Lila thing?"

"T-the second one," I said, nearly gasping for air. "You can do whatever you like to me now."

Barry brought his mouth back to mine, his hand running through my hair and grazing my scalp. I let out a gasp. That part of me was sensitive, a fact I'd never known before since it was used to the abuse from being under a wig so much. I was pressed into the cool counter, the sharp edge digging into my back.

"B-bedroom?" I managed to ask.

Then suddenly, I was there, being flopped onto the bed by the man who had my whole attention. His mouth returned to me as he settled between my open legs.

I was ready for this. So ready it almost hurt.

"Fuck, sunshine," he said into my neck. "You don't know what you do to me."

I gasped as he tugged down my shirt. His mouth found my nipple, teasing it gently with his tongue.

All thoughts were lost to sensation. His other hand slid past the waistband of my sleep shorts, finding my aching core.

He made a noise when he touched my slick folds and I wanted to tell him it was all for him. I couldn't, though, because I lost the ability to speak once his finger dragged across my clit.

I didn't often have time for myself with the tour going on, but sometimes I remembered that night when he'd given me the best orgasm of my life. This felt like it could pale in comparison.

I jerked into him, wanting more, and he sucked on my nipple harder and pressed his fingers in tighter.

"Yes," I said. "Just like that."

I was soaring, pleasure building up inside of me, making my toes curl. I arched off the bed, feeling myself break as fire erupted from my core and spread through me. Gasping, I was consumed until I was only a puddle in Barry's arms.

"Was it good?" he asked.

"Y-yeah," I said. "So good. Better than last time."

His lips came down on mine again, and I angled my hips up. I could feel the details of his cock as he pressed against me, despite the jeans he wore.

I wanted him inside of me. I *needed* him inside of me. Last time, I was too tired to take anything further, but I was wide awake now.

"Fuck me," I said.

"Are you sure?"

"Very." I pressed into him again and dragged my hands under his shirt. I only got a touch of warm skin before he pulled back and took off his shirt. "You're not wasting any time."

"With you in my bed? Absolutely not."

His pants were next, but I stood as he went for his underwear.

"I want to do this part," I said, placing my hands on the band.

"You can do whatever you want."

I hooked the elastic in my fingers and dragged it down his toned legs. His cock sprung free and my mouth went dry imagining it inside of me.

When I straightened, his eyes were dark. "Your turn," he said. He gently pushed me back down on the bed and grabbed at my shorts, pulling them off my body. Once that was done, my shirt was next.

"You're beautiful, you know that?"

"And you are too. How did I get so lucky?"

"How did *I* get so lucky?"

I kissed him, needing to feel him on me again. He hovered over me as he maneuvered his cock right at the entrance of my pussy, ready to push inside of me.

"We should get a condom," he said.

"I have an IUD and I get tested. I don't have anything."

"Neither do I, but I don't usually do this without other forms of protection."

"You can get one," I said. "But I would also love to feel you bare inside of me."

His eyes darkened as his mouth came down on mine again. "Only with you," he muttered into my lips, "would I do this."

I hooked my legs around him, bringing him closer and moving him slightly inside of me.

My core clenched, desperate to feel more. He slowly slid in the rest of the way. I gasped, breaking the kiss as my head fell back on the pillow.

"Are you okay?"

"More than okay," I said.

"Good," he replied. "Because I don't think I can hold back anymore."

He pulled out and slammed back in. His hips jerked as his cock sank inside me repeatedly. He tried to kiss me again, but our lips barely touched as both of us were lost in how good and right this felt.

There was nothing as good as this, I decided. Nothing. I was floating again, my body enjoying each of his thrusts. I could feel the heat building.

"I'm gonna . . ." I trailed off, lost in sensation.

"Do it, sunshine. Come on my cock."

And I did. I let out a near yell as my vision whited out. Pure pleasure danced up my spine and took over my brain.

"Fuck," he said, and his thrusts became erratic. I felt him come just as my orgasm faded away.

"You're good at sex, singing, and guitar," I said as my mind came back online. "Is there anything you're not good at?"

"Not thinking of you."

Barry

While I wanted nothing more than a round two with Rose the next morning, I didn't get a chance because she had to spend the day getting ready to meet Max and everyone else as Lila. It took a long time for her to become a completely different person, and while I knew why, I also wanted more time with her.

The plan was to meet in the middle of the day at Tom and Selena's place. Tom wasn't in much of the public eye, making his place safer than any of ours. Despite it being a weekday, everyone made the time to see Lila Wilde—other plans didn't matter when she was involved.

I was sent to wait with everyone while she arrived. Rose told me it would make us look less close.

"Whew," Max said, nearly dancing on his feet. "What do I say to not look like a fool?"

"She's nice," I promised. "Just like any other person. You don't need to worry about everything you say to her."

"Yeah, but I want to tell her I've listened to all of her songs. Is that too much?"

"I don't think so."

Tom watched from where he was sitting on the couch. He and I hadn't talked yet, but I was sure he was wondering why I was letting it slip that I knew Lila, especially since I'd been so tight-lipped about it before.

I wondered when he was going to corner me to ask all of his questions, but Selena walked into the room, her face looking exactly like Max's, and that took his attention.

"How do I not be weird?" she asked.

"I just asked that! Well, kind of," Max said. "And it's no use. We're both about to be *so* weird."

Tom tried to placate the both of them, but as time went on, Selena and Max only seemed to grow more nervous, as if they could possibly mess this up.

They didn't know it yet, but I doubted this would be their only chance to see her. They'd already charmed Lila when she was someone else.

Ruth walked in, hair down, chatting animatedly with Lynn. "And she has so many cool lyrics," she said. "I love everything she's written."

"I'll have to ask what her favorite song is," Lynn said. "And I'll start there."

"Thank you for coming, even if you don't know her all that well."

"You like her, though; that's what matters to me."

I couldn't resist smiling at the two of them. It was nice seeing Ruth so comfortable with Lynn. It was the connection she never had with Mom.

We saw Juno's blacked-out car pull up and a hush fell over all of us. Even *my* heart pounded, but for different reasons.

Lila got out of the car, all dark hair and sunglasses. From far away, hardly anyone would recognize her.

When she walked in the door, the sunglasses came off and she smiled at everyone.

"Hi," she said warmly. "It's good to meet you."

Her makeup was heavier than usual, casting a stark difference between her and Rose. Her voice was also clear and loud, adding another thing that set her apart from her alter ego. I let out a breath of relief as Ruth smiled with no sign of suspicion.

Rose had been right. She *had* been doing this long enough to know exactly what to do.

"Hi!" Max was the first to speak. "I literally can't believe this is real."

Tom laughed. "Don't forget to introduce yourself."

"Right! I'm Max, and this is my mom." He dragged Selena by her arm.

"Hello," she said weakly.

"Hi. I don't bite. I promise."

Selena let out a mix of a laugh and a gasp.

"It's nice to *meet* you for the first time," Ruth said with a wink.

For a second, I cursed. Was this Ruth's way of hinting that she knew?

"Oh yeah," Lila said, not missing a beat and winking back. "We've definitely never met before."

How was she not freaking out? How did she not see what Ruth was hinting at?

But then Ruth caught onto my expression and she mouthed *the bar*.

Oh. They were talking about the day Ruth and Lila had met. It had nothing to do with Rose at all. I nodded, trying to remember that Lila knew exactly what she was doing.

"Hi," Lynn said. "I'm Lynn."

"She's my boyfriend's mom that I steal sometimes."

"I've heard your songs on the radio at my salon," Lynn said. "You're incredible. I haven't listened to any of it in my own time, though, so you'll have to tell me your favorite place to start."

"Thank you. I would say my oldest album."

"I totally agree," Max said. "By the way, it's so cool that Uncle Barry knows you. How did that happen?"

"I was on the run from paparazzi and he was at the wrong place at the wrong time." She smiled at me and she was a mirror image of Rose for a split second.

"We've been *friends* ever since," I said, but I could already see Ruth looking between us.

Considering she'd just seen me with Rose last night, I knew it was better to clarify our status so she didn't get nosy about the two women in my life.

"That's so cool," Max said. "And also, *Goodbye, Hello* is *amazing*. Especially your mysterious singer."

"Oh yeah, he's a friend . . ." She trailed off. "I mean, not a friend. He's more."

It was a genius move, playing off the man who had sung that song as someone more. I knew it was only to cover herself, but it kicked my heart into gear.

"Could you maybe sign mine?" Max asked. "Oh! And the record my dad gave me. We really bonded over you."

"Of course," Lila said. "Does anyone have a pen?"

She spent time signing things and getting to know Max. I thought we were in the clear until Ruth and Tom found me.

"So . . . friends, huh?" Her voice was light, but I froze anyway.

"Yep."

"And Rose?"

"More than friends."

"Do they know about each other?" Tom asked.

"Of course. We all communicate very well."

She nodded slowly, but her lips were pressed together. "You were really torn up about Lila, though."

"In the end, she was right. Doing all of this would be too much."

"But—"

"Ruth," Tom began, "I trust Barry to be telling the truth."

"He's acting weird. I've noticed you've been glancing over at me. Did I do something wrong or something?"

"No," I rushed to say. My brain finally came up with a reason. "You're just also a fan of Lila, so I'm watching your reaction because I want to make sure you're happy."

She blinked. "Really?"

No. And I felt like shit for lying. I *did* care about her reaction and wanted her to have fun, but I was more invested in her not figuring out Rose's secret.

"Come on," Tom urged, "we have Lila Wilde here for only a little bit. Let's not worry about Barry and focus on her being here."

"God, you're right. I need to get out of my own head. Sorry, Barry. I just wouldn't be a true girl's girl if I saw you with two women and didn't ask."

"I wouldn't dare hurt any of them. Trust me, lines have been drawn in the sand."

"Keep them that way," she said. "Both Rose and Lila are nice. I wouldn't want them to get hurt."

"Me either," I said. "I promise you that."

She seemed pleased and walked over to have Lila sign something. I let out a breath of relief.

Lila chatted with everyone, including getting caught up in a conversation with Lynn about hair care. I lingered on the sidelines.

"So, everything work out like you hoped?" Tom asked. I had completely forgotten about telling him anything that had happened.

"Yeah, I'm happy with it."

"Good. That's all we wanted for you, Barry."

When we got back, it was late, and Rose went upstairs, saying she had a song idea she wanted to write down. As much as I wanted to go and help her, there was something else I needed to do.

I'd promised that I would ask Liam and Audrey if they would be okay with me going to LA for a few weeks. I doubted it, considering the line that spilled out into the street. I'd only left them for a few days before, and even then, it had been nerve-racking to come back.

Audrey was heatedly discussing something with a bouncer, her brow furrowed. When I saw her expression, I knew nothing good could be happening.

"What's going on?"

She looked up, mouth still pressed into a thin line. "Some woman was way too drunk. She got angry when we cut her off. Don't worry about it. I have it taken care of."

"Still, I—"

"It's all good," she said, shaking her head. "Now, what did you come over here for? Do you need me for something?"

"Yes, but more for a talk. I need you and Liam for this."

"All right. Let me get him."

"Where is he? I didn't see him at the bar."

"He put one of the new guys you hired on it. The cooler *desperately* needed organizing." She waved for me to follow her, but I had to take a second. The cooler had been on my to-do list since I returned from LA. I hadn't even asked Liam to work on it.

Was I paying them enough? Maybe they needed another raise.

"Oh, hey!" Liam said, a bright smile on his face as he popped out of the walk-in cooler. "I thought I heard you come in."

"I can't believe you're not dancing tonight."

"And miss out on being in a literal cooler? I'm good. Besides, Jeremy's incredible anyway."

I'd known he would be. I was good at sniffing out new hires who would be perfect for the team.

And I wouldn't be able to do that in LA. *Fuck.* Just another reason that made me have to stay.

"I believe you have something to bring up with us?" Audrey asked.

Shit. Right. The thing I'd been dreading.

Clearing my throat, I said, "So maybe you were right."

"You'll have to be more specific," Liam said. "There're a lot of things Audrey's right about."

She preened under the praise. "You know me so well."

I sighed, knowing she'd be like Ruth and not make admitting this easy at all. "You were right about me having another chance at *something* in LA."

Both of them froze for a moment. "What is it?" Audrey asked.

"Someone . . . famous needs a fill-in guitarist. It's not a permanent thing and it's only for a few weeks, which is longer than I think I can leave for."

Audrey and Liam glanced at each other. I wondered if they were working on how to tell me no. I had stuff to do anyway. I could probably work on adding more bouncers to the staff or maybe look into hiring another person to help Audrey with clerical work. They did a lot, but I couldn't expect them to do it all.

Audrey pulled out the walkie-talkie that she only used to communicate with the security staff.

"Hey, Joe?" she asked.

"Yeah?" his deep voice answered.

"Can you be sure Barry Murray doesn't come back for a few weeks?"

I opened my mouth to ask her what the hell she was doing, but she put up a finger.

"Uh, sure. Why?"

"Because he has something he absolutely has to take care of in LA, and knowing him, he'll try to find a reason to stay."

"Oh, is it that thing you wanted him to do? That you said he was being a stubborn ass about?"

"Yep. And I was right. Go figure."

Joe laughed. "I'll keep a lookout for him. You'll have to deal with his wrath, though."

"Oh, I'm prepared." She put away the walkie-talkie and finally looked at me. "Sorry, boss. But you're kicked out. It's for your own good."

"Am I being pranked?" I asked.

"Nope." Liam shook his head. "I'm the one who pranks. She is stone-cold serious."

"Not to say I told you so," Audrey added, "but I told you so. We already had a plan for this. Now get your ass to LA and enjoy yourself. We'll call you if we need you."

Chapter Twenty-Nine

After dinner, I eagerly awaited Barry's return from talking to Audrey and Liam. I meant to change out of the wig, but I was too busy writing a song about spending time with a family you find rather than the one you're born with.

It didn't take him long to get back, though. I was only through writing the first verse when he opened the door.

"Oh, hey. That didn't take long. What did they say?"

"They kicked me out of the bar," he grumbled. "Those assholes."

"What do you mean they kicked you out?"

"I only halfway mentioned I was helping a friend with something in LA when Audrey called security and told them not to let me back in."

I couldn't help but laugh. "I think I owe her some flowers."

"She's too much like Ruth. If those two met, they'd either kill each other or plot world domination."

"So, you can go to LA?"

"Yes, I can. But I'll be on call in case they need anything, which they probably will in the end."

"That's totally fine. You can step away whenever you need to. And we'll make it work if you have to come back. I promise."

"All right, then, I guess I'm packing tonight. What do I even wear to be a stand-in guitarist?"

"Comfortable clothes. It's hard work. Here, I'll help you."

Song momentarily forgotten, we went to his room and I helped him pack. We spent the night talking about the tour and what he could expect.

I could tell he was nervous up until he fell asleep.

Sleep evaded me, too, and I went over exactly how I was going to tell everyone about our new addition. Near midnight, Mom texted me.

Mom: So, no one else knows?

I hadn't talked to her in a few weeks, and while I hated to admit it, not having her talk my ear off about my secret identity helped ease my worries.

Dad had called to check in, but once he found out that I was busy, he was quick to tell me he would give me space to work. It all seemed too good to be true. He had to be busy with something that he forgot about. Or maybe there was something else up his sleeve.

Rose: No. No one knows.

She didn't answer and I felt terrible for the fact that I was almost grateful.

I finally fell asleep early into the morning, and when we woke, the plane was ready. While we were driving to the airport, my phone lit up with a call from Malia.

"I know you're supposed to be relaxing," she said, and I heard a smile in her voice, "but I have something you need to hear."

"Is it about the new guitarist? Because I have news for you."

"No, not at all, but what's the news?"

"Barry agreed to step in so we can continue practicing while we find someone else."

"That's fantastic. Justice will be so relieved."

"Yeah, we're really lucky he could step away from his other job."

"I'll be sure to give him my thanks in person. Now, enough about work. I need you to listen to Blaze's new album."

"It already came out?"

"Yes. He surprise-dropped it. And it's . . . hilarious, honestly. But I wanted to tell you first because you're mentioned in it. A lot."

I'd been dreading whatever he was planning, but I knew I couldn't stop him. He had Mia behind him and I wondered if they were working on something devastating. I didn't think they were going for comedy, however. "Why's it so funny?"

"It's terrible," she said. "The worst album I've ever heard."

"Really? But Mia produced it."

"And you can tell she's a PR agent trying to make music. Give it a listen. It'll brighten your day."

"I will," I said. "Thanks for the warning."

We got off the phone moments later, and I could see Barry watching me.

"I heard Mia's name. That doesn't usually mean good news."

"This time it is. We have an album to listen to. A very bad one, apparently."

Blaze Matthews FINALLY Releases His Side of the Story
. . . And It's Bad

By Perez Adder

We were all waiting for Blaze Matthews to release something detailing what went down with Lila Wilde. According to him, it takes two to ruin a relationship and she seemed happy pushing the blame onto him.

At midnight, Blaze dropped his album as a complete surprise, and fans clamored to listen to it. Since it was produced by most of the same team that made Lila's music, we all had an expectation of quality. But Blaze is made to be the muse, it seems, because those lyrics do NOT work. He whines about how Lila found someone else, how he did everything for her and got nothing in return.

Now, I'm not the biggest fan of Lila myself, but even I can admit that SHE wrote her own songs. Blaze didn't do EVERYTHING for her.

He was in a position to turn the tables and make everyone see his side of the story, and unfortunately, it looks like he fumbled the bag.

5642 Comments

H8terfister69: Lmao we knew this would happen eventually

BuzzBuzz: This doesn't make sense! He helped her with ALL of her original stuff! How could his album be so bad?

RealLilaFan247: Because SHE wrote it, you doofus.

NomChompy: Ah, the garbage taking itself out. Perfect.

The album played on the plane while Barry and I laughed until we couldn't breathe.

It was truly awful. It was all the worst parts of my old songs—the repetitive lyrics and the synthetic pop beats combined with Blaze's pitchy singing—making it more of a comedy routine rather than an emotional album. He tried to drop mean one-liners about me in every song, but paired with his voice, they all sounded cringey.

There were tears in my eyes from it. When he'd threatened to release an album, I knew it would have been bad for me if the album were *good*. But this? This was the best-case scenario.

"He tried to get picked up when I did," I said when we finally managed to calm down. "I knew he was a bad singer, but I thought he would at least take some lessons. Or that Mia would be able to whip him into shape."

"It just proves that she never made your songs good. Only you did."

Warmth spread through my chest. "Yeah, I think you're right."

As we got close to landing, I asked if he could put his hair in a hat. I hated to even bring it up, because I knew he wasn't a fan of hiding, and yet he didn't complain as I tucked his long strands away.

And when he looked totally different, it was time to disembark. As usual, people were dying for photos of me. Juno had been relaxing for most of the time, preparing for the chaos of LA.

When we got out, it was definitely that. There were yells of Lila's name, asking for my opinion on Blaze's album, or if I was seeing someone else. Photos were snapped of the three of us as soon as we got off the plane until we were driving down the road. Barry grabbed my hand the second we were alone.

"It's so good to be back," I muttered. "There's more security at the practice arena. And we'll take the long way to throw them off the trail."

Barry's hand didn't leave mine and his eyes were on the windows.

A terrible thought hit me.

"You can always tell me if this is too much," I offered softly.

His eyes finally settled on me. "It's not too much."

"Your grip on my hand says otherwise."

Barry's eyes trailed down to our intertwined hands. "Sunshine, I'm holding your hand because I *want* to, not because I'm worried about some strangers I don't know. I'm more worried about how they make *you* feel."

"But it's so hectic. No one can handle it."

"I can, and I will. And I'll do it without complaining once."

"Why?"

"Because I want to, the same way *you* want to give everything to those around you. I'm going to return the favor, and then some."

His hand squeezed mine, and for a brief moment, I thought he might not be real. How could one person want to do so much for me? How could he want to be in this loud, wild life I had?

"Thank you," I managed to say.

"You don't need to thank me. Just let me do it." He gave a half smile and my heart nearly stopped.

I could have written a song about that moment if only I'd had more time. But we pulled into the venue and I had to force myself to focus on what we were about to do.

"Ready to see behind-the-scenes of a tour?"

"I am. Let's do this."

"Don't worry about what they think of you. They're all nice people."

"You know I won't worry about what they think." But his eyes roamed over the building.

"Do you need a minute?" I asked. "I know these kinds of things can be overwhelming."

"It's not overwhelming. It's just . . . you know how it feels when you've somehow managed to do something you dreamed of?"

I had that feeling when I played on my first tour. "Yes."

"That's what I'm feeling right now. It's not nerves, it's . . ."

"Excitement. The purest form of excitement."

"Yeah. That." He took one more moment to look, but then turned to me. "All right. I'm ready."

As we walked in, the band was mingling around their instruments. They were all relieved to see a new guitarist was temporarily joining so we could be sure that we had every part of this right. I only had time to give them his name before we practiced all of the songs for the new setlist.

Barry blended in, knowing every part of every song. We sounded perfect together, as if Jason were here.

"That's it," Justice called as we finished up. "That's the sound I was missing!"

She ran over to me, eyes on Barry the whole time. "Where did you find this guy?"

"Barry? He's a friend of mine."

"He knows *every* one of your songs," she said. "He fits in like he's really on the tour."

"It's only temporary. He, unfortunately, has a life back in Nashville."

She sighed. "They always do. Don't worry, though. We have some interviews set up in ten minutes."

"Oh, okay. Do you need me to go?"

"Definitely."

"Then I need to go say bye to Barry. Give me five minutes."

"Of course. I'll grab Juno."

When I approached Barry, he was talking to the drummer, Steven, who was telling him about the best restaurants in LA.

"Hey," I said. "Sorry to interrupt, but I have to go do interviews."

"Do you need me to go as well?"

I shook my head. "It'll be boring. You're welcome to hang out here or I'll send a car for you."

"I'll get to know these guys," he said. "They're going to a local dive bar and I'd love to see how another one is run."

"Are you sure?"

"I like them. If I'm only doing this for a few weeks, I might as well enjoy it as much as I can."

I smiled and told him to have fun. He got to live his dream for a bit. I would let him do it however he wanted to.

I got home from the dive bar around nine. It had been fun, but it wasn't *my* bar. The company was excellent, though. I didn't mention my usual profession solely because I didn't want them looking me up, but I was very tempted to.

Lila walked into her mansion a half hour later and fell right onto the couch, wig still on. "I'm fucking exhausted."

"How did the auditions go?"

She heaved out a sigh. "Some of them were good, but none of them knew the material. This is going to be an uphill battle. I'm so tired I can't even take the wig off at this point."

"Has this happened before?"

"Usually after a show. Or a bunch of interviews. I'll be fine. I've slept in it before."

"Fine is not good enough," I said.

"Barry, I literally can't get up right now."

"That's fine. I'll take it off for you.

Her couch was so big that I could sit next to her lying down. When I did, she sat up only long enough to move her head to my lap.

"Can't get up, huh?"

"Shut up. I'm only moving so I can get cuddles and to see if you'll actually take the wig off for me."

"I'm a man of my word."

"It's a whole process."

"I'm guessing wig and cap. Did you use glue?"

"How the hell do you know how wigs work? Are you about to tell me you wear a wig too?"

I laughed. "No, but I looked it up once I learned the truth. It seemed like it would come in handy."

Taking my time, I removed the layers of Lila, careful not to tug her beautiful copper hair. Once the strands were free, I ran my hands through it, rubbing her scalp.

"Thank you," she muttered. "I needed that. Sometimes it restricts my ability to think."

"Happy to help," I said lowly. Knowing I was the only one who knew her like this, who could take off her mask and return her to who she was, made my heart skip a beat. "We should get your makeup off too."

"Why?"

"So I can see your freckles again."

She laughed softly. "Fine. I'll get up to do it, but only because the relief of getting the damn wig off added ten years to my life."

She got up to head to the master bathroom. I followed, waiting patiently as she scrubbed her face with cleanser.

"I really need to make a routine of getting un-Lila-ed every day." She wet her face and scrubbed all the soap off. "Shit, I didn't grab a towel."

There was one on the farthest wall, which would feel like a mile away to someone with a soaking wet face.

"I have one," I said, walking to her. "I'll do it."

I pulled her into my arms and helped her dry her skin, but my eyes were stuck on her freckles.

"What?" she asked. "Did I miss something?"

"No." My fingers brushed across one of them, and then another. "You're just beautiful."

Her cheeks reddened under my touch. "I'm supposed to be tired," she grumbled. "But now you're waking me up."

"Should I apologize?"

"No. Just kiss me."

I captured her lips with mine. The world melted away, leaving only her. There weren't two sides—Rose or Lila—when she was like this. There was just my sunshine, the woman who made breathy noises when I moved my lips to her neck.

"You're going to spoil me," she said.

"As much as I can," I replied before kissing her again. I wanted to promise every single one of my days, but I couldn't.

Eventually, I'd go back to the bar and she'd set out on an unforgettable tour with her new rhythm guitarist. We had a lot of time before we would be alone together again, but it didn't matter. I had her now.

I deepened the kiss, knowing it was just the two of us and we were free of any of the burdens that weighed us down. At this moment, I wasn't going back to the bar anytime soon and she didn't live a double life, one of which I couldn't be with.

Pulling her closer, I felt the cotton leggings and tank top she'd been practicing in. My hand moved to where I cupped her ass, bringing her impossibly closer. My tongue met hers and she sucked in a breath.

"Should we go to the bedroom?" I asked.

"That's too far away," she said.

And it was. This mansion was too huge, and too empty.

"We can stay right here then," I said. "Even if it's uncomfortable."

She nodded and brought her lips back to mine. I lifted her onto the marble countertop and her hips jerked down on my hardness.

"I think I like that," she said breathlessly. "Being moved around like I'm nothing."

"Really?" I asked. "So, if I just threw you over my shoulder one day . . ."

"We'll *definitely* have to try it out."

I noted that for later and took off her shirt, moving my lips down. I thought about taking her pert nipples into my mouth, but I was craving something else on my tongue.

As I grazed her stomach, she tensed.

"I might be sweaty from practice," she said.

"I don't care."

"But it might smell."

"I still don't care. You might be insecure about it, but I promise you I won't notice. I'll only care about making you feel good."

She blinked as if she'd never heard those words before. "Okay, but only if you're sure."

I was. I went downward, pulling off her leggings and underwear. I knelt on the ground as I brought her pussy to my face.

I hadn't lied. I didn't fucking care about the smell. I cared about the way she tasted, the way she gasped when I touched her for the first time, how wet she was for me.

Sucking on her clit, I listened for the sounds of her pleasure. I was rewarded with gasps and moans, her head thrown back.

Rose's thighs tightened around my neck, moving me in closer. Any more and I would have suffocated, but I didn't mind. It would have been the perfect way to go. Her body shuddered and her hips moved as she chased exactly what she needed. I knew she came when she nearly screamed and fluid rushed out of her. I drank in the moment because there was nothing more perfect than this.

"Oh my God," she said as words finally came back to her. "I can't believe we did that in the bathroom."

"We can find all sorts of places to do this and more."

"I hope you're talking about doing some of that now. I think it's very unfair that I'm naked and you're not."

"Say no more, sunshine."

My clothes came off in a flash and I was back on her again, hips hovering over hers as I pressed my desperate cock into her entrance. I pushed in, feeling her tightness surround me. She gasped against my lips as I bottomed out inside of her.

The world melted away as I was lost in her. Sex hadn't felt like this before, not with anyone, and it never would again. Rose would be ever-present in my mind and I couldn't wait to have more memories to be tortured with.

I moved, unable to hold back any longer. I rammed into her, feeling her pussy flex and flutter around me.

"I don't know how long I can last."

"Fuck lasting long. I want you to come."

My movements grew rougher and she stopped talking, only moans escaping her open mouth. I felt heat building from everywhere as I tumbled toward an orgasm.

She was close too. I could tell by the way her body moved under mine. I bit my tongue, desperate to hold out for her. And when she sucked in a shocked gasp and her eyes closed, I finally let my own orgasm hit.

It was blinding. All-consuming. I had to catch myself to avoid falling on top of her.

"Wow," she said as she caught her breath. "I wonder what place will be next."

CHAPTER THIRTY

I was deep in blissful sleep when my phone rang. It was eleven a.m., which was late enough that I should have been up, but early enough that I was still exhausted from the night before.

"Hello?" I answered, my mind resistant to the idea of being awake.

"Rose!" Mom's voice was loud. "I need your help."

"Mom?" I asked. "What's happening?"

"I need you to tell your father that I'm *fine* and don't need him here."

"What?"

"Let me have the phone," Dad's voice said. "Sorry about this, Rosie."

"Are you visiting Mom?"

"Yeah, I'm in Canada."

I blinked. Dad didn't go to that corner of Canada at *all*. He had avoided it ever since he left. "Why are you there?"

"I was—"

"I'm tired of being babysat," Mom snapped. "Rose, please tell your father that I'm *fine* and I don't need help."

That was even more confusing. Dad didn't babysit. At all.

"*Are* you okay?" I asked.

Barry sat up, his sleep disturbed. He gave me a questioning look.

My parents, I mouthed to him.

"Of course I'm fine! Well, as much as I can be, considering you're letting people know about your secret. I saw this man at the store and he *looked* at me like he knew who my daughter was."

Even though I knew there was no way Barry had told, I checked Google anyway. "No one knows. All I see is an article about how I'm a Hollywood sellout."

Barry's hand covered my phone and I pulled it away to close the internet tab.

"People know, Rose. I knew this would happen when you finally broke."

"Linda," Dad said, his voice tight. "She's being responsible. The only people who know aren't going to tell anyone."

"Why are you with Mom?" I asked.

"Don't worry about it, Rosie. You have a lot going on."

"Telling me not to worry about something isn't going to make me not worry. You never go see Mom."

"You're right. I don't. And look at what's happening."

"I'm *fine!*" Mom shouted in the background again.

"I've got things here," he said. "You focus on work."

"But—"

"Rosie, I'm your father. Let me handle something for you. I love you and I'll talk to you later."

He hung up without another word.

My jaw was on the floor. Since when did Dad even have an authoritative tone, much less use it?

"What happened?" Barry asked.

"My dad's being responsible," I said slowly. "Which is *not* what he does. He travels the country and leaves his kid behind."

"Is that what he did to you?"

"Yes," I said. "I mean, we're fine now. Mom always said he was never meant to be a dad, but this doesn't make sense. It's unlike him."

"Maybe he grew up." Barry shrugged. "What did your mom say?"

"She's panicking as usual. She thinks you're going to tell everyone who I am."

"Not happening."

"I know, but she can be unreasonable when she's like this."

"Maybe it's good that you're not dealing with it."

"Yeah," I said. "It is. It's just unlike Dad to do anything about these moods. Usually, it falls to me."

"Take the help," Barry replied. "You don't need to take on anything else right now."

I looked at my hands. I felt like I should be doing more for Mom. Dad didn't like being there with her, and if I stepped in, maybe I could shorten the time he was stuck.

But then Barry's hands covered mine.

"Rose, you don't need to give everything to make others happy."

"I don't know how to stop."

"You can start by letting your dad handle this for now and focusing on the tour."

"What if he messes up or it gets worse?"

"That hasn't happened yet," he said. "And we can't live our lives thinking about what isn't happening."

He was right. I knew he was. It wasn't even like I wanted to worry about everyone else. I just did.

Taking a shaky breath, I nodded. I wanted to be better.

"Okay, I'll focus on the tour for now."

"Good, the guys said we needed to be there at one, and judging by how awful LA traffic is, we probably should get ready."

Barry

"You did amazing today," I told Lila, but I knew words weren't enough to describe how she moved onstage. We weren't even on the real one where she'd be performing, but she owned the small practice theater like she was made to be here. Her strong voice was undisturbed by however she moved and she had energy for days.

"I was off in a few ways," she said, "but it wasn't bad."

"Off? You were perfect."

"There were a few notes that I messed up."

"You're way too hard on yourself."

"But it makes me better." She gave me a bright smile. "That's how I keep doing this."

"Lila," Justice said as she walked up. "Have I told you how *great* it is that you found a stand-in? Thank you for being here, Barry."

I liked Justice. She'd taken my temporary help with a smile and rolled with it.

"You're welcome," I replied.

"And I bet you have a good voice. I can just tell."

"He does," Lila said, nodding.

"So good that maybe he could perform 'On This Night'?"

I blinked. I thought I'd never perform it again. That had been a one-time thing, and I wasn't even named.

"That song isn't on the tour for a reason," Lila said.

"People will love to hear it."

"I can't perform it by myself."

Justice gestured to me.

"But I'm just here for a short time."

"Maybe you can make an appearance. Without the hat, you could be a real presence onstage."

I glanced at Lila, whose eyes were wide. I knew why it couldn't happen but hoped it somehow could. I loved the stage at Movers and Shakers and knew I would love this one too.

But Barry Murray would never make it up there.

"Think about it," Justice said. "I have a meeting with Malia for another first round of auditions for the guitarist. I'm sure you'll be in them tomorrow, Lila."

"I'll be there," she replied. She smiled at Justice, but it didn't reach her eyes.

"Are you okay?"

"She's right," Lila said. "The setlist feels empty without that song. It's the last song on the album for a reason. It's supposed to wrap everything up."

"I'm sure if you did it, you'd nail it."

"I don't think I could sing it by myself. I've tried and it's not the same without you there."

"I doubt that."

"Then let's play it," she said. "And you'll see how perfect it is as it was on the album."

She moved into position and gave me an extra mic. I played what I remembered. Lila started us off, singing her part in a high-pitched tone. I came in on the second verse, and then we sang together.

And yeah, she was right. When performed live, it was meant to be a duet.

I'd never hated the bar before, but this was as close as it would come. My first dream had been to be a rock star. My second was the bar.

But I wouldn't leave what I'd created the moment something better came along. I refused to.

It still hurt to make that choice, though.

We sang the last note together and a slow clap rang out from the front of the room.

"I see why you're hesitant to perform that by yourself," Malia said, walking forward. "It really is better when both of you sing it."

"I thought you were with Justice," Lila said.

"I swung in for a second to chat, but you were busy."

"It was just practice," I replied.

"That's still important. You're the singer on the original, right?"

"Yeah."

"I'm not the tour expert, but you would be so perfect onstage."

"No," Lila rushed to say. "I'd rather keep it out of the tour."

Her tone was sharp and I wondered if Malia would snap back. But she didn't.

"Okay, I won't push it. I respect your decision."

"Thank you," Lila said, some tension leaving her shoulders.

"I do need to head out. Our chat can wait." She made a move to leave but paused and looked in between us. "You two are good together."

"We aren't *together*."

Malia's eyebrows raised. "Could've fooled me. Let's meet tomorrow. We need to talk."

CHAPTER THIRTY-ONE

Lila

Malia was true to her word and added a meeting to my calendar for the next day. I wondered just how much I was about to be questioned about Barry and my reasoning for not including "On This Night" on the tour.

Barry offered to go with me, but I turned him down. He'd looked stricken when Justice had mentioned him joining the tour, and I refused to make him feel forced to stay longer than he had to.

I told him to check on his bar, and even he couldn't hide his sigh of relief when I said those words. This was the longest he'd ever been away from it.

However, walking into Malia's office made me regret telling him not to come. I was *so* not ready for the interrogation.

"Hi, Lila," she said. "Sit down. Want some water?"

"No, I'm good." I tried to sound casual, but my voice shook. "If this is about Barry, then—"

"This isn't about Barry at all. It's about you."

My heart stuttered. "Wh-what about me?"

"Have you ever heard the name Rose Hill?"

And now my heart completely stopped. *No way.* How did she know? Could I get out of this with my secret intact? "Um, no?"

Malia raised an eyebrow. "Really? Because she's seeing your man. Or not really, considering you *are* her."

Fuck.

I didn't have anything to say to her. I just knew I was in trouble. Big trouble.

"Don't look so worried," Malia said. "It's a good thing that I know. I can bury the lead I followed, and the only reason I *did* figure it out is because Barry introduced himself."

"I'm sure you have questions."

"Questions? About how you can disappear and feel normal for a bit? I think it's obvious why you did this and it was smart to start from the beginning."

"And you won't tell anyone?"

"Absolutely not. I know your last agent would have used this against you, but not me. I only care about your well-being, and if this is how you keep your life safe and sound, then I will do everything in my power to keep this secret for you. You deserve peace."

"So . . . you're cool with it?"

"Yes."

"You don't think it's weird?"

"Maybe if you came to me when you were up-and-coming and said you wanted to create a new persona, but even if you had a good explanation, I would have accepted it. I'm assuming Barry knows?"

"Yes. And Juno."

"Anyone else?"

I shook my head.

"Blaze?"

"No. I never trusted him like that."

"You made the right choice, considering he's *still* using your name to his advantage."

"Did he do anything else?"

"Do you really want to know?"

"Yes."

"This morning he insinuated that you were once married."

"What?"

"He wants to make his side of the story as painful as possible. It would have helped if he could have produced a good album, but fortunately, he didn't. People are going to be following you for a while, though."

"When aren't they?"

"Good point. But they know I represent you now and they know you're here. You might want to call someone to pick you up once we finish."

"Juno should have it covered."

"Then let's go over how we keep this secret just that—a secret."

"Thank you," I said, blowing out a breath of relief.

"I'm on your side. Never forget that." She smiled before turning around her laptop, showing me how people could link Rose to Lila. I listened, intent on getting rid of all the evidence I could, and when the meeting was over, I walked out of Malia's office feeling like my secret was safer than ever before.

Barry

Taking an uncertain breath, I pulled up Audrey's name on the phone. She wouldn't be working yet, but I didn't know when I would get another free moment.

"Hey, Barry," she said. There was a rustling sound on her end of the call. "What's up?"

"Have a minute? I just wanted to check in."

"Yeah, I'm just waking up."

I didn't have a sleep schedule now that I was traveling, but it wasn't *that* early in Nashville.

"Late night?"

"Later than usual," she said. "Or earlier, depending on how you look at it."

"Who is it?" a voice asked. It sounded like someone I knew, but who the hell would be with her in bed?

"Barry," she muttered back.

"Oh, that's perfect. You needed to talk to him."

My eyes narrowed as I finally placed the voice. "Wait a second, is that *Liam*?"

"Uh, no?" Audrey laughed awkwardly. "Maybe he's on the other line."

"Are you trying to hide me?"

"I fucking knew it," I said.

"I hate you both," Audrey muttered. "But to answer your question, every-thing is fine."

"Mostly," Liam added.

"That is *not* how I wanted to ask him this," she hissed.

"What is it? Do you need me back?"

"No. We were just thinking about upping the number of people allowed in."

"Why?"

"The bar is busy, in a good way. The change to the dance night has really made things explode. And I sent out a survey that confirmed that most people would rather deal with crowds than wait."

"But if we up the maximum guest list, we can't keep an eye on things."

"We have the money to double the staff. I'm serious, Barry. The change to the dance nights has been good."

"If we double the staff, then I need to be there to hire them."

"I mean, we could hire them. If you trust us, of course."

"I trust you," I rushed to say, because I did. "But hiring has always been my thing. I'm good at it."

"You're also good at guitar and you deserve to take time with it."

"Wait, can you teach *how* you hire?" Liam asked. "We can try replicating it and send you who we're thinking about."

"But you guys are taking care of the whole bar."

"Yes, but we can handle some interviews. We'll come in early and do them before we open."

"You deserve time off."

"And do *you* take time off?" Audrey asked.

"That's not the point."

"Barry, when we said yes, we knew we'd be working more. You pay us so much so it isn't a problem."

"It doesn't feel like enough."

"Why not?" Liam asked. "We're happy, and we want to help. Why is that so hard for you to understand?"

I knew why. I did everything alone and asking for help made me feel like I wasn't doing enough.

"We can drop the idea," Audrey said. "It's a big change, and I know—"

"What was the plan?" I asked. "To add a larger guest list."

"I was going to hire more staff and then do it. We'd start with adding fifty occupants, which is still way under the fire safety limit, and see how the guests like it."

"And if they don't?"

"We go back to the way things were and still keep the staff."

It wasn't a bad plan at all. In fact, it was a good one. I wasn't there, and as much as it killed me, I needed to trust their judgment.

"Okay," I said. "Do it, but I want to see the reviews."

"Yes!" Audrey cheered. "Thank you, Barry. We'll send you everything."

"Thanks, man," Liam added. "We won't let you down."

"I know you won't."

"And now no more talk about work. It's personal time. How are things with you and she who must not be named?"

"Amazing."

"And the two of you are . . ."

"Still friends."

"Are you sure?"

"How are you and Audrey?"

"Cold move, man," Liam said. "But I can respect it. Once we figure out this new guest list thing, we *will* come for answers from you."

"I'll be waiting."

There was a knock on the door and I knew my time was up. I told Liam and Audrey that I had to go and said my goodbyes.

"Yes?" I called.

"Please tell me you have clothes on," Juno said through the door.

"Yes, of course. What's up?"

"Blaze was a fuckhead again," she said. "And now there's *more* interest on Lila's name. I'm going to get Lila since the paparazzi know where she is. Want to come along and be waiting in the car for her?"

"Of course," I said. "I'll get ready. Hey, do you know how to braid?"

"I started learning when I found out about Rose. Need help hiding your hair?"

"Yeah. One of these days, I'll learn how to do it myself, but today is not the day."

Chapter
Thirty-Two

I once thought I would adjust to the lights and cameras, but I never did. And sometimes, after a long day of work, they just became too much.

I knew when I saw the crowd outside of Malia's office that it was going to be a lot. I felt raw, both from her figuring out my secret and the way we had to go through every connection someone could find. Talking about my double identity so openly wasn't something I was used to. By the time I was done, I hoped the crowd had diminished to the point that I could dart to the car and get out of there.

No luck.

My usual armored car was waiting for me, and everyone knew exactly what that car meant. Juno was inside, anticipating a speedy getaway.

Another one of my security guards, hired by Malia, flanked me as I was led to the car.

It was a frenzy of lights and sounds. People called my name, they said Blaze's name, and they even called me a whore to my face to get a reaction. LA paparazzi were of another breed, and it felt like they were sapping away all of my energy today.

At first, it was chaos that I could manage. But then as I neared the car, they upped the intensity.

One got too close, shoving my security guard so they could get a picture of my face showing any emotion. I jerked away, but my obvious fearful expression egged them on because now they had a photo they could sell.

My guard shouted, which meant nothing good for me, and I nearly fell against the car as I tried to escape. The guard pushed, and then someone yelled at him for stepping in. A new kind of chaos erupted behind me.

But then the door to the car opened and a hand—a lifeline—pulled me to safety. I looked up. Barry had gotten halfway out of the car and pulled me to him. He was in sunglasses and a hat, thankfully disguised, and I collapsed into his steady, warm weight.

He slammed the door behind me and everything was muffled by the car.

"Juno, can we get some privacy?" he asked.

I'd had a privacy glass installed long ago, back when I thought I might change in cars.

"Of course. I swear, if I didn't have to be the dang getaway driver . . ." She trailed off as she rolled up the window.

I let out a breath of relief as the car moved.

Barry's arm tightened around my waist and I realized I was sprawled into his lap.

"Thank you," I said. "We may have to pay for that later when we explain it to Malia, but thank you."

"They're fucking vultures. I shouldn't have ever left you by yourself."

The realization that he'd saved me from them did unfair things to my body. Barry had no problem being in all of this with me. He was interwoven in everything now, and I couldn't bear to even dream of life without him in it. I usually loved touring, but the idea of him returning to Nashville made me want to follow him and set up camp there.

"I'm fine now," I said, leaning into him. "All because of you."

My hand rested on his neck and it hit me how intimate this position was. "Do you want me to move?"

His hands tightened on my hips. "Absolutely not."

My heart rate slowed as I listened to his heartbeat. Was this what love was? Feeling so calm and protected that I could be myself anywhere?

I shifted slightly, pulling myself closer to him. It was then I felt his hardness beneath me.

"Sorry," he said. "I know you're stressed, so don't worry about—"

I kissed him. My stress was gone, taken away by his embrace, and now that it was just the two of us, I wanted him, just like I always did.

He pulled away, hand on my cheek. "Are you okay?"

"I am. I think I just needed you."

"I'm always happy to be of service to you, sunshine."

"You're just saying that because you know people are going to call you my bodyguard again."

He cracked a smile. "And it's funny even now."

"You know," I said absentmindedly, "no one can hear anything back here. Or see anything. It's a thirty-minute drive back to my place."

"And what do you propose we do?" His voice was low now and his breath ghosted over my ear.

"Anything you want," I said, rolling my hips back into him.

"It's a good thing you wore this dress. Pink is a stunning color on you."

I opened my mouth to say something, but his hand had found easy access to my inner thighs. All I could muster was a gasp as his finger brushed my underwear.

He could have asked to fuck me right then and there and I would have said yes, but he took his time, touching the areas so close to where I wanted him while his lips kissed my neck. "You're so fucking beautiful in dresses."

Maybe I should go through my closet and get rid of all of my T-shirts and pants. That sounded like a great idea.

But then, all thoughts flew out the window when his fingers slid under my underwear.

"B-Barry," I moaned.

"What?"

"I need you to touch me *now*."

With a chuckle, he moved my underwear aside and his fingers finally did what I wanted them to. I was more than ready for his touch. Barry grazed up and down and I rested my head on his shoulder. Heat pulsed from my core, making me ride his hand even as the car moved.

But I knew this wasn't going to be enough. My thighs clenched around nothing and I was desperate to be filled.

"I want you to fuck me."

"Not until you come first."

"I won't until you're inside of me. Please, Barry?"

"You're impatient today."

"If we're going to do this in a limo, then I want to fuck."

"Whatever you want. Lift your hips, sunshine."

I didn't need to be told twice. The second I moved, he unzipped his pants. I held my underwear aside so I could feel his cock press in at my entrance.

"Don't take it slow," I said. "I want it all."

And he didn't. He pushed into me with one ruthless thrust. My body burned in pleasure as I made room for his cock.

"All of these people want a look at you," he said, pushing impossibly deeper inside of me. "But I have you like this."

Oh, fuck. How did I form words? I'd forgotten.

"Touch yourself, sunshine," he said. "Come on my cock."

His hips rocked up, sending him even deeper inside of me, and I found my clit, letting his movements move me into my hand.

This was the most pleasurable form of torture. My body was wound up, desperate for release, and his cock was hitting the most sensitive parts as he ground upward.

"I won't last long," I said, my voice desperate.

"Neither will I." His strain finally hit his voice. The car was moving, going up a bumpy road that disguised his thrusts. He moved harder and I gasped as I tumbled over the edge of a cliff.

My body exploded, tiny fireworks shooting out from my clit, through my core, up my spine. My vision whited out and my orgasm continued for as long as he was moving.

"Fuck," he said, and with one last thrust, he came too.

Barry and I only had seconds to catch our breaths before we pulled into the driveway. We rushed to get all of our clothes back into their proper places before anyone caught onto what we'd just done.

That was staying our little secret.

Barry

Pulling Lila into the car had been a split-second decision, just like having sex with her right then and there had been too. While I knew no one—not even Juno—could see us, the other things I'd done were far more obvious.

The photos from outside Malia's office were everywhere instantly and I foolishly thought my disguise would work. It mostly did.

I was known as a mystery man, exactly as planned.

But I forgot about my family who wouldn't be fooled by a hat and sunglasses.

Ruth called three hours after the photos had dropped.

"Hey," I said as I picked up the phone. Lila was in another room, working on a virtual meeting about her costumes for the concert. "If this is about family dinner, I can't come this week."

"I figured because I'm pretty sure you're in LA right now."

I froze for a second. "And why would you say that?"

"Because you're pictured pulling Lila Wilde into a car, with the caption, 'Her new savior,' which is really fucking sexist, by the way."

"Who the fuck printed that?"

"Did you forget the part where you deny it's you?"

"Would you believe me if I did?"

"Absolutely not. Your disguise isn't going to work on me *or* Tom."

I let out a long sigh. "First of all, no one was supposed to see me."

"That's how it always starts," she said. "But that's not the biggest problem here. What does Rose think about all of this, Barry?"

"Rose?" I asked. "Why would she care?"

"Because you said you're *with* her," Ruth snapped. "You're my brother and I'd like not to have to kill you for cheating."

I'd completely forgotten I had said that, but then again, I never thought I would be in LA helping Lila practice for her tour.

"She knows, Ruth. Of course she knows. She's fine with it."

"And does she know about your past with Lila?"

"Yes."

"Really? I don't get how she wouldn't be worried about this."

"You can even call her up and ask her when she's free. I'm an open book."

"Maybe I will. Give me her number."

I pulled the phone away from my ear to send a message. "Sent it to you through text."

"Thanks. I'll follow up with her soon. Why are you in LA anyway? I thought you were done with Lila."

"She . . . she needed help on something with her tour, and considering I know most of her songs, I was a good stand-in while they look for someone else."

A gross feeling settled in my stomach. I hated not telling the whole truth to Ruth. She didn't deserve to not know the whole story, but this also wasn't my secret to keep or not keep.

"Interesting. Where's Rose?"

"Here too. We've figured it all out. Everything's fine."

"It better be," she warned. "And besides, I have more questions for you. Mom called."

"God, what could she want?"

"She wanted to know if you and Wilfred had met. Obviously, he isn't talking to her, and I didn't say anything either. But *I* want to know more at least. So, how did it go?"

"I already told you it went fine."

"Come on, other than threatening to kill you if you cheat on your girlfriend, I haven't done anything to warrant you going back into your shell. Can't you talk to me? You've been so tight-lipped about Wilfred to me *and* Tom. Even at the party."

"There isn't much to say." Another lie. Wilfred might have been the coolest person I'd met in a long time, and despite how busy I'd been, I'd wondered what he would think of all of this. Would he be proud? Or would he be like the man who I thought was my father?

I shook the thought out of my head the moment I had it. Wilfred was not like Todd Murray in any way. It was almost unfair to him even to think that.

Ruth sighed. "Fine. Then, is there anything we can catch up on? I've mostly been talking to Tom, and he's only been talking about kids and marriage, which is fun for a while, but I need him to propose already so I can start planning with Selena."

"You're going to plan it?"

"I'm going to help, at least. Selena is a kind and sensitive soul. I'm worried she'll get eaten alive by the wedding industry and I want to be the kind sister-in-law on her shoulder telling them all to fuck off."

"Uh huh, and what about *your* wedding? When is Knox going to ask?"

"Probably soon, considering we've been talking about kids."

"What?"

"Didn't I tell you?"

"You absolutely did not."

"This is what you get for going to help your super famous friend. You get left out!"

"When did this get decided?"

"Like a few weeks ago, I think. But it's not something we're going to actively try for or anything. If it happens, it happens."

"That's a very relaxed way of going about it for the woman who once tracked how many times I came out of my room."

"I can be relaxed. Mostly. I only had a few freak-outs about it, and then I was fine."

"That sounds more like the Ruth I know," I said, chuckling.

"Now, what the hell is going on in your life? I feel like I haven't talked to you in forever and seeing you in the news really didn't make any sense."

"Nothing much, other than helping Lila and checking in on the bar. It feels weird to be away from it. I can't wait to get back."

"Enjoy your LA time. I bet the people you work with have it covered. You only ever say good things about them."

"They're great, but it's my bar. I can't just up and leave."

"So responsible," she said. "Who even are you anyway?"

I rolled my eyes. "Very funny."

"Glad to hear from you, Barry. Seriously. And if you break Rose's or Lila's hearts, I will end you."

"And I would let you," I replied, knowing it was the truth.

Once I got off the phone, I went to mine and Wilfred's texts.

Barry: Hey. Hope you're okay.

It took him a few minutes to respond.

Wilfred: I'm goob.

Wilfred: These buttons on this danm keyboard are too small

And then he called.

"I can't text, kid," he said, sighing. "I can't do it for the life of me."

I laughed. "It's fine. I was just checking in."

"Things are good here. I've got the plants planted. Been spending time outdoors, which is always good for the soul."

"I haven't been spending any time outside, but I've also been doing something good for the soul. I didn't realize how much I liked playing music until now."

"Really? You're playing more?"

"All the time. I could really do this kind of thing forever."

"Sounds like it's a dream come true then. I don't know if you want my advice—"

"I do," I cut in, surprising even myself with the sincerity of it. "I do want your advice."

"When you find something that you love as much as breathing, do whatever you can to follow it. You've only got one life, kid. And if you do it right, you'll only ever need the one."

"Even if it's not what other people do?"

"*Especially* if it's not what other people do. Be different. It's what makes us all interesting."

"Thanks," I said. "I needed to hear that. But I have ties in Nashville. I don't think any of this is simple."

"It's often not. But life has a funny way of working out sometimes. Maybe things will end up exactly as they should. Give it time and give it your all. You don't know if you don't try."

"Yeah, maybe you're right." I couldn't see myself leaving the bar, but I couldn't see myself walking away from this forever, either. My life felt split in two, an echo of what Rose had to go through every single day.

And I would have to figure out how to do it without creating a secret identity.

CHAPTER THIRTY-THREE

Lila

Rose's phone rang right after my meeting ended. It was a number I didn't recognize. I bit my lip, no clue who it could be—but it was a Nashville area code.

"Rose!" Ruth's voice said the second I pressed accept. The name sounded wrong when I still had the wig on my head. "Hi, sorry to bother you like this, but I have something to bring up with you in the interest of the girl code."

"The girl code?" I asked. I checked my watch and saw I only had ten minutes until my next meeting, but this was Ruth. I'd make do.

"Yes. Listen, I may love my brother, but I will ruin his life if he's a cheater. You know what I mean?"

I blinked, confused. "Um, that's really nice?"

"Did you know he's in contact with Lila Wilde?"

My eyes widened. "How did you know?"

"I can recognize my brother even if he's disguised. And if we're being honest, the disguise is so fucking suspicious. Why would he need to hide?"

"Probably all the cameras?" I offered. "And it's okay. I know."

"You do?"

"Yeah, of course. Barry and I are fine."

"Are you *sure*? I know how to kick his ass, you know."

"It's fine. I trust him. He doesn't feel that way about her."

"But they had a thing not too long ago."

I winced. On the one hand, it was sweet that she cared so much, but on the other, I wished she didn't notice *everything*. "Yeah, I knew about that too. Things are different now."

"How so?"

"Um." I struggled to come up with an answer. The only thing that made sense was one reason that was very untrue. "We talked about it, and he said she was . . . too much."

This was a terrible excuse. Worst one I could have thought of.

"Really? He seemed so ready . . . Never mind. I'm sure you don't want to hear about his ex."

"No, it's okay. I know how he felt. We're all good."

Ruth hummed. "Okay, then. If you're cool with it, then I have nothing to worry about."

"It's really sweet that you called," I said. "Most people would have just kept it to themselves."

"I'm definitely not that kind of person. Not when someone could get hurt, that is. And besides, I like you. I think you're good for him."

"Thanks," I said. I rechecked my watch; I was running out of time. "Can I maybe call you later? I have a work thing to do."

"Oh, shoot. I do too. I was too busy making sure my brother wasn't an asshole that I forgot about my next ass to kick. I'll keep your number if that's okay."

"Yeah, of course. We'll talk soon."

I hung up after saying goodbye, nervous about how close Ruth was to both sides of me and how much Barry had been seen with Lila.

This was getting messy again and I had no idea how to begin cleaning it up without telling everyone who I was.

Thankfully, I was distracted by Lila's phone ringing this time.

"Hey," I said to Malia, trying to put on a happy smile, pushing away my thoughts. "Nice to talk to you for the second time today. How did talent scouting go?"

"For once, very good. Are you free to meet me right now? I know this was supposed to be a phone meeting, but I think Justice found the perfect guitarist."

I peered into the living room where Barry was lounging, practicing chords as if they were second nature. I waved to get his attention and pointed to the door. He nodded and grabbed his hat.

"Yeah, Barry and I will be there as soon as we can."

Mickey Richardson had dazzled everyone else around me. He was a man with greasy black hair pushed back, reminding me of an unwashed Blaze. His face made me wonder what he was truly thinking about.

With the way his eyebrows kept wiggling at me, I wondered if the thoughts were appropriate.

But he knew how to play all of Lila's songs.

"I think he's the one," Justice said, leaning over to me.

Something in my chest turned. I wasn't so sure, but after working with almost a hundred people throughout my career, I knew we had to choose someone, and fast.

And I knew I was being influenced by how his wiry frame and flirty expression reminded me of my ex.

"Yeah, I think he could work." The lie felt wrong on my tongue, but when Justice turned to ask about his availability, I gave him a smile.

Mickey's eyes were on me and they felt hungry in the grossest way. I looked away, unable to keep eye contact.

It's just his looks. Everyone else likes him.

Mickey wound up having the perfect availability and could start immediately. I hid my disappointment.

"Welcome to the band," I said. "We're lucky to have you."

"No, we're lucky to have *you*. I can't wait to get started."

I looked back down, ignoring my instinctual reply to his words, and instead, turned to Barry. He was in the very back of the auditorium. His lips were pursed and I wondered what he thought of this new man.

Maybe Barry was happy to leave. I knew he was itching to get back to his bar and his work, and I didn't blame him for that. I only hoped he was going to miss me as much as I was going to miss him.

Mickey left shortly after, promising to see us all again, and I beelined for Barry.

"What did you think?"

"He knows the stuff."

"Do you get a weird vibe from him?" I asked lowly.

"Yes, and as much as I'd love to tell you not to hire him based on that, I might just be jealous that someone else is going on tour with you."

"You know he's not going to replace you, right? We'll talk every night."

"I know, which is why I'm reining it in. I have the bar and you have this. We have to be separated sometimes."

"It sucks, though." I smiled at him, but we could both tell I was forcing it. "When do you need to go back?"

"I have no idea. Audrey and Liam haven't had any issues. Every update they give me is good. But I do know they're the kind of people who would take on way too much to give me a break."

"Do you think they'd be okay with you staying one more night?" I wouldn't have been angry if he told me no, but I was desperate for just a little longer with him. "You could head out first thing in the morning."

He thought about it for a moment. "I think I can do that. I couldn't get back in time to help them with tonight's rush anyway."

I nodded, grateful for every extra second he would give me.

As we drove home, my mind was bustling with all the things I wanted to do with him, whether it be sex, cuddles, watching a movie, or simply writing a song together.

Once I had the last idea, however, it wouldn't leave.

"I know this is our last night," I asked as we pulled into the garage, "but I have this song idea . . . about saying goodbye. Would you kill me if I said I wanted to write it with you?"

"Absolutely not. Where's your notebook?"

I dreaded every second of the drive to the airport. Somehow, I managed to keep my cool even as we pulled up.

Lyrics we'd just written last night played in my head, things like *I don't want you to go* and *come back forever*.

"Well, I guess this is it for a while." My voice cracked. "At least for you staying with me. I have a week-long break two months into the tour. I'll come see you then."

"Of course. I'll be waiting."

My lip wobbled, and as much as I didn't want to cry, I could feel the tears forming.

"Come on," he said, his hand trailing my face. "Don't cry, sunshine. I won't be able to leave if you do."

"I just . . . like having you around. I hate separating."

"It's just for a few months. We can call each other."

"It's not the same," I protested. His lips pressed together and I could see him take a second look in the direction of the security line.

But as much as I wanted him to stay, I knew he couldn't.

"I'm sorry," I said. "I know it'll be okay. I'll just miss you, and I'm not used to that."

"I'll miss you too," he replied. "Every day."

My eyes watered again, but I nodded, pulling him into a tight hug. I took in everything I could, his scent, the feel of his shoulder pressing into my cheek, in some hope that I would remember this forever.

I love you.

The words sprung forth in my mind and I immediately knew how true they were. They settled into me, a realization that I had been barreling toward since the second I met him.

I could have said so, but something else told me he wouldn't board his plane if those words left my lips.

And I refused to be the reason he walked away from something he'd spent years building.

"Have a good flight," I said instead.

"I will. I'll call you when I land."

But I wished he had said *I love you.*

"One more thing," I said, clearing out the emotion from my throat. "I have something for you."

"What is it?"

"Tickets to *you know who's* first show here in LA."

"What are these for?"

"You worked hard on this album and on this tour. If you can swing it, I'd love for you to see it. I've included enough for you to invite friends if you want to."

He slowly took the envelope. "So, I'll be seeing you again sooner."

"If you come," I said. "I'd love to see your reaction to all of it."

"I'll be there, I promise."

And that sounded as close to an *I love you* as I would get.

It was almost enough.

Barry

I usually found my home charming and comforting. I liked seeing the tourists in cowboy hats or the neon signs of Broadway.

But I quickly realized I didn't want to be here.

I gripped my phone like a lifeline, letting Rose know I was back safe and sound. I had a mountain of work to do to get reacclimated to the bar. My first stop should have been checking in with my employees to be sure everything was okay. I probably should've reached out to Ruth and Tom to make sure everything was fine with them too.

Instead, I went straight to my apartment.

Lying on my bed, I thought back to the last few weeks in LA, about how much I loved to play with Lila's band, and how much I enjoyed spending every second with Rose that I could. It had been heaven, like living in a dream I didn't even know I had.

I was reaching for my guitar before I could stop myself.

The routine for Lila's tour was second nature. I went through the opening chords, feeling it all flow out of me as if I were really there.

I didn't hear the knock at the door or the turn of the key. I only noticed anyone was in my apartment when I heard clapping.

I jumped, my focus broken.

Liam and Audrey were in the living room. "What the—how did you two get in?"

"The key under the doormat. It works for both the back door *and* your apartment." Audrey shrugged as if she hadn't broken in.

"We saw your car," Liam explained. "You're back now?"

"Yep. My work is done."

They shared a look. "Is it? You were still practicing."

"Yeah," I replied. "I was just doing it out of habit."

"It sounded great," Liam said.

"Thanks. I'm certainly better than I was."

"Gonna use it onstage?"

The idea of stepping on a stage, even the one I'd made at Movers and Shakers, sent a wave of nausea through me.

I couldn't deny the fact that I knew exactly what stage I wanted to be on.

"No, I'll probably take a break."

"Are you okay?" Liam asked. "You seem . . . down."

"I'm good," I replied. "Ready to get back to work."

They exchanged another look, but I stood and put my guitar down. "Okay," Audrey said. "Let's go downstairs. I don't have *much* to catch you up on, but I'm sure you're eager to know how everything went."

"I am. Let's go."

I followed them down to the first floor. She went over the new schedules she made and how we'd done financially. I could see for myself how well the higher guest list count was working.

But I wasn't all there. I'd left a part of me in LA with the woman of my dreams.

And my soul was longing to be put back together.

CHAPTER THIRTY-FOUR

Lila

We worked until we couldn't anymore. The tour finally came together. I dealt with the looks Mickey kept giving me, and eventually, I figured out how to ignore them.

Barry and I talked every night. Some nights, we texted, especially when my voice was raw from all the singing. As the opening night loomed, I counted the seconds until he flew back to LA.

"Have you decided who you're bringing?" I asked one morning as I was preparing for another day of practice. "Tom and Ruth might love to come."

"I don't know," he said. "I still haven't told them about Wilfred, and every time I look at Ruth, I feel bad for lying."

"I agree, but maybe Max would like to go."

"He would. I'm just . . . struggling with talking to them."

"I could call them and offer."

"As who?"

"Lila. I could say you gave me their number. I have Ruth's."

"Okay, yeah. Maybe find a way to remind her that we're *friends*. Any more questioning and I'll feel worse."

"Of course. I won't let who I am slip."

I finished my makeup while we talked more about what I would say. When I was done, he had to go to the bar, and I said my goodbyes as I got Ruth's number from Rose's phone.

"Hello?" she asked, in the same suspicious voice I would if I got a call from a random LA number.

"Hi, Ruth. It's Lila. Barry's friend."

The line was silent. "Lila?" she asked. "How did you get . . . What—why?"

"I know it's a lot. I got your number from Barry because he's really busy and wanted me to invite you on the tour in a few weeks. The whole family could go, actually. You could invite Tom and Max, and Lynn if you wanted to."

"What about Barry's girlfriend, Rose?"

Shit. "Rose? Um, of course, she's invited. I called her earlier, actually, but she's not a big concert person, and she's busy with work anyway."

"Oh, okay. That makes sense, I guess."

I cringed, hoping I'd covered for myself well enough. "She's just so busy right now. Oh, do you have a way to contact Barry's coworkers, Liam and Audrey? I would ask him to mention it to them, but I'm sure he would say something about how they're needed at the bar."

I twirled my hair in my fingers, hoping the diversion would work. She was silent for so long I worried that it didn't.

"I can figure out a way to talk to them. It'll be like one big party."

Whew. I was covered. "Right? I hope everyone can come. Barry is such a good friend that I want everyone he cares about to be there."

"Of course. I guess I'll be seeing you in LA, then?"

"Yeah," I said, letting a relieved laugh escape me. "I'll see you soon, Ruth."

Barry

Ruth: Family meeting. Now. At my office.

I should have seen it coming. Ruth would either be excited that Lila Wilde had called her or there would be more questions. If I were unlucky, then it would be both.

Her text was oddly cryptic, but I hoped she was just about to say how wild it was that a huge pop star had called her.

Either way, it was unlike her to call a family meeting over something like this. I knew she and Tom loved seeing me in person, but this seemed out of pocket.

Which meant she probably had more questions.

Damn it.

I pulled into the garage for the PATH office just as Tom did.

"What do you think this is about?" he asked as he got out of his truck.

"I gave Lila Wilde Ruth's number."

"Ah," Tom said. "So less of an emergency, then. Weird. She sounded mad."

"She's probably just being Ruth about this. We can't worry too much."

I *was* worrying too much, but I refused to let it show.

Tom nodded. He knew where her office was and led us there as if he knew the place like the back of his hand. As much as I wanted to pay attention to the place Ruth worked, all I could think about was all the ways she could question me about Lila again.

I really needed her to miss hints sometimes.

"Hey," I said. "We made it."

I readied myself for another barrage of questions as I stared down my sister. With her pursed lips and narrowed eyes, she didn't look excited at all.

"So, Lila Wilde called."

"Why do you look so upset about that?" Tom asked. "I thought you liked her."

"Oh, I do. But I'm also not an idiot."

"I'm not cheating on Rose with her," I said before she could finish.

"Why would Barry see two people?" Tom asked. "He's not that kind of guy. If you're still thinking he's—"

"Oh, he's seeing both Lila and Rose—"

"Ruth," I hissed, shaking my head. How the fuck did I convince her that I wasn't a scumbag?

"Let me finish," she snapped. "He's seeing them both because they're the same fucking person."

Oh.

Fuck.

I thought I'd thrown Ruth off the trail well enough to where she wouldn't pick up on any similarities.

Obviously not.

Time ticked by, the seconds agonizing.

"I figured it out when Lila called me," Ruth said, leaning back in her chair. "I knew there was something off, but I couldn't put my finger on it. The second she spoke, I was thinking about how much she sounded like Rose, just with a projected voice. Then I asked if Rose was coming to the concert, and she stuttered out some excuse about how Rose will be busy *working*. Which, *duh*. She's onstage. How did I not see it when I met the two of them? They look *exactly* alike."

Goddammit.

"I knew Barry wasn't cheating, but I couldn't deny that he looked at both of them like they were the moon and stars. It's the only explanation."

"That seems far-fetched," Tom began.

"Okay then." She looked at me. "Barry, tell me I'm wrong."

"You're wrong." I managed to strangle it out.

"Sound a little more sincere next time."

Was there any way to deny anything to Ruth once she had it figured out?

I knew the answer. *No.*

"Did you have to bring Tom here for this too?" I asked instead.

"Honestly, yes. Because I was thinking about strangling you for lying to me."

"It's not my secret to tell."

"Wait," Tom said, looking in between us like he was watching a tennis match. "They really *are* the same person?"

"Yes," I said lowly.

"How?"

"Wigs, Tom." Ruth rolled her eyes like it was the most obvious thing in the world.

"But *who* is wearing the wig?"

"Considering the bangs? Lila. Definitely her."

Tom slowly covered his mouth, the truth dawning on him.

"You can't tell anyone," I said quickly. "Seriously. No one."

"Haven't we proven you can trust us?" Ruth asked. "We won't tell a soul. And I'm sure Tom will agree once he stops internally calculating everything over there."

"She always wears a wig *as Lila*?" he asked.

"Yes, she does."

"Can someone *do* that? Like onstage?"

"Uncomfortably, yes. A lot of lace wigs require glue."

Tom's face twisted. "That sounds like torture."

"It probably is," Ruth said, "but her having it means she can go out in public and no one follows her. That's why she does it, right?"

"Mostly. And some of her family can't deal with all the attention that comes with it. This is why no one else was supposed to know."

"And no one will," Ruth said. "We've not let anything slip, ever. I thought we were getting closer, not *lying* to each other, Barry."

And now I saw why she was mad. We had been getting along and feeling more like a family than ever before.

And this felt like something the old us would do.

"It had nothing to do with the three of us. I didn't even know until a few months ago, either."

"What?" Ruth asked. "She didn't tell you?"

"No."

"Even when you met her at the bar?"

I shook my head.

"Is that why you were mad at her?" Tom asked.

"When was Barry mad at her?" Ruth's eyes went wide.

"The day I told you that Barry and I went to the gym and got breakfast with Max. I told you he was out of it."

"Yeah, that's when I found out."

Ruth blinked. "But you knew her for months. You wrote an *album* with her."

"And I knew Rose separately. It was . . . bad. And she admitted it was. Publicly."

"The apology song," Tom said. "That was about . . . She mentioned someone getting to know both sides of her. How did no one catch onto the meaning of that?"

"Thankfully, it's not a person's first thought to think of a secret double life. But I'm telling you, there's a reason she hid it like she did. Until me and her bodyguard, *no one* knew."

"No one?" Ruth repeated.

I nodded.

"Okay, that makes sense, then."

"You're going to let it go that easily?"

"Fame sucks, Barry. I get it. And besides, I have another thing to bitch at you about. Why did the offer of tickets for her opening night for all of us come from her and not you?"

"Tickets to opening night?" Tom repeated, raising an eyebrow. "What?"

"Would you believe me if I said it was because I felt bad for lying?"

Ruth crossed her arms. "If you said it sincerely, yes."

"Okay. It did feel bad to lie. I hated it, and I know Rose did too. I'm sure if it wasn't for the tour and us being separated right now, we would have been able to discuss all of this more, but neither of us is in our best mental state right now. Being across the country from each other isn't fun."

"Wow," Ruth said. "You really like her, don't you?"

"I *love* her," I said. "I've known it for a long time."

"*Love?*" Ruth's eyes went wide. "All right, then. I mean, I should have seen it coming when you met her. What do I call her?"

"Whoever she is in that moment."

"Seems simple. Now, we need to figure out how to get to this concert."

"You're really gonna accept the double identity that easily?"

"*I* haven't accepted it yet," Tom grumbled.

"It is . . . different, but ever since that time that I was caught with Knox, I've learned that people can be invasive. Especially when she has a tour about to start that I am *definitely* going to."

"She'd also understand if you're busy."

"Are you kidding?" Ruth scoffed. "I'll cancel a meeting with the president if it means I can go. This album is her best and the whole tour sold out in seconds."

"And Max would love the opportunity," Tom added. "I can use his noise-canceling headphones to be sure he doesn't get overwhelmed, and I'm sure Selena would enjoy getting out of the house. If she doesn't want to go, she has a friend she's been visiting in Atlanta. We can make it work."

"It's across the country, though," I reminded them. "It's a lot for anyone to try to make work, especially since you're both executives of your companies and one of you has a family."

"Barry," Ruth said, leaning forward. "We'll make it work. I'm sure Lila is proud of her album. Plus, *you* worked on it. Why would we miss seeing it live?"

"You don't need to make it some huge deal."

"Why not?" Tom asked. "You're our brother."

An uncomfortable feeling crawled up my neck at his words. "*Half* brother. I have a different dad, remember?"

"Why would that change anything?" Ruth asked, frowning.

"It means I'm the odd one out. You guys don't have to care as much as you do."

"We do care," Tom said. "Even if you think we don't."

"But you don't *have* to," I huffed out. "I'm different than you guys. I always have been. It's okay if me having someone else as my dad means you feel differently."

It *wasn't* okay, but I would deal. I couldn't imagine the jealousy I would have felt if they had an out and I was stuck with Todd for a father.

And if they were jealous, it would fester and break us. And when it did, I would be alone. They didn't *need* me. They had incredible lives I'd never been a part of because I was too busy making my own.

But now, as the words hung in the air and my heart pounded in my chest, I realized that maybe this time, I needed *them*.

"Barry," Ruth began. "We're *never* going to figure out that we don't need you. Even if you weren't related to us at all, we will *always* care."

"Yes," Tom said. "We've been through a lot together, and no matter how much you say you want to be alone, we know you still care. Why else would you have come to those stupid dinners?"

"But—"

"No buts," Ruth interrupted. "We love you, Barry. Nothing you say can change that."

My mouth snapped shut. The words hit hard, harder than I ever thought possible.

"Is this why you've not told us about Wilfred?" Ruth's voice was soft.

"I just thought it would add insult to injury if I said I liked him. Especially since he's nothing like Todd."

"There's no anger at all," Tom reassured.

"If he's a good guy, why would we be anything but happy?"

"I don't know. Maybe you'd be jealous or something."

I couldn't look either of them in the eye, so I looked at the floor, begging that this be the one time that they were not like me.

"We would never be jealous," Tom said. "Do I wish Todd had been different? Sure. But that doesn't change the fact that you have something better."

"And we're not shit out of luck anyway. We've *made* better families. We're not bitter because you have someone better who's related to you. It's far easier just to be *happy* for you."

"Really?"

"Yeah. The competition is over. It's time to live now."

"I wasn't a competitor."

"No, but you saw it. And you walked on eggshells for far too long because of it."

I closed my eyes. I needed to hear what they were saying more than anything, but it still *hurt* to talk about our past.

"Are you—" Tom began.

"I'm *not* crying. Just give me a second."

It took far longer than a second, but eventually, I was able to breathe again.

"I like Wilfred," I admitted. "A lot. I should probably see him now that I'm back in town."

"Definitely," Ruth agreed. "And you can invite him to family dinner! We'd love to meet him."

"Just no text chains. The man absolutely cannot text."

"Aw, why is that kind of adorable?" Ruth asked.

"Because it is. He's a dork, but he's my dad, so . . . he's not all that bad."

Tom only laughed. He sat on the office's extra chair and Ruth leaned forward at her desk, asking me more about him. I gave in, deciding not to be alone with my thoughts for once and to enjoy the company of the two people I'd waited so long for.

Barry: Hey. How are you? Maybe we can meet up soon?
Wilfred: Is there a way I can come see all your hard work on your bar?
Barry: Sure. When?
Wilfred: Tomrrwo?
Wilfred: dang it
Wilfred is calling . . .

After the plan for Wilfred to visit was finalized, I had a text from Rose that she was free. I immediately called her, knowing that she needed to know about Ruth and Tom.

"Hey," she said. "Good timing. I just got home."

"How was your day?" I asked. She'd been growing increasingly stressed about the tour, and while I would never keep anything from her, I wanted to know if we should FaceTime about this. Sometimes, seeing each other helped, but other times, it was a painful reminder of the distance.

"Busy as always. I'm going to take the longest bath after this."

"If only I could be there."

"There're only a few more days," she said, laughing.

It trailed off as I tried to work out how to tell her about all of the things happening at once.

"Are you okay?" she asked after a long silence.

"I know you're busy, but I have something to tell you. Are you sitting down?"

"Uh, yeah?" she asked. "Is everything okay?"

"It *is* okay, but you should know that Ruth figured out your secret."

"Which secret?"

"The *big* one."

"What? How?"

"Ruth figured out that you two sounded the same on the phone, so she called Tom and me for a family meeting to talk about it."

"Damn it. How many people are going to figure it out before *everyone* knows?"

"I stand by what I said before about Malia. She *needed* to know. And my family won't tell. They know how much you need privacy. Ruth has a famous boyfriend, remember?"

"But they can't be happy about the lying."

"They were angrier at me for that, but we're all good now. Tom was more confused about how you wear a wig onstage."

I heard her take a stilted breath. "This could be bad."

"But it won't be," I insisted. "I trust them."

"And I do too, but it's complicated."

"Yeah, it is. But that's the thing about having people on your side: they'll help you too. Don't just think about how this could go wrong. Think about how it could go right. Malia can now bury leads and Ruth can stomp on anyone who thinks twice about it."

"Okay, yeah." She was trying to sound confident, but her voice was still shaking.

"Everything's fine."

"It's easier to believe that when you're here in front of me. When I'm alone, all of this feels . . . heavier."

"I know, and I would be there if I could."

"Just a few more days until the concert. I'll try to keep my shit together until then. Thank you for telling me, though."

"No secrets, remember? And besides, there's more."

"How can there be more?"

"I haven't even told you about how Wilfred's coming to the bar or how I finally opened up to Ruth and Tom about him."

"*What?*" she nearly yelled. "Okay, start from the beginning and tell me *everything.*"

"How much time do you have?"

"For you? I'll *make* time."

I didn't want to be nervous about my biological dad seeing my bar, but I was. He'd agreed to come an hour before opening and stay a while to see it in action. I'd never had a parent in before, and despite his constant kindness over the last few months, I was terrified he'd tear it down like Mom and Todd did.

Rose had given me plenty of positive reinforcement, giving my own advice back to me.

I needed to focus on how this could go *right*.

Unfortunately, it was easier said than done.

I'd been disappointed by this part of my life a lot, and yet, each time, it felt like a little more of my soul died. As much as I wanted to pretend it didn't matter, it did, and I was starting to realize that.

And now that Ruth and Tom *hadn't* disappointed me, I needed the trend to continue.

"Why do you look like you're about to shit your pants?" Audrey asked as she walked in. "Is *you know who* coming here or something?"

"No, but my dad is."

She froze. I didn't mention my family very much, if at all.

"Like, your asshole dad?"

"Nope. Apparently, I'm not related to him. My *real* one is coming."

"What? You have a different dad?"

"It's new to me too."

She blinked. "Okay. Wow, um, so how did you take the news?"

"Terribly. But I'm adjusting to it now."

"And do you need us to do anything?"

"No. In fact, don't even listen in on anything."

She gave me a look that told me she wouldn't be doing that. "Yeah, right. I want to make sure you're okay. And if I'm not around, Liam will be."

"I should be fine either way."

"But if it goes south, we'll be here."

"I'm not worried."

"Do you remember when I said you looked like you were about to shit your pants?"

"I blocked it out because you sounded too much like my sister."

"Who I need to meet, by the way," Audrey said. "But seriously, we're your friends too."

What was with people caring about me? Would I ever get used to it?

"Okay," I grumbled. "I'll let you know if I need you."

"Really? You're not going to fight us?"

"I'm trying out the idea of *not* being alone for everything."

"Finally. It only took me like four years of knowing you."

I gave her a smile before I saw him at the front door. My heart stuttered in my chest.

I don't want to be hurt again. I don't think I can take it.

"You've got this," Audrey said, smiling. "I'm going to get Liam and catch him up. He's gonna be *so* mad he was in the back for this."

I watched her leave before I turned back to the door.

"Hey," I said as I let him in.

He whistled. "This place is *nice*. People are already at the front door."

"They line up early."

"Wow," he said. "I saw all the buzz, but it's wild to see it in person."

"Hi," Audrey said, returning with Liam on her arm. "I'm Audrey, his favorite employee."

"Don't lie," Liam said. "*I'm* his favorite employee."

"You're both equal."

Wilfred laughed. "Really? I heard the boss was strict."

"Oh, he's the *worst*," Liam said. "A real hard-ass. Did you know he didn't even tell us about you until today? He actually didn't tell me at all."

"You're falling down the list, Liam." But I wasn't mad.

"He's a little quiet," Wilfred said. "But I'm starting to see that he opens up over time. Now, can I get a tour? I want to see it all before the people pack in here."

Liam gave me a thumbs-up as I led Wilfred away. We went to my apartment first, to the back kitchen, and then to the front where I turned on the lights for him.

"This is *something*," he said in awe.

"It's pretty good for a guy who didn't attend college," I said.

"Not everyone needs that. You did what makes you happy."

"Some people think everyone needs college."

Wilfred raised an eyebrow. "Who?"

"Did you see the Murray building on the way over here?"

"That's Todd's business, right?"

"Not anymore. Tom took it over."

"He retired?"

"No, he was fired."

"Why?"

"Because he was a terrible fucking person." It blew out of me, shocking Wilfred into silence. "And I don't want you to feel bad about it because it isn't your fault, but he was . . . He almost broke us. All of us. He's the one who told me I was one of the biggest disappointments in the family and that I'd never make it if I didn't go to college."

"I . . . I thought he was good to you all."

I shook my head.

A frown pulled on Wilfred's face, a stark contrast to the smile he usually wore. "I'm sorry. I never liked the man, but I assumed I was just jealous because your mom chose him."

"She thought he was the better option, but money didn't buy my peace. It only bought us more misery."

He blew out a long breath. "Damn it. I was hoping that . . . Never mind."

"You were hoping I was at least happy?"

"All of you, even the two older ones. I thought . . . I thought your mom *loved* Todd."

"I don't know if she did. He was a shit father and she was his enforcer. If there was love between them, I'll never know. I got out early, but Ruth and Tom . . . well, they *just* figured out that life isn't your parents yelling at you to be the best at everything. For a while, I didn't know if they would ever figure it out at all."

"I hate that," he said, his voice shaking. "I would have been there. For all of you."

There was that damn emotion again, the one that weighed me down and made it hard to speak. "You didn't know. It wasn't your fault."

"Look, I'm far too late and I don't exactly know what I'm doing, but if you need a dad . . . I'm here."

"I know. That's more than Todd was. More than Mom was, even."

"I always thought that if she came back, I'd be with her. But I don't think I can now that I know about you."

"You could do whatever you want."

"She hurt me by telling me. What's worse, she hurt you. I'll always think of these years and wonder what could have been. I don't think I'll move past that."

"Me either. But on the bright side, we have time now."

"We do. So, let's make the most of it."

Chapter Thirty-Five

Lila

I was confused when I heard a knock at the door. Barry wouldn't arrive until later today and I wasn't expecting a visitor. Juno was already here, going through the plan for all the people coming into town. She raised an eyebrow at me before opening the door.

In the rare event that I had a guest, she gave a spiel about how this was private property. Paparazzi usually weren't bold enough to knock, but sometimes salespeople or neighbors did. As light spilled into my home from the open door, I listened for any hint as to who it was. And when Juno muttered an, "Oh, uh . . ." I knew something was up.

I peered around her and saw red hair tinged with gray, and hazel eyes like mine.

"Mom?" I asked.

"Hi, Rose," she said, bypassing Juno to walk in and hug me.

"W-what are you doing here?"

She smiled. "I'm here to see your first concert. Your dad is coming too."

"But you never come to my concerts."

Her smile fell. "I know, and I've been thinking a lot about how I've let my nerves stop me from everything. I want to see you perform, even if it's only once."

My first thought was that I was being pranked. This was bold, especially for her. She didn't just get on planes and surprise me. She always stayed home.

But I wanted her to see a show of mine.

Badly.

"And you must be Juno," Mom said.

"Nice to meet you in person," Juno replied.

"Yes. I must apologize for my anxiety about my daughter's secret. I should have never put that pressure on you."

Juno's eyes widened and she looked at me with an expression that mirrored my own feelings.

What the *fuck*?

"Wow, this house is beautiful," she said. "I can't believe I've never seen it."

"H-how are you not terrified right now?"

"Oh, I am. But your dad found me a doctor who recommended some medicine to help, and it has. I want to see *this* part of your life. Even if I choose to stay away from cameras."

"Yeah, okay. We can make that happen." Juno walked back to her list of plans. "You can ride in separately from everyone and arrive early."

"That's perfect." She looked around. "Is Barry here?"

"Um, he's home. Back in Nashville, I mean. He has a life there."

"That's a shame. I was hoping to meet him."

"He'll be flying in later today, though."

She smiled, and it hit me that I'd *never* seen her like this. What the fuck had Dad done?

My watch went off, a reminder that I had to get to the stadium and do my dress rehearsal.

"Work calls. Do you mind if Juno and I go?"

"Of course not. I'll be here. Maybe Rose and I can get up to something tonight?"

"Yes, definitely."

I nodded to Juno, who was waiting for me. I asked her to get another guard here in case Mom saw anyone, and she called someone in.

"So," Juno started after we got on the road, "that was not the same woman I talked to on the phone."

"Yeah, I was thinking the same thing. Dad visited her after he found out what she'd done to you. Apparently, he helped."

"We've gotta thank him."

"This isn't like him, though. He spent all of his time on traveling and avoiding responsibility. Why would he help with the family issues now?"

"Some people change. It's best not to question it."

"Is it?"

"Let me rephrase, it's best not to question it when the biggest tour of your life starts in a few days."

She was right. I needed to focus on my job, but I couldn't help wonder what Dad had done. If I didn't know and couldn't replicate it, I would be blindsided when he returned to his old ways.

It was still on my mind when we pulled into the arena. Since today was the full dress rehearsal, I had to force myself to put it behind me. This was when we would finally see everything come together.

My skin buzzed with excitement. Malia said that despite all the drama surrounding me, my tickets had sold out instantaneously, which made me even more excited to get this started.

The second I arrived, my team got me in my first outfit, and I walked out onstage exactly how I would if the tour was going on. I danced and moved, pretending a crowd was in the empty seats.

I could feel Mickey's eyes on me as usual, but I once again told myself it was nothing. It didn't help that my costumes were more revealing than what I usually practiced in. I was probably feeling exposed from that alone.

Despite my weird feelings, he was good at what he did. He played the whole thing almost as good as Barry would.

Almost.

Two hours later, the show felt real, and Justice had clapped for the performance.

I was panting but feeling ready to share this with everyone. I couldn't wait to see Barry and tell him about the rehearsal or hang out with Mom and show her the life I'd made here.

"Lila! Hang on!" Mickey called as I was heading to get undressed. I turned to see him jogging over to me.

"Good job today," I said, giving him a polite smile. "I need to head out, though."

His hand landed on my arm. "Let me take you out after this. You must be starving."

Oh *no*. "Um, no thanks."

He didn't seem deterred from me turning him down.

"So you want to do a slow burn? I can get with that."

I frowned. "What does that mean?"

"You do a whole romance thing with *someone*, and I'm the newest guy. I knew what I was signing up for and it's gonna be great"—his eyes slid up and down me—"as long as we start soon."

"I'm . . . I'm not single. I'm seeing someone."

"Yeah, right. I know how show business works. I know what we have to do to keep the public interested."

"We're not going to be together."

"My agent told me we would."

"Your agent lied."

"Then I guess I need to be persuasive. I won't take no for an answer."

My eyes slid to Justice who was talking with one of the stagehands. I desperately waved her over.

"Hey, what's going on?" she asked.

"Um, can you tell Mickey that we aren't doing a romance thing onstage?"

"What do you mean?" Justice asked.

"Come on." Mickey rolled his eyes. "Lila Wilde needs a boy toy to flirt with to make her fans happy. That's me."

"No," she said immediately. "We're not doing that. The little thing with Blaze went way too far. We're here to celebrate her talent and let Lila do what she's comfortable with."

"But I'm supposed to be the new Blaze."

"I don't want another one of him," I cut in. "I just want a guitarist."

"You *need* another Blaze Matthews. You can't do this on your own."

"That's enough." Justice stepped in front of me. "I will not tolerate you speaking down to her like that."

"Blaze did."

"And he better be glad I didn't see it. Her team is on *her* side, so you can buzz off."

"Oh, so you *don't* need me?"

"Wait, we do," I interjected. "It's two days before the show."

"That's right," Mickey said. "And I'm not doing this without some sort of romance."

"Then you're fired. Get out."

Mickey shook his head, standing up straighter. "Yeah, right. You just said you needed me. I don't have to leave."

"Hey, buddy." Juno's angry voice made even my hair stand on end. "Leave or I will throw you out."

"You can't—" Mickey stopped as his eyes finally fixed on Juno and he remembered how much bigger she was than him. "Whatever. When you crash and burn, I'll be watching."

He strode out without another word and Juno followed to make sure he actually left.

"What was that?" I asked, panicked. "We can't fire him."

"He's looking at you like a piece of meat. And treating you like one too."

"I mean, *yes*, but the tour—"

"You're not sacrificing yourself for this tour. We want you to *enjoy it*."

I didn't expect that answer.

"Let me talk to Malia," Justice said. "I'm sure we can figure something out."

"But we had a hard time finding Mickey. And now we have to do it again right before the tour?"

"We have other options. Don't worry about it. Get some rest before this actually starts. Let us figure out the rest."

"But—"

"Lila," Justice said, "you're at the top of your game and deserve to be *happy* onstage. I already have some ideas to discuss with Malia. We have this. Go enjoy rest."

I wanted to. The conversation with Mickey had exhausted me.

I nodded, pushing past the desire to fix everything for everyone or to pull an all-nighter until I solved this problem. I knew I wanted to focus on Mom being here and on Barry's arrival. Malia and Justice had been fantastic to work with and I needed to let them handle this. "Okay, I trust you."

And I did. But I didn't see a way out of this. We were down a band member *again*, all because of me.

"She did the right thing," Juno said as she walked up to me. "And don't worry, if anyone can handle it, it's Justice and Malia."

"Why did he have to be weird?" I groaned.

"Some guys make it their goal to be as weird as possible. He should have taken the hint."

"Let's just go. The more I stay here, the more worried I get."

Juno nodded, giving me a sympathetic look as we walked to the car.

We drove silently until we returned to the house where Mom lounged on the couch.

"Hey," she said with a smile. She didn't seem worried, and I was glad she didn't. Our roles had been reversed in the span of a day. "How was the practice?"

"Um, fine," I lied. "So, you wanted to see LA?"

"I do."

"Let me get the wig off, then we can go."

I went to the bathroom, hoping that meticulously taking off my disguise would put my Lila worries away.

It didn't.

Barry

There was a limo waiting at the airport. I blinked at the driver standing outside of it holding a sign that read, *The Murray Family*.

"Is that for us?" Max asked, gripping my shoulder.

"I guess Lila wanted to spoil us." I was hoping to see her here, whether as Lila or Rose, but with two days left before the tour, I knew she was more than likely practicing.

We piled in, and as we rode through the busy streets, Max excitedly talked about every aspect of our trip.

I played it cool, but I counted down the seconds until I saw her again.

We were all staying in a nice hotel close to the event. Everywhere was packed for the first night of her concert. Even our hotel was clogged with other fans coming into town. This morning, she'd mentioned all of us staying at her mansion, but I turned her down, knowing that the members of this party would not take it well if I couldn't keep my eyes off of Lila.

And Ruth had reiterated that I had a terrible poker face.

It was better for our story if we stayed somewhat apart. Lila paid an excessive amount for the hotel to get us all rooms, plus offered extra tickets for the hotel to giveaway.

"Wow," Selena said. "This is . . . huge. And loud."

"You can rest for a bit if you feel like you need to," Tom said.

"I think I will. I want to enjoy the concert, not overdo it beforehand. Max, do you want to join me?"

"Yeah. I need some quiet time."

"As do I," Lynn added. "Will you kids be okay without me?"

"We'll be fine," Ruth said, her hand in Knox's.

"I actually have to go too," Knox said. "Work calls."

"Boo." Ruth groaned. "But I understand. Just stop before dark, okay?"

I hated to admit it, but the weight was off my shoulders at the fact that the only people with me knew who Rose was. There would be far less to worry about with just the three of us.

"So, what's the plan? Rose is obviously here, right?"

"Yeah, she is. But she might be practicing. I'll text her and see if she's free."

I pulled out my phone and scrolled to our text chain.

Barry: Are you busy?

Rose: My mom is in town and I'm out as Rose.

Barry: Your mom came to LA?

Rose: I know. It's wild, but she wants to see the show. Who are you with?

Barry: Tom and Ruth. We were talking about going to dinner.

Rose: I can't wait to see you. Want to join us?

"So, how would you guys feel about seeing Rose and her mom?"

"Rose and not the other one?" Ruth asked. "I thought she was practicing."

"Her mom is here, and being Rose is the only way she can get some peace. It should be far more low-key than if we were with *you know who*."

"I think we can make that work," Ruth said. "As long as there's some food. I'm fucking starving."

"You're always starving," Tom remarked dryly.

"I can't help that the plane had terrible food. Who serves salmon on a plane?"

"First class does," I remarked. "It's why I prefer the lower classes."

"This time, I agree with you. We should get going. Judging by the traffic, it's gonna take us hours to get anywhere."

Chapter Thirty-Six

My leg wouldn't still. I was trying to focus on what Mom was saying about her therapist and doctor, but all I could think about was how my tour was fucked and it was all my fault. I hoped that the addition of Barry, Ruth, and Tom would help.

I saw the black limo I'd sent for them pull up. My eyes followed it as they climbed out.

"Who's that?" Mom asked. "I thought this was a low-key place."

"Just some friends of mine." I got up when I saw Barry, nearly running to where he was getting out of the limo.

His long hair framed his face and he looked gorgeous in the light. My entire body loosened as I got close.

"Hey—"

He didn't get to finish because I jumped into his arms.

"God, I've missed you," I said into his shoulder.

"Likewise, sunshine." Even his voice was soothing.

"Hi," Ruth said as Barry reluctantly let me go. "It's so good to see you again."

"You too. I'm sorry I can't go to the concert. Work is so—"

But then Tom walked up, offering up another Murray grin. "Hi, Rose."

"Hey. Okay, so when we meet my mom—"

Someone grabbed my arm and I turned to see the very woman I was talking about had followed me.

"Who's this?" Mom asked, but her voice shook this time.

My stomach dropped. She was getting nervous.

"I'm Barry." He held out his hand. "I'm sure you've heard about me."

"A little."

"And this is my brother and sister, Tom and Ruth."

"W-what are you in town for?"

"Oh, just a concert," Ruth said. "Kind of like everyone else is."

"Lila fans?"

"Very much so," Ruth said, and her eyes looked over at me for one second. It was an innocent move, but Mom picked up on it. A frown came onto her face, the same kind as when I'd told her my plans to pursue music in the first place.

I was in trouble.

"Why don't we sit and eat?" Tom asked. "I know Ruth is starving."

"'Fucking starving' was the phrase she used," Barry added, a smile going over to his siblings. I wished I could join in, but I was receiving a death glare from Mom.

"We have a table," I said.

"Oh, yes. Where is it?"

"In the back."

Ruth nearly beelined for the table and Tom followed. Mom's grip on my arm tightened as they walked off.

"Everything okay?" Barry asked.

"You go ahead. I need to talk to Mom."

"Okay. Let me know if you need me."

Mom waited until he was gone before she spoke.

"Ruth *looks* like she knows."

I shook my head. I didn't want to lie, but Mom wouldn't take it well if she knew the full truth. "Come on, Mom. You came all this way. Let's not let one look ruin it."

Her lips pursed. "I thought today was for *us*."

"It is, but I knew they were coming weeks ago, and I really like these people. Can't we all get to know each other?"

"It's like you don't know me at all." She shook her head. "I'm going back to the house."

"Wait—"

"I don't want to hear it. If you can't value me coming all this way, then I won't put myself through the misery."

She took out her phone and called for a cab, saying nothing else. I opened my mouth to tell her to stay, but she walked away.

A hand gently grazed my shoulder and I turned to see Barry.

"So, everything is *not* okay," he said softly.

"No," I muttered. "Mom's mad that I invited you guys."

"Wasn't she a surprise guest?"

"Yes." I rubbed my face. "I can't get it right with her, or anything else in my life, it seems."

"Is there more going on?"

"Guitarist stuff." At his worried expression, I shook my head. "Malia and Justice are on it. I'll tell you when we're *not* in public. I'm just *so* worried, and Mom is making it worse."

"Come here," he said, pulling me into his arms again. I closed my eyes and leaned into him. "Why is she here anyway? I thought she stayed in her hometown."

"Dad connected her with a therapist and she got on medication. She really was fine until just now."

"How did your dad get through to her?"

"I have no idea, but she said he's coming into town too."

"Can he help her through this?"

"He's already done so much," I said. "I can't add another thing."

As I said it, my phone buzzed with a text from him.

Dad: Rosie, I just got into town and your mother is upset. I would love to meet for dinner, but I'd rather you relax and not worry about her like I know you're doing. I'm going to meet her at your place and talk to her.

"He's already handling it," I said. "Who is this man?"

"What was he like before?"

"He's always cared and answered when I called, but I felt like he had this whole other life to live and that I was an afterthought."

"Maybe he got tired of that way of living."

"I should talk to him."

Barry shook his head, his hand grabbing mine. "You can later, but for now, he's right. You do need to relax, and if you see your mom again, it might not end well."

He wasn't wrong. "Why is everyone doing all of this for me?"

"Because we care," he replied. "Do we need another reason?"

"I . . . I guess not. This is why I should keep you around, Barry. You know exactly what to say."

"Let's enjoy dinner."

"Do you think Ruth is mad that I made her wait?"

"I'm sure she's already ordered an appetizer." He smiled. He pulled me close again, his mouth right next to my ear. "She's gonna have to be patient when we're waiting for Lila Wilde."

No one heard it, yet my face exploded in flame.

"They don't have to be patient because of that."

"Then we'll be patient because it's *you.*"

A few minutes ago, my life had felt like it was falling apart. But because of him, it now felt like it would turn out okay. How did he do that? How did he level me out?

"So," I said as we walked to the table, "I hear one of you figured something out?"

Ruth was in fact digging into an appetizer, but she paused when she registered what I said. "Do you want me to pretend I don't know? I can be a good liar."

Tom shook his head. "No, you can't."

"I can *try*."

"It's okay," I said. "Barry trusts you, so I'm going to try to as well."

"Good. I've had my run-ins with the media because of Knox. I completely understand why you did it."

"Does Knox still have that problem?" I asked.

"Not as much anymore," she explained. "He's boring now that he's been with me for months. But we'll be careful. I won't tell him the secret, but I can steer him away from being seen with you."

"I can also have my agent handle some of it. She's been burying leads ever since she found out."

"So," Ruth started, putting down her chip, "is your mom why you do this?"

"I'm sure you caught onto some tension. I'm sorry you had to see it."

"It's no problem," she replied. "We're very used to family drama, but usually it's *our* family drama. And it's more explosive."

"Mom's just stressed about everything. My dad is handling it."

"That's good," Tom said. "You have a big day coming up."

I blew out a long breath. "Yeah. I do. It's not my first rodeo. I know the show inside and out. *Mostly* everything is figured out."

Other than the guitarist.

"Then we shouldn't think too hard about it," Ruth said. "Tonight is for *fun*."

"No alcohol, though," I said. "I don't drink before shows."

"I don't drink at all," Tom said. "I've been sober just under a year. So, we'd be avoiding it anyway."

"What should we do?" Ruth asked.

"Don't look at me," Tom said.

"Yeah, really don't," Barry piped in. "You know what I've always wanted to try? Topgolf."

I stepped away from dinner to make a reservation at the local Topgolf range. When I returned, Ruth was telling Barry and Tom about something nearly catching fire in the kitchen.

"Carmen was in shock," Ruth was saying. "She said she'd never seen something do that in the oven and now it had happened *twice*."

"Who's Carmen?" I asked.

"Selena's mom," Tom interjected.

"She's been helping my mother-in-law learn to cook," Ruth said. "And it's going hilariously."

"I don't know if you can call Lynn your mother-in-law if you're not married," Barry teased.

Ruth glared. "I absolutely can. Knox and I are basically there anyway."

"Where *is* Knox?" I asked. "Didn't I give you all enough tickets to bring your significant others?"

"He had some work to do," Ruth said. "But I was thinking about dragging him to Topgolf. If you were okay with that, of course. He can enter separately and with a disguise. But I don't really think people care about him when the concert of the year is in two days."

"It'll be fine. You all can invite whoever you want. I, um, might have reserved the entire floor."

"You can do that?" Barry asked.

"With enough money." I shrugged. "Sorry if it's a lot. It would give us some privacy and would give us enough room to invite everyone."

Ruth snorted. "You and Knox will get along. He would have done the same thing." She pivoted. "So, who here has actually golfed?"

Tom and I raised our hands.

"Really?"

"Dad was into it," Tom said. "But I'm willing to try it with people who aren't assholes to see if I enjoy it."

"Same. My old agent liked it too."

"So you're gonna kick our ass," Ruth said.

"Doubt it. Topgolf is *very* different than golf."

"As long as I get to threaten Knox," Ruth said, "I'm good."

"Is he okay with that?" I asked.

"He's probably into it," Barry replied. "They have a very odd relationship."

Ruth lowered her voice so no one could hear. "You don't get to lecture me about odd relationships, Mr. Almost Cheater."

I laughed. "At least you tried to tell me."

"The fact that I told you about *you* will mortify me for months." Ruth sighed. "But it'll be one for the storybooks."

Barry

I quickly decided that having the entire place to ourselves was the perfect way to spend the evening.

Rose introduced herself and greeted everyone who arrived. I took stock of all of my family and friends here, noticing that she didn't invite anyone she knew.

"Couldn't Malia or Justice come?"

Her lips pressed together. "I let them know they could join, but I highly doubt they'll be able to—"

As she said it, Malia ascended the stairs, dressed in what looked to be slacks and a fancy blouse. She must have come directly from her office.

"Rose," Malia said, smiling. "It's good to see you."

"You could come? I mean, is everything okay with . . . you know, the *thing*?"

"We're working on it," Malia reassured. "I can't stay for too long, but I wanted to see you and ensure you were doing okay."

"Anything I can help with?" I asked.

Malia smiled. "We can talk in a few. Let's try and have fun."

I didn't know if I wanted to wait until later, but Rose was the first up, and I tried my best to focus on her. It was hard to care about hitting a ball when I could see the tense line of her shoulders from a mile away.

The first shot she took flew across the field with more force than I'd ever seen from her.

"Whoops," she said, laughing awkwardly.

"Holy shit," Ruth muttered.

"I think the club is light. Does anyone else want a turn?"

Ruth took it and announced the club definitely was not light. I raised an eyebrow at Rose, but she shook her head and she sat next to me.

I turned to see Ruth miss the ball on the first swing.

"Not good at golf?" I teased. I was worried, yet I couldn't help but egg on my sister.

"Hang on. I'm trying to remember how to coordinate my hands and eyes."

The second time she hit it, the ball went about half the distance that Rose's first shot did. Her score, however, was remarkably high, far too close to Rose's.

"They have to inflate that," I said.

"It's the angle she hit it at," Rose explained. "Mine went straight to the back."

Knox went next, but didn't hit it as far as Ruth.

As they teased each other, I checked on Rose one more time; she was watching Tom teach Max how to hit a ball in the other bay. The soft smile on her face told me I needed to watch too.

It took a bit of trial and error, especially when Max missed the ball on the first shot. Tom showed him again. Max's excited face was worth it when he finally got the hang of it.

My eyes slid back over to Malia, who hadn't yet taken the offer of a turn. She was on her phone, biting her lip.

"Do you want a go?" Rose asked, breaking my focus.

"Oh, yeah." I took the club from Juno, who had just finished her turn. I'd never played golf, but it wasn't hard to smack it across the field.

I only took three shots before I let Rose go again, and while she was distracted, I knew I needed to talk to Malia.

She obviously had the same thought because she gestured for me to follow her before I could even ask. We went to the opposite end of the level, out of Rose's sight.

"What's going on with the tour?" I asked.

"Mickey is no longer the guitarist."

I blinked. "What? Is that why you two are off?"

"I'm supposed to be figuring out a replacement, which is why I've been on my phone."

"What happened?"

"He hit on Lila and Justice fired him."

"The concert is in *two* days."

And I could now see why Rose had nearly lost it in front of the restaurant.

"Yes. Justice thought she could strong-arm you into taking his place, so she didn't think twice about letting him go."

"You know I can't step on that stage."

"I do."

"What are the other options?"

"We could use a studio recording temporarily."

"But if you get caught, fans would be pissed the whole show isn't live."

"Exactly," Malia said. "So, I'm brainstorming. Or at least trying to."

"What, like I sit backstage playing guitar?"

"It's an option."

"She wanted me to see the show."

Malia sighed. "I don't know if this is a situation where we can all have everything we want. Either you watch the show and we use a recording, or you do it backstage. You're our *only* option with this short of notice."

"Have you asked her what she thinks of it?"

"Rose is barely hanging on. She was near tears when Justice told her not to worry about it."

"And her mom is in town," I added.

"What?" Malia asked. "That too? God, I know I said I would tell her everything, but I'm afraid she won't be able to go onstage if we do."

"What have you told her?"

"That we'd handle it and she needed to take care of herself."

"All true things. We *will* handle it."

"So, you'll play? It can be just for the first show. *Maybe*."

I opened my mouth to say I'd do it for as long as they needed me, but I couldn't exactly promise that. I was supposed to be back in Nashville in a few days to work on some burnt-out lights at the bar.

"I can promise opening night."

Malia sighed in relief. "Thank you, Barry. I'll need to get going to figure out some things, but I do have one question for you."

"What is it?"

"If there was a way to keep your identity a secret *and* be onstage, would you do it?"

The question hung heavy.

"It's not possible. I have the bar and—"

"I'm not talking about forever. I'm talking about right now. Do you want to be on the stage?"

"Of course I fucking do. She shines out there and being backstage feels like I'm missing the sunrise."

"That's what I thought." She gave me a half smile. "We'll talk later."

CHAPTER THIRTY-SEVEN

I almost forgot my worries, but they lingered, especially after Malia disappeared. I was surprised she showed up at all, considering the mess we had on our hands.

"Were you talking to Malia about . . . the issue we're having?" I asked Barry when he finally walked up next to me. He'd disappeared with her for a good few minutes.

"For a bit. But it's nothing we can talk about here. We'll need to get you home first."

"Oh my God, *home*. Mom's there. I need to deal with that too."

"We only have thirty minutes left. Let's finish this out and deal with things one at a time."

I nodded, forcing a smile as Ruth teased Knox about beating his score. I tried to play the happy, easygoing woman I wanted to be.

But when the game was over, Ruth hugged me tight and told me to call her if I needed any help. Tom also offered his.

Yep. They saw right through me.

I had to admit that it was nice having a bigger support system. I believed both of them when they offered their help, and it eased my nerves to know I had at least a few more people on my side.

Barry was looking off into the distance as everyone drove away.

"You're thinking about what you and Malia talked about, aren't you?" I asked.

"I am. She's bringing me in to help with your guitarist problem."

"That makes sense. It's probably the only way we'd be able to play live, at least for this show."

"You're disappointed that I won't see it, right?"

"A little, but I'll just get you tickets to the Nashville show. Hopefully, I'll have a new guitarist by then."

"It's going to work out. First things first, you should check on your mom."

"Yeah, I should. I would invite you, but the last thing you need is family drama while also dealing with Lila's drama."

"You're dealing with it all."

"Not really. My team is on one of them. And I trust whatever they come up with."

"Good. We won't let you down."

I gave him a soft smile and stood on my tiptoes to kiss him on the cheek. "The limo with your family is still waiting. Go with them."

"But if you need me, call me."

"I will," I said. "I promise."

He pressed his lips to mine one more time before reluctantly leaving. I let out a long breath.

"Where to, boss?" Juno asked.

"My house," I said. "It's time to face the music of my family."

When I pulled into the driveway, the blinds were drawn and Mom was huddled on the couch. Dad was next to her, talking to her softly.

"I can't do this," she muttered. "I can't do this."

"It's okay, Linda. You can go back home."

"But *why* can't I do this? Why can't I just be happy for her?"

"Mom?" I asked as I walked in. "Is everything okay?"

Mom saw me, her eyes wide. "Why are you back?"

"I came back to make sure everything's okay."

"You should be enjoying your time with your friends," Dad replied. "Your mom told me you were hanging out with them."

"And I did, but I'm also worried about things here. Mom snapped at me in public about inviting them and then left in a rush."

"I'm handling it."

"And I just . . . I just got worried," Mom added. "Like I always do."

"Your therapist said this might be too much," Dad reminded her. "And it's okay if it is."

I blinked, still not understanding this new side of him.

He sounded . . . like a dad. Like the man I wanted to be *my* dad.

"Wh-why are you doing all this?" I asked him slowly. "For years, you were fine with traveling all the time and letting Mom stay alone."

"H-honey," Mom said. "Don't be mad at him, I—"

"It's okay. She needs to know what happened." He turned to me and my heart kicked into high gear as I thought of all the words he could say. We didn't do this. We didn't confront each other. We just pretended things were fine. "I didn't know how bad your mother was. Whenever I talked to her, she said things were fine. You said they were fine too."

"Because you didn't seem to care."

"Rosie, I always cared. I answered all of your calls. I would have come back if I knew how much you were doing for her. I always said I would be here if you needed me. It was the deal I made when your mother told me no to taking you with me."

"W-what? Taking me with you?"

Mom looked at her hands. "Rose, he . . . When he left, he told me he was worried it would be too much for me, that raising you after the divorce would be difficult, and that you would be better with him, either half the time or all the time."

"But you said he didn't want to be a dad. He wanted to travel."

Dad looked at Mom, his lips pursed. "I wish you hadn't said that."

"I-I know, but I thought you were lying when you offered."

He sighed and then looked back at me. "Sure, I wanted to travel, but I was a parent first. I thought you two were fine, and the minute I saw how Linda really was, I came back to help her find the help she needed."

I couldn't wrap my head around this. He wanted me to go with him? And Mom had told him no? All my life, I'd thought he'd left because he didn't want to be a parent. It made his sudden return impossible to believe.

But this changed everything.

"You really said no because you thought he was lying?"

Her face crumpled. "That, and I thought you would be better off with me. I thought I could handle it, but as time went on, and you wanted fame . . ."

"Hey, it's not because she wanted fame," Dad reminded her.

"Well, what else could it be?" I asked. "This all started getting worse right after I became Lila."

"There were hints of it when you were born," Dad said. "But we all thought it was postpartum depression. Instead, it's something else. Have you ever heard of borderline personality disorder?"

I shook my head.

"It's a mental disorder that makes it very difficult for her to manage emotions, especially her anxiety. After you told me what happened with Juno, I knew she needed help, and now we know why."

"But I've been going to therapy," Mom said. "I did everything they said and I'm still so scared. I've done so many stupid things because of my own emotions, and I want to be better."

"I don't think that's how getting better works," I said.

"It's not," Dad agreed. "And while I wanted you to enjoy your time in LA, if you're not, then it's okay."

"I liked part of it, but the minute I met those people—"

"Ruth and Tom?"

"Yes. Them. I was so nervous they knew."

I wanted to lie and say they didn't, just so she would feel a little better.

But that wasn't the right thing.

"Mom, a secret like this is huge. People are going to know."

"But—"

"I need a support system. I need people I trust so that I can be myself with them and so they can help me keep everything straight. I know you didn't want me to tell anyone, but they have to know."

The words hung heavy in the air. Mom's eyes were wide and I saw the spark of defiance in them. She was going to argue.

"Linda," Dad started, "you know she's right. She's kept this to herself and it's gotten more complicated over the years. This is *her* life too. Not just yours."

"And even if it all blows up someday, I have people who can protect both me and you. You haven't met her, but my new agent, Malia, is incredible. She works so hard and even helped me cover my tracks so no one knows. And today, Ruth saw me stressing about the show and made me have fun so I could breathe for a second. And it *helped*. Living a double life keeps people safe, but what's the point if no one actually knows me?"

"You're right. I *know* you're right, but I'm so . . ." She shook her head and turned to Dad. "Can you call an emergency session? I should talk to my therapist about this."

"Of course."

"And . . . I don't know if I can see your show."

"It's okay. I have a ton of other ones. I'd rather have you take care of yourself."

"Thank you," she said. "I'll get better. I *need* to."

"And I'll be here until she does," Dad added. "No more miscommunication. If I return to traveling, I'll be sure everyone is okay with it."

A weight lifted off of my shoulders. Dad wasn't going to flip a switch and leave.

It wasn't just *me*.

"Thank you," I said. "I've been *so* stressed—"

"Come here, kiddo," Dad said in that same soft voice he'd used with Mom. "You look like you need a hug."

I really did. He wrapped his arms around me, giving me an embrace I didn't know I needed. Mom joined in, and for once, this didn't feel like a split family. Things were shifting.

And we were entering an era of healing.

Barry

The second I got back, I went to my hotel room to grab my guitar. I'd brought it on impulse, but something in the back of my head told me I would need it.

I'd taken to playing the setlist whenever I missed her, which meant I was in perfect practice for this. I could step in like I was never gone, even if I remained backstage.

But then what? How long would it take for them to find someone else? How long did I have before I was needed back at Movers and Shakers?

The future wasn't clear, which was terrifying.

I got through four of the songs before there was a knock at the door. I paused to answer it and found Tom on the other side.

"What are you doing here?" I asked.

"You were off after Malia talked to you. I'm worried. And Ruth is too. She would have joined, but I told her not to. She's a little more intense than I think you need right now."

"I'm fine," I muttered.

"Are you sure?" he asked. "Because Selena and Max are hanging out with Lynn, and I have nothing but time."

"Why are they hanging out with Lynn?"

"I sent them to. I wanted to be sure you were all right."

"Oh." I blinked. "You care that much?"

"We've been through enough that you *know* I do."

"It's still weird, you know. We've fought or ignored each other for so long that I'm still shocked when it's not like that anymore."

"It's going to take time to adjust, but the more we talk, the easier it'll get. Can I come in?"

I nodded, stepping aside. I shut the door behind me, knowing we were free to discuss whatever we needed to.

"Something is going on with the tour," I admitted. "Something I can fix in the short-term."

"Then do it."

"But this problem will still be there after, and I can't do this and be at Movers and Shakers simultaneously."

"I'm guessing this is music-related."

"Yes. And I care about it so much that I could almost leave Nashville for it. But I made something back home. I need to stay there."

"Wow," was all he said.

"You think that I should stick with the bar, right?"

"Why would I think that?"

"It's my responsibility."

"It's still your bar . . . unless you're thinking about selling. And from what I've heard, you have a good team."

"But I should be there in the flesh, working."

"Working? That sounds like something Dad would say."

"You know what I mean. I'm sure Todd and Mom were waiting for me to step away, but they'd want me to go to college. I promised myself I could never do this."

"Things have changed, though. You have an opportunity that you want. Go for it."

"For the record, I'd be backstage. I'm not . . . No one will *see* me."

"Do you want them to?"

Yes.

But I couldn't say that out loud.

Tom got the message anyway.

"If I know one thing about you," he said, "it's that you're the most creative of us. This problem you have? I have no doubt you'll find some way out of it."

"But I have no ideas this time."

"Give it time. Put away any expectations you have. No matter what you do, we'll be proud."

"Even if I streak across the stage in the middle of the show?"

"Is that an option?"

"No, but it would be wild."

He laughed. "Then we'd make fun of you, but ultimately be proud because you'd be happy."

"You have that much faith in me?"

"I do. You'll find some way to make it work. You always have. And you know what? I can't wait to see what you figure out."

Chapter Thirty-Eight

Lila

The day before the show was always terrifying, even when I had a full crew. But this time, I had genuine reason to panic.

I paced the floor, mind going through the endless routine of what all we could do to fix this. The final dress rehearsal tonight was figured out. But what about the future? If we didn't find someone in a week by some miracle, would we have to use a recording for the guitar?

God forbid if anyone found out about it. I was known for doing everything live, but I'd been the victim of lip-synching scandals for many years. Even my backing track was controversial. If the guitar were recorded, then people would assume everything else was too.

"Lila!" Juno called as she walked in. "It's time for your last dress rehearsal."

"Coming."

"And I have a surprise for you."

I didn't know if I could handle a surprise, but then Barry walked into the living room in his usual LA disguise.

"Hey," he said. "Ready to practice?"

"You're stepping in for today?"

"We have to have some sort of run-through."

"Thank *God*. I would have understood if you wanted today off, but more practice is better." Words poured out of me and I couldn't stop them. "But if you want to spend time with Ruth and Tom, we can make this go faster and—"

His hands came to cup my cheeks. "Breathe," he said. "It's going to be okay."

Here, with him close to me, I could almost believe it.

"S-sorry. It's been a lot."

"I know. Let's start with practice and we'll go from there."

I nodded and let him lead me to the car.

"You okay?" Juno asked. "I gave you extra space in case you needed any time to . . . melt down."

"We came close," I replied. "But we're good."

She smiled and nodded at Barry. Juno had been worried about me as my stress piled up, but even she knew he would pull me out of it.

And everyone else, apparently.

When we got to the arena, my entire team was relieved to see Barry. The news had traveled quickly and Justice had been fielding questions for a while. One of my backup singers hugged him so tightly I thought he might burst.

"Ready to start?" he asked after everyone finished fawning over him.

"Are you? You're the first instrument to open us."

"I'm always ready, Lila."

I smiled, knowing it was true. I got into position and started singing my first notes and he joined in right after.

As we got into the show, I realized this practice felt different than all the others. Instead of avoiding looking over at my band, I did more often than ever. Seeing Barry there filled me with more joy than I ever imagined.

In the plan for this tour, I only went over to sing to my band members once, but it didn't feel like enough now that Barry was back in it. I smiled at him brighter than I would have ever smiled at Mickey.

If he were staying onstage, I'd work in much more time to be next to him.

But he wasn't, and I needed to remember that.

Barry

After the rehearsal, everyone looked less stressed, and I didn't have the heart to tell them this was a one-time deal.

Rose and I went home where she was finally able to un-Lila herself. She took melatonin and fell asleep right after. I lay awake, still thinking about tomorrow.

I was happy she'd managed to sleep because she needed all the energy she could find for her show the next day. I should have done the same, but I had far too many thoughts swirling in my head.

"You'll find some way to make it work," Tom had said.

But I hadn't. I'd been listening to Lila Wilde, admiring her creativity, all my life. And if we had more time, I was sure we could somehow figure something out. But it was the eve of the concert and we were in the eleventh hour.

When Lila had wanted this, she'd donned a wig and made a new version of herself. And it wasn't like *I* could do that too.

I froze as the thought hit me.

Was there a reason I *couldn't* wear a wig?

I got out of bed, mind reeling. How did I not figure it out sooner? If I followed Lila's lead, then I could be a different person onstage. I'd never admitted my identity in LA and had hidden my hair.

It was like I was planning for this.

Pulling out my phone, I dialed Malia. She answered on the third ring.

"I have an idea," I said.

"You do?"

"Yes. What if I had a wig too?"

The line was silent and then she chuckled. "I was about to call you and mention the same idea. I had it last night."

"Last night? And you didn't bring it up?"

"Wigs are hard to make, especially if fitted to you. I was spending the day seeing if it was even feasible."

"What did you find?"

"Someone who would work overnight to get it done. She's got a good reputation too. I hope you didn't have plans."

"I can be free," I said.

"Thank God. You'll have to come up with a new name. You never did before."

"I'll think about it once I see my new persona."

"Meet me at my office then. We have a lot of work ahead of us tonight."

Chapter Thirty-Nine

Lila

As the clock ticked down before the start of the show, I hoped I wouldn't disappoint my fans. I hoped that, despite all of the changes that had happened over the last few days, I could put on a good performance.

This wasn't going to plan, but I would make it work.

I was in position under the stage, about to be lifted up into the lights and the screams of everyone who'd bought a ticket. My heart was pounding, adrenaline coursing through me.

With less than two minutes to go, Malia ran to my lift, ducking under the stage supports.

"I have good news," she said, out of breath. "You'll have a guitarist."

"Barry, right? He'll be backstage."

"You'll have someone onstage, actually."

"What?" I asked. "And they know the routine?"

"Every note."

"Are you sure?"

"Surer than I'll ever be."

"How did you make this happen?"

"Magic and a few strings being pulled."

"Barry gets to see the whole show too?"

"Yes," she said with a smile. "He has the best seat in the house."

I shook my head, trying to understand how she had made the impossible happen.

"Lila!" one of the stagehands said. "You've got to go up."

"Don't worry about a single thing. Just focus on your performance. You've got this."

I nodded and got back into position.

I only had one second to take a breath. This was all happening so fast. All I knew was that I was going onstage and I was singing.

I wouldn't let it show that I was meeting my guitarist like this. I tried to channel Barry and all of his calmness. If he were here, he'd tell me I was *Lila fucking Wilde*. I could do this.

And I would.

The crowd screamed as I appeared, loud even through my inner-ear speaker. I gave them a wave, twirling on the stage as I'd practiced.

The first song was "Goodbye, Good Riddance," which I stood in the center stage for. It was a guitar-heavy song, but I started it out with only my voice. A few seconds in, the guitar began. I breathed out a sigh of relief. It was definitely live.

My band was in the back on the right. I was too busy singing and interacting with the crowd to get a glimpse of the new person. Soon, I'd be able to spare a glance, but for now, I wanted to find Barry.

I spotted the Murrays in the front row. I'd been looking forward to seeing Barry there, but I'd put away that hope when Mickey was fired. All I wanted to see was that shocked expression he'd worn when I'd shown him the album.

As my eyes drifted over their familiar faces, I recognized Ruth, Tom, Max, Selena, Knox, and Lynn. I even saw Liam and Audrey all cheering at me.

But no Barry.

Disappointment hit me, but I tried not to let it show on my face. Where was he? Was he backstage for some reason? Was he late?

The song came to a close and I fought the frown trying to tug on my lips.

My next number was an older one, a pop song that would get people dancing. I performed the routine in the back of my mind, glad I'd practiced it many times. In my head, I was replaying what Malia had said about Barry. He'd have the best seat in the house. But *where*?

I looked at Ruth and Tom as if they could give me some answers from all the way out in the crowd.

But they weren't even looking at me. They were looking behind me at my band.

Ruth's jaw was on the ground. She was shaking her brother, moving his entire body as he looked in a similar state of shock.

What the fuck? What was going on with my band?

Screw my usual steps, I had to know. I turned to face them. Everything was in order. My drummer was rocking out as usual. My background singers were having the time of their lives. I knew them all.

Except for my rhythm guitarist.

The newest member of my band was buff with shoulders that looked familiar. If it weren't for his long, black hair, I would have said it was . . .

Barry.

My mind blanked and I missed my next moves. All I could do was stare at the man who played my music. He looked up, joining the thousands of eyes that were on me.

And I saw stormy-gray irises, the same ones I'd stared into for many hours.

Holy *shit*.

He was in a wig, almost unrecognizable. Like this, he was messy in ways he usually wasn't. His arms were on full display while he was in a tight black shirt. He looked the part of a rock star.

And I realized exactly what Malia and he had pulled off.

I couldn't help the smile on my face when I saw him.

The crowd, watching my every move, cheered at my newfound good mood.

The happy love song I was in the middle of suddenly was far easier to sing.

As energy sank into my every atom, the crowd got louder, as if they were feeding off of it too. My choreography was entirely forgotten as I ran over to Barry.

I wanted to ask him so many questions, but I could only mouth things unless I wanted the whole audience to hear them.

Luckily for me, the one thing I wanted to say was easy.

I love you, I mouthed at him.

His eyes widened and he almost missed a note. He recovered far faster than I would have.

I could have waited, but these words had been in my head for too long. And if he had found a way to be *onstage* with me, then he needed to know.

I love you too, he mouthed back. I wondered if I could say more, but he reminded me that I was performing by bobbing his head to the music and giving a pointed look to the crowd of excited fans.

Shit. I was about to miss an important mark. I reluctantly moved to go to the left side of the stage, but I couldn't stop glancing over at him at every turn. It didn't feel like I was singing for the crowd anymore. The world had fallen away, leaving only him and me.

It took another two songs for me to find a moment to get back over to him. I couldn't say anything, but our matching smiles said everything we needed to. I danced to the rhythm, my feet moving of their own accord, and Barry joined me, moving his feet in sync like when I was Rose in his bar and we'd lost time dancing together.

I had to pull my mic away to let out a laugh of pure joy. I hadn't felt this light onstage since I was just starting out, and all the lights and cheers felt new to me. We finished the song together and I reluctantly left, knowing I had to make my way to center stage to get ready for another song. I interacted with the crowd as much as I could, but he was constantly on my mind.

As the show went on, I pointed to him for every single love lyric I'd ever written. The crowd melted down each time.

Four songs later, it was time for a quick change, and while I was getting into the new outfit, Malia ran up to me.

"Like who I picked?" she called. She must have been waiting for me.

"He's perfect," I said. "If only he could do this every night."

"This crowd gets a special show," she said, smiling.

I only had time to give her one nod before running back out onto the stage.

Picking up where I left off, I sang my heart out for the crowd and flirted with Barry every second I could. I almost didn't want the show to end, even though I was covered with sweat and out of breath.

When it was over, it didn't *feel* over. I was set to leave the stage in the same way I appeared at the start of the concert.

As the lift descended, I was running to where I knew Barry would walk off with everyone else in the band.

The crowd was begging for an encore. For this tour, I hadn't planned one.

But I couldn't deny that it felt incomplete.

"Barry!" I called as I ran to him.

"What did you think?"

"I don't want it to end," I said desperately. "We have one song we didn't do."

He paused. "'On This Night'?"

I nodded. "We have to do it once. Please?"

"Anything for you."

"Thank you," I said before turning to the band. "We'll do the encore by ourselves."

The crowd was deafening as we returned to the stage.

"Now, if you don't mind, I have one more song for you. Please welcome my very special guest."

I gestured to Barry and he took a second to absorb the thunderous roars of everyone in the arena. I elbowed him, mouthing, *Have a name?*

He nodded, giving me a heart-stopping smile.

"I'm Nyx," he said into the microphone. He used a deeper, more sensual voice that made my knees weak. "I'm a little new to all this, but I hope you like this song we wrote together."

He strummed, and as the crowd screamed both of our names, I could see his genuine, elated smile.

I started the song, wishing I could slow it down to make this moment stretch on forever. When Barry joined in, I wondered if he was thinking the same thing.

For a piece we only performed twice, we got it almost perfectly. Our voices enmeshed, even when I took lower notes to save my exhausted vocal cords.

And when it finally ended with Barry's last guitar strum, I couldn't hide the sadness I felt when the lights went out.

I let myself feel it for three breaths before I put my smile back on, determined to celebrate what Barry had just done.

He deserved it.

Barry

"I can't believe you did that!" Lila yelled as we went backstage for the final time. "You went *onstage*! And you killed it!"

"Thank you," I said. "It was . . . life-changing."

And it was. The way she moved, getting to dance with her onstage—it was one of the greatest moments of my life. I could see myself doing this forever if I got the chance.

I was pretty sure Lila wanted that too. In the darkness after our encore, I saw how her shoulders slumped. She didn't think I would see, but I noticed everything about her.

I had a lot to figure out.

Especially about my future.

"Barry," Malia said, interrupting my train of thought. "I know you just got offstage, but some visitors are waiting in the tour bus. Want to see them?"

"Is it my family?"

"I believe so."

I hadn't had a second to look and see their reactions. Tom and Ruth wouldn't be fooled by my disguise.

"Let's go then," I said. "It's time to face the music."

Lila grinned. "Pretty sure we did that onstage."

"Very funny." I grabbed her hand. "Come on, sunshine. Let's go see Tom and Ruth.

We made it outside, where security led us to the tour bus. I was ready to face a barrage of questions from my siblings.

Instead, I heard someone else speak.

"I fucking told you so."

That was not Tom's or Ruth's voice. My eyes shot to the couch where Audrey and Liam sat.

"What the—how are you two here?"

"We have enough staff to where we could take a night off when Ruth asked us to come to the show."

"*Ruth* asked you?"

"I gave her enough tickets to," Lila said. "They're your family too."

"Oh, wow. Lila Wilde." Liam looked red in the face. "I should have known you'd be here. I love your music."

"It's nice to meet you," Audrey added, but her arms were crossed. "Even if I have questions for Barry about why he's with Rose and holding *your* hand."

I snapped to attention. *Shit.* I'd thought it was safe if it was just Ruth and Tom. "Um, Rose is . . ."

"Also here," Lila piped in. "I *am* Rose. Surprise. This is a wig. I'd take it off, but it's kind of glued on."

Audrey stared for a long time, but Liam burst into laughter. "Oh," she said as he cackled. "Well, that explains *so* much."

"You're okay with telling them?" I asked.

"It's my secret, and they kept Lila on the down-low for so long that I know we can trust them."

"And it's a good secret," Audrey said. "We were all fooled, even when you came into the bar."

"Thanks. And sorry for lying."

"It's okay. I'm about to get even."

"Get even?" I asked.

"Yep. Because now you're *fully* banned from Movers and Shakers."

"What did I do now?"

"You became a rock star overnight." She rolled her eyes as if it were obvious. "This is what you were meant to do. We all know it. You're amazing onstage, but for some reason, you keep acting like you have to be at the bar every night."

"Because I started the bar. I need to finish it."

"You're still the owner. But we can run it."

"And we *want* to," Liam added.

"Running it is different than me leaving it with you, even if I did it for a few weeks."

"Yeah, but knowing you, you'll give us a raise and it's not like you'll be dead. We can call you with problems. Hell, if we can't handle it, we can talk about you coming back. But I don't see that happening. You can live your dream. Just trust us enough to let us help you. Permanently."

I opened my mouth, but no words came out. I looked to Lila as if she would give me answers.

"Barry," she began, "I would never ask you to leave the bar, but I would also *love* for you to join this tour. Working with you is when this feels right."

"And the tour doesn't last forever, right?" Liam asked. "He can still visit. If Audrey lifts the ban, of course."

"I'm only lifting the ban if he says yes to joining."

"Why are you two so okay with this?" I asked. "You've done more for me than you ever should have."

"Because we saw your smile onstage. You've never looked that happy."

"Yeah," Liam added. "And all we want is for you to be happy."

"Wow, good answer," I said quietly.

"We admittedly practiced this."

"Yeah," Liam replied. "We were kind of going to do this when you came back."

"Kick me out?"

"Offer to take over so you could do this full time. We saw it."

I wasn't used to being noticed. It was a consequence of being alone, I supposed. Who could ever notice anything when you chose to be by yourself?

But slowly, I'd broken down those walls, and I'd done it for the right people.

"Thank you, guys," I said, voice cracking. "Seriously. I can't thank you enough."

"Emotions are running high, huh?" Audrey asked.

"Shut up."

"I'm not judging. But I almost feel bad for what I have to do next."

"You've already kicked me out of my own bar. What else could you do?"

"Invite the rest of your family in. I'd wait, but I met Ruth and she seems like she'll kick down the door after too long. She seems like a badass. We told them to give us ten minutes alone with you before they came storming in."

"You guys can come in!" Liam called. The rest of my family piled into the tour bus.

"Oh my God!" Ruth yelled. She, of course, got in first. I only had a second to react before she pulled me into the tightest hug of my life. "That was *so* incredible! I had no idea you were so talented! And the wig! That was so fucking smart, dude!"

"I knew you'd come up with something amazing." Tom walked in behind her.

"Get in this hug, Tom."

"I don't want to crowd."

Ruth pulled him in with a glare.

When was the last time we'd hugged? It had to have been the night of the tornado when I didn't know if I would make it to see the next day. But this was different. This was *joy* I felt.

"So, you guys liked it?"

"We *loved* it," Ruth said. "I wish I had come into the bar more to see you live because then I could have told you that you were *made* to do this."

"You are," Tom added.

"Thank you," I said. "I was worried it would be too much."

"My brother's going to be a rock star. It's never too much!"

"And you get to have exactly what you wanted," Tom reminded. "I told you that you're the smartest one of all of us."

"That's really Uncle Barry under there?" Max's voice asked from the door.

"I think it is," Selena replied.

"Sorry," I said, extracting myself from Ruth and Tom. "I didn't see you come in."

"You got a massive hug from Ruth and Tom at first," Selena said, smiling. "I don't blame any of you. But honestly, you were great."

"Did you enjoy the show?" Lila asked.

"Oh my God," Max said. "I didn't know you were here."

She laughed. "It was Barry's moment."

"It's so good to see you again. And it's so cool that you're with Uncle Barry. I know I can't tell anyone—Dad already gave me the lecture—but it'll be my little secret." He glanced at me. "Does this mean you and Rose broke up, though?"

Everyone held their breath. Was it wrong to lie to a kid? Because it *felt* wrong.

"Max," Lila said, getting down to his height. "How good are you at keeping secrets?"

"Very. I didn't even tell Tess I met you because I didn't want it getting out."

"Good. Tom, are you okay with him knowing?"

"I trust him," Tom said. "He really didn't tell anyone about that meeting."

"What's happening?" Selena asked. "What did I miss?"

"Yeah, I feel like a whole conversation is happening that we're not a part of," Knox added. I didn't even know he was in here, but it made sense considering he never left Ruth's side.

There was a beat where Lila bit her lip, and I wondered what she was about to choose.

"Max," she began, "I'm Rose too. I'm wearing a wig right now."

Max stared and then laughed. "That's a funny prank."

"I'm not kidding. I met you as Rose first. You told me you loved Lila Wilde, and I came to meet you as Lila."

Max's jaw dropped.

"Huh?" Selena asked. "You—what?"

"Holy *shit*!" Max yelled.

"Normally, I would tell you not to use that word," Selena said, "but this is a good occasion."

"You're all a part of Barry's family, which one day will be mine. I hope I can trust all of you."

"I'm still really lost," Knox added, "but I won't tell a soul about your double life. I will, however, ask my girlfriend how long she knew without telling me."

"You don't wanna know the answer to that question," Ruth replied.

"So, this means I get to hang out with Lila in secret as Rose?" Max asked.

"Yes."

"And we don't have to deal with all the weirdos with cameras?"

"Yes."

"This is the coolest day of my *life*! I know I previously said meeting you was, but this is better."

"Does this mean Lila Wilde is gonna be my sister-in-law?" Selena asked.

"If things go well, yes. But Rose Hill is just as cool, I promise."

"She's *way* cooler than me. Both of you are! I think I need to sit down and process this."

"I'll give you the couch," Audrey said.

"Would it be rude if I asked if you're gonna make another album?" Max's voice was hopeful.

"Not at all, and I *will* be." She looked at everyone on the tour bus before her eyes landed on me. "I've got some incredible inspiration."

Lila Wilde's New Boyfriend? See the Stills of Her Concert That Show Us She's in LOVE

By: Perez Adder

Lila Wilde has been in hiding, and it's apparently been with Nyx Ronan. He's a newcomer but rocked the stage and even stayed with her to pose for photos hours after the show. This writer has certainly never seen Lila look as happy as she did at that concert, especially with the dance moves they perfected onstage. Nyx has been added to her website and announced as her official touring partner. As for him, his agent (the same as Lila's) released this statement he made about Lila: "For a while, I thought I'd only be with Lila behind the scenes, but I quickly realized I wanted to be there for her in every part of her life. I'm so lucky to have a woman like her and I can't wait to see the world with the perfect person by my side."

7,843 Comments

RealLilafan247: THIS IS WHAT I WAS WAITING FOR

Poproxxx: SHE LOOKS SO HAPPY! HAS SHE EVER LOOKED LIKE THIS?

Fangirlsweaty: seriously like I can't get enough! Look at how loose she is! Look at that gorgeous smile!

Lilafan08: I just know they're so wild together.

BlazeandLila1: he's so basic. This is all for pR

Epilogue

ONE YEAR LATER

Lila

After the tour wrapped, Malia set up interviews. We'd been too busy for them while going around the world, but we all knew people wanted to know more about us.

There had been a lot of speculation, most of which Malia kept us updated on since I'd turned over all of my social media to my team. Most people had correctly assumed we were dating. Some still believed this was PR, and almost all enjoyed the new music. I found that I cared less and less about what others thought. I wanted to do what felt *right*, and touring was exactly that.

I was a bit nervous about this interview, especially considering the host was a journalist who had a love-hate relationship with me. He used to love the gossip of my life, and I knew many Lila fans would recognize the name, but I was worried he would ask something I didn't want to answer.

Barry, sensing my nerves as usual, grabbed my hand. He was in his whole Nyx getup, which had only evolved over the last year. His wig was now perfect and he sometimes temporarily darkened his beard to match his hair, especially on a day like today when we'd be on camera.

He was still ridiculously attractive in this form, but in a messy, rock star sort of way.

"Perez agreed to all the topics to avoid that Malia sent him."

"I know."

"And his articles have been respectful in the last year."

"I know that too." I took a breath. "It's so hard doing interviews."

"I could do the talking for you."

"And somehow, you'd charm everyone," I said with a smile. "How do you manage to do that again?"

"The same way you do. By being myself."

I shook my head. My charisma onstage and in person would never feel as natural as Barry's, but even I had to admit that it had bled over to me too. Outings were easier, and I even looked forward to them.

"Are you guys ready?" a producer asked.

"Yes," we both said.

The interview was in a small room and would air on a major news network in a few days. Perez was in the running to get his own late-night show, which was why he had practically begged Malia to let him do this.

I could only hope he wouldn't resort to awful ways to get it.

Nyx's hand squeezed mine, reminding me once again that everything was okay.

Perez entered the room, his face glistening with sweat as if he were as nervous as I was. "H-hi," he said. "Nice to meet you both."

"Nice to meet you too. In person, I mean."

"Have you read my articles?"

"I used to torture myself in the comments of them, actually. I stopped, though."

"Probably for the best. I'm . . . sorry about the older ones."

"It's fine. It's all fair in celebrity news."

"Yeah, but it still couldn't have been fun. I was always a fan, but I guess I lost track of it when the repetitive albums came out."

"I'll admit that I did too." I turned to Barry. "I just needed someone to remind me that I could do what I want. Don't worry, Perez. The past is in the past. We're turning a new page."

"You're as kind as they all say," he said with a smile. "Thank you." He sat across from us, shuffling his note cards in his hands. Once the cameras were rolling, he put on a dazzling smile, all signs of his nervousness gone.

"Welcome, welcome," Perez said for the cameras. "You two have caused quite the stir."

"Why?" Nyx asked, putting an arm along the back of the couch. "Did we do anything?"

I rolled my eyes at his fake innocence.

"Oh, only traveled across the globe on your new tour, which was *incredible*, by the way. I was at the LA show and the feeling in that arena was electric."

"Thank you," I said. "It was different than my last one."

"That's right. It's the first time you've performed with your significant other. Can I call him that?"

It was a test, one I had practiced for.

"You can because that's what he is."

"Congratulations," our host said. "I know your fan base had some . . . hard times accepting the change."

"It was a lot of it all at once, and I know for a long time I shared *everything* about my last relationship. And while Nyx is the inspiration for so much . . . some things are just for us."

"Also," Nyx added, "I don't need to stroke my ego and make her fame about me. She's the talent here."

My cheeks heated as they always did when he talked about me.

But I was going to drag him in.

"You're just as talented. You helped me write most of the album."

"Will he continue helping you?" Perez asked.

"Of course. We work best when it's the two of us."

"So, you share touring and music? When's the wedding?" Perez laughed.

I wasn't going to answer, mostly because we hadn't discussed a wedding. I knew I wanted to spend the rest of my life with him; the tour had only proven that. But I was okay with waiting for life to slow down.

"Probably sooner than later," Nyx answered. "I'll ask when she least expects it."

My jaw dropped. "Seriously?"

"What? Can't I drop hints?"

"You're ridiculous."

"Always."

Perez laughed again. "The people are going to *love* that. Now … I *have* to ask. I'm sure you've seen what Blaze has been saying …"

I rolled my eyes. What a mood killer.

Blaze *still* tried to make my fame about him. I knew both he and Mia had to be getting desperate. After the tour started, however, I heard many of her clients didn't renew their contracts and that she and Blaze were running out of money.

It's what they deserved.

"For those who don't know," Perez continued, "Blaze has gone on social media and said that Nyx is only a replacement for him, the original man who made Lila Wilde." He turned to Nyx. "I get the feeling he's the kind of man who has a response."

Nyx leaned forward. "You think right."

The entire studio waited with bated breath, but Nyx glanced at me, raising one eyebrow to ask permission.

"Say whatever," I said.

"All right. He can call me a replacement all he wants. But one thing is for damn sure. I keep my woman happy and satisfied. And I know for a fact that he never did. So, I wouldn't call myself a replacement. I'd call me an upgrade."

If there were an audience, they would have gasped. I'm pretty sure I did.

"Maybe I gave you too much leeway," I said, running a hand over my hot cheeks.

"It had to be said," he replied.

"Wow." Perez's eyebrows were at his hairline. "You should put that in a song."

"Don't worry," Nyx said, a devious smile on his face. "I'm working on it."

Barry

"People are gonna be talking about Nyx's little line for weeks," Juno said. We were climbing into the jet, heading for Nashville, all evidence of Lila and Nyx gone from our faces.

"Yeah," Rose replied. "He just *had* to call Blaze out."

"It's what he deserves." I grinned. "If only I could see his face when it airs."

"We're gonna be busy," Rose said. "And perfect timing because everyone will be looking for our alter egos."

"Do you guys have everything?" Juno asked. "You'll be in Nashville for a bit."

"Yep. And a lot of my stuff is at Barry's place already." Rose sat in one of the seats of the jet, letting out a long breath. It had been a long year touring, and while I enjoyed it, I was happy to be heading home for a while.

Neither Rose nor I would be relaxing for another week, however, because I would be helping Rose's mom move into a house in the city. After two therapists didn't work out, Rose mentioned that she might have more options in a bigger place. And Linda didn't want to move to a big city without someone she knew.

Nashville was the best option, considering all of our support systems were there. She'd reintroduced herself to Ruth and Tom and had also gotten to know Lynn and Carmen. Linda needed to be around more people who cared about her, and she'd found it.

Even Archie was going to stay in Nashville part-time, especially when Rose was around. All of these plans were waiting for us to return and we were more than ready to set them in motion.

"I'm going to the back. If you're going to *do* anything"—a shadow crossed Juno's face—"please block the door."

She'd walked in on us once, which was more than enough for everyone involved. Rose's and my tendency to have sex *not* in a bed had caught up to us.

"I'm too tired," Rose said. "You have nothing to worry about."

We'd stayed up nearly all night working on a new song. I was used to it from running the bar, but it always hit her harder.

While her eyes closed, I took my phone and texted Liam, telling him I was on my way.

Movers and Shakers had flourished despite my absence. My two best employees told me most of what was going on, but only when I had the time. Audrey had told me to enjoy touring, and I did, but I wanted to be back in action at the bar.

After the move, I was going to take on some shifts to give the two of them a break so they could go on a long vacation. Even Rose was willing to help out if she had the time.

However, with how busy she'd been performing practically every night on the tour, I refused to put more on her than I had to.

"Come here, sunshine," I said. "Don't fall asleep alone."

She huffed out a laugh and moved to my seat, putting her head on my shoulder. "I love you," she said.

"I love you too." I kissed her forehead.

"So," she started, her eyes still closed. "Do you have a ring yet?"

My heart skipped a beat. "No."

"Then let's go find one together while we're home. The perfect one. Then you can shock me with the proposal of a lifetime."

"Do you want two rings or one?"

"No idea." She snuggled in closer. "But let's figure it out together."

WANT MORE?

Visit the Murray's one last time with a bonus epilogue set five years in the future!

Get it here:

THANK YOU

When I set out to write this novel, I didn't know what a beast it would become. For starters, I had an entirely different idea, one where Lila's double life played far less of a role. But then I realized I wanted her secrets to be a big part of the story, so I rewrote EVERYTHING to make it what it is now.

I'm not gonna lie: it was harder than I expected. I basically started from scratch and I didn't realize how difficult it would be to tie the third book into everything else. So, with that in mind, I'd like to thank Kasey because, as always, she combed through this with amazing detail and helped me fix all of my fuckups. You're a QUEEN.

Also, I'd like to thank the newest member of my editing team, Amanda. Thank you for finding the last-second typos. They haunt me.

My readers don't get out of this thank-you unscathed either. There are so many of you who sign up for ARCs and cheer for me on social media. I cannot thank you enough because it reminds me to KEEP GOING! As a writer with a growing list of mental illnesses (I'm collecting them like Infinity Stones), it helps to know that people actually love my work and that I am not just a goblin pretending to be a writer.

And last but not least, I'd like to thank my IRL support team. Josh, Lizzie, Morgan, and Cass, you always listen when I bitch about what to do next in my novel. All of your advice saves me every single day. THANK YOU.

About the Author

Elle Rivers writes fun romance books filled with real-world problems wrapped in beautiful, heartwarming happy endings. When not writing, she can be found speed-reading other authors' amazing romance novels, curling up next to any warm object she can find, or singing obnoxiously loud to Taylor Swift.

Elle was born and raised in Nashville, TN, and she considers herself one of the few native Nashvillians who does not like country music. She has eight cats who fight for the spot on her lap, and eight chickens who couldn't care less about her unless she is bringing them food. She lives with her romance-hero of a husband who endlessly supports her writing endeavors, and her son, who is the biggest, but most adorable, distraction.